As I am Known

by Kim Pearson Wiese

To Bob—
without whose longsuffering,
no story of mine would ever see the light of day.
You are the best!

"Then shall I know, even as I am fully known."
I Corinthians 13:12

© 2006 by Kim Pearson Wiese. All rights reserved.

No part of this book may be reproduced, stored in a retrieval system, or transmitted by any means, electronic, mechanical, photocopying, recording or otherwise, without written permission from the author.

Library of Congress No. 2006902120
ISBN: 0-9779176-0-6

This book is printed on acid free paper.

Prologue
Jerusalem, AD 33

Gallus Septimus risked a glance at his companions. None of them met his eyes. His commander stared straight ahead, the muscles bulging in his jaw as he clenched and unclenched his teeth. Desiring to emulate him, Gallus trained his eyes forward again, as beads of sweat prickled his upper lip. *How long will they make us wait?*

His fate, along with the fates of the three others with him, would be decided this morning. He shifted one shoulder under his breastplate, and as he often did when forced to wait, let his mind wander, let it take him home to Gaul. He'd been gone four years. Far, far too long. But if he held himself still enough, if he turned his eyes inward, he was there again, roaming the shaded forests of his childhood, breathing the loamy earth scent under his feet. Sunlight dappled the trunks of the elms and oaks. Off to his left a creek sent water chuckling, sparkling over smooth stones. Overhead a lark called out, its song piercing and sweet....

The shout of a peddler on the other side of the wall snapped him back to the present. How did he end up in this god-cursed place? He'd been eager enough to join the regiment. The discipline and efficiency of the Roman armies beckoned him like a siren's song, and gave him a chance to see something of the world, to find out what lay beyond the rivers that bordered his own country. He was housed and fed, and even paid at each moon's turn, paid in coin and salt. This allowed him to buy drink when he was off duty, and occasionally a woman. On the whole, a soldier's life wasn't bad. But this place....

His company, the Eighteenth Auxilius, had been sent to Palestine the summer before. Gallus hated it from the moment he disembarked the ship and set foot on its dusty shores. How, he wondered, could anyone live in this sweltering heat? His opinion of the place from that first day had not improved. Since they came, the Eighteenth had no respite, no relief. Between riots, and bandits, and the unreasonable demands of the religious leaders, they stayed busy night and day. And did the people appreciate their efforts to keep the peace? Gallus chewed at the inside of his cheek and ignored the wet trickle snaking down the side of his face. This assignment was like babysitting a pack of wolves. Just last week a man in another auxilius was knifed in broad daylight. The murderer was caught and crucified, but Gallus found himself glancing over his shoulder all the time now.

Training his eyes on a blank spot on the stone wall opposite he mused, *Why can't these people behave? Do they think they are the only ones to be defeated and ruled by Rome? My village was taken by them. I was only a child, but I remember.*

Kim Pearson Wiese

I remember the cries and the screams of combat. He closed his eyes briefly again, and felt himself running, running. And then came the odor of burning as his village was torched. Gallus opened his eyes. *The smell of the smoke lingers still, and many died in the fighting—my grandfather, two of my uncles. If anyone had reason to hate the Romans, I would. But things changed, got better, and my people learned to live with the Roman presence, even to benefit and profit from it.*

But these Jews! They can't get along with anyone. They even hate each other. To a man they are wounded in the brain. Gallus sighed. *It's their religion. Or maybe it's this hellish heat. Whatever it is, now it's affecting us.*

Who was that man at the tomb? Marcus thinks he was no man, but a god. Maybe he was. Gallus shivered at the memory. *I've never seen anyone so tall, so frightening. And how did we all fall asleep at the same time? I wasn't tired when I was posted. We even joked about how easy the assignment was. How hard can it be to guard a tomb?*

Gallus was plenty familiar with guard duty, and he knew his responsibility. If a prisoner escaped, his own blood would be demanded. That he understood. That was logical. But if a corpse escaped? What then? *Will I have to die for a dead man?*

Chapter 1
Jerusalem, AD 47

"No, Prisca!" Jacob exclaimed. "Don't let go!" He tightened his grip on his little sister's hand. "Here, let's get out of this." He pulled her into the niche of a doorway. "Remember what I told you?"

"When there are too many people, get in a doorway until they are gone," she recited.

"That's right. That way no one can shove you around or step on you." He leaned down. "Are you all right?"

The child rubbed at her shoulder. "A man hit me with his elbow," she complained, but gave him a reassuring smile. "I'm all right."

Spotting a gap in the mass of bodies, Jacob said, "It looks clearer now. Let's go. Hold my hand tight." They wove through Jerusalem's marketplace, threading in and out among the jostling throng and the vendors' stalls. Jacob didn't want to risk losing his sister in the crowd. A couple of years ago he would have picked her up and carried her, but now she was nearly nine, too big to carry. Not that she would let him anymore. Over the last few months she had developed—in Jacob's view—an overblown sense of propriety. No, picking her up was out of the question.

Prisca tugged at him. "Jacob, I'm hungry."

He grinned down at her. "You just had breakfast an hour ago. Are you really hungry—or just hungry for honeyed almonds?" She turned her wide, pleading eyes on him, and he laughed and pulled out his purse. "Oh, all right, but just a few this time, or you'll make yourself sick again." When he paid for the treat, he led her to a narrow strip of shadow cast by a building where they could squat down in relative comfort out of the traffic.

"How long will we have to stay away from the house?" Prisca popped the first of the almonds into her mouth.

"I don't know, Baby. Aunt Deborah said to check back at sundown."

"Do you think Mama's baby will be all right this time?"

Jacob swallowed the truth and tried to sound more optimistic than he felt. "I hope so." He handed her another nut.

Prisca let out a long sigh. "I hope so, too. The last time, Mama cried and cried, and she wouldn't let me go anywhere for weeks."

Yes, and she slapped me for no reason. His hand strayed to his face where the memory of his stepmother's stinging blow remained. But Prisca didn't know about that, and he would never tell her.

"Maybe you could take me to Tamar's house," Prisca interrupted his thoughts. "Then you could go sit with Papa in the Temple."

"That's a good idea, Baby." He smiled and stood up. "Here's the last almond."

"I'm not a baby," she reminded him with a ladylike sniff as she smoothed the skirt of her sky-blue tunic.

"Sorry, I forgot." He suppressed the urge to tickle her right there—still, he grinned at the thought. She'd be outraged.

Fingering the thick, black braid at the nape of her neck, Prisca said, "Maybe there will be a real baby at home when we get back."

He took her hand again, and they started up the street. "Maybe so."

* * * * *

Jacob arrived at the Temple less than an hour later, having safely deposited Prisca at her best friend's house. He smiled and shook his head. The two girls were already giggling about something before he left. Once inside the Outer Court, he spotted his father and grandfather hard at work exchanging money, and stopped as a jolt of shock hit him in the gut. *Grandfather looks like a corpse!* Until now, Jacob hadn't noticed the sick, yellow cast of the old man's skin. A few weeks before, he overheard his aunt Deborah confide to his father that Grandfather wasn't well, but until that moment he hadn't seen any difference in him. Jacob swallowed. Then mentally shaking himself, he ducked behind a column to dust off and straighten his robes—*That's better*—and ran his fingers through his unruly hair. *One less thing for Grandfather to fuss about.*

Satisfied that his appearance would get passing marks, he put his shoulders back and, accomplished actor that he had become, strode to the table like a young man who had all the confidence in the world. "Shalom, Father. Shalom, Grandfather," he greeted them as he neared the table.

"Jacob." His father, Caleb, greeted him and moved over to make room for him. "How goes it at home?"

"I don't know," he answered, sitting to Caleb's right, relieved that his father was a buffer between him and his Grandfather Lathan. "Prisca and I left more than an hour ago."

"And where is Prisca now?"

"I took her to Tamar's house."

Lathan narrowed his eyes in Jacob's direction without really looking at him and growled, "Shoved your responsibility off on someone else, did you?"

Caleb intervened. "It's all right, Father. The boy did the right thing. If he brought her here, she'd just be underfoot."

Lathan grunted in reply and turned to his next customer.

"I'm glad you're here, son." Caleb handed him a scroll and with a quick glance at the older man, leaned toward Jacob and murmured, "I need you to deliver this to Zerah."

"The priest?" Jacob whispered, tucking the roll into a sleeve.

"Yes, and if he has a reply, I want you to wait for it."

He nodded, and as he stood to go, his grandfather said, "Get on with you, boy, and don't be all day about it." Caleb and Jacob exchanged a knowing glance. Grandfather (never a man of great patience) grew more surly with each passing week, and for reasons Jacob could only guess at, turned most of his ire on him. But his father tempered much of the old man's abuse, counseling Jacob to hold his tongue and be patient.

Passover was still a week away, and the biggest crowds were yet to come. Nevertheless, Jacob had to elbow his way out of the Temple. He started for Zerah's home, his curiosity piqued. He had seen the man often, but had never actually met him. The rumor was that his grandfather and the priest had once been great friends. They weren't anymore. Grandfather steadfastly refused to speak of Zerah—or to him—for as long as Jacob could remember. He wondered what separated them, and what business his father had with the priest.

Jacob also heard that the priest's man-servant was a retired Roman legionary, but he wasn't sure he believed that. He'd caught glimpses of him, and though the servant's fair hair and blue eyes marked him a gentile, he looked too young to be retired from the army. Besides, why would a Roman soldier lower himself to serve a Jew—even a priest?

Moments later, Jacob knocked on the door of Zerah's home. It swung open, and he found himself face to face with the stone wall that was Zerah's servant. "Yes? Was there something you wanted?" the man asked with a heavy accent. He stood, apparently immovable, his hands tucked into his sleeves. His angular face, square at the jaw and brow, looked as if it had been chiseled from granite, and Jacob guessed that the body beneath his tunic was as hard and unyielding as his countenance. The servant's hair, yellow as sun's fire, contrasted sharply with his ice-blue eyes.

"Uh, yes..." Jacob stammered, a little unnerved by those pale eyes. "My father asked me to deliver this message to the priest."

"Your father? Who is your father?"

"Caleb ben Lathan."

"Let him in, Gallus," boomed a voice from inside the house. "I have been expecting him."

The servant stepped aside, and keeping his right hand tucked inside the sleeve of his tunic, gestured with his left for Jacob to enter. In the main room, a tall gentlemen with hair that fell like snow in thick waves around his face greeted him. "You are Jacob, yes?"

"I am, sir." He clasped his offered hand.

"Shalom, Jacob, and welcome to my house," Zerah smiled. "It's good to meet you at last. Please come in and sit down."

Grandfather had warned him not to waste time, but Jacob sensed his father would want him to accept the priest's hospitality. "Thank you, sir."

Where Zerah's servant resembled stone, Zerah himself reminded Jacob of the plump cushions on which they now settled, soft and comfortable. This was a man unused to much physical labor, a man who made his way with his mind, as Jacob guessed by the way his piercing black eyes studied him from under bushy eyebrows. "You have the look of your father, but your mother's eyes, I think. How old are you?"

"Fifteen, sir." Jacob ducked his head to hide the flush rising to his face. No one ever mentioned his real mother—at least not in a good way.

"You are tall for your age." The servant set a bowl of dried dates between them. Zerah selected one and bit into it. "How is your grandfather?"

Jacob cleared his throat. "To be honest, sir, he isn't well."

The priest grunted, and Jacob noticed for the first time that their conversation seemed to echo in the room. "I am sorry to hear that. Well, let's see that scroll of yours."

Jacob handed the document over and took a date for himself while he waited. He glanced around him, all the while trying not to look like he was looking. Even in full daylight, the room seemed dim. And where were the tapestries and the rugs? Only one mat covered the floor beneath them. The bare stone walls, devoid of color and warmth, amplified every sound. Even the sibilant scuff of the servant's sandals resonated on the tile floor. He couldn't help comparing the austerity of Zerah's house with Grandfather's, which was loaded with every kind of luxury and comfort imaginable. Had the priest suffered a downturn in his fortunes? What other reason would cause him to live like a poor man in a mansion?

He chewed at the sugary date as Zerah opened the scroll, read it, and set it aside. "Tell your father I will be pleased to meet with him tomorrow." He smiled, "Does he want you back right away?"

"I don't know, sir. I suppose so."

"Then you had better go." They both stood, and Zerah held out his hand again. "But feel free to come and visit, Jacob. I would enjoy the company."

"Thank you, sir." Jacob followed the servant to the door. Once outside, a thoughtful frown creased his brow as he hurried back toward the Temple. The priest seemed genial enough. What business did his father have with him, and what did he do to make Grandfather hate him so? He knew Grandfather Lathan bore a vicious loathing for anyone who was a member of that sect, the ones who were followers of Jesus of Nazareth. Was Zerah one of those? Mark, his best friend, was—a fact Jacob kept a close secret. Though Mark was about three years older, the two boys had forged an amiable friendship, a friendship Grandfather would destroy if he suspected Mark's religious leanings. Fortunately, Lathan paid little attention to him or his friends. It made the secret easier to keep.

Jacob spent most of the rest of the day running errands for his father, something he was happy to do, since it kept him out from under his grandfather's nose and gave him a measure of freedom to wander. That afternoon he heard a familiar voice hailing him, and stopped and turned to see Mark running down the street toward him. "Shalom, Jacob!" Mark panted as he caught up. "What are you doing? Working for your father?"

"Yes. He has me delivering messages today—and invitations. He's throwing a banquet during Passover."

Mark stopped in his tracks. "A banquet? After what happened last time?"

"My aunt Deborah begged him not to." Jacob sighed and hung his head. "She's afraid this baby will die like the others, but Father is convinced it won't. My stepmother's time has come. I guess we'll know soon enough."

"I have to go now," his friend glanced around, "but if you need a place to hide out for a few days, you can always come to my house. Mama likes you." Mark clapped him on the shoulder and trotted off down the narrow street.

Jacob colored at Mark's casual use of the endearment. He himself never called his stepmother by such an intimate term, nor would she welcome it if he did. Diana would never be 'Mama' for him.

*   *   *   *   *

"It's nearly sundown," Caleb said that evening. "Why don't you go ahead and get your sister? We'll meet you at the house."

"And do something about that hair," Grandfather added, grimacing as he stood up. "Your appearance is a disgrace."

"Yes sir." Jacob knew it was a lost cause even as he ran his fingers through the mass of curls on his head. He hurried out of the Temple to avoid further comments from his grandfather, wondering—as he had countless times before—why he could never please the old man.

When he stopped for Prisca, spurred by echoes of Lathan's disapproving words, he raked at his hair again and dusted off his robes. Tamar's mother answered the door. "Shalom, Jacob," she smiled, and called back over her shoulder, "Prisca, it's your brother." She turned to him again. "Any word?"

"Not yet," he told her. "I'm on my way home now."

"I see. Well, if you need a place to bring Prisca, she's welcome here." She gave him a bright smile, "But I'm sure everything will be all right."

He thanked her as Prisca came out to him, her hands behind her back. As they walked away, she sang, "I have a surprise for you, Brother," and whipped one hand out to reveal a honey cake. "Tamar and I made them."

He took the cake and broke off a piece. "All by yourselves?"

"Well, no," she answered. "Tamar's mother helped."

He smiled, savoring the sweetness in his mouth. "You did make good use of your time."

They arrived at the house moments before Caleb and Lathan did. Jacob pushed open the door and stepped in. All was quiet. Did that bode good or ill? Just then Aunt Deborah, pregnant herself with her third child, appeared out of the kitchen. She wiped her hands on a towel and gave them a tired smile. "You have a new little brother."

Prisca gasped in joy and tugged at Jacob's hand. "Let's go see him!"

"You go on up," he said, glancing at Deborah. "I'll be there in a minute." When Prisca was out of earshot, he asked, "Is everything all right?"

Deborah answered, "This baby is stronger than the others. I think he will survive. Your stepmother is worn out, of course...."

"And so are you," Jacob observed. "I'm here now, and Father and Grandfather are coming. You should go home and rest."

Deborah took his hand between her own and sighed, "I will soon."

The door swung open again, and Caleb entered with Lathan leaning on his arm. Jacob frowned, puzzled. His grandfather had always been a slender man. When did he acquire a belly? Jacob averted his eyes so as not to stare. *Why, Grandfather is bigger around the middle than Aunt Deborah!*

"What news?" Lathan asked.

"It's a boy," she told him. "Both Diana and the baby are well, and they're resting."

Grandfather's grin showed all his long, yellow teeth. He poked Caleb in the ribs. "What did I tell you? Finally—you have a son!"

Without another word, Caleb sprinted up the stairs. Chuckling and muttering under his breath, Lathan followed at a much slower pace, leaving Jacob alone with his aunt. He didn't miss her look of understanding and pity, and he sighed and tried on a smile. "I guess I'd better go up, too."

* * * * *

Prisca was madly in love with the baby. She sat and held him for hours on end, rocking and crooning lullabies. Four days after his birth, she brought the baby downstairs where Jacob had just finished his breakfast. Slowly, and with care she lowered herself down next to him. Jacob reached over and tweaked the end of her nose. "What do you have there?"

Prisca rolled her eyes in feminine disdain. "Our new baby, you great ox! Your brother." She smiled and chirped, "Just think—in a few years you can take us both to the marketplace."

"And I'll have to buy sweets for two of you." He pulled a long face and let out an exaggerated sigh. "I'll end up a pauper, begging in the streets."

Prisca giggled, "You will not. You'll be rich, like Father and Grandfather." In the next breath she said, "Do you want to hold him?" Even as Jacob hesitated, she bundled the baby into his arms. "Isn't he beautiful?"

The infant's nose was all mashed, and his head misshapen. Privately, Jacob guessed he'd improve with age. "He's not bad. He has hair like yours." He fingered the fuzz that covered the baby's crown like ebony feathers. *It'll be nice to have a little brother.*

Just then Diana appeared on the stairs. Her eyes widened with alarm when she saw her baby in Jacob's arms. She hurried down the steps and snatched the infant from him. The sudden movement startled the baby, who puckered up his face and began to wail. "Prisca," she scolded, raising her voice over the crying, "when I let you hold your brother, he is your responsibility. I don't want you to give him to anyone else."

"But it's just Jacob," she protested. "He's his brother, too."

Jacob saw the shadows that marred his stepmother's lovely eyes, shadows of fatigue and worry, and he swallowed his hurt. "Mother is right, Prisca. You have to be careful with him." Confused by her mother's anger, and upset by the baby's screaming, the little girl's lower lip trembled.

Diana's expression softened somewhat. "Of course, I didn't mean to say Jacob couldn't hold him, dear, but when you tell me you have him, that's what I expect." She sighed, "It's time to feed him anyway, so I'll just take him now."

When she had disappeared again into her room, Prisca buried her face in Jacob's shoulder and wept. "It's all right, Baby," he soothed. "You really didn't do anything wrong. Mother is...well, she wants to be extra careful with him, that's all. You can understand that, can't you?" She nodded, but couldn't speak for sobbing, so Jacob held her. Before long, he was rocking her and crooning under his breath.

* * * * *

The week of the Feast brought with it a state of controlled chaos to the household. Servants scurried back and forth seeing to the usual Passover chores of cleaning and sweeping to rid the house of leaven, all the while trying not to run over each other in their haste to finish preparations for the banquet. The finest families in Jerusalem were invited, and Diana's father and mother were coming in from Ephesus.

Jacob pitched in everywhere he could. He helped clean out the garden, ran errands to the marketplace for Diana, and trotted back and forth between the house and the Temple delivering messages. At the back of his mind a question appeared, took shape and persisted. It nagged and hammered at him, growing in strength and weight. *Did Father have a banquet to celebrate when I was born?*

He asked Susannah, one of the older servants as he helped her sweep out the kitchen. She lifted an indifferent shoulder and shook her head, coughing at the dust they stirred up. "I don't know. You weren't born here. Ask your father."

Ask my father. Jacob's head told him that would be the reasonable thing, the logical thing to do, but in his heart he couldn't bring himself to do it. His mouth tasted of dust, so he leaned over and spat into the cook fire.

The flame sizzled and snapped at him, and Susannah whirled around. "What did you do?" She glared at him, her eyes narrow and angry. "Don't you know it's bad luck to spit into a fire?" She poked at him with her broom, backing him out of the kitchen. "Go on. Get out of here. Take your bad luck somewhere else."

*　　*　　*　　*　　*

The next day as he entered the Temple, he spotted a familiar face in the crowd, a pair of green eyes, the left one overshadowed by a brow cut neatly in half from an old injury. Below the wide grin, a tuft of sandy-brown beard. Jacob's heart leapt up, and he called out, "Uncle Joel!"

Joel turned and bellowed, "Jacob, shalom!" and pulled him into a hearty embrace. "It's good to see you, boy!" He released him and held him at arm's length. "I believe you've grown a head taller since last year. Another year or so, and you'll pass me. Come." He led him into Solomon's portico out of the heavy press of celebrants. "What are you doing? Running for your father?"

"Yes. He's hosting a banquet at the end of the week. Mother's had another baby—a boy this time, so I'm chasing all over the city."

His uncle's answering smile seemed forced. "I know how it is. I did enough running for your grandfather when I was a boy."

"Will you be with us for Seder?" But even as he asked, Jacob knew full well what the answer would be.

Joel put an arm around his shoulder. "I suspect not, unless your grandfather's heart has changed. I am no longer welcome in his house."

Jacob swallowed his disappointment. "How long will you be in Jerusalem?"

As I am Known

"I intend to stay through the Feast of Unleavened Bread, and then I'll leave and go back."

"To see my mother?" Jacob blurted out, and instantly regretted the question.

Joel's eyes searched his. "Well, no—not immediately, though I plan to see her later this year." He tugged at his beard. "I'm staying at the home of Zerah the priest. Do you know him?"

Stunned—what did his uncle have to do with the priest?—Jacob stammered, "Yes... yes I do."

"Then why don't you come see me there after this banquet of your father's is over?"

"I will," he replied, resolving to find a way to make the visit without arousing anyone's suspicions. "Uncle Joel, do you know...did my father have a banquet for me when I was born?"

Joel shot him a questioning look, then sighed, "I don't know. All I remember is that you were born in Capernaum, and that your grandmother left me with my uncle while she went to attend to your birth. She never mentioned a banquet, or I don't recall that she did, but I was only a lad, younger than you are now, and I didn't have much interest in babies, or in women's talk." He shrugged. "Perhaps he did. He might have had a banquet fit for Caesar himself, and I wouldn't have noticed." Jacob nodded, forced himself to be satisfied with an unsatisfying answer. Joel gave him a friendly squeeze. "You'd better get back to your father before he wonders where you are. Come and see me at Zerah's. We'll have a nice, long talk."

* * * * *

Diana's parents, Gedeon and Eunice, arrived the next morning. Eunice swept into the house and took over as soon as she set foot in the door, announcing, "I want to see my grandson. Where is he?"

Prisca tugged at her robe and held out a jonquil she plucked from the garden. "Shalom, Grandmother, and welcome to our house."

Eunice gazed down her long, patrician nose at the little girl. "I suppose you are Prisca."

"Yes, Grandmother." Prisca, who had never met her grandmother, and had been counting the days until her arrival, smiled hopefully at the older woman.

"Well, don't just stand there, child. Show me where your mother and the baby are."

"I'll take you to them." Caleb stepped forward and kissed her cheek. "They're just upstairs."

She followed him without sparing another glance for Prisca or another word to anyone. Prisca's face fell in disappointment, but Gedeon came to the rescue, hoisting her in his arms and exclaiming, "Here's my girl at last!" Then he grunted, "But you're almost too big to pick up anymore."

Prisca giggled and twined her legs around his waist, and her arms around his neck. "Oh, Papi, I thought you'd never come!"

"Well of course I came, Little Monkey," he laughed. "The same as every year, but a bit slower this time." He set her down and putting a finger to his lips whispered, "It was your grandmother's fault. She made me bring crates and crates of things. I thought our poor camel would collapse and give up the ghost."

Prisca giggled again. "Camels don't have ghosts, Papi. That's silly." She took his hand and led him to a chair. A servant brought him a cup of wine, and as he sipped at it, Prisca asked, "What kinds of things did you bring?"

He leaned his head back and blew out a long sigh. "Baubles."

A delicate line creased her forehead. "Baubles?"

"Oh, you know—girl things. Nothing important."

Prisca had been leaning against the chair. Now she straightened up, her hands on her hips. "I'm a girl, too, Papi."

He grinned. "You are? Well, that's convenient." He reached into the folds of his robe and pulled out a leather pouch. "I happen to have something here that I believe was made for a girl about your size." From the pouch he produced a bit of cloth which he unfolded to reveal a gold bangle. Prisca gasped in surprise and delight as he clasped it onto her slender wrist. "Will that do?"

"Oh, it's just beautiful!" Prisca climbed into his lap and snuggled her head against his shoulder, holding her arm out so they could both admire the gleam of gold against her skin.

At this point, Jacob, who had been standing apart from the others, turned and slipped unnoticed out the back door.

*   *   *   *   *

The morning of the banquet dawned cloudy and chill. Prisca was sent to Tamar's early in the day at her mother's urging. She wanted to stay at the house, but Eunice decided she would only be in the way. The men were all gone to the Temple, and Jacob sat at the table tackling his breakfast so he could go there himself. The baby, now named Andrew in honor of Caleb's maternal grandfather, had been circumcised the day before—his eighth day—in accordance with the Law. He wasn't taking it well. He slept fitfully, only an hour or so at a time, and would only be comforted at his mother's breast.

"Oh, not again!" Jacob heard Diana moan just after breakfast when the baby's mewling wails reached her from upstairs. She rubbed her face with both hands. "If I don't get some rest soon....."

"Get hold of yourself, daughter," Eunice commanded. "He is only a babe, and in pain. Another day or two, and he'll settle down."

"But Mother, he's hurting me...." Diana started, then glanced at Jacob and flushed red.

Embarrassed himself, he stood up. "Would you like me to bring him to you?"

"Oh, Jacob, would you?" Diana turned her most charming smile on him, the smile that made him feel he could conquer the world and offer it to her on a platter. "What a wonderful help you are."

As he climbed the stairs, he heard Eunice say, "Then rub olive oil on them, dear. I'll get Susannah to make you some willow tea."

Jacob picked the baby up from his pallet. "Hello there, little man," he murmured. "Oh! Your cloths are all wet." He spotted a pile of freshly laundered ones, folded and ready, on a table. At first he thought he'd take one down to Diana with the baby, but then decided to handle it himself. "It can't be that hard to change a baby," he murmured. He laid the infant on the table and removed the damp cloths. "Oh good," he sighed, "you're only wet." But the site of the circumcision was raw and sore. Jacob let out a low whistle of sympathy. "That has to hurt. It's a good thing you're so little, and you won't remember it." A vial of olive oil sat nearby on the table. He opened it and sprinkled a few drops on the baby's wounds. "Maybe that will help."

He picked up the clean cloth, unfolded it and turned it this way and that in his hands. "Now how do these go on?" He glanced at the baby with a smile. "You aren't going to tell me, are you, Andrew?" Andrew's initial wails quieted to a low fussing as he tried to stuff a tiny fist in his mouth. Jacob shrugged and wrapped the cloth around him the best way he could figure out, and tucked the end in. "I guess that will have to do." Once the diaper was on, he swaddled the baby in a fresh blanket and picked him up. Seconds later, snuggled in his older brother's arms, Andrew fell asleep again. Jacob stroked his feathery hair a moment with the tip of one finger before laying him back down on his pallet and tiptoeing out of the room.

"What took you so long?" Eunice demanded when he came down again. "And where is the baby?"

"He's asleep," Jacob answered. "He was wet, so I changed him, and he went back to sleep."

"He went back to sleep?" Diana echoed, mystified. "How did you do that?"

He started to answer, but Eunice fixed him with a glare. "I do not believe it. What have you done to him?"

With a cry of dismay, Diana sprang to her feet and bounded up the stairs. Moments later, the baby's angry wail sounded from her room. She came down with the screaming child in her arms. "He's all right," she announced with a crooked smile. "Just hungry, I suppose."

Furious hurt drove discretion from Jacob's mind. "Why?" he asked, looking back and forth from Diana to her mother. He spread out his hands in question. "Why do you think I would hurt him? He's my brother."

"He is your *half*-brother," Eunice corrected him with a sniff. "And he is your rival."

"My rival. So you think...." He didn't finish. The thought made him physically ill. He turned to Diana. "I never hurt Prisca, did I?"

"No, of course not...." she began.

"That is different," Eunice cut in. "Prisca is a girl. She is no threat to you."

"And I am no threat to him!" Jacob had to shout to be heard over the baby's screaming.

"How dare you use that tone of voice with me, young man!" Eunice exclaimed. "Get out of this house this instant!"

He turned on his heel and muttered, "Gladly," as he slammed the door behind him. He rubbed at the back of his neck and sighed, "Well, I've gone and done it now." Jacob put his head down and started up the street. "That woman is going to get me for this." He watched his feet carry him away from the house. "What did I do wrong—except for shouting?" He shook his head. "They think I want to hurt the baby. I guess I'll have to stay away from him." The thought filled him with sadness.

His eyes were still downcast, so he didn't see Gedeon coming toward him until they were nearly past each other. "Good morning, Jacob."

His head snapped up. "Oh, good morning, sir."

The older man paused. "You don't look like you're having a very good morning, boy. Is something wrong?" Jacob shrugged and shook his head. Gedeon glanced toward the house. "Let me guess. Woman problems?"

Diana's father had always been nice enough, but he doubted he could count on him as an ally against his own wife and daughter. When he didn't reply, Gedeon said, "Maybe you'd better tell me about it."

Jacob's face flushed red. "Sir, if it's all the same to you, I'd rather not."

"Did you do something wrong?"

He clenched his right hand while his left reached up to rub at his cheek. "I... don't know," he stammered. "I don't think so."

Gedeon frowned, but nodded in understanding. "I see. That bad, eh? Well, I intended to go in and get a scroll to show to your father, but now I'm not sure I want to go in at all." He turned with a hint of a smile. "Will they eat me alive?"

Jacob bit his lip and looked away. "They might, sir."

Gedeon adjusted his turban. "Maybe I should make you go with me—as a shield."

"I wouldn't make much of a shield, sir." Now he could almost smile at the image of his step-grandfather under fire from the females in the house. "I'm already full of holes myself."

Gedeon did smile, and clapped Jacob's shoulder. "In that case, I'll have to go it alone." Then he sobered. "My wife is not an easy woman to get along with. Leave it to me, lad. I'll get whatever this is smoothed over."

Jacob wanted to hug him in gratitude. Instead he answered, "Thank you, sir. I am in your debt."

"No," he said quietly, "I am in yours. I see how you are with Prisca. It sets my heart at rest knowing she has you for a protector." With that, he set off again toward the house.

* * * * *

Jacob kept a wary eye out for Gedeon in the crowded mass inside the Temple. About an hour later, he spotted him coming to the table. As the older man approached, he gave Jacob a firm nod. To Caleb he said, "I found the scroll I was looking for. It was in the bottom of my bag." He winked at Jacob. "I have one bag for my things, and my wife brings enough to furnish a house."

Caleb glanced at the scroll, then said, "You'd probably better go on home, son, and help your mother get ready for the banquet."

Jacob heaved himself up like a prisoner going to his own execution, but Gedeon caught his arm and said to Caleb. "Actually, I was hoping to borrow the boy for a couple of hours. I have some things to attend to, and could use his assistance. Besides," he raised his eyebrows, "it would be cruel to throw any living man into that den of wolves at your house!"

Caleb laughed. "Fussing about the banquet, are they? I might have guessed. You are welcome to him for as long as you need him."

On their way from the Outer Court, Jacob asked, "Where are we going, sir?"

Gedeon scratched at his chin in a thoughtful manner. "I have no idea." Then he brightened. "Want to look at some horses?"

They headed north through streets jammed with visitors who had come for the Feast. "I don't know whether it's me, or whether this city really is more crowded every year," Gedeon said as they passed through the Damascus gate under the watchful eye of a brace of Roman legionaries. "This many people packed in one place makes me uncomfortable."

"Me too, sir." Jacob shouldered and squeezed around a knot of men arguing about their accommodations for the Feast.

Once outside the city walls, their going wasn't so hampered, and in a few minutes they came to the gathering place for buyers and sellers of livestock. No one was buying on this day, not during Passover, but he and Gedeon were among a small crowd of lookers. They paused a moment at the camels, and Jacob ran his hand along the coarse, brushy mane of a donkey tethered with them. A few dozen paces further down were the horses. Gedeon passed the heavier mounts the legionaries favored with barely a glance. "Ah," he finally said, "here's what I was looking for." More than a dozen horses, all fine-boned and petite, pranced and cavorted in a makeshift corral.

An Arab sat under a canopy nearby. He stood and greeted them when they stopped. "Salaam, my friends." He made a bow. "Have my beauties caught your eye?"

Gedeon smiled, "They have indeed." He turned and pointed. "How old is the roan?"

"You have excellent taste, sir," the Arab answered. "She is but a yearling. That's her sister there with the star on her forehead. She's two years old."

"Very nice," Gedeon agreed, "but alas, I can do nothing today."

"Nor I, sir," the Arab nodded. "Heaven forbid that I should violate your sacred feast and profit from your presence here."

"How long will you be in Jerusalem?" Gedeon asked.

"At least another week." He gestured toward his canopy. "I was just about to have some coffee. Would you and your grandson do me the honor of joining me?"

Gedeon agreed, and Jacob, noticing that he didn't correct the man about their relationship happily followed them into the shade and sat down. The Arab poured black, steaming liquid into three tiny cups and passed them out. Jacob took his and sniffed at it. Did sitting under the canopy and drinking this man's coffee make him unclean? For a moment he envied Gedeon his race. The Greeks didn't worry about such things. He touched the rim of the cup to his lips and took a sip. The potent coffee barreled into his throat, making him cough and splutter.

"Careful, boy," Gedeon grinned. "This is heady stuff. It'll rush you like a bull."

The Arab laughed and winked at Jacob, who was wiping his eyes on his sleeve. "We like our coffee bitter and our women sweet." Gedeon cleared his throat, and the Arab added, "Of course, you're too young to know about such things. How old are you, lad? Seventeen? Eighteen?"

"I am fifteen, sir," he replied.

The Arab's eyes widened. "Fifteen? You are well-grown for your age. I took you to be older."

Flushed with pleasure at the flattery, Jacob took another careful sip of the coffee. By the time they left about an hour later, his head buzzing pleasantly from the potent drink, he said, "You never asked him the price of his horses. Did you decide not to buy one?"

"Oh, I want one, all right," Gedeon answered. "Not the roan, but her sister." He gave Jacob a sly grin, "I seem to have a weakness for high-strung females. But

I don't want the Arab to know that. It's all part of a complicated process—something like a dance. When I come back in a few days, he'll greet me like a long-lost brother, and then try to sell me the roan at double her value. I will balk at the price and let him think that I might settle for the one I really want, but that I expect her to go for less. He may take the bait, he may not. Depends on how experienced he is." Gedeon chuckled, "He's probably already seen through me."

They stopped a moment before going back through the gate, and Jacob asked, "Have you talked to Phillip lately, sir?"

Gedeon nodded. "I saw him in the fall. Your uncle is well, and he did tell me to send you his greetings."

"And my cousins?" Both he and Gedeon chose for the moment to ignore the fact that he was not related by blood to Phillip or his children.

"They're well, and thank Heaven for that. Lyssa was sick for a time, but she's recovered. Arin—she's what? Two years younger than you? She wanted to come with me, but her father said she was still too young. Maybe next year." He glanced at Jacob. "You've never met the girls, have you?"

"I met Arin once," he answered, "when I was six, I think. Uncle Phillip brought the whole family to Jerusalem. Lyssa was just a baby. He continued to come to Jerusalem every year for a while, but he didn't bring his family again."

"Yes, well.... these are perilous times for men of his, er... faith."

Both Jacob's uncles were members of the Galilean sect. Four years ago Phillip and Caleb had an argument. He didn't know what the fight was about, but Phillip had not been back since, and Joel came but once a year. Jacob missed his uncles.

"I have a thought," Gedeon said. "I know Phillip would like to see you. Next year when I come for Passover, perhaps you can go back with me—if your father will permit it."

"Go back with you? All the way to Ephesus?"

"Phillip is in Capernaum, but why not? Traveling is greatly improved with a companion. I would take you this year, but Eunice is with me."

"That's all right, sir," Jacob hastened to say. "Next year is soon enough."

Gedeon laughed, "I understand. Now what else can we do before we have to go back?"

*   *   *   *   *

The two of them managed to kill several more hours before returning to the Temple. "We should join forces with your father and grandfather before we face the women," Gedeon explained. "Present a united front."

But Gedeon underestimated his wife's desire to repay Jacob's offense. The men had picked up Prisca on the way, and Jacob had her by the hand when they came in the door. Diana met them and took hold of Prisca's arm. "I need you to come upstairs with me, dear."

"But why?" she whined. Tired and hungry, she continued to cling to his hand.

"Let go, Prisca, and come with me," her mother insisted.

As she led the child away, Eunice stepped up to her husband. "There is a problem. We need to talk." She glanced once at Jacob, a look that was almost a sneer, and he felt his stomach drop with dread.

Gedeon frowned. "What's the matter?"

"It's the baby. No, Caleb, he is all right—now." She glared at Jacob. "But this morning, after *that boy* had him, Diana went to feed him, and he wouldn't wake up to nurse. All he wanted to do was sleep."

Gedeon gave her a taut little smile. "Babies sometimes do that, don't they?."

"No, you don't understand. We couldn't wake him." She wagged a finger at Jacob. "He went right back to sleep after you changed him. Diana says he's never done that. Did you drug him?"

"No!" he exclaimed. "I told you this morning, I didn't hurt my brother." He turned, pleading, to his father. "I would never hurt Andrew."

Caleb started to reply when Lathan rapped his walking stick on the stone floor. "I have heard enough! As master of this house, this is my judgment." He turned his glare on Jacob with eyes that had gone yellow as his skin. "Boy, you have clearly done something wrong, or this fine woman would not be upset."

"But I didn't...."

Lathan cuffed the side of his face with a gnarled fist. "Talk back to me, will you?" Jacob hung his head in shame, noted how his grandfather's sandals were cutting into his swollen feet. "I have had enough of your insolence and disobedience. You will not take part in the banquet tonight. As a matter of fact, I don't want you in the house at all. You will sleep in the barn with the animals until I say otherwise."

Jacob looked to his father, but Caleb only nodded and said, "Go get your things, son."

Fuming with anger and hurt, he wheeled around and went to his room. He picked up the seashell Arin had given him during that one visit, two scrolls—gifts from his uncle Phillip—and his cloak. As he passed through the house on his way out, he saw Gedeon in one corner, whispering furiously to his wife. She wrenched her arm from his grasp and started to reply, but stopped when she saw Jacob. Unwilling to endure the triumph in her eyes, he turned away and went outside.

He had to tamp down the temptation to kick dirt onto the rugs spread out in the garden for the banquet. Everything in him screamed, "Unfair! Unfair!" When he reached the cool dimness of the barn, he paused a moment to look around, thinking, *Sleep with the animals? Grandfather thinks we still have animals?* He had slept in the barn before, many times. Lathan often used the barn as punishment, but Jacob normally didn't mind it. Sometimes he even slept there on his own, preferring the peace and quiet of the animals' company to the turmoil that too often reigned in the house. Tonight, though, was different. Guests would soon fill the house and the garden, and he'd have to sit in the dark and listen to their merriment far into the night. Besides that, the goats and the donkey that once kept him company had died off, one by one, leaving the barn empty and cold.

Still holding the scrolls and the cloak, he flung himself onto a pile of hay, and lay there staring at the handful of pigeons perched on the rough beams that crossed the ceiling. Without moving from his resting place, one hand groped inside his purse until it found Arin's seashell. His fingers tightened around its familiar shape, found the places worn smooth where he'd handled it, and he remembered when she gave it to him. *Grandfather sent me out here as punishment during their visit.* He frowned, trying to remember the reason for his earlier exile. *I think I spilled something, or maybe I broke something.* Arin slipped the shell into his hand as he went out. Even now he could see her eyes, gray and solemn, watching him go. *And when I came back, we played as if nothing had happened. She didn't shun me just because I had been naughty.* He chewed on his lower lip. *What would she think of me now?*

"I'm not staying here," he told the pigeons. "I don't care what anyone says. Not anymore. They don't want me, so I will go away." They cooed and cocked their heads as if to ask, "But where?" With only a few coins in his purse, he really had but two options. He could go to Zerah's and ask Joel to take him in, or he could go to Mark's. After a moment's debate, he decided on the latter, since he'd been invited—in a way. Hearing voices in the garden, he pushed himself off the hay and went to the door to look out. A half dozen guests had already entered the garden. The banquet was officially underway. Jacob scowled, and throwing his cloak around his shoulders, slipped out and around to the back of the barn and stole away.

* * * * *

"You're certainly welcome to stay," Mary told him. "John Mark isn't here just now. He and his cousin are visiting a friend, but I expect them back any minute. Why don't you come in and take off your cloak?" She took it and hung it on a peg. "Are you hungry?" Then she laughed at her own question. "Of course you are! Boys your age are always hungry. Let me fix you a bite to eat." Before he knew it, she settled him on a cushion with a round of freshly baked flat bread and a bowl of lamb stew. "Here's a little wine to wash that down," she said. "Now tell me, how is your mother? And the baby?"

Jacob, until that moment unaware of how hungry he was, tried not to stuff too much in his mouth at once. "They are well," he managed when he swallowed the first bite. "The baby is named Andrew."

"Andrew," she repeated. "I like that. Who is he named for?"

"My grandmother's father." He dipped the bread into the stew and took another bite.

"Oh yes," she answered. "I knew your grandmother when I was a little girl. Your aunt Deborah is a lot like her."

"You knew both of my grandmothers?" Jacob asked.

"I did. Your grandmother Abigail and my mother were good friends. Oh, here are the men now!"

Mark strolled in with an older man at his heels, exclaiming, "Well, look what wandered in out of the night! No, don't stand up. You remember my cousin Barnabas, don't you?"

Jacob and Barnabas clasped hands, and Barnabas said, "I think we met last year."

"Mama, is there any more of that stew left?" Mark settled down across from Jacob. Within minutes the men were all eating together.

"So, Barnabas, what did you two decide?" Mary asked as she poured their wine.

Jacob thought she meant the two kinsmen, but Barnabas answered, "Saul and I talked it over, and I persuaded him."

Mary paused, the pitcher of wine in her hand. "When will you leave?"

"As soon as we may," Barnabas answered. "Probably within the week."

"I see." Mary glanced at her son and chewed a moment at her lower lip, then turned away, leaving Jacob to wonder why Barnabas' leaving troubled her.

*   *   *   *   *

That night, Jacob and Mark went up to the roof of the house. "What happened today?" Mark asked. "What made you decide to come?"

He told him the whole sorry tale. "I thought Gedeon, or maybe my father would defend me," he concluded, "but Grandfather would have none of it."

"That's too bad." Mark shook his head. "Your grandfather has always been harsh with you."

Jacob nodded, his face red with misery. "I cannot please him."

Mark, playing with a bit of straw, wound it around one finger and said, "I have to tell you something." He sighed and looked at his friend. "I am going with Barnabas."

"What?" He tried to swallow the panic rising in him. "Why are you going?"

"To assist them any way I can. We may be gone a long time, a couple of years, maybe more."

Suddenly Jacob remembered something Mark had told him before. "The man you're going with, what did Barnabas say his name was?"

"Saul," his friend answered. He pulled at the straw until it broke in half. "He's from Tarsus, up in Syria."

Jacob paled, "I have heard of him." He didn't add that Grandfather reviled the man regularly, spitting his name, rather than speaking it. "You're going on this journey to...?"

"To preach," Mark replied. He had already told Jacob what he believed, that a man named Jesus from the Galilean town of Nazareth was the Messiah, that he was crucified when Jacob was about a year old, that he was buried and came back to life after three days in the tomb. It was too much for Jacob, but Mark was his friend, and he loved him and respected his faith. After all, his uncles believed it, though Grandfather insisted it was blasphemy. "I'm glad you came. It's good that we'll have a little time together before I leave."

Jacob nodded, thinking the year ahead would be a long one without John Mark.

* * * * *

Early the next morning, Mary woke him. "Your father is here."

Sick with apprehension, he went to the door where Caleb waited, his face grim and stern. "Father, I'm sorry...."

"No, son. This isn't about you coming here," his father answered, "but you have to come home now. It's your grandfather. He's dying."

Chapter 2

"How did you know where to find me?" Jacob asked as they left Mark's house.

"I saw you sneak out last night, and I followed you until I knew where you were going," his father answered. "Your grandfather fell ill during the banquet and took to his bed. I think he will not survive another night."

He hung his head. "I am sorry for what happened yesterday, Father."

"I'm sorry, too, son. I don't think you did anything wrong." His brow creased in a frown. "I understand your mother's nervousness about the baby, but I can't imagine what set Eunice off. Of course, I couldn't go against my father's orders, but I really wanted you there with us at the banquet."

"Father...." Jacob hesitated a moment, then plunged in. "Did you host a banquet when I was born?"

"Well...." Caleb's expression told him the answer before he spoke it. "Things were different then, son. Your mother was.... " He blew in exasperation, leaving Jacob to wonder yet again what she did to disgrace herself. "She was different, that's all. Everything was different. We weren't living here in Jerusalem, you see, and I didn't know many people in Capernaum." He glanced at him and added, "That doesn't mean I wasn't happy you were born." He smiled and laid a hand on the boy's shoulder. "It was one of the proudest days of my life."

He nodded and managed a smile for his father's words. *Maybe things will be better when Grandfather is gone.* He immediately chastised himself for the thought, but the idea persisted, and he allowed himself to daydream of a time when the two of them would work side by side in the Temple with no one to interfere or criticize. *Soon,* he told himself. *Soon I will have my father to myself during the day. I will help him with his work, and he will be proud of me. And eventually Mother will see that I mean Andrew no harm.*

When they reached the house, Caleb said, "Come with me, son. Your grandfather wanted to speak to each of us before...." His voice caught, and he passed a hand over his eyes.

Jacob swallowed, wanting to kick himself for his traitorous thoughts. *Father will miss him.* Determined to try one last time to win his grandfather's approval, he ran his fingers through his hair and straightened his robes. "Do I look all right?" he whispered.

Caleb smiled sadly. "You look fine. Don't worry." He opened the door and led him through the main room, under the scrutiny of the family gathered there. Suddenly ashamed for having run away, thus forcing his father to come after him, he didn't raise his eyes. *I have been weighed in the balance and found wanting.* He followed his father to Lathan's room where Caleb stopped him. "Wait here a moment."

He stood just outside and heard his father say, "Father, are you awake?"

A groan and a rattling cough answered, and Lathan said, "Here, my son, take this. I want you to wear it."

"Your ring?"

"I had it made...." Another spasm of coughing. Jacob cleared his own throat. "I had it made long ago. You take it now."

A short silence followed, then, "Jacob is here to see you, Father."

"No," came the raspy voice. "No, I don't want to see him."

"But Father...."

"I said no. That boy is a burden and a curse around your neck. Don't interrupt me, son...." Another cough. Jacob's hands curled into fists on their own, and he felt the blood rise hot in his face. Could the others hear what Lathan was saying? "You have a true son now. Like our father Abraham...a son of promise. Remember what the Lord told Abraham about the son of the Egyptian? He said Ishmael would never share in Isaac's inheritance. So it must be with you." Lathan's voice wheezed, "Now, I know you're fond of the boy, just as Abraham was of his...."

"Father, he's my son...."

"Yes, just as Ishmael was Abraham's son. But he sent him away, and that is what you must do."

Tears scalded Jacob's eyes as he heard his father say, "Send him away? But he's only a boy."

"He will not share in Andrew's inheritance," Lathan insisted, and a spasm of coughing overtook him. "Aaagh!" he groaned in pain. When he recovered, he said, "Swear to me, son. Swear you will do this."

No...no! Jacob's heart cried in the ensuing silence. *No, my father, don't send me away!* Caleb's answer came quiet as doom. "I swear it."

* * * * *

But Lathan did not die—not that night, nor the next. He lingered on, hovering between his bed and the grave. Deborah and Susannah likewise hovered. When he was asleep, they bathed him with vinegar and kept watch. When he was awake, they bore his feeble abuse. The constant demands of caring for him began to take a toll on Deborah.

"Aunt Deborah," Jacob said, pulling her aside after three days. "Are you all right?"

Her smile didn't quite light up her face. "I am a little tired, that's all."

"Let me help you with some of it," he suggested. When she hesitated, he said,

"I know Grandfather doesn't want me in there. *No more than I want to be in there with him.* But I can help in other ways. I can bring things for you, and when he's asleep, I can help turn him over. You shouldn't be doing that anyway. He's too heavy for you."

"You're right," she murmured. "I keep thinking of you as a child, and look at you! You're taller than I am. You've grown into a young man. Yes, I could use your help, when your father can spare you."

"I'll go talk to him," he said, and bounded down the stairs.

"You would do that for your grandfather?" Caleb asked when Jacob recounted his conversation with Deborah.

He shook his head. "No, sir. I want to do it for Deborah."

"I see." Caleb looked at him long and hard, as if trying to read his mind. Then he sighed, "I guess I can understand that. For the next week or two you can stay here and help her."

And then what, Father? Where will you send me? Unable to bring himself to ask that question, he murmured his thanks and went back upstairs.

So instead of running for his father, he began running for his aunt—up and down the stairs, more than a dozen times a day. But though he missed wandering Jerusalem's streets, his reward came from seeing Deborah's pallor lessen as her countenance eased from its strain and fatigue.

Finally, after about a week, she told him, "I don't need you this morning. Your grandfather is better. He's sitting up and taking a little food. Why don't you go out and get some fresh air?"

"Are you sure?" he asked her.

Now her smile was genuine—the smile he remembered. "I'm sure. Just be back in time for dinner."

Jacob went out, closing the door silently behind him and turned up the street toward Zerah's house. He doubted anyone else in the house would miss him. His father was away at the Temple. Diana had her hands full with the baby, and Eunice had taken command of the household and servants. Gedeon and Prisca were off somewhere at Eunice's request. *Now is the perfect time to see Uncle Joel,* he told himself.

Much of the Passover crowd was already dispersed, leaving the streets of upper Jerusalem relatively quiet under the gentle spring sun. He took no comfort in its warmth. His father had barely spoken to him since his talk with Lathan—not that Jacob expected him to—but he took it as a bad sign. *Father swore, made an oath.* Jacob couldn't imagine that he would go back on his word. As he turned up the street toward Zerah's house, a worry that had nagged at the back of his mind pushed forward. *Is Uncle Joel still in Jerusalem? He may have already left.*

The pale-eyed servant met him at the door. "I am here to see my uncle Joel," Jacob told him. "Is he still here?"

"He is." The servant stepped aside. "You are expected." He ushered him into the main room where Zerah and his uncle were just finishing breakfast.

"There you are!" Joel stood to embrace him. "When I heard about your grandfather I wondered if you'd be able to come and see me."

"Would you like something?" Zerah asked, gesturing to the food spread out between the cushions.

"Thank you sir, but no," he replied as he sat down. "I just ate."

With a wry smile Zerah patted his own generous middle. "That's never been a problem for me."

Joel took his seat again. "I didn't want to leave Jerusalem without getting a chance to talk with you. I'm glad you were able to get away."

Jacob bowed his head as the emotions he was trying to tamp down rose unbidden to the surface. "I...I hoped you might still be here. Thank you."

Joel laid a hand on his arm. "Something is amiss, isn't it? Something other than your grandfather's illness." Jacob glanced at Zerah, and Joel added, "It's all right, lad. You can tell us. Zerah is trustworthy."

He swallowed. How was he supposed to speak with this brick lodged in his throat? "My father...that is, I...." Without warning he burst into tears.

Joel wrapped an arm around him and pulled him to his chest. "Oh, lad, I'm so sorry," he murmured over his head.

"Let it out, son," Zerah added. He reached out and laid a hand on Jacob's shoulder. "Let it all out."

Great, choking sobs seized him. The rage and hurt he had hidden away exploded from deep inside. His crying grated in his own ears, the only sound in an otherwise silent room. He wanted to stop, but his fierce hurt clutched him in an iron grip and wouldn't let him go. He felt foolish, and at the same time oddly comforted by the rough feel of Joel's wool garment against his face. When at last the tempest of his tears subsided, he sat up and wiped at his streaming eyes. He saw Zerah accept a cloth from his servant, which he now offered, saying, "Here. Use this."

"Thank you sir," Jacob's voice sounded strange—deep and harsh, as if it belonged to someone else. He dried his face and wiped his nose, wondering how he could ever speak of what his grandfather demanded—and what his father swore. At the moment he wanted to talk about something else—anything else. "Uncle Joel, tell me about my mother."

Joel frowned in puzzlement. "Your mother?"

He nodded. "No one ever speaks of her. Aunt Deborah could, but she won't." He shrugged and wiped at his nose again. "I think she's afraid."

"Very well. It's time you knew," Joel took a sip of his wine. "But I want your promise that you won't repeat what we've told you to your father or your grandfather."

"Grandfather will have nothing more to do with me," he murmured. *And soon my father will turn me out.* "I promise."

"Your grandfather is not long for this world, but he still may seek to do me harm. I do not fear your father—only that he might say something to Lathan." He cleared his throat and said, "Your mother's name is Miriam. She married again—a man named Reuel. They have a vineyard in Antioch. I was about ten when we—your Grandmother Abigail and I—brought her to Jerusalem to wed your father." He sighed, "She was a pretty girl, but of course as her little brother I didn't have the eyes to see it. Your father actually confessed to me once that he loved her the moment he saw her." He sat hunched over, staring into his cup, and now he rolled one shoulder, as if the memory burdened him. "Perhaps he did...I don't know. Anyway, they married about this time of year, just before Passover. The marriage was unusual because your mother was deaf."

"Deaf?" Jacob's mouth fell open. "My mother is deaf?"

"She *was* deaf," Joel corrected him. "But soon after you were born...."

"In Capernaum," he heard himself murmur, shocked and puzzled by his uncle's words.

"In Capernaum," Joel nodded. "After you were born, your mother met Jesus of Nazareth, and he touched her and opened her ears. My mother told me later that Caleb didn't seem to be offended by her healing, or even much surprised. I think if they'd been left to themselves, the two of them might still be husband and wife. The problem lay with your grandfather. I still don't know all the particulars, but he hated Jesus—violently hated him."

"Perhaps I can fill in some of the gaps," Zerah said, grunting as he adjusted one of the cushions under him. "Jesus came into the Temple the same Passover your parents married and chastised the money changers, including your grandfather. He turned their tables over and denounced them for making a profit of worship. Lathan came to me to find out what I knew about the Nazarene, and whether the Sanhedrin was planning to do anything about him. I was a member of the council," he explained, "though no longer. He wanted us to take immediate action—I think to kill Jesus. Sometime after that, your grandfather fell ill while your parents were in Capernaum. He sent for Caleb to come home, which he did, but he didn't bring your mother right away. I think he knew how your grandfather would react to her association with Jesus and wanted to hide her healing from him."

By the time she did come, your grandfather was near death. It took me a while, but I have managed to piece together what happened. She brought Jesus to the house, and he raised Lathan from his deathbed."

Stunned, Jacob raked at his hair. "But...I don't understand. This makes no sense. If Jesus was a prophet, why did he heal him? Didn't he know Grandfather hated him?"

"I do not doubt that he knew," Zerah's eyebrows knit together, "though I still don't understand that part myself. Your grandfather denied that Jesus had anything to do with his recovery. Later he met privately with me and said your mother had shamed herself, that she carried a child of adultery, and Caleb wanted to put her away."

"But I was already born," Jacob protested.

Zerah nodded. "I speak of your brother."

Brother! He leaned forward with a groan and covered his face in his hands.

He heard Joel say, "Perhaps this is too much at once for him. We should leave the rest for later, when he is able to hear more."

"No." He sat up again, his eyes dark with misery. "I am able now. Tell it all. I want to know."

"I am ashamed to say I took part in the divorce." Zerah spat out the bitter words. "And I lost track of her afterward, though I knew she was forced to leave you with your father. Later on when I understood what really happened, I confronted Lathan with it." His lips pressed tight in a grim expression. "My friend became my enemy."

Jacob turned to his uncle. "What about my brother?"

"His name is Jonathan. He is a year younger than you."

"And are you sure he is my true brother?" His face went red with embarrassment for asking, but he had to know.

Joel smiled and laid a hand on his head. "I have no doubt. You two are as alike as any litter mates I've seen."

Zerah said, "Your mother was no adulteress, my boy. Your grandfather accused her so he could send her away. Her healing—and his own—were an indictment against him."

"There is more," Joel spoke into the silence that followed, "but it can wait for another day. Now I want you to tell me what's happened with you and your father."

Zerah's servant handed him a cup of wine. "Thank you," he murmured, then blinked in surprise. The servant's right arm ended in a stump. His hand was missing. *So that's why he keeps it hidden in his sleeve!* Distracted by the sight and wondering what the man's story might be, he took a gulp of the wine and told them everything, beginning with his attempt to help Diana with the baby. "Father swore," he concluded, hanging his head. "Grandfather made him swear to send me away."

Joel and Zerah exchanged knowing looks. "I told you this would happen," Zerah said. "Even now Lathan reaches out from the edge of the grave to destroy another life."

"One of us should talk to Caleb," Joel answered, "though I doubt he would willingly speak to me."

"Uncle Joel," Jacob broke in. "You and Uncle Phillip both had arguments with my father. Were they about my mother?"

Joel sucked at his teeth a moment, considering. "On the surface, yes. We both tried to make him see the evil behind what Lathan did." He stared into his wine cup and sighed. "Perhaps that was a mistake. Neither of us made any headway with him, and we both lost the freedom to see you."

"I understand now. The reason Grandfather never liked me was because of my mother."

"I'm afraid that is true," Joel patted his back, "but she was innocent of wrong-doing. I didn't know that at first. No one spoke of her, and I assumed she had disgraced herself and was afraid it might rub off on me. So I didn't speak of her either and was happy to keep it that way, but just before my mother died, she told me the truth and made me promise to tell you when you were older, when it was safe."

"When it was safe?"

"Lathan used various threats against all of us should we be tempted to tell you about your mother. We suspect he had a hand in killing one of his own servants, though we couldn't prove anything. So we kept quiet and bided our time." Joel shrugged, "Now he is perhaps going to his reward. In any event, we can be free with the truth."

Jacob glanced toward one of the windows, and noting the length of the shadows, knew it was time to go. "I told Aunt Deborah I'd be home in time for dinner."

Zerah drained his cup and said, "Come to us and let us know what your father decides to do. If he sends you out of the house, we are here for you. Joel, you and I may need to remain here longer than we planned."

"It is no loss to me," he smiled. "Your hospitality is more than adequate."

Zerah chuckled, but the muscles in his face tightened as if in pain. "Enjoy it while you can, my young friend."

* * * * *

Two days later, Mark came to the house, his manner solemn and careful. Jacob asked, "This is it, isn't it?"

Mark nodded. "Can you come and walk with me a while?"

"I can't. Father told me to stay close at hand today, but we can go up on the roof." His friend agreed, and presently the boys sat on top of the house, buffeted by an energetic breeze riding in off the Great Sea in the west. "It looks like we may not be able to stay up here for long," Jacob gestured to a bank of high, dark clouds approaching in the distance like an invading army. "So when do you leave?"

"This afternoon," Mark answered. "We will travel to Antioch first, then set out from there."

"Antioch!" Jacob clutched his arm. "That's where my mother lives! My Uncle Joel told me so. You remember Joel, don't you?" Mark nodded, and Jacob said, "He lives in Damascus now, but he's here for the Feast." He closed his eyes briefly. Almost he could feel the wind lift him up and carry him away. "I wish I could go with you." Then seized with an idea he said, "You could find her and give her a message from me, couldn't you? Her name is Miriam, and her husband's name is Reuel. They own a vineyard."

"A message?" Mark glanced behind him toward the stairs leading from the lower floors. Was anyone listening? "Do you think that's wise?"

"I don't care, Mark. My uncle told me all about her, and I want her to know. It's important. Will you do it?"

"Well...." Moved by the intensity in Jacob's eyes, he answered, "For you, I will. Do you want to write it down?"

Jacob shook his head. "She's a woman, Mark. She won't be able to read it. Just tell her this...." He narrowed his eyes at the gathering clouds and said, "Tell her that I know everything now." He told him of Gedeon's offer to take him traveling and added, "And tell her I will try to come and see her—and my brother, perhaps next year."

"Brother?" Mark exclaimed. "You have a brother?"

"My uncle says I do, and...."

"Jacob, I need to talk to you now." Startled, both boys jumped to their feet. Jacob's father said nothing more, but stood waiting across the roof from them at the head of the stairs, his face gaunt and pale with weariness and worry. *Did he hear?* Jacob wondered. *How long has he been standing there?*

Mark stuck out his hand. "Take care of yourself, my friend."

Jacob clasped his hand in his own, then they embraced briefly. Mark pulled away with a nod and turned to go. As he passed Caleb at the stairs, he paused to make a polite bow. "Goodbye, sir."

"Goodbye, John Mark. Good journey."

"Thank you, sir." With that, he was gone.

Caleb trained his gaze on his son. "I think you and I had better talk." He crossed the roof. "Sit down, son."

The wind now carried a heavy mist with it. Jacob sat down again and waited for his father to speak. "I suppose...." Caleb cleared his throat. "I suppose you are wondering about the conversation I had with your grandfather last week."

Unable to meet his father's eyes, Jacob stared off toward the west. "Yes sir."

"I made a promise, a vow to him, but I have been looking for a way to fulfill that vow without injury to you or me." He wiped at his dampened face with one sleeve. "I think I have found a way. I talked to Simon, Caiaphas' steward, and he has agreed to take you on as an apprentice."

Jacob felt the blood drain from his face. He had to bite his tongue to keep a cry of dismay inside. He had met the man on a number of occasions, each time quailing under the disapproval and contempt that radiated from him. To make matters worse, a schoolmate of his had been apprenticed to the steward—briefly—the year before. The boy was sent home in disgrace after only a few weeks, though Jacob knew him well enough to know he was neither lazy nor stupid. Simon's name was a by-word among the boys Jacob's age. "You don't want to work for him," the rumors insisted. "He'll eat you for dinner."

".... a good situation for you," his father was saying. "You'll be doing the same kinds of things you did for me, and you can stay in Jerusalem. You won't have to go off..." Caleb gestured vaguely toward the horizon, "...somewhere."

"Yes sir." Jacob chewed at the inside of his lip.

"This way I can keep you close by." Caleb draped an arm around his shoulders. "You heard what I swore to your grandfather. I can't leave you an inheritance, but I can make sure you are well situated, that you can make your own way. And if you need it, I can help you out—from time to time."

Jacob looked away and wiped at the tears that had gathered in his eyes. "When am I to go?"

"I will take you to Simon tomorrow morning, so get your things together tonight."

Tomorrow. Jacob's heart fell to the pit of his stomach. *So soon!* "Then may I have this afternoon, sir?"

"You want to go wandering?" Caleb smiled, "I understand. Of course you may. Just be home in time for supper." He stood up and gazed at the sky. "Be careful, though, son. Looks like rain is coming."

"Yes sir." Jacob watched him go, then turned back to face the storm clouds.

*   *   *   *   *

An hour later, he was at Zerah's again, his hair whipped wildly around his head by the capricious wind. Rain had just started coming down, slapping at the walls and pavement of the city in angry bursts. "Father found a place for me here in Jerusalem," he told his uncle when he was inside. "I am to be apprenticed to the High Priest's steward."

"That's good, isn't it?" Joel looked at Zerah, who gave his head an almost imperceptible shake.

Jacob, who missed this exchange, plunged ahead, trying to put a good face on

As I am Known

his situation. "I am sure I'll learn a lot, and I will be able to see my father from time to time."

"Well, I'm glad you could come," Joel said. "I'm leaving Jerusalem the day after tomorrow, at first light."

"And I will be with him," Zerah said. To Jacob's exclamation of surprise, he added, "I have planned this for months. Your father found a buyer for my house. That was the business I had with him."

"Where will you go?" Jacob felt like he was losing yet another ally, though he scarcely knew Zerah.

"We're going to back to Damascus," Joel answered. "I bought a house and land just north of the city with the inheritance Mother left me, and I have a good-sized herd." He grinned, and added, "You may have some cousins soon. I am betrothed to a girl there. We're supposed to wed this summer."

Jacob managed a smile. "Congratulations, Uncle Joel."

"And I will go to interfere and be underfoot," Zerah declared in his most serious tone. "Your uncle will tire of me, forcing me to purchase a house in the city so I won't pester him and his bride to death."

Jacob laughed despite his melancholy mood. Then he asked, "But isn't Jerusalem your home, sir?"

"Until now it has been." He glanced around him at the near-empty room. "Ever since my Ruth died, I have felt less at home. And the last few years have been—difficult. It is time for me to go."

"Sounds like the storm is passing," Joel remarked. Jacob stopped to listen. The rain had reduced to a patter. The wind had spent most of its energy, and now circled the house, moaning softly with fatigue.

* * * * *

The next morning, as Caleb, Diana and Gedeon looked on, Prisca clung to Jacob's waist and cried. "Why? Oh, why are you leaving me?"

"Prisca." Grateful that Eunice wasn't there to sneer, he went down on one knee and held his sister close as she wept on his neck. "I'm not going very far, and I'll come and see you sometimes."

"Do...." she hiccupped through her tears. "Do you promise?"

"I promise." He fought through his own pain to offer her a smile. "I'll take you to the marketplace and stuff you so full of honey cakes and almonds you won't be able to walk for a week. Now I want you to promise me something."

Prisca sniffed and pulled away to look at him. "What?"

"Promise you'll be a good girl and obey Mother and Father, and that you'll take care of Andrew the way I took care of you." Out of the corner of his eye he saw Diana bite her lip and look away.

"Yes, I promise," Prisca kissed his cheek, and turned and fled upstairs.

Jacob picked up his pack and reached out for Gedeon's hand. "Thank you for everything, sir."

"Thank you, son." Gedeon grasped it firmly and smiled, though his eyes were grieved. "I hope to see you next year."

"I hope so too, sir." Diana stood behind Caleb as if she needed protection. Jacob said, "Goodbye, Mother." He lingered, hoping for some sign of affection from her.

"Yes, well...." She stepped forward and gingerly patted his shoulder, then withdrew her hand, almost as if she'd been burned. "Good fortune to you, Jacob."

It wasn't a kiss on the cheek, but it would have to do. He went to the door and stepped out. Caleb followed him saying, "I'll see you all tonight."

Jacob heard the final thud of the door as it closed behind him. He paused, took a deep breath, and tucked away his hurt and his fear.

"Let me give you this before we go, son." Caleb handed him a leather pouch. "Simon will supply your food and shelter, and your clothes are in good condition, so you won't need money for much. This should be enough to get you through the first year if you use it wisely."

Jacob accepted the pouch and hefted it. It felt about half full. He opened his pack and buried the pouch in the bottom under his clothing. "Thank you, Father. I will be careful with it."

"I know you will," Caleb smiled. "You're a better steward of your money than I was at your age." He gestured up the street. "I promised I'd have you to Simon before the third hour, so we had better be going."

Simon met them in the courtyard of Caiaphas' palace. He watched their approach with deep-set black eyes. A prominent blue vein ran down the center of his forehead, from his hairline to the bridge of his nose, like an angry river. Though a Jew, he was clean-shaven and had cut his gray hair short, Roman-style. And he wore his tunic like a Roman, with no outer coat. A ring of keys hung from his belt. He swung them absently in one hand as his cold black eyes searched Jacob's, probing as if to see into his very soul. "So this is the boy?"

Feeling a desperate need to make a good first impression, Jacob waited for his cue in the little orchestrated courtesy. When Caleb laid a hand on his shoulder, saying, "This is my son," he made a low bow. "Shalom, sir."

Simon's lips stretched in what Jacob supposed passed for a smile. "You are a most fortunate young man." The keys jangled and clashed. "Your father has secured you one of the best apprenticeships in the city," his lips stretched thinner, "perhaps in all Israel. If you are intelligent and obedient, you will do well."

"Yes sir." The steward's invasive stare made Jacob want to fall at his father's feet and beg him to take him home. He swallowed. *But I am no longer seven years old,* he told himself. *I have to be a man now.*

"All right then, son." Caleb embraced him briefly. "I have to get to work—and so do you. Come and see me when you can."

Scarcely had his father turned away when Simon said, "Follow me."

He followed the steward across the courtyard, through one of the white stone archways and into the darkness of the palace. He had to trot to keep up with Simon's hurried pace. They passed through a massive main hall that gave Jacob a brief impression of sumptuous luxury, where Simon stopped to pick a lamp up from a table. Gesturing with his chin, he turned left into a hallway that led to a storage room filled with crates and baskets. At the back of the storage room, a door opened to a flight of stairs descending into a dark cellar. Jacob followed the bobbing lamp light down and down. *Why are we here?* He wondered when he reached the bottom. The cellar stood empty, its stone walls carved out of the bedrock upon which all Jerusalem rested.

"Turn around and face the wall," Simon commanded, setting the lamp on the floor.

As he did, he felt the hairs on the back of his neck stiffen and rise. Halfway up the wall, just out of the edge of his own shadow, a set of iron manacles dangled from the stone. This room was not used for storage.

"Lift your robes and let me see your legs."

Gooseflesh prickled Jacob's arms as he obeyed, raising the hem to his knees.

"Higher."

When his thighs were exposed, he heard a sound behind him and had less than a second to brace himself before the whip lashed his flesh. He yelped once in surprise and pain.

"Quiet, you little cur," Simon growled behind him. The whip whistled in the silent room, landed another stinging blow, and then a third. Jacob, grinding his teeth with the pain, felt a trickle start down his right leg. "Let your robes down and face me." He did as he was told, his face flushed with anger and humiliation. Simon studied him with cold, hard eyes. The flickering lamplight from the floor made him look ghoulish "You are a son of wealth and privilege. All your life you've been pampered and petted. Well, no more. Here you are little more than a slave, and you will obey me without question. If you are derelict in your duties, if you are lazy, or slow, you will feel the sting of the lash again, but next time I will not be so merciful. You will receive a dozen lashes—on your back. This was merely a warning." The corners of his mouth curled up. "And do not think to run to your father. Whatever you did to earn his disfavor...."

"But I didn't...." Jacob began. Another biting lick of the whip on his ankles made him curse his indiscretion.

"Do not argue with me, boy! I know you have displeased your father, or he would not have brought you here." Simon eyed him with a cold smirk. "Obedient sons are taught by their fathers. Whatever you did will only be compounded if you disgrace him by running home. He will send you back to me, and you will have another taste of this." He held up the whip, then tossed it to the floor. Picking up the lamp once again, he turned and started up the stairs, calling back over his shoulder, "Come along."

* * * * *

That night, Jacob stood in a bare little room, empty but for a narrow cot and a rough table with a lamp, and stared out the window. He had trotted at Simon's heels all day long, had fetched and carried for him, and endured the pitying stares of the servants in the house. He learned nothing. Simon didn't bother to explain anything, and he didn't dare ask questions. Except for "yes sir" and "no sir" he hadn't spoken a half-dozen words. After a thin meal of bread and cheese, he was locked into this room.

"Go to bed, boy," Simon admonished him. "You have another long day tomorrow." He nodded toward the latticed window. "And don't try to run away. I will find you, and the punishment will be more than you can bear."

Gazing out the window, he began to doubt. *Did Father really think this would be a good place, or was he just trying to get rid of me?* He swiped at his eyes with the back of one hand and tried to ignore the burning pain in his legs. *I'd be better off anywhere else but here.* He tugged at the edges of the lattice, and the nails on one side squealed lightly as they gave way. Jacob backed away, and wiping his sweaty palms off on his robe, sat down on the edge of the cot to stare at the lattice. Getting out wouldn't be hard. *But where can I go that he won't find me?* Going home was out of the question. *That will be the first place Simon looks. Mark is gone, and Uncle Joel is leaving. Aunt Deborah and Uncle Nicanor might hide me.* Then Jacob checked himself. *I can't do that. If Simon or Father came looking for me there, she'd tell him. Deborah doesn't lie.*

He wrestled with himself. *If I run away, it will hurt my father, and he's been through so much already.* His eyes filled again. *But then he really would be rid of me. He wouldn't have to worry about me anymore. Besides, he has Andrew now.*

Then he remembered the money his father gave him. *Do I have enough to get away?* He dug into his bag, pushed aside the clothing and the scrolls. His heart thudded dully in his chest as he searched, becoming more desperate with each passing second. Finally he dumped the bag out onto his cot and went through everything. Something hard came to his hand, something folded inside an extra tunic. With shaking hands he pulled it out. Not his money, only Arin's seashell. Now he shook every piece of clothing, moaning under his breath. Even in the dim light of his cell, the horrible truth was clear. The pouch was gone. *Someone took my money!* With a groan, he knelt on the stone floor and laid his forehead against the edge of the cot. *I am trapped.*

But he didn't sit still for long. The memory of Simon's lash against his legs filled him with angry determination. He went to the door and lay down on his stomach, and peered out underneath. He didn't see any feet, and didn't hear anyone. *Simon probably thinks his threats are enough to keep me here. Well, there's only one way to find out.* He stood up and pried his fingers under the edges of the lattice. After three or four firm tugs, the bottom nails came out. A few more, and he had the lattice in his hands.

He set it down, leaning it against the wall, and stuck his head out the window, then clapped a hand over his mouth to stifle a gasp of astonishment. A pair of ice-blue eyes watched him from below. Zerah's servant. What was he doing here?

"Can you get down?" The servant's words, though little more than a whisper, reached him perfectly from the stone courtyard.

He leaned out and looked down. His room was on the second floor. He suppressed an urge to whistle. It was a long way to the ground. "I don't know," he whispered back. "I'll break my legs if I jump."

"Can you make a rope of something? Look around—and hurry!"

Hurry, yes. Dusk was falling rapidly. He needed to quit the city before nightfall. His eyes strayed to the threadbare blanket covering the bed. Its rough texture caught his attention. *I could tear this up and make a rope. Five strips, and that's all. If I tear it any thinner, it won't hold my weight.* He leaned out the window again. "Give me two or three minutes." Gallus nodded.

Jacob worried at the edge of the blanket with his teeth and fingers until the fabric gave way with a dull, ragged sound. When he had reduced the blanket to five strips, he knotted them together and tied one end around the door handle. Working feverishly, he stuffed his clothing and scrolls back into his bag, and dropped it down to Gallus. Praying no one in any of the neighboring houses would spot him and raise the alarm, he tossed the homemade rope out the window, and taking a deep breath, he followed it. He managed to shimmy down without incident, but discovered to his dismay when he reached the end that he was still a good six feet from the ground.

"There's nothing for it but to jump," Gallus said from just below him. "Kick off against the wall and let go."

He took a deep breath, swung out, and released the rope. The shock of his feet hitting the pavement stung like a thousand angry hornets. Jacob blinked back tears and rubbed his legs furiously.

"Come on, boy, run!"

He scooped up his pack and shouldered it. Breaking into a staggering run he kept his eyes on Gallus' impossibly yellow hair as they ducked into the darkening labyrinth that was Jerusalem's streets.

* * * * *

When dusk fully fell that evening, a traveler stopped to drop an armload of dead wood and kindling near the site of an old fire. He knelt and brushed away the remaining ashes and laid down a handful of dry grass for kindling. That done, he reached into his firepot with a pair of metal tongs and removed a pair of smoldering coals. He set these on the grass, and blew on the coals until they came to life with an eager red glow. In moments, the kindling was enveloped in flame. The traveler added a handful of slender twigs to the infant fire, then bigger ones as the flame grew, illuminating and warming his face. He had just laid on one of the bigger logs when his companion came and sat next to him, asking, "Any sign of them?"

"Yes, I think I see them coming up the path."

"What if his father comes looking for him? Or his master? I haven't the heart to send him back."

"Nor I. We will just have to pray that doesn't happen." Joel stood up. "I'll go get them."

He returned to the fire with Jacob and Gallus in tow, announcing, "They made it. Our company is now complete."

"Did you run into any trouble?" Zerah asked his servant.

"No. Mina created a diversion for the sentry to pull him away from his post, and the lad was quick and courageous. We got away cleanly."

Jacob felt his face redden to the roots of his hair at Gallus' praise. He said to Zerah, "Thank you, sir for waiting for me. And thank you, Gallus, for your help."

"It is our pleasure," Zerah beamed.

Joel remarked, "We will have to make a short night of it tonight and be on our way as early in the morning as we can." He opened their pack of provisions.

"We cannot wait for morning," Gallus sat down. "We need to keep going until we reach Jericho."

"Tonight?" Zerah regarded him with an expression of alarm. "Travel in the dark?"

Gallus nodded. "There is risk in it, but the risk is greater if we remain. We still have the moon to travel by." He turned to the priest and a rare smile quirked the corners of his mouth. "I would hate to see your venerable self thrown in prison for kidnapping."

The food in Jacob's mouth went suddenly dry. Until that moment he had given no thought to the consequences the others faced for helping him. "I...I will go on ahead," he stammered. "I was going to run away anyway. You shouldn't get into trouble on my account."

"You'll do no such thing," Joel said as he tore his bread in half. "As your uncle, I'm taking authority, and I order you to remain with us." He glanced at him and winked.

"You can't leave us now," Zerah added. "I haven't had this much fun in years."

The four of them ate a quick meal and set out again. A few hours later, they were inside Jericho's ancient walls, where they found an inn for the night. Jacob lay down on his rooftop bed and stared at the stars. *I hope we've come far enough. I hope we don't get caught.* His thoughts turned to his father. *I've shamed him by running away.* A tear trickled down the side of his face just before he closed his eyes. *I'm sorry, Father.*

* * * * *

The morning after Jacob escaped from Caiaphas' palace, Deborah was busy feeding her children breakfast when a pounding at her door made them all jump. "Hannah," she called out, "will you go and see what that's about?"

Hardly had the servant opened the door, when a man dressed in an iron-gray robe burst in, pushing her aside. He paused a moment to look around, and when he spotted Deborah he demanded, "Where is the boy Jacob?" A pair of manacles dangled from his fist.

Deborah scrambled to her feet to face him, keeping her voice in check, though her heart pounded in terror. "Who are you, and what do you want with him?"

He ignored her first question. "The boy ran away from his master last night." The stranger's hair and eyes matched the color of his robe. Had his face been gray also, he could not have looked harder or more uncompromising. "His father is disgraced. He sent me to you." He didn't add that the boy's father was in tears when he left, or that he overheard the mother hissing in the father's ear, "I told you he would do something like this."

Deborah swallowed both her tears and her fright. *Oh, Jacob, where are you? And how can I help you?* Her children, whimpering with fear, clung to her skirt. She touched their heads to reassure them and lifted her chin. "He is not here."

The stranger's gaze narrowed on her, assessing her honesty. His answering smile, cold and sardonic, didn't touch his eyes. "Then you will not mind if I search your house."

He started past her, but Deborah took a step to block him. "You will do no such thing," she declared, her voice trembling with rage. "My husband isn't home."

He snarled, "Out of my way, woman!" and cuffed her. The manacles he carried struck her temple, and with a cry she fell to the floor as blood seeped scarlet from the wound on her face.

The servant cried, "Mistress!" as she rushed to her side. Deborah's children bent over her, weeping, and the stranger turned on his heel and went from room to room to search. He knew she had spoken the truth, that the boy was not in her house. It only fueled his rampage. In his wrath at the woman's defiance, he overturned furniture and smashed pottery. The light in his eyes resembled something close to joy as he tore each room apart. In one room he found a pair of golden earrings lying on a table. He swept them to the floor and ground them under his heel until they lay scarred and misshapen on the tile. That done, he pitched the table over on its side. From the window he heard the servant running down the street screaming for help. He grinned and murmured, "Squall away, you old hen—for all the good it will do you."

Fortunately for John Mark's mother, she wasn't home when the stranger knocked. He kicked open the door and took her house apart, all the while muttering under his breath, "You're not here, are you, little man? You're not even in Jerusalem. You've fled the city." Finding the house empty, he climbed to the roof and walked a deliberate, unhurried circuit around its perimeter, shading his eyes as if to pierce the distance with the force of his gaze.

Simon had sent him on this mission that morning, saying, "I want you to find the boy and bring him back. Today, Phineas."

Phineas appraised Simon's reddened face. "So the boy got the better of you, did he? You've lost boys before. What makes this one so important?"

"I don't have to answer to you," the other growled. "Do you want the job or not?" He pulled a leather purse from his sleeve. "It's gold," he said, and dangled it in front of Phineas' eyes to entice him.

Phineas crossed his arms and grinned. "Depends. Who's paying for it?"

"What does it matter to you as long as you get your money?"

"Ah, I see," he nodded, stroking his beard. "Does Caiaphas know this is coming out of his pocket?"

The blue vein that bisected Simon's forehead bulged as his face darkened. "You dare question me?"

He made to return the purse to its hiding place, but Phineas snatched it from his hand. "Easy there, friend," he chuckled. "I will take that—and the job as well. Don't worry, I will find him for you."

When he came away from his meeting with Simon, a figure cloaked in a dark robe beckoned to him from the shadows outside the palace wall. "I have a message for you." His eyebrows raised. The voice under the hood was a woman's. He took the scroll she held out to him and opened it. When he had scanned the message, he asked her. "Does he want to meet with me?"

"No," came the reply, "I am to return to him with your answer."

"Tell him I will do it—for a price."

"How much?"

She gasped when he told her. Phineas smiled, "He can afford it."

"I will ask him and give you his answer tomorrow."

Not bothering to disguise his contempt for the amateurish attempt at intrigue, he sneered, "You know where to find me." As she walked away, he mused over the situation. *How is it that so many people are interested in this boy?*

Now he continued his circuit on the roof of Mary's house, disappointed that she hadn't been there to witness the destruction of her possessions. It was always more satisfying when he could see the fear. *So, little man, Simon wants you back. Why? Why are you so important to him? What makes you different from all the other boys who have run away? I think I should find out before I return you to him. And what about this other one? He wants me to find you, too—but for a very different reason. Perhaps I can pit the two of them against each other, with you as the prize.* He smiled, confident of his ability to track his prey. *I know you're out there, and sooner or later I will find you. Which way did you go?*

Chapter 3

I am nothing like my sisters.

Arin hauled the bucket up, listening to it rattle and slop as she pulled the coarse rope hand-over-hand from the depths of the well and emptied the water into her jar. Lyssa stood in line behind her, along with another dozen girls and women who gossiped and laughed while they waited to fill their jars. She hefted the heavy clay vessel to her right shoulder and stood aside while her sister lowered the bucket again.

She watched Lyssa work at the rope, and one corner of her mouth twitched up. Surely the Lord loved her father and mother to bless them with such a sunny disposition. She sighed inwardly. Content with her own company, Lyssa enjoyed everything—and lingered at everything

"Be swift," Arin urged. "Remember, we have guests." She shifted from one foot to the other while she waited and wondered what the evening would bring. A man and his grown son, old friends of her father's, had stopped in on their way home from Passover. They had stated their intention to resume their journey after a brief visit, and Papa had properly insisted they stay the night before going on. She knew this was likely to happen often over the next few days as people left the Holy City to return to their homes. The visitors would stay and talk, then they would all worship and pray together. *Will the Lord speak tonight?* He often did in these times, a word of encouragement, or of admonition or correction coming through her father, and now more frequently, through herself or through Lyssa.

She hoped any prophecy that came tonight would be in her father's mouth. After all, he knew these people. They were his friends. But most importantly, he had known the Christ, had seen him with his own eyes. *Envy is a sin,* Arin had to remind herself, yet she couldn't help wishing she had known him as Papa did.

"You *do* know him, little one," Papa insisted the one time she confessed her yearning. He gathered her in his arms and laid his head against hers. "His Spirit lives in you. Doesn't he reveal himself to you?"

He did, in countless ways.... "Papa, tell me about Jesus. What did you see him do?"

Papa shifted her in his lap and sighed, "I only saw the Master a couple of times, and I wasn't yet a follower. I was there in Jerusalem when he healed a blind man." Though Arin had already heard the story a number of times, she settled in to hear it again.

"The thing I remember first was that Jesus squatted down to talk to the beggar. He didn't make him stand up, though the blind man surely would have done so. Instead, the Master lowered himself to meet the beggar face to face." Her father's voice went soft with the memory. "Perhaps that was when I first began to believe. Anyway, he spat in the dirt and made a bit of mud which he daubed on the man's eyes. And I noticed his hands—strong hands, rough, accustomed to physical labor—but so gentle on the beggar's face." About this time, Papa began to stroke Arin's face, and she closed her eyes as his fingers touched her eyelids, light as a hummingbird's feathers.

She shivered a little and lost herself under his soothing hands. She was no longer Arin, daughter of Phillip and Leah. She was a blind beggar, and the Master was touching her, healing her. "The blind man knelt at the edge of the pool and scooped up water in his hands and splashed his face...." Tears gathered under her closed lids. "Then he stood up and turned, looking all around him...." Arin blinked and opened her eyes. The room in which they sat, though dim in the fading afternoon, seemed awash with newborn light. She stared about her in wonder. The walls looked as clean as if they'd just been whitewashed. The rug beneath them, its geometric blue-on-yellow pattern, faded and familiar, stood out in sharp relief against the swept stone floor. And Papa's hands. She could see every vein, every freckle and hair, the rough edges of his cuticles. She was seeing them for the first time. She turned to gaze into her father's solemn, handsome face and was arrested by his eyes, gray and turned up at the corners, eyes like hers....

"Arin?"

Standing there at the well, enfolded in remembrance, she had closed her eyes. Now she opened them and found a steady pair of hazel eyes—eyes like her mother's—staring back. Her sister had filled her jar and was ready to leave. Arin flushed with embarrassment and turned toward home. "Let's go."

"Are you all right?" Lyssa asked her, tucking an errant, light brown curl behind her ear. "Was it the Lord?"

"No...it...it was just a memory," she stammered. "I was thinking of something else."

The girls skirted Caesarea's walls and headed north along the seashore. Arin normally enjoyed this walk. She relished the smell of the salt air and loved listening to the breakers crash and hiss against the beach. But today her mind was elsewhere. *Oh Lord,* she pleaded silently, *please choose someone else tonight. I don't know these men. Please let Papa bring them your word, or even Lyssa. She isn't shy.*

Last time.... Arin cringed, shied away from the memory that wouldn't leave her alone. The Lord had given her a word for a believer in Caesarea, a woman she knew fairly well, but it was a word of admonition. Her stomach twisted in knots. *I can't say this to her!* In the end, she beckoned her father aside and gave him the prophecy. He didn't scold her for her reticence. He only laid a hand on her head and said, "It's a true word, Daughter. You must learn to trust the Spirit when he speaks to you." And he had gone and given the word in her place.

Just ahead on the shore a gull screamed in protest at her intrusion, and taking to his wings, sailed out over the waves. Arin hardly heard him. Her foot nudged a shell half-buried in the sand. Its whorls and ridges glowed orange and coral in the morning light. She hesitated, tempted by the brilliant colors, then passed it by. Ordinarily, she would have picked it up to add to her collection, but now.... *Perhaps I should put such childish things away. In another year or two, if the Lord is willing, I'll be married and have children of my own.*

Head down, she trudged home, her heart heavy with burdens she did not yet bear.

*   *   *   *   *

"Arin!" Salome stood in the doorway and shouted over her shoulder to her mother. "Mama, they're back!"

"Salome, shush!" her mother scolded, "You make enough noise for three little girls."

Undaunted, Salome grinned up at her oldest sister, displaying a wide gap where her two front teeth were missing. "Arin, I can't find my bracelet. Can you help me look for it?"

She paused and rested her free hand briefly on the child's head. "Maybe later. Right now we need to help Mother." She came in the door and nodded to the men sitting to her right on the rug. Even that simple gesture took all the power of her will, and though she kept her eyes averted from theirs, she couldn't stop the furious blush that rose up hot in her face. She turned to hide her discomfort, crossed the room and eased the jar from her shoulder, setting it carefully on the floor near her mother. "What do you want me to do first?"

Her mother shot her a grateful look as she stood up. "We need bread. I'm taking Salome to the market to get some."

"I can grind the wheat for you," Arin began.

"I do want you to do that—for tomorrow's bread," she answered. "For today, there's no time. We'll have to buy it. Come, Salome." She held out her hand. "Lyssa, I want you to tend the garden while I'm gone. Weed it, and make sure you water those melons."

"Yes, Mama." Lyssa went out the back door as her mother led Salome out the front, leaving Arin alone with the men. She bit her lip as she pulled the grain sack out of the corner. She hoped they would ignore her. And they did. The rest of the morning passed quietly enough. Arin dropped wheat, one handful after another, into the stone mortar and ground it to flour with the smooth, round rock that served as a pestle, all the while keeping one ear attuned to the conversation between her father and his friends.

"I fear the whole of Judea is in for a bad time," the older man shook his head as he spoke. "The latter rains were sparse, almost non-existent, and the grain fields are parched. Doesn't look like there will be much of a harvest this year. Added to that, last year's harvest was far less than ideal."

"The price of grain has already gone up," his son added. "If the rains don't come soon, the poor will be left with nothing to eat."

"I will talk to the others here about sending a gift to the church in Jerusalem, and we will pray for rain." Phillip laid a hand on the younger man's shoulder, and turned again to the father. "Linus, what is the situation in Antioch?"

"As to the weather, nothing is amiss," he replied, "but our people face other trouble—most of it from the synagogues."

Phillip nodded, "It's the same everywhere. Our fiercest opposition comes from those who should embrace us."

Arin heard a long silence follow before her father asked softly, "What is it?"

The younger man, Andrew, answered, his voice harsh with emotion, "My father-in-law was stoned last year."

Another silence fell, and Arin had to strain her ears to pick up Linus' explanation, which came just above a whisper. "He preached the Christ in one of the synagogues, using the prophesies of Isaiah to prove Jesus was the Messiah. The leader of the synagogue was incensed and ordered him thrown out. We thought that was the end of it, but later that day the Romans came, arrested him for disturbing the peace, and threw him into prison."

Andrew picked up the thread of his father's story. "The centurion in charge was known to us. Father spoke to him and won my father-in-law's release, but the very next morning when he left his house a mob from the synagogue ambushed him. They dragged him out of the city and stoned him to death."

Heavy sighs punctuated his words, and the house went quiet as a tomb. Arin's hands shook as she pounded the wheat. *Papa's thinking about his friend, Stephen.* Her gaze focused on the rock in her hand, and she faltered and laid it down in the mortar. She stared at the tool—such a simple thing. In her hands it ground wheat for bread to feed her family. But in another's hands.... She had never seen anyone stoned, but she had heard stories.

She tore her gaze away and looked at her Papa, wonderful and gentle, and completely unafraid to preach. His sad eyes met hers momentarily and he smiled. Arin swallowed against a new fear rising in her throat. How long before he suffered the same fate? Reluctantly she picked up the pestle again and resumed her work. Soon she heard her baby sister's voice piping a song as she and Mother neared the house. She was glad they were home—gladder still they hadn't heard.

* * * * *

That evening after dinner, Phillip asked, "Tell me, how are our friends in Antioch?"

Linus smiled. "Reuel and Miriam? They are doing well. Reuel offered to buy me out last year. I was only too happy to let him do it. Now he and Miriam have sole ownership of the vineyard ."

"That is wonderful news," Phillip nodded, and took a sip from his cup.

Andrew added. "I've never seen anyone with a greater gift for growing things, or with more dedication than those two."

"How are their children?"

Linus peered at Phillip. "Jonathan, you mean? He's about eleven now, I think. Or is he twelve?"

Andrew said, "He just turned fourteen, Father."

"Did he?" Linus shook his head with a rueful smile. "Seems the older I get, the faster the years pass me by."

Phillip chuckled, "It's the same for me." He paused, considering. "Does Miriam still worry...?"

"About the boy? Not as much as she used to, but he is the image of his father. If Caleb ever sees him, he'll have to acknowledge the truth—about his paternity, at least."

"Did you see Caleb while you were in Jerusalem?" Phillip asked.

"Briefly. I went to his table during the Feast, and we exchanged pleasantries. That's about all. He did say your sister just bore him a son."

Phillip tore a piece of bread from one of the loaves. "Perhaps you should tell Miriam that bit of news when you get to Antioch."

Linus frowned. "Why would I burden her with such tidings?"

"If Caleb has a son to occupy him in Jerusalem, he is far less likely to ever show up on her doorstep demanding to see the one she took with her. It might ease her mind."

"I see your reasoning," Linus answered, "but new son or no, Caleb is entrenched in the city. He has his work and family there. I can't imagine him ever leaving, not even to venture as far as Caesarea." He studied Phillip's face a moment, then gently rapped at his knee with a fist. "He is not the man he used to be, my friend. He's not so malleable. He has something of his father in him."

"I am truly sorry to hear that," Phillip sighed, and drank from his cup.

"Lathan is not well," Linus added. "I saw him when I spoke to Caleb. He was yellow—his eyes, his skin. He looked terrible. I doubt he will live much longer."

"And what of Jacob?" Phillip asked.

As I am Known

"He wasn't in the Temple when I was there," Linus answered. "As a matter of fact, I believe Caleb said he was out running around with your father."

Phillip's eyebrows shot up. "He was? Well, that's interesting. Has my father taken a liking to him, then?"

"Caleb didn't elaborate." Linus shrugged, "We didn't have much time to talk. But I hope so. The boy needs a grandfather. The one he has isn't worthy of the title."

* * * * *

Evening fell gently on Caesarea. The sun sank into a billowing bank of clouds over the Great Sea, setting them ablaze in orange and pink, brilliant hues that deepened to violet, and then faded altogether as the first star winked in the dusky sky. Arin sighed and crossed her arms against the chill breeze flowing in off the waves. She needed to go inside.

I wish I could stay out here. She tilted her head to the darkening canopy overhead and picked out another star, and then another. A few months before, her father told her that he had once preached to an official in the Ethiopian government. "After I baptized the man, I was taken by the Spirit of God, just lifted up and set down again many miles away in another city." Then he had gone still and quiet, shaking his head, and refused to say more.

What would that be like, she wondered, to be in one place, and a moment later find yourself in another? She closed her eyes and imagined her feet touching down somewhere else, somewhere far from home. The wind caught her skirt and played against her ankles. Arin sighed and smiled ruefully at her own thoughts. *What a goose I am! I can hardly open my mouth when I'm with family and friends. It's well enough for Papa—he's fearless. I'd be terrified in a strange place among people I don't know.*

"Arin? Is that you?"

Startled, she turned to see three men walking up the beach from the city. She checked her first impulse to flee back to the house when she recognized the man who had called out to her. "Saul!" she exclaimed, and she ran to him and took his hand.

"I'm glad to see you, little one," Saul chuckled, and he bent to plant a kiss atop her head. "How is everyone? Has Lyssa recovered?"

"She has," she answered, momentarily forgetting her shyness in the presence of her friend. "She started getting better just a few days after you left."

Saul tightened his grip on her hand. "Ah, the Lord has answered our prayers." He indicated his companions. "Does your family have room for us tonight?"

"We have other visitors," Arin answered, "but there's plenty of room on the roof, or you can always sleep on the beach."

Saul glanced up at the stars. "It looks like a fine night. I think the beach would suit me. How about you two?"

The older of the two, who Arin noted stood a full head taller than Saul, answered, "I could sleep anywhere tonight."

The younger, who appeared to be hardly more than a boy, grinned. "You may sleep, Barnabas, but none of the rest of us will."

Saul murmured, "He snores. Rather loudly."

Arin stifled a giggle when Barnabas protested, "I do not snore!"

"Actually, it comes in handy when we sleep outside," the young man added. "Keeps the wild animals away."

Barnabas kicked up a plume of sand in the young man's direction and chuckled, "Insolent puppy."

They entered the circle of light spilling from the front door, and Arin called out, "Papa, Look who I brought home!"

"Saul! Barnabas!" Phillip exclaimed as he rose to embrace his friends.

Arin stood aside and watched the men greet each other. Her father introduced Linus and Andrew, then asked, "Are you hungry?" When they assured him they had eaten in the city, he said, "You've come at just the right time. We were just about to pray."

Arin sat down with her mother and sister across the room from the men. Little Salome dropped into her father's lap and laid her head against his shoulder.

"Please remember us in your prayers," Saul said as he took his seat. "We are on our way north to carry the message of Christ to the gentiles in Asia."

They began with a hymn, following Barnabas' lead. His fine baritone filled the room like incense.

All at once, Arin's mind was flooded with an image of the blind man Papa had seen healed in Jerusalem. She saw him fall to his knees and grope his way toward the pool. *My people who are called by my Name are blind....* Her breath left her, and she leaned forward until her forehead touched on the floor. She pulled her veil close around her. *Oh, Lord,* she pleaded, *choose someone else!* Dimly she was aware of her mother's hand on her back, stroking and soothing. *My people who are called by my Name are blind....* There would be more. Once she opened her mouth, the words would spill out, though she didn't yet know what they would be.

All at once a tremor seized her, making her body shake from her bones. Arin clenched her teeth to keep them from chattering, and held on to herself. Her father once told her that the earth shook after Christ was crucified, shook so hard the graves around Jerusalem opened and gave up their dead. She believed it. She took deep, shuddering breaths, trying to make the trembling stop, *willing* it to stop, but to no avail. *Oh Lord, you shake the heavens and the earth as easily as you are shaking me now.*

"My people who are called by my Name are blind."

Arin gasped, for the voice came this time not from within, but in the sweet, childish tones of her littlest sister. Her head snapped up. Salome, still cuddled in her father's lap with her head against his shoulder said, "When one leads the other, both fall into the pit. They call themselves my children, yet they do not know Me." The words, seared with grief, still left Salome's face unperturbed and calm. "They will reject you because they have rejected Me. They will hate you because they have hated Me. Do not fear them, for I am sending you to those that they have scorned and despised." Salome popped her thumb back in her mouth and closed her eyes.

The men all stared at the child in stunned silence, then looked at each other. "So," Linus murmured, "we see the words of the prophet Joel being fulfilled before our eyes. 'Your sons and daughters will prophesy'."

Phillip nodded and tightened his arms around his little girl.

Pierced with anger and grief, Arin jumped to her feet with a strangled cry and ran to the door. She stumbled out into the night, hearing her mother say behind her, "Let her go, Phillip."

She ran down the dimly-lit path from the house and out onto the darkened beach. A three-quarter moon's silver glow gave her enough light to make her way along the familiar ground. Her steps slowed as she neared the water. She wandered to the beach, right down to the water's edge where she stopped to close her eyes and breathe in the bracing, salty air. The cool breeze off the sea dried Arin's tears and calmed her racing heart.

A tiny wave caught her toes and kissed them. She retreated a few steps and lowered herself to the sand, where she sat hugging her knees. "Why, Lord?" she whispered into the darkness. "Why Salome? She's just a little child—a baby." She covered her forehead with one hand and chewed on her lower lip. "Was I too slow?" Fresh tears welled in her eyes. "I...I do love you, and I want to know you as Papa and Mama do, but it's so hard." She swallowed. "It's hard to speak your words."

The incessant hiss and splash of the waves on the shore, a sound that had surrounded Arin since her birth, soothed and comforted her. A lullaby from Heaven itself, it held her still, covered and enfolded her. After several long minutes, she sniffed and loosened her grip on her knees. *I should go back inside.*

"Arin?" She raised her head as Saul sat down next to her. "Are you all right?"

She nodded and stared out at the sea. "I...I'm sorry about interrupting prayers like that."

"What happened? Can you tell me?"

Arin sighed and tugged at a dark tendril that had escaped the confines of her veil. "I had a word," she murmured. "I was supposed to speak it, but the Lord gave it to Salome instead." She hung her head. "I was disobedient."

"Ah." Saul pried a half-buried bit of shell out of the sand and hurled it back into the waves. "Why did you hesitate to speak?"

Swallowing her misery, she whispered, "There was so much pain in it."

Saul nodded, "The Lord grieves over his people." Beneath the ruff of his beard, his jaw clenched and bulged with emotion. "But unless we...."

Arin glanced at her friend, noted a familiar searching stare in his eyes, and waited.

"Unless we hear him," he finally resumed, "how can we know his will? The gospel must reach all ears, whether they will listen or not." He laid a momentary hand lightly atop her head. "Tell me, little friend, I know you believe in the Lord, but what exactly do you believe about him?"

"Well," Arin scooped up a handful of sand and watched it sift through her fingers. "I believe he is the Anointed One, the Messiah."

Saul nodded, "Go on."

"I believe he did miracles. He healed sick people." Her inner vision of the blind man washed over her once more. "I believe he was crucified..." Arin passed that thought quickly, unwilling to dwell on its brutality, "and that he came alive again and ascended to Heaven." Here she stopped, assessing her own words. Was that enough?

Saul grunted, but did not comment, leaving her to wonder if her answer somehow displeased him. Finally he asked, "Do you believe he is good?"

Startled, she answered, "Oh, yes." But it was her father's face she held in her mind. "I know he is good."

"Then...." Again the searching stare. His inability to find his own words was the very thing that made Arin comfortable in his company. She felt a kinship with him that she had with no one else, not even her father. "....then if he is good, he means everything for good. Do you understand that?" When she nodded, he continued, "Everything, Arin. You may not always see it. Some things—many things—don't seem good to our eyes, but they serve his purposes. And his purposes are good. Always." He smiled and gave one end of her veil a gentle tug. "Trust him, Arin."

Trust him. Papa said the same thing. She turned her eyes back to the ever-rolling waves, to the tender play of moonlight on the water. She took a long, deep breath and released it slowly. *Trust him. Perhaps I am making it harder than it is.* Content in the silence of their company, preacher and prophetess soaked themselves in the noise of the tumbling waves under a star-lit sky.

As I am Known

* * * * *

The next morning all their guests prepared to depart. Linus and Andrew went first, the two of them saying their goodbyes just after dawn. "Come and see us when you can," Linus said, wrapping Phillip in a hearty embrace.

Soon after they were gone, Saul and his two companions trooped up to the house from the beach. Arin was already at the fire cooking flat rounds of bread from the flour she had ground the day before. Salome stood just behind her, thumb in her mouth, her other hand resting on Arin's shoulder. Another day Arin might have gently coaxed her out of the way and given her something to occupy her, but this morning, the weight of her sister's hand on her shoulder—no more than a baby bird's—was welcome.

"Good morning, little one." Saul stopped to lay a light hand on Salome's head. Turning to Arin he asked, "Where is your father this morning?"

"I'm here," Phillip announced as he came in the back door. "You will eat with us before you go, won't you?"

"Of course, and thank you." The two men with him followed him in, and they and Phillip sat down to wait for breakfast.

"We didn't get to talk much last night," Phillip said. "What are your plans? Where will you go?"

Barnabas answered, "The Lord has called us to preach to the gentiles. We go north from here. I intend to stop first in Antioch."

"And then to Tarsus?"

Arin nodded to herself. Tarsus was Saul's home town, and not far from Antioch. But Saul's answer startled her.

"No. If the Lord wills it, we'll sail to Cyprus, and from there go north into Pisidia."

Arin's mother asked, "Are there any believers in that region? That is, any you know about?" She set slices of cheese and a bowl of dried fruit in front of the men.

"Cyprus is my home," Barnabas replied, "but I have been away for a long time. Whether there are believers there yet or not, I haven't heard."

"But by the grace of God there will be some soon!" Saul said with a laugh.

They gave thanks and ate, and soon after got ready to leave. Phillip embraced each of them. "Greet our friends in Antioch."

Barnabas smiled. "We will, but you really should make the journey there yourself. You would be encouraged by their faith, and they by yours."

"It's a long journey to make with three young ones...." Phillip began.

"About two weeks," Saul agreed. "Much farther than Jerusalem, but your girls' gifts would greatly edify the church."

Arin, who had been intrigued by the thought of traveling to another city, suddenly decided she'd rather stay home.

"Perhaps you're right," Phillip answered. "I will think on it and bring it before the Lord. I have to admit I've lately felt an urge to roam. It's been a long time since I traveled."

"We should...." Saul began, and stopped. No one interrupted his silence. They knew to wait. "...We should be going. A long road lies ahead of us."

"We will send you off with a prayer." Phillip lifted his hands. "Father, in the name of our Lord Jesus, I bless my brothers. Keep them in your hand. Strengthen them for the work, that your kingdom may grow, that the fame of the Lord will spread throughout all the earth."

"Amen," Barnabas said. "And may your grace and peace rest upon Phillip and his household until we meet again."

Until we meet again. Arin was suddenly struck with the knowledge that it could be years before she saw any of them again. *And with the persecution....* She didn't allow herself to finish that thought. Now she wanted to prolong her time with Saul. "Papa, may I walk a little way with them?"

Phillip smiled. "If your mother has no objection."

Leah said, "You may go, but only as far as the crossroad. Then you come straight back."

"Yes, Mama." She took Saul's proffered hand, and they set out down the path from the house."

"You've never been to Jerusalem, have you?" he asked as they turned north along the beach.

"Only once, when I was four or five," Arin admitted. "We have relatives there—my father's sister and her husband. They have a son named Jacob. He's about two years older than I. And they have a daughter named Prisca who is about four years younger."

Mark, who had been following close behind them exclaimed, "Jacob is your relative?"

She glanced back. "Yes, he's my cousin. I've only seen him once, though, and I doubt he remembers me. Do you know him?"

"He's my best friend!" Mark's eyes were bright and eager. "You may get to see him next year."

"Really?" Arin raised one hand to shade her eyes from the glare of the morning sun. "How so?"

"Jacob told me that Prisca's grandfather—I guess he's your grandfather, too—offered to take him traveling next year after the Feast. I presume they will come this way."

Arin frowned. Mark's words sounded odd. *Prisca's grandfather? Why not*

Jacob's grandfather? But her heart lightened at the thought of a visit from Gedeon. He did stop by nearly every year. Maybe he would come within a few days. "So," she ventured, "what is he like?"

"Who? Oh, you mean Jacob." Mark grinned and rubbed at his forehead. "What's he like? I don't know...."

"You know him too well to describe him properly," Barnabas broke in. To Arin he said, "He is younger than Mark, though nearly as tall, with a great heap of curly hair on top of his head, and enough sense inside it for two young men," he gave Mark a sidelong glance, "which is fortunate."

Arin was shocked by Barnabas' good-natured abuse of his young cousin, but Mark only laughed. Just then Saul stopped, and Arin realized they had reached the crossroad. Barnabas and Mark bade her farewell and went ahead, leaving Saul another moment alone with her. He bent down and kissed her forehead. "Remember what we talked about last night."

"God is good," she replied, blinking back her tears.

"All that he is, and all that he does, Arin."

She nodded, and though it wrenched her heart, she stepped back from him, murmuring, "Go in his mercy."

"And you also." With a final nod, he turned and started up the road toward the town of Dora. Beyond that—far beyond—lay Antioch, the gateway to the rest of the world.

Chapter 4

"Yes, like that. Now cut it." Gallus was showing Joel how to give Jacob a Roman-style haircut. Jacob watched with mild alarm as a handful of curls cascaded past his eyes to the ground. "Now do the next section the same way." Another clump of hair floated to the ground.

"Don't worry, boy," Joel teased from above and behind him. "It's not so different than shearing sheep, and I've had plenty of experience with that."

Zerah asked with a chuckle, "Was that meant to reassure him?"

Jacob blew at a lock that stuck to his nose. "How short are you cutting it?"

"Short," Gallus answered. "We want to eliminate as much of the curl as we can, so if anyone is following you, you'll be harder to spot."

"How are your legs this morning?" Zerah asked.

"Much better, thank you sir," Jacob answered, brushing the hair off his right arm. "That one stripe is finally healing. I can hardly feel it now."

The priest nodded, his smile tight. "You young ones heal quickly." He took a swallow from his water skin and stood up. "I need to stretch my legs. Call when you're done. I'll stay within earshot."

Jacob fingered a lock that landed on the back of his left hand. "How does it look?"

"Odd," Joel answered, then added quickly, "but I'm sure it will improve when I've finished the second half. Trading clothes with that boy yesterday will also help deflect anyone who comes looking for you."

They had left Jericho and gone west, crossing the Jordan River into Perea, where they turned north on the road toward Damascus. Yesterday they'd passed through a village and met a boy about Jacob's size. Jacob hadn't wanted to trade. His own cloak was nearly new, and Prisca had declared it her favorite. But Gallus threatened to dress him as a girl if he didn't comply, so he traded. And now about half of his hair lay around the stone where he sat, a circle of circles.

If Father comes looking for me, this haircut won't fool him. He'll know me. Then with a pang he corrected himself. *But he won't come. Not now. I've disgraced him by running away. And he has Prisca and Andrew to think about.* He calmed his aching heart with thoughts of the future. *Someday I'll see him again, when I'm a man and on my own. I'll go to Jerusalem for Passover and surprise him.* He toyed with the idea of sending his father a message, just to let him know he was safe, but Simon's face loomed in his mind. *No, I dare not—not yet. But maybe soon.* A falling lock of hair brushed his cheek. *Old Simon probably has too much work to be chasing after me. I bet he won't even bother to look.*

*   *   *   *   *

"You're sure he's left the city? Absolutely sure?"

Phineas poured himself a drink from the wine bottle and tasted it. He glanced at Simon's darkening expression and raised his cup in salute. "Your master keeps good wine." He sauntered to a chair and sat down. "The boy is out of your reach. Better forget about him."

"Where do you think he went?" Though Simon feigned only a casual curiosity, his face and neck had gone scarlet.

"My sources tell me he probably went north with a friend of his, a boy two or three years his senior. This friend left just after Passover with two other men, so the timing would be right."

"And what is their destination?" Simon had gone to a window and now stood with his back to Phineas, gazing out over the courtyard.

"The best I can ascertain, they are heading for Antioch." He finished his wine. "A long journey. As I said, the boy is beyond your reach."

"No," Simon muttered. "There is no place on earth that boy can go to get away from me." He turned. "How much?"

A lazy smile spread across Phineas' face. "I beg your pardon?"

"Oh, stop toying with me!" Exasperated, Simon folded his arms across his chest. "You know very well what I mean. How much money do you need to track him down and bring him back?"

"Ten more talents should do it." Phineas had to suppress the urge to laugh when the vein on Simon's forehead bulged out. *Someday he will have a fit and die. I hope I'm there to see it.*

"I've already paid you five gold talents!" the steward raged. "Do you take me for a fool?"

Phineas rubbed his thumb and fingers together. "Information does not come cheap, you know."

With a low growl, Simon braced his hands on the arms of Phineas' chair and leaned down until his florid face was mere inches away. "After what you did to ben Lathan's sister, Deborah, I could have you whipped."

"You could," Phineas agreed. "So why didn't you? I heard her husband came beating at your door."

Simon leaned in even closer. "If that woman dies, I'll make you wish you were dead, too."

Phineas exhaled to clear Simon's sour breath from his nostrils, and made a dismissive gesture with one hand. "She is out of danger." His gray eyes bored into Simon's black ones. "You never answered my question. Why didn't you have me whipped?" Simon stood up again and turned away. With a sardonic smile, Phineas said, "Let me guess. As much as you loathe me, you need me. I am the only one you can trust to find this boy for you." When he did not reply, Phineas added, "He's obviously not worth it, friend. Why don't you just forget about him?"

Simon's hands curled into fists. "I have my reasons."

Phineas, thoroughly enjoying the conversation, swirled the wine in his cup. "Perhaps," he drawled, "I might be persuaded to settle for a bit less if you shared those reasons with me. After all, I should know what I'm getting myself into."

"It's a personal matter." Simon's eyes narrowed on him, sizing him up. "It has to do with his father. I have an old debt to repay."

Phineas entertained no illusions that Simon's "debt" had anything to do with honor. *He's out for revenge of some kind. How very interesting! I wonder if the other one is involved?* Aloud he said, "All right. I'll do it for six. For that amount you have me for as many months. I will go to Antioch, and if the boy is there, I will bring him back."

Simon pulled a purse from his sleeve, weighed it in his hand, and sighed, as if with great reluctance to part with it. "How sure are you of your information?"

Phineas watched, amused. Simon could easily pay twice what he had asked. *And he will pay—later, when he gets himself so entangled in his need for revenge that he can't move. I can see him now, an unhappy spider caught in his own web.* He said, "His friend's whereabouts are no secret. If the boy isn't with him, I will learn why. Don't fret, Simon. I will sniff him out."

* * * * *

Prisca woke up crying the night Jacob left. Caleb heard her and got up. "What's wrong, love?" He took her in his arms. "Did you have a bad dream?"

She nodded against his shoulder and gasped between sobs, "Papa, why did Jacob have to go away?"

Caleb sank to the edge of her bed, still cradling his daughter. "Your brother is a man now, Prisca. He has to leave home and make his way in the world. That is what men do."

She continued to weep, and Caleb held her close, as though she might somehow shield his own wounded heart. *I did the best I could,* he told himself. *My father is ill, probably dying, but I still have my son close by. Everything will work out. Jacob's a good boy, a fine son. Father just never understood him.*

When Prisca's sobs subsided, Caleb tucked her back into bed and kissed her, promising, "You'll see your brother again soon." But the next morning his hopes for his son were shattered when Phineas showed up at his door.

"I told you," Diana hissed at him, while Phineas searched the house. "I told you that boy would do something like this."

Caleb thought, *No you didn't. You haven't mentioned him once since he left yesterday,* but he held his tongue. An argument with Diana now would only multiply his grief. And when Phineas was gone, he found Prisca cowering in her grandfather's arms, her face swollen and streaked with tears.

"He frightened her," was all Gedeon said, but that night Prisca woke the whole household with her screaming.

"The bad man is hurting Jacob!" she wailed, when he rushed in to her. "Make him stop!" When he tried to pick her up, she cringed away from him and screamed, "No! I want Jacob!"

"Let me see if I can help," came Gedeon's quiet voice from the door. He bent over Prisca and stroked her hair. "Papi's here, baby girl." Sobbing, she allowed herself to be gathered into his arms. After that, Gedeon was the only one who could comfort her. She woke twice more that night.

The next night, after she had wakened the household with her piercing screams, Lathan called out to Caleb from his room. "Son, I want a word with you."

Deeply dreading what his father would say, Caleb stood at the foot of his bed. "Father, I'm sorry about this...." he began.

"Sorry will not do," Lathan rasped. "Sorry will not bring peace to this house. You must do something about that child. What is she screaming about anyway?"

"She's having nightmares," Caleb answered, scratching at his disheveled hair.

"I can hear that," Lathan snapped. "I'm not deaf."

"I think the fellow who came looking for Jacob frightened her," he explained.

"Then it is a good thing the boy is gone," Lathan announced. "And the sooner she forgets about him, the better. But something will have to be done about the screaming."

"Listen—she has quieted already. Gedeon is in there with her now."

"Is he? Well, much good may it do him. Much good may it do us all." Lathan yanked at his blanket, pulling it up under his chin. "I need my sleep...."

But the nightmares did not subside, and in the morning Eunice announced, "This is absurd. No one is getting any sleep." She said to Caleb, "Why don't you send her to the servants' quarters at night? Let them deal with her."

"Absolutely not," Gedeon interrupted. "She's a frightened little girl. I will not have my granddaughter shuffled off on someone else—someone who doesn't love her." His eyes, puffy with fatigue, bored into his wife's. "She misses her brother, and she's worried about him."

Eunice drew herself up and faced him, her voice shaking with rage. "Are you blaming me for his absence? Because if you are...."

Gedeon waved her off with an impatient hand. "Hush, woman. Don't weary me with your indignation."

Caleb sat cross-legged on the floor cushions, his head in his hands. "This is my fault. I never should have sent him away." He sighed and sat up. "If I knew where he was, I'd bring him back."

"You made a vow," Diana broke in like a petulant child. "You promised your father. You can't just go off and leave me alone with Prisca and the baby."

He gazed at her, her once-lovely face now pinched and drawn. What was it Phillip said about his sister so long ago? *"I pity the man who marries her, for she will give him no rest." You were right, my friend. I should have listened to you.* "Where is Prisca now?"

Gedeon said, "She's asleep."

"In our bed," Eunice muttered, her eyes casting daggers of accusation at her husband. "He insisted it was the only way to settle her down."

Miriam used to have nightmares. Though he wasn't hungry, Caleb took a fig from the bowl in front of him and broke it open. *I wonder if she still does?*

"Perhaps we should call in a physician," Gedeon said. "He could give her something to help her sleep."

"Just until she's used to Jacob being gone," Caleb nodded. "That is a good idea. I'll find him and talk to him before I go to the Temple."

*　*　*　*　*

The wind off the sea felt much colder than it had two days before. It snapped and bit at the travelers. Jacob's ears ached from exposure, and he pulled his cloak tighter around him. Winter might be losing the contest with spring, but it seemed determined to have the final say. With one hand he jammed his turban as far down as it would go on his shorn head. *They might have waited a few more days to cut my hair,* he grumbled to himself, now painfully aware just how insulating his thick mop had been.

As he gritted his teeth against the next gust, Joel called out, "Pick up your feet, boy. Don't lag behind."

He trotted a few paces to catch up with Zerah, who intoned, "Lagging is a privilege reserved solely for me, owing to the weight of years I carry on my back."

Jacob had to laugh, in spite of his sour mood. Zerah's fine, dry humor had lightened the long journey.

The priest draped an arm across Jacob's shoulders. "It's a foul day, to be sure, but Joel says there's a good inn up the road. We should reach it before sundown."

Joel turned with a grin. "Gallus and I will reach it, but I'm not so sure about you two. Slow as you are, you'll end up passing it in the dark."

Zerah heaved a ponderous sigh. "Do you believe it—a man of my stature, taking this rank abuse?"

Joel didn't reply, but Jacob heard his chuckle just before it was whipped away on the wind. They did make an odd pair, Zerah and Uncle Joel—simple farmer and wealthy priest. "Sir," he said to Zerah, "how did you and my uncle come to be friends?"

"Ah, well as you know, he used to be employed by your grandfather."

"Yes. He ran messages for him."

Zerah nodded. "The same sort of thing that you did for him and your father these last few years. That was how I first met Joel, but in those days, he was a skinny little stick of a boy...."

"I heard that!" Joel exclaimed without looking around.

Zerah winked at Jacob and called back, "I was not attempting to be secretive. Do you care to refute my words?"

"Not at all." Jacob couldn't see his uncle's face, but he heard laughter in his reply. "Your powers of observation are above reproach."

"Ah, yes, I have always had a firm grasp of the obvious." Chuckles erupted from the men ahead of them, and the priest continued, "As I was saying, your uncle was but a boy when he first came to see me, and soon afterward your grandfather discovered that I had undergone..." Zerah paused and squinted at the ground in front of him for several steps before he finished, "...a change of heart."

Jacob, itching to know what the "change of heart" was about, kept quiet, remembering his father's instructions. *"Don't ask too many questions, son. A man will tell you what he wants you to know when he's ready."*

"It was the end of my friendship with your grandfather, but I still saw Joel from time to time, trotting around the city. His mother—that is, your grandmother Abigail—and my wife were friends, so I kept up with him through her. I think the reason I took interest in him was because he was a little older than my son, and I'd watch your uncle, thinking, 'So that's what Justus will be like in a few years.'"

I went to see your grandmother just before she died. 'I'm going to tell Joel everything,' she said, 'and he will need your help.' Sure enough, three or four days later, he came to me. He wanted to kill your grandfather."

"I did want to," Joel tossed back, "and I might have actually tried if you hadn't stopped me."

"Is that when Grandfather fired you?" Jacob asked his uncle.

"No, Zerah counseled me to stay, to remain close for your sake, and I did for a while, though many times my contact with him left me sick in my spirit."

"A couple of years ago," Zerah continued, "your grandfather discovered that Joel was associating with me, and that he was a follower of Christ. That's when Lathan forced him out."

Joel spat, "Best thing that could have happened."

"Quite possibly," Zerah agreed, "but it made me all the more concerned about you, Jacob—how you were being treated—which was one of the reasons I asked your father to help me sell my house. I thought it might put me in contact with you."

A long silence ensued. The bitter wind had made Jacob's nose raw and sore. He sniffed and wiped at it. "Why, sir?" he asked after several more steps. "Why were you interested in me?"

Zerah folded his arms across his chest and made a low sound in his throat, half a growl, half a moan. "I felt...I *feel* responsible for you. I was there to oversee when Caleb divorced your mother and sent her away. And I was still in the house when you were taken from her arms. Your cries haunted me, and a few weeks later when I learned the truth about Jesus of Nazareth, I vowed before Heaven to do whatever was in my power to help her. But she was gone from the city before I could locate her. All I could do for her was to help her son. Till now what I've done has been in secret, hidden even from you."

Jacob, walking about a half step behind the priest gazed at him in silence for several minutes. Finally he asked, "What did you do, sir? Will you tell me?"

Now Zerah sniffed. His nose was as red as Jacob imagined his own to be. "Do you remember when father tried to get you into Rabbi Eleazar's synagogue school?"

Jacob hung his head, and despite the chill wind, his face flushed hot with embarrassment. Rabbi Eleazar's school was supposed to be the most prestigious in Jerusalem. His father had been so disappointed when Jacob was refused, and Grandfather had of course blamed Jacob. "The boy can't get into that school, Caleb. You're wasting your time. He's lazy, and he doesn't pay attention." Grandfather had not bothered to lower his voice when he said this. He made sure Jacob heard him, and the memory of it still stung. Maybe it always would. Had Zerah tried to get him in? Tried and failed? "What happened, sir?"

"I know Eleazar, know the kind of man he is. You were not received into his school, but even if you had been, you would not have prospered there. More than any man I know, he looks down his nose at Galileans. If a man wasn't born in Jerusalem, or if his father or even his grandfather wasn't born here, Eleazar considers him a waste of time. Your father and grandfather were both outsiders in his eyes. I can't imagine sitting at his feet would have done you any good. Your rabbi Sameas, on the other hand, is an old friend. I spoke to him and had him ask specifically for you."

"I liked him," Jacob answered. "He was harsh at times, but fair."

Zerah nodded, "Just so. You didn't get the teacher your father wanted for you, but you got the better teacher, all the same."

Jacob swallowed hard. All his life he'd had more friends—and finer ones—than he realized. "Sir, thank you for not leaving Jerusalem without me."

"I wouldn't dream of leaving you with Simon, lad, no more than I would my own son."

"You know Simon?"

Zerah's reply to this was terse. "I know enough."

* * * * *

"No, not that nag. I want the best horse you have." Phineas turned from the animal the trader had shown him and studied the other mounts. "I have a long journey. I need a horse that's strong and swift. And it'll have to bear the weight of two on the way back."

"Then perhaps my lord should take a camel instead. My cousin...."

Phineas cut him off. "Are you deaf, or merely stupid?" He turned his iron gaze on the trader. "Show me the best you have."

The trader, one Zenas by name, was caught in a vise. The last time he hired a horse to Phineas he barely broke even on it, and Phineas so mistreated the animal it had to be put down. Now here the gray man was again, offering next to nothing for the pick of Zenas' string, and Zenas couldn't refuse. With Phineas' connections, Zenas would never be able to sell another horse in Jerusalem, perhaps not in all Judea. "Which animal pleases your eye, my lord?"

"How about this mare?" Phineas ran a hand along her shoulder. "She looks capable."

"My lord has a good eye," the trader made a slight bow. "And she is certainly capable, but she would not be the best choice for the long journey my lord will have to make."

Phineas rounded on him. "Why not?"

The trader tried without success to meet his steely glare. How much did this son of a pig really know about horses? "She...well, she is breeding, my lord. Hard to tell it yet—it is still early, but she could not endure the kind of riding my lord has in mind."

Phineas smiled, and Zenas felt death crawl up his spine. "Then which one do you recommend?"

He wiped his dampened palms against his robe and gestured. "That gelding, the gray one, will be more to your liking, I think. He is young and strong." Zenas didn't add that he was also unpredictable and unstable. He thought, *Maybe the gelding will throw him and wipe him from the face of the earth.*

"Very well." Phineas' voice went soft as a caress. He paid the trader precisely half the gelding's worth. "I'll take him." As he turned the horse to lead him away, he added, "And if he doesn't suit, you will be hearing from me."

When Phineas was out of earshot, Zenas muttered, "Not with any luck, I won't." He leaned over and spat on the spot where Phineas had stood.

Less than an hour later, a rider set out from Jerusalem heading west. Dressed all in gray and sitting astride a gray horse, he passed like an ill shadow, racing through the valley, onto the road toward Emmaus, and into the countryside beyond.

* * * * *

The inn just south of the city of Pella was no more than adequate, but at least it was warm. Jacob lingered as close as he could to the cook fire, flexing grateful fingers until his hands and feet began to thaw. After a dinner of fresh bread and steaming stew warmed their bellies, the four of them stretched out on mats in their room.

Zerah sighed with satisfaction. "This reminds me of when I was a child. My father took us once each year to visit my grandparents—my mother's people. My cousins and I would go out and sleep with the goats in the barn."

"Actually, a barn would be better than this," Joel grunted as he pulled his cloak over him. "Hay's a lot softer than this mat."

"Hay smells better, too," Gallus added with a grimace. "Still, it beats a tent tonight." Everyone murmured agreement.

"I've slept in our barn a lot." Jacob yawned widely and adjusted his cloak over his feet. "It's not bad. It's quiet and warm, and the animals are good company."

The silence that followed lasted so long he thought his companions had fallen asleep. But then Zerah said, "Ah, lad, if I could have gotten you away from there I would have. I prayed about it often enough, but in my heart I heard Heaven counsel me to wait. The Lord chooses His time."

Zerah's continued concern for Jacob emboldened him to ask, "Sir, are you a follower of Jesus of Nazareth?"

"I am." The reply came quiet and firm. "If you like, I will tell you about it in the morning."

"I would like that very much."

Just before he fell asleep, he heard Joel's voice murmur, "It's a story worth hearing."

* * * * *

The next morning, though not much warmer, dawned sunny and still. A fine, clear sky arched overhead, and the travelers set out with gladdened hearts. Joel said, "We should reach Damascus in about three days, if the weather holds."

Zerah said to Jacob, "This is as good a time as any to tell you the story I promised you last night. Now let me see...." He stroked his thick, white beard, considering. "Where should I begin? Well, I already told you that your Grandfather Lathan had talked to me about Jesus of Nazareth, and that he wanted the Sanhedrin to do something about him—meaning of course, he wanted us to kill him. A large faction of the Council favored that plan of action. As for myself, I had been studying, poring over the prophesies. I wasn't convinced this Jesus was Messiah, but on the other hand, neither was I certain he was not."

The Sanhedrin ruptured under the debate regarding him. Each side commanded allegiance, demanded loyalty. Still I wavered. I had friends and respected colleagues on both sides. And I wasn't the only one caught in the middle. Even Gamaliel, possibly the most learned scholar among us, wanted to wait and see, though now that I think about it, I don't know what we were waiting for."

It was cowardly of us—of me. Soon events spiraled out of control. Jesus was arrested and subjected to an illegal trial. The faction that wanted to kill him was powerful and determined. After he was crucified, I learned that two Council members took his body from the Romans and prepared it for burial. This made them unclean, and therefore unable to celebrate Passover. I marveled at their loyalty, for our law says, 'Cursed is anyone who hangs on a tree'".

Early in the afternoon on the first day of the week I heard disturbing rumors that the tomb where Jesus had been laid was robbed, that the body was gone, and his disciples were claiming he had risen from the dead. I hurried over to the Temple to find out for myself what I could. I got there just in time."

This seemed to beg the question, so Jacob asked, "Just in time for what, sir?"

"In time to overhear the meeting between some of the Sanhedrin members and the commander of the Roman guard who had been posted to watch the tomb."

He frowned. "The tomb was guarded?"

"Oh, yes. The Sanhedrin was afraid of the very thing that appeared to have happened. But the commander told a different story. I can still hear the sound of his voice, tight and frightened. The guard had been confronted at dawn that morning by a shining man, he said, a man all in white, tall and terrible to behold. 'It was one of the gods,' he insisted. 'I think it was Mars himself.' He said the next thing he knew, he was waking up where he'd fallen to the ground. The boulder that sealed the tomb had been rolled back, and the body was gone. At that moment I knew the truth. It exploded into my heart before my mind could take hold of it. Jesus of Nazareth had risen from the dead. And why not? We all knew he had raised his good friend Lazarus only a few weeks before."

One of the priests accused the guard of lying. 'His disciples came and stole the body while you slept. You were derelict in your duty.' But the commander was adamant. 'Even if we had all fallen asleep,' he said, 'no one man could have rolled that stone away, and no group of men could have done it without waking us.'"

I remained where I was while the priests conferred among themselves. I knew the guards' lives were at stake, and if the priests went to Pilate—he was procurator at that time—to demand their execution, I planned to intervene. But they surprised me. Their plan was clever, hatched by the devil himself. They called the rest of the soldiers in—there were four in all—and handed them each a purse heavy with gold. 'Here is what you will say happened,' and they repeated the story that the disciples had taken the body while the guard slept. 'Say this and we will keep you out of trouble with Pilate.'"

Never in my life had I experienced such anguish in my spirit. As the soldiers took their blood money, I tore my robes and fell to my knees. I bowed my head to the floor and begged Heaven to forgive my blindness and my part in the death of the Messiah. I was on the floor for a long time; when I came to myself again, the Roman guards and priests were gone. I decided to go see Joseph of Arimathea. He was one of the two who had taken Jesus' body for burial. I ran to his house, but he wasn't home, and his servants would not tell me where he was. Then I ran to find Nicodemus. He was the other of the two, and Joseph's closest friend on the Council. When I arrived at Nicodemus' house—which fortunately for me wasn't far from Joseph's—I found both of them there. They didn't want to talk to me at first, but when they saw the state I was in, they were willing to hear what I had to say."

Zerah paused and wiped away tears that were tracking down his cheeks. "I told them, 'I believe. I believe. His claims are true....'" The priest faltered and stopped in his tracks, put his hands to his face and bending over at the waist, cried aloud and began to sob. Jacob, stunned by the intensity of Zerah's weeping, backed one step away. He was used to seeing men cry—it happened all the time in the Temple—but this was different. This was more than a memory of Zerah's, more than his reliving the moment.

Jacob stood back while Joel and Gallus moved toward the priest. They put their arms around him, murmuring consolation. Moments later, Joel lifted one hand in prayer, though he spoke so quietly Jacob couldn't catch what he said. The two men covered Zerah like ministering angels until his weeping was past. Then, with their arms around his shoulders, they walked alongside him for a mile or more, encouraging him until he could continue on his own.

Jacob trailed several steps behind them, staring numbly at his feet as he walked. Zerah made no apology for his outburst, and after a few minutes he gestured to Jacob to catch up with him. When the two of them were in tandem again, the priest picked up the thread of his story where he left off. "That was all I could get out at first to Nicodemus and to Joseph—that I believed. I was weeping, just as now. They gave me water and helped me sit down. We spent the rest of the day together, and I told them everything I had seen and heard that morning; they in turn told me how they came to believe." Zerah wiped his eyes on his sleeve. "That night I went home and told my wife and my son. My whole household was saved."

They walked in silence for a good half hour, each absorbed in his own thoughts. Jacob pondered Zerah's story. *The priests paid the soldiers to lie?* That alone was enough to stun and shock him. And the lie was generally accepted as truth. He had heard others repeat it any number of times. Grandfather used to rage whenever the matter of the empty tomb was brought up. "Galileans!" he would spit, choosing for the moment to forget that he himself had grown up in Galilee. "Nothing but ignorant farmers and fishermen! Do they really think any intelligent man will buy their story of a resurrection? Bah! They stole the body away themselves. We have the word of the Roman guards who witnessed it."

Even Jacob's father believed the tale, though he was more sanguine. "That happened a long time ago, son," he once said when Jacob brought the story home from school. "You were just a baby. Don't believe everything you hear. The man died, and his body was stolen from the grave. That's all there is to it."

He believed his father then, but now he wasn't so sure. Would a man like Uncle Phillip give up his wealth, risk the ridicule of family and friends, and put his life in jeopardy for the sake of a story, or a rumor? Would John Mark travel so far away from his home, leaving his mother alone in Jerusalem, and go live among strangers? And would a man of Zerah's age and status abandon his fine home and strike out for an unknown city and an uncertain future?

At that moment it dawned on him that nearly everyone he had known who had cared for him, everyone who had ever shown him kindness was a follower of the Christ. His father wasn't, nor was Gedeon, but he thought his Aunt Deborah and Uncle Nicanor probably were, and his grandmother Abigail. Mark was, and here Jacob was surrounded by men who believed. Part of him wanted to shrug off his doubt and join them, but he couldn't take that step yet. He was disgraced for running away, and now he had to find his place in the world somehow. He had to make something of himself, so he could return to his father with his head up, so his father would be proud—so his grandfather would be proven wrong.

I have my whole future to think about, he told himself.

*   *   *   *   *

At that very moment, a shadowed rider on a gray gelding pulled up outside an inn just east of Joppa. The proprietor, normally a devout man, looked out the window and cursed. "Rachel," he called over his shoulder. "Gather the children and take them to your sister's." She stopped only a second to glance out the window herself before running to do his bidding. "Hurry now," he urged her as she herded them out the back door. "I'll send for you as soon as this fellow is gone."

Chapter 5

Early the next morning, without bothering to knock, Susannah yanked open the door to Caleb and Deborah's bedroom. "There's a man here to see you," she said. "Says he's a client of yours."

Caleb jumped at the intrusion, then frowned. "So early?" He had gotten up with the sun, and had not yet finished dressing. "Who is he? Did he give you his name?" He bent down to tie his sandal.

"No, he didn't."

Her tone was as short as her answer. He glanced up, and straightened in shock. *Did she just roll her eyes at me?* "And I suppose he didn't say what he wanted?" When Susannah shrugged, he sighed, "Very well. Make him comfortable and tell him I'll be with him shortly." He turned his attention back to his sandal.

"Mistress!" Susannah's sudden exclamation made him jump again. "You should not be lying down like that to feed the baby!"

Diana yawned, and with a disinterested air asked, "Why not?"

"It's terrible bad luck," Susannah had gone shrill with anxiety. "You'll bring evil on that child. Here," she offered, "let me help you sit up."

With a deep sigh of reluctance, Diana gathered the baby and let Susannah pull her into a sitting position. When the maid had finished fussing, she left the room, but not before stopping to make a warding gesture around the door as she went out.

"She is losing her mind," Diana drawled.

Caleb said, "We need to discharge her."

"*You* need to discharge her," she corrected him with a sniff.

Caleb used his most authoritative demeanor. "My love, the household is your domain. The servants are yours to hire and discharge as you please."

Nonplussed, Diana cocked one eyebrow at him. "Your father hired her. That makes her your servant."

"So neither of us wants to do it, but still it must be done." He winced at the thought of the nasty scene that would surely follow. Diana said nothing. "She was never a very good servant," he mused aloud. "Deborah complained of her more than once, but Father would never let her get rid of Susanna. And since Father's illness, she's gotten worse—lazier, more disrespectful." *Father favors her—too much for a servant.*

Diana smirked, "I'll do it for you, Caleb."

Surprised, he turned with a smile, "You will?"

"I will," she purred, "but it will cost you."

Caleb fisted his hands to keep from wrapping them around her pretty neck.

"Never mind," he growled. "I'll do it myself." Ignoring the light laughter that followed him out the door, he remembered what Susannah had told him. *A client? Who could it be at this hour?* Caleb tried to cheer himself. *Do I smell an opportunity?* Then he grinned. *No, that's breakfast.* Still smiling at his own jest, he went downstairs.

* * * * *

"You're serious about this?" Caleb felt his stomach sink when his visitor stood to leave.

"Yes, Caleb, I am." James finished off the cup of wine Caleb poured for him. "I'm sorry for the trouble this causes you." He didn't sound the least bit sorry.

"And you're certain you want *all* of the money you invested with me?"

"Every last shekel."

James was one of Caleb's wealthiest clients. The thought of losing his business made him physically sick. He took a quick mental accounting of the money he had on hand. Nowhere near enough. "I can have it for you by the end of next week."

James' eyes narrowed on him, and shock hit Caleb like a dash of cold water in his face. *He doesn't trust me!* He swallowed hard, praying that their long business relationship would win him over. "I can give you a fourth of it now," he began.

"Half," his client countered. "Half now, and the other half on the first day of the week."

"I don't have half on hand," Caleb answered, hating himself for revealing even that much. "One third. I can give you one third today, and the rest by the end of next week." Inwardly he cringed. It would leave him woefully short of reserves. "You understand, of course, I have to sell off your investments. That takes time, and you'll lose a good deal of your profits." His stomach did another slow roll. *And I'll lose, too.*

When James didn't answer, Caleb asked, "Are you in some kind of difficulty? Is there any way I can help you?"

His client replied in chilled, measured tones, "The only help I need from you is for you to return my money."

"I understand," Caleb nodded and tried to smile. "Give me a moment and I will bring you what I have on hand." He left the room and hastened to his own where he kept his cash hidden away. "What is wrong with him?" he muttered as he pulled the tapestry back from the wall. "We've done business together for years. He came to Andrew's banquet—why he even raised a toast to my son!" Caleb's brow furrowed as he remembered that night. He searched his memory for some clue, some hidden gesture of James' that might have indicated displeasure, but he came up empty. With shaking hands, he counted out the gold and silver.

"What? What is this?" He was missing what amounted to a month's profits. A knife of dread sliced through his gut. Frantically, he felt around in the hole. Nothing. "Do I still have enough? He laid aside what he would have to surrender to James, and when he was done, he was left with only three silver staters.

"Three staters. That will be enough to get me through the week," he muttered as he piled James' money into one purse. "Except, of course, I'll have to pay my part to Caiaphas in two days." With another jolt he realized his three staters would barely cover that expense. *Who else would have gotten into my money? Father is sick, so he couldn't have. Diana?*

On his way back to where James awaited him, he pondered his dilemma. *Should I raise my rates—just until the end of this week?* With shaking fingers, he twisted the gold ring on his right hand—Lathan's signet ring. He had given it to Caleb saying, "My fingers are too swollen to wear it. You keep it safe for me until I'm better." Now he considered talking to Lathan about his dilemma, but decided against it. *I have to make these decisions—and mistakes—myself. Father would never allow any man to empty him out.* He sighed and shook his head. He had learned much in the past dozen or so years, but he would never have his father's head for business, or his negotiating skills.

When James had taken his money and gone, Caleb got ready to leave for the Temple, still chewing on his problem. The Feast of Unleavened Bread was over, and The Feast of Weeks was still a month away. Business would be slow. Ruefully he recalled the banquet he had given to celebrate Andrew's birth, and the money he spent on it. *I should not have invited so many.*

Gedeon and Eunice were still with them. He toyed with the idea of asking his father-in-law for a small loan to tide him over until the next week, but quickly dismissed it. *I can't go crawling to my wife's parents. There's no help for it. I'll have to skim a bit more of James' profits when I've recovered the rest of his money. He will never know.*

Caleb stopped to looked in on his father. Lathan was awake, and Diana was standing over him. He asked, "Father, did you give Diana money?"

Lathan barely managed a nod. "Did."

He turned to Diana. "What in the world did you spend it on?"

"Things for Andrew, for the banquet. A few things for the house."

Staggered by her cavalier attitude, he told her, "No more. I have just had to meet a large expense. You may not spend any more money without my permission."

She tossed him a withering look. "Your father is still the head of this house."

He came in close, his voice low. "And you took advantage of him. It will not happen again." He said to Lathan, "Father, do you hear me? Do not give Diana any more money without telling me first." There was no response from Lathan, and Diana merely arched her eyebrows at him.

As I am Known

Enraged, he stalked out of the house. When he came in through the Temple gate, he bumped into a priest coming the other way. "Sorry," he muttered into the other's glare. *I've always kept short accounts with Caiaphas. Perhaps he'll let me put off paying this week's fees until next.*

Convincing himself he would be able to work it out, Caleb set up his table in the Outer Court and prepared for his day. *If Jacob were still with Simon, I could at least have gotten his silver back from him. That would have helped.* Thoughts of money faded as his grief over his firstborn, still fresh and raw, settled heavy as iron in his bones. He sat down to begin his work. *Oh, my son, where are you?*

* * * * *

"Where are they now?" Phineas poured another helping of wine into his informant's cup. "Are they still in the city?"

The old man wagged his head. "No, my lord. Those men left Caesarea, I'd say three days ago."

"And which way were they going?"

The man shrugged and tipped back his cup. "I didn't pay much attention, my lord, but if they came in from the south, it stands to reason they'd continue north. Unless, of course, they took a ship." He squinted up at Phineas, "But I doubt that. Weather's been ugly. To the best of my knowledge no one's set sail from here for more than a week."

Phineas had no reason to doubt the man's word. Before he left Jerusalem, he had found out the names of the men Jacob would be traveling with. He was slightly acquainted with Saul of Tarsus, having met him a dozen or so years before—before Saul lost his mind and ran off to join that Galilean sect. The old man he now spoke to described Saul perfectly, as well as Saul's companion, Jonathan, also called Barnabas. As luck would have it, this Barnabas stood at least half a head taller than most other men. His handsome, strong-featured face and booming baritone made him stand out.

"And the boy, Jacob—are you sure he was with them?"

The old man took another swallow of wine. "I cannot say as to any boys, my lord," he answered. "I only mention that I saw the men because they are known in this city. If they had a lad or two with them, I didn't notice, so I don't know." Plied as he was with wine, the informant still had wits enough about him to know he didn't like Phineas' looks or his manner. He remembered only one young man traveling with Saul, but chose not to say so. Feigning ignorance seemed the safest course.

Sensing the old man's reticence, Phineas' smile broadened. "Do they have friends in Caesarea? Someone they might have visited or stayed with?"

Phillip's face floated before the old man's eyes. He didn't know Phillip well, but he had welcomed him into his tanner's shop more than once. Phillip's quiet kindness seemed to shout a warning against this stranger's questions. The informant's knuckles and back were starting to ache. He groaned and flexed his fists. "Must be a storm coming," he muttered. "No, my lord. As I said, they are known in the city, but I know of no one here in particular they might have gone to."

You're lying. Phineas' grin was positively radiant. *If we weren't in a public place.... Well, I'll find you later and deal with you when no one is watching.*

* * * * *

Arin gasped and sat up. Blinking sleep from her eyes, she gazed around at her sisters, all still napping. Her sudden movement hadn't wakened them. The rays of the early afternoon sun streamed in through the window and settled on Lyssa's curls, firing them gold and copper. Arin picked up one of the transformed tresses and rubbed it gently between her fingers. Then she remembered her dream. Rising carefully so as not to disturb the others, she padded out into the main room where Papa was busy mending a sandal with an awl. Arin watched a moment, and laid a hand on her father's shoulder. "Papa?"

Phillip looked up and started to smile before he saw her expression, and his brow furrowed with concern. "What is it, Arin? Is something wrong?"

"I had a dream," she began, and sat down beside him. "I don't remember all of it, but it was about Sheliel."

"The tanner?" Phillip laid down his awl and gave her his full attention. "What about him?"

"I dreamed there was something in his house." Arin swallowed. "Something black—like a man, but not...." She rubbed at her face with both hands. "I don't know how to describe it. It was terrible."

"Were you thinking about Sheliel before you went to sleep? Or were you praying for him?"

"No, Papa." Arin was sure of that. She had been thinking about Grandfather Gedeon, hoping he would stop by and visit soon.

"What do you think the dream means, beloved?" Phillip asked gently.

The way her father took her at her word gave her the confidence to say, "He shouldn't go home tonight."

He stared at her a full minute, then got to his feet. "Then I will find him and tell him." He took his staff from beside the door and started out.

"Papa?" she called out. When he stopped and looked back at her, she asked, "What if I'm wrong?"

Phillip's eyes on her were full of concern and compassion. "I think the proper question is, what if you're right and we say nothing? He could be in danger of his life." Then his expression brightened and he chuckled, "If you're wrong, all that will happen is that Sheliel will spend the night in a strange bed." He looked out toward the sea. "I think I'll invite him to stay here with us. Tell your mother where I've gone."

As her father disappeared through the door, Arin ran her fingers through her tangled curls and blew out a long breath.

*   *   *   *   *

Her father was as good as his word. A couple of hours later, as she was helping her mother prepare dinner, she spotted him returning from the city with the tanner at his side. *Did Papa merely invite Sheliel, or did he tell him the reason for the invitation?*

Arin got her answer when they came in the door. Sheliel met her with a sharp look and asked, "Is this the little girl who dreams?" Coloring under the intensity of the tanner's gaze, Arin bit her lip.

"This is our oldest daughter, Arin," Leah said, coming up behind her and putting an arm around her shoulders.

"Well, Arin," Sheliel sketched a short bow, "I am thankful to you for your caution." He smiled at her mother, "And to you, dear lady, for your hospitality."

"Someone was in the city today asking about Saul," Phillip said.

Arin gasped, and Leah asked, "About our Saul?"

Sheliel said, "That's why I was so quick to come with your husband this afternoon. When the stranger asked who Saul and his cousin might have stayed with, I lied—may Heaven forgive me—and said I didn't know of anyone here who knew them well. I was afraid he'd be looking for your family next. I didn't know the man, but I had a feeling he was up to no good."

Arin shivered in the warm room. Even if her dream meant nothing, it frightened her to know someone was looking for Saul. It occurred to her then, that though Sheliel had kept his own counsel, others in Caesarea might not. "Papa..." she began.

"We will all go to Uncle Jonas' house tonight," Phillip answered her unspoken fear. He added to Leah, "I have already talked to your brother, and he says we are welcome. But first," he glanced around the room, "why don't we pray?" He closed his eyes and lifted his hands, and after a moment's hesitation, Sheliel did the same. "Oh Lord, we thank you for your provision and protection, and we ask you to shield us from those who would do us harm this night."

In the ensuing silence, Sheliel added, "Throw our enemies into confusion, as you did the army of Midianites in the days of Gideon. Amen."

Phillip and his family added their amen's to his prayer, and Leah said, "Well now, we have work to do. Arin, help me gather our dinner. We'll take it with us."

"Yes, Mama." Arin hastened to obey.

"Lyssa, fetch blankets for everyone. Salome, help Arin." While Leah marshaled her family, Phillip hitched their donkey to a small cart. He and Sheliel loaded it as the girls brought bundles from the house. When they were done, the men walked beside the donkey's head, talking quietly between themselves all the way into town. Salome rode atop the blankets. Lyssa followed the cart, with Leah and Arin bringing up the rear.

Arin's relief at being away from the house lasted only until they reached Caesarea. Once they entered the city, she seemed to feel danger looming around every corner. Evil intent lurked in the shadowy doorways. She clutched her veil close around her face and walked right at her mother's elbow, until Leah put an arm around her shoulder and whispered, "Don't be afraid, daughter, only pray."

Arin's eyes darted back and forth, searched every face, every figure that passed them in the growing dark. *Oh Lord, as You hid Moses in the cleft of the rock, hide us now with your hand. Cover us with your shadow.* To her enormous relief, no one seemed to pay any attention to them.

When they neared Jonas' house, Phillip stopped suddenly and turned. "Arin, come here a moment." She trotted up to the men, and Phillip said, "I know John Mark and your cousin Jacob are friends. Did he say anything to you about him when he was here?"

She nodded. "He said that Jacob told him he might come this way with Grandfather next year. Why?"

Sheliel explained, "The stranger wasn't looking specifically for Saul. He seemed more interested in locating a boy he thought was traveling with him. I remembered a young man with Saul and Barnabas, but he didn't fit the description the fellow gave me. He said the boy he was looking for was named Jacob."

"And the description fits our Jacob perfectly." Phillip frowned in puzzlement, and stroked his beard. "I don't understand. For some reason he expected Jacob to be with them, but why in the world is he looking for Jacob here, if he's in Jerusalem?"

*   *   *   *   *

Joel stopped in the road as the travelers crested a rise, and made a sweeping gesture with one hand. "There she is—Damascus."

Just below them at the bottom of the hill ran a wide river, gleaming in the late afternoon, and about ten miles beyond that rose a plateau. The city crowned the tableland and completed it, as if it had sprung up from living rock. The sun, now past its zenith, and lowering toward the western mountains, washed the desert that lay to the east in golden light, making it appear almost translucent.

Jacob, who had never in his memory traveled farther than Jericho, stood stunned. *It looks like it's sitting in a sea of amber, or honey.* "It's...it's beautiful," he finally managed to stammer.

"One of the oldest cities in the world," Zerah murmured, and Gallus, who had wrapped the end of his turban around the lower part of his face to protect his fair skin from the sun, nodded his head.

"It is?" Jacob frowned, his pride in his heritage slightly bruised. "But not older than Jerusalem...."

Joel grinned at him. "Were you asleep in school, lad?"

"The ancient name of Damascus is Sham," Zerah added, "for Noah's second son, who settled here."

"My house is north and east of the city." Joel turned and shaded his eyes, squinting at the sun. "We won't make it before nightfall, and there won't be enough moonlight to travel by. My betrothed's family lives in the city. We can stay with them. Make haste," he called over his shoulder as he headed down the hill. "We don't want to be caught outside the walls in the dark. Too many bandits."

They followed him, Zerah grunting with exertion on the slope. The road led to a massive stone bridge that straddled the water. "This stone work looks new," the priest remarked as they started across.

"It's Roman," Gallus answered. His cloth mask did not hide the note of pride in his voice. "Our engineers are the best in the world."

"Ah, son of my heart," Zerah answered, laying a friendly hand on Gallus' shoulder, "you are about as Roman as I am." Jacob thought Zerah's manservant would be offended, but Gallus laughed.

A pair of sentries stood watch on the far end of the bridge. When they reached it, one of the soldiers put out a hand to stop them. He looked them all over, then peered at Gallus' icy eyes and barked out something in Latin, which Jacob did not understand. Gallus gave him a short answer, one which apparently didn't satisfy the soldier's questions, for he grasped the hilt of his sword to unsheathe it. Gallus put out his left hand in a gesture of conciliation, then showed him the stump of his right arm. The sentry sneered and backed away one step, as if the old wound were contagious. Still grasping the sword's hilt, he waved them all on.

Jacob let out the breath he was holding, and followed his companions. The men made no comment about the incident, leaving him to wonder if it happened often. But he had little energy to spare for wondering, for Joel now hurried along the road toward the city, leaving Jacob hard-pressed to keep up with his pace on the slight, but steady uphill grade. Zerah huffed and puffed alongside him, his face growing redder with each passing minute. After about two miles, Jacob became alarmed at the wheezing sounds coming from the older man, and he called out, "Uncle Joel, wait a minute."

Joel stopped and turned, scowling at the delay. "What is it?"

"I have a rock in my shoe," Jacob answered, and bent down to untie his sandal. As he did, he nodded toward the priest, who was now leaning heavily on his staff with his eyes closed.

Joel followed the gesture, and his expression softened. He turned to Gallus, and the two of them conferred quietly before Gallus unshouldered his pack, handed it to Joel, and took off toward Damascus at a trot.

"Where..." Zerah wheezed, "where is Gallus going in such a hurry?"

"He's going to see if he can hire a donkey," Joel answered, taking the older man's arm. "Are you all right?"

"A donkey." He thrust his chin out, but his eyes gleamed with good humor. "You don't think I can keep up with you?" As Joel hesitated, Zerah chuckled, "You are absolutely right." Planting the end of his staff firmly in the road, he turned toward the city. "But we should keep moving, or we'll never make it through the gates by nightfall, donkey or no donkey."

The three of them started forward again, more slowly than before, but still at a determined pace. Jacob trailed behind his uncle and the priest, now absorbed in his thoughts. He searched his memory for what he could recall about Damascus and its people, the battles between this place and Jerusalem. King David collected a tribute from the king of Damascus. Or was it Solomon? And the leper—the army commander that Elisha healed—was from here. Jacob remembered that when prophet told the commander to wash in the Jordan river, he protested that the rivers of Damascus were cleaner than the Jordan. Jacob glanced back over his shoulder. The wide stream behind them was, no doubt, one of the rivers he had referred to.

He gazed up at the city again, at its high, imposing walls, still far away, and all at once he was stricken by a crushing wave of homesickness. At that moment he would have traded the company of his uncle and his friends for five minutes with his father. He bowed his head to hide his gathering tears and plodded on.

*   *   *   *   *

Gallus returned less than an hour later. Joel spotted him first, trotting up the road toward them with a donkey in tow. "Look who's coming!" he called out.

When he reached them, panting from exertion, Gallus said, "Heaven was with us today. I found a merchant with a string of animals. He was happy to sell this one—perhaps too happy."

The donkey gave Zerah a sidelong look as he approached, snorted, and tried to sidle away. Joel caught the animal by his rope bridle and turned him. "No you don't. We need you to behave."

The priest laughed and patted the donkey's neck. "You think I'm too heavy to carry, don't you, my wise little friend? You must be descended from Balaam's ass."

Joel held him steady while Zerah mounted, then stepped back and eyed them both dubiously. "Well, at least your feet aren't dragging the ground."

Chuckling, the priest said, "We'd better go on. The day will not wait for us."

The company started moving once again at Joel's preferred pace. Jacob wondered how Gallus could keep up, when he had already been running, but the former soldier showed no signs of fatigue, even when the road began its ascent toward the city gate. Jacob supposed Gallus' military training had toughened him for such travel.

They were still about a mile from Damascus when the sun began to sink into the mountains behind it. "It is well," Jacob heard Joel mutter. "We are close enough. We'll be there before dark."

Their pace had slowed somewhat as they labored uphill. Jacob trudged alongside the donkey, trying not to look up at the massive, yawning gate above him. It reminded him of a mouth, a ravenous, gaping maw lined with stone teeth, open and ready to swallow him whole. Somehow he knew if he entered that gate, he would be lost forever to his father, to his home, to everyone he loved. The memory of Prisca's anguished cries stole unbidden into his heart. *Why? Oh, why are you leaving me?* Fresh tears prickled his eyes.

From ahead of him, Zerah began to sing,

> "Those who trust in the Lord are like Mount Zion,
> Which cannot be shaken, but endures forever...."

The priest's gravelly voice suffered some unsteadiness as he was bounced along on the back of his donkey. After the first few words, Joel, who was hopelessly tone deaf, joined in, and somehow his tuneless droning worked a counterpoint to Zerah's tenor.

> "As the mountains surround Jerusalem,
> So the Lord surrounds His people...."

A song of ascents. Is it proper, Jacob wondered, *to enter a pagan city singing one of the celebration songs for going up to Jerusalem?* He knew the words by heart, but could not make himself join in. He continued up the road, his feet slowing with every step, until they stopped altogether as Zerah sang the benediction. "Peace be unto Israel." He looked up. Everyone had stopped. Roman soldiers at the gate were halting people as they came into the city. Jacob craned his neck for a better look, and everything he might have expected to see going up to Jerusalem was here also—the soldiers, the shuffling throngs of people. He stood on tiptoe, and a moment later he spotted them—the tax collectors. They wove in and out among the crowd, inspecting merchandise in order to levy tribute to Caesar's government, arguing with the merchants over the amounts they charged.

Just like at home! The scene before him was so familiar. In running for his father, he had been in and out of every gate in the Holy City—the Sheep Gate, the Beautiful Gate, the Damascus Gate—Jacob knew them all. For the first time since the night he shimmied down the wall of Caiaphas' palace, he had the sense that he was arriving somewhere, rather than just leaving home. He squinted his eyes enough to blur his vision a little, and found he could almost make himself believe he was entering Jerusalem. But instead of comforting him, the thought disquieted his spirit. He felt like a traitor, comparing Jerusalem to this benighted place, this pagan place.

Then from somewhere behind him, another voice lifted up a song.

> "Hear us, O Shepherd of Israel,
>   you who lead Joseph like a flock;
>   you who sit enthroned between the cherubim,
>   shine forth before Ephraim, Benjamin, and Manasseh...."

Startled, he turned around to try to locate the source of the song, but because of the dark and the size of the throng, he couldn't see the singer. "There are other Jews out here."

"Damascus has many Jews," Joel answered. "Our people are scattered like seed all over the world."

Our people. Something in Jacob unclenched at that, and he lifted his head and squared his shoulders. *I am far from home, far from my family, but I am not alone.* His thoughts turned to John Mark. *I wonder where he is now? He left before I did. Perhaps he is already in Antioch. I hope he will be able to find my mother—and my brother.* The traffic moved forward several paces. They were nearly at the gate.

*   *   *   *   *

In less than a half hour they were inside the city walls. It was now fully dark, so Joel lit a torch and held it aloft. "Come." Jacob fell in behind his uncle, and Gallus followed, leading Zerah's donkey. Jacob kept his eyes fixed on Joel's striped robe, the only thing he could discern clearly in the circle of light cast by the torch's flame. In single file they navigated the stone maze of Damascus' streets.

"Here we are," Joel finally announced when he stopped in front of an unimposing house on the western edge of the city. He rapped on the wooden door, and stood back to wait. When no one answered, he frowned. "Surely they haven't all gone to bed yet."

Gallus pointed to a faint flicker in a second story window. "I think I see a light. Try again."

Joel knocked more loudly the second time, and moments later, the door cracked open. Jacob caught a glimpse of a young woman, who peered out with the wide, frightened eyes of a doe. She whispered, "Who is there?"

"Mary," Joel said, "Will you let us in?"

"Joel!" With a sobbing gasp, the girl flung the door open, fell into his arms, and burst into tears.

Chapter 6

After an unfruitful search in the city of Tyre, Phineas mounted the gray gelding and continued north, relying on his earlier information that Barnabas and Saul were headed to Antioch. He was in a foul mood that the sunny day did nothing to dispel. *If they truly have friends there, they will linger, and I will catch up with them. And if I have somehow gotten ahead of them, I will await them there. They'll have to turn up sooner or later.* He kept telling himself that, as if sheer repetition made it true.

But he had been thwarted by that old man in Caesarea.

Determined to repay him for his lies, Phineas had asked around until he found the home of Sheliel the tanner. Breaking into his house was an easy matter, and after surveying the humble contents of the one-room dwelling and adjoining shop, he settled down to wait for his prey.

But Sheliel did not come home, not all that night, nor the following morning. Finally at noon, convinced the old man had somehow been warned, and aware that he was wasting precious time, Phineas tore into Sheliel's belongings. Trashing the house and shop did not satisfy his lust for revenge. *But I will come through Caesarea on my way back to Jerusalem,* he promised himself. *This time I will catch him unaware and repay him—with interest. While I'm at it, I'll find out who he was protecting and deal with them as well. And I'll make the boy watch.*

As black as his thoughts were, Phineas had to admit that the horse trader, at least, had not deceived him. The animal was young and full of energy, and he trotted along the road at a steady pace. He had shown signs of skittishness at the beginning, but Phineas took a firm hand with him, and now it seemed they had an understanding. At times he let the horse have his head and run, which the gelding was eager to do. Today, however, Phineas held him to a brisk trot, all the while combing the road ahead and the surrounding countryside for signs of the boy. He passed a few small caravans that day, and a handful of others driving carts or walking north.

Each time he passed a traveler, he slowed the horse and asked after Barnabas and Saul, describing them, but withholding their names, and telling the lie he had decided to use. "They had a couple of near-grown boys with them. I have a message for one of the lads. His father is sick, and at the point of death. His family sent me to find him and take him home."

The leader of the last caravan he passed that day reacted much as the others had. He clucked his tongue in sympathy for Phineas' plight. "I have not seen any such party, but if I do, I will pass the message along." He shook his head. "How terrible for the boy...."

"Indeed." Phineas answered, his tone grave with feigned regret. "I must find him as soon as possible."

"I wish you good journey." The merchant waved as Phineas snapped the reins and galloped away.

The day wore on toward evening, and he began having second thoughts. *No one has seen them. Does that mean they're still ahead of me? They must be, but....* He shifted uncomfortably in the saddle and glanced behind him. *Have I passed them by?* He hated not knowing. He was usually sure of himself, certain of his ability to track men down, but now doubt nagged at him. *Ever since Caesarea....*

By the time he came within sight of the city of Sidon that afternoon, he was convinced that Barnabas and his companions must be behind him, that he had missed them somehow. Unwilling to go ahead of them into Antioch and wait—hadn't his waiting in Caesarea been a colossal waste of time?—he turned his horse around and started back toward Tyre. *I won't make it before dark.*

Blinded by anger at his own indecision, he didn't see the viper until it was too late. Out of the corner of his eye he caught a flash of black and brown. The horse screamed in terror and reared, throwing Phineas to the ground. Searing pain sliced through his left shoulder, and the last thing he heard as his head hit the stony pavement was the sound of the gelding's hooves tearing away across the adjacent field.

* * * * *

Is there a millstone on my chest? Aaagh!...My head...! Phineas started the slow ascent to consciousness like a disoriented swimmer engulfed in a sea of dark misery. He felt suffocated. Every breath was an agony. *Where is the surface?* He wanted to claw his way up... somewhere... but his limbs refused to move, as if he were bound hand and foot. And the sea was cold...so black and so cold. A crushing dread almost stopped his heart. *The Sadducees are wrong. There is a resurrection. There is, and I am in torment somewhere in the bowels of Gehenna. But Gehenna is a fire that never goes out. Why is it so **cold**?* A racking shudder ripped though him. Then he heard a voice, but instead of the demonic hisses he feared, this sounded normal and solid. And it was singing. He cracked one eye open.

"Ah, you're awake at last."

Awake? Then I'm not dead? He opened both eyes. A wood-beamed ceiling stretched above him. When he tried to move his head, pain slammed like a sledge hammer against the inside of his skull. He cried out.

"Easy there, friend. You've had a rough time of it. Don't try to move."

Phineas' eyes canted left toward the voice. A white-bearded man sat on cushions next to his pallet. *I know you...from somewhere....* He wanted to speak, but all that came out was a groan.

The man nodded as if he understood. "You want to know where you are, and what happened. My name is Joseph. You probably don't remember me, but you passed me on the road. You were asking after a boy. You told me his father was at the point of death. Remember?"

Phineas tried to fix his gaze on his visitor, but the man kept sliding in and out of focus.

"Well, no matter. What is important is that you and your horse were both bitten by a snake. I came upon you lying in the road, probably less than an hour after you were thrown. Your horse, I'm sorry to say, had to be destroyed. We found him in a field nearby." He didn't add that the horse's condition had dismayed them all. He was standing, just barely, splay-legged, and foaming at the mouth. "I think the snake bit your horse first, and then it got you after you were thrown. You were lucky, my friend. We only found one set of fang marks on your leg. Your horse got most of the poison."

"Where...?" Phineas croaked.

"Where are you?" Joseph smiled. "You are in Sidon, and this is my home. I brought you here because it was the closest city, and because you were headed this way." He took a sip from a steaming cup he held. Phineas' eyes followed the movement, and his tongue, swollen, dry and insensate as old leather, crept out to touch his cracked and blistered lips.

"Ah, forgive me. You must be very thirsty. I'll help you sit up to drink, but," he added with a chuckle, "you'll probably wish I hadn't."

He slipped an arm behind Phineas' shoulders and sat him up. Every muscle and nerve screamed in enraged protest, and Phineas almost passed out again, but through the sheer force of his will, he held onto himself. Gritting his teeth, he accepted the cup. The steaming liquid—an herbal infusion sweetened with honey—nearly scalded his tongue and throat, but the heat went down like the promise of life. Another shudder shook his bones, rattled them as if he were hollow inside, as if everything in him had dried to dust. He finished off the cup and held it out. "More."

"Not yet," the older man answered, taking the cup. "Let's see if you keep that down first."

Too sick and weak to harbor thoughts of rage, Phineas allowed himself to be laid down again on his mat. "How long?" he whispered.

"How long?" Joseph frowned in puzzlement. "Oh, you mean how long have you been here?" When Phineas managed to nod, he answered. "You heal quickly, my friend. It's only been two days."

* * * * *

Jacob did not want to follow Joel and the others into Mary's house. Her reaction to their presence at first startled, and then shocked him. She stood there in the street—in public!—clinging to Joel and weeping. The girl was crying so hard, that even with Joel's gentle probing, she was incoherent. Unwilling to watch, Jacob looked away. Her weeping reminded him far too clearly of his own when his father abandoned him to his grandfather's hateful demand. He couldn't bear any of her pain while he yet carried his own.

"Let's get her inside," Zerah finally suggested. "Once she has calmed down she'll be able to talk."

So Joel pushed the door open, and with one arm around her, led his still-weeping bride into the dark house. Zerah followed them with the torch, and Gallus started in, but Jacob stopped him. "What should we do with the donkey?"

"Tie him up here for now," Gallus answered. "We will bring him food and water later."

Jacob did as he was told, but when that small task was finished, he still didn't want to go inside, though Gallus was holding the door for him. Jacob stroked the donkey's head. "Are you sure he'll be all right?"

"Come on in, lad," Gallus answered, glancing about him. "It's best if we do not linger out here."

With deep reluctance, Jacob left the donkey and stepped over the threshold, where he stopped as Gallus pulled the door shut behind them. Inside, he shaded his eyes against the light from a half-dozen lamps Zerah had ignited with the torch. Joel and Mary stood in the center of the room, locked in embrace, and now Joel wept, too. Turning away, Jacob removed his turban and raked his fingers through his hair. *He shouldn't be touching her like that. It's not proper. What kind of woman is she, to permit it?*

When Zerah had finished with the lamps, Gallus took him aside and said, "There is nothing to eat in the house. Half a jar of water, but that's all. No flour, nothing."

"Do we have provisions enough for tonight?" Zerah asked.

"More than enough," the servant answered. "It's a good thing. Who knows how long she's gone without food?"

For the first time Jacob noticed the hollows in the girl's pale cheeks. Stricken with shame for his condemning thoughts—and didn't they sound just like Grandfather?—he hastened to help Gallus open the packs and set food out.

Drying his eyes on the sleeve of his tunic, Joel led Mary to the cushions. "Sit down, Beloved," he urged her. "We'll eat, and then you can tell us what has happened."

She refused at first. "It isn't proper." Her words, spoken in a bare whisper, were a hammer blow to Jacob's heart. "I should be serving you."

Zerah said, "You'll have plenty of opportunities to wait on us, my dear." The smile he gave her was full of pain, almost a wince. "Let us serve you tonight."

With that, she acquiesced and sat down next to Joel. Gallus set flat loaves out for them while Jacob unwrapped the rest of the smoked fish they had purchased earlier in the day. That, along with a bowl of olives and some dried dates made up their dinner. After Zerah gave thanks, Joel took one of the loaves, tore it in half, and gave a piece to his betrothed. Jacob tried not to stare as she accepted it with shaking hands. And when, after the first experimental bite, she devoured the rest of her bread like a ravenous animal, they all averted their eyes.

A little later, her initial hunger satisfied, Mary looked around the table and stammered, "I apologize.... It's been so long...." Her pallid skin flushed with embarrassment.

"How long?" Joel asked. "How long have you been alone here?"

"Five days," she answered.

"Five days," Zerah echoed, shaking his head.

Joel covered her hand with his own. "Can you tell us what happened?"

Fresh tears sprang to her eyes, but she nodded. Her hands still trembled as she grasped her wine cup and gulped down its contents. She said, "They came and arrested my parents...they took them away...." Her voice trailed off. She stared into the empty cup.

Joel touched her hand. "Where is your brother, Mary? Where is Jonas?"

"I...I don't know." Her dark eyes were pools of misery. "He hasn't been here. Maybe they got him, too."

Zerah asked, "Do you know who betrayed them?"

She shook her head. "No, and that's why I've been afraid to go out."

Joel's hands were in his lap, the fingers so tightly interlaced they looked like one hardened fist. "So your mother and father are in prison?"

"Mama is. At least, I think she is still there." Mary raised her eyes to meet Joel's. "Papa is dead. They stoned him."

Joel's mouth dropped open. He quickly covered it with one hand, but could not stop the groan that followed. He stared blankly for several seconds while tears fell unheeded from his eyes. Then with a cry, he grasped his own tunic at the neck and yanked at the fabric until the cloth gave way and tore open to his waist. He fell forward, weeping aloud and covering his head with both hands, until his face was to the floor. Mary draped her veil around her face and cried with him, all the while clutching herself and rocking back and forth.

Jacob dropped his gaze and found his own eyes flooded with tears. He ached for Joel and Mary, but their pain resurrected the awful truth he'd tried to bury on the long road from Jerusalem. Even as he pushed it away, it erupted again in his heart. *Why? Why does it have to be like this? Why did my father send me away? If he really loved me, he would have kept me with him....*

*   *   *   *   *

On the first day of the week after James' visit, Gedeon met Caleb as he came down for breakfast and said, "We will be leaving tomorrow." When Caleb protested, Gedeon held up one hand with a weary smile. "Your hospitality, as always, has been flawless, but since Prisca is sleeping better now, since her nightmares are not so numerous...well, I have business to attend to at home. And of course, I want to stop off in Caesarea to see my son."

At the mention of Phillip, Caleb turned away, embarrassed.

"You and Phillip were friends once," the older man continued. "I know you had a falling-out, but perhaps this would be a good time to mend it. True friends are hard to come by. The older I get...well, many of my friends are gone now." He sighed. "I don't always see eye-to-eye with my son, but he is a true man, and as true a friend as you are likely to have. You should make peace with him."

Caleb's throat had grown thick with his father-in-law's gentle counsel. Unable to speak, he nodded. He could scarcely remember now what he and Phillip had argued about.

Gedeon added, "I intend to tell Phillip about Jacob—unless you forbid it. The boy might turn up in Caesarea. In fact, he may be there already."

Caleb turned and met Gedeon's steady gaze. "I had that thought myself, that he might go to him, or to his uncle Joel. I even thought that he might go looking for his mother."

Gedeon's expression hardened. "You didn't tell any of this to that Phineas fellow when he came searching, did you?"

"No." Caleb rubbed at his forehead with both hands. "I was so shocked...I didn't think of it until later."

"It is well that you didn't. He is not the kind of man I want looking for my grandson."

Caleb's head snapped up. "You would own Jacob for your grandson? After the trouble that happened with him and the baby?"

"I didn't tell you," Gedeon let out a long breath, "but I met Jacob that morning right after it happened. The boy never did his little brother any harm, nor did he mean to. The women were overly fearful for the baby, and they made an incident where there was none." He shook his head sadly. "And for that I am heartily sorry. I should have stood with Jacob, and if I ever find him, I will tell him so. He deserved better." Gedeon's voice broke with those last words.

He loves Jacob, but my own father—Jacob's flesh and blood—made me send him away. Gedeon is right about Jacob. He's a good boy. The truth of it sliced Caleb to the heart. He put his face in his hands as the first sobs escaped him. With tears spilling down his own face, Gedeon put his arms around his son-in-law, and heedless of who might hear or see, they each wept for the boy they lost.

* * * * *

After Gedeon and Eunice left Jerusalem, the week raced by, and on the evening before the Sabbath, Caleb rose from his money changer's table in the Temple and straightened his robes. *I did it,* he told himself. *I made it though the week with a little money to spare.* And that, after one of his smaller investors withdrew his accounts. He cursed the coincidence—the timing was terrible—but he still managed to keep his head above water. *Of course,* he reminded himself, *I'll have to be extra careful about the household spending for a while, but we'll survive.* Satisfied that he had done the best he could, he gathered his scrolls and money box.

The sun was lowering out of sight behind the Temple. Any moment now, the priest standing lookout atop the wall would blow the shofar to signal the beginning of Sabbath.

"Shalom, ben Lathan."

Startled, he turned and found himself staring into the dark, angry eyes of Caiaphas' steward. "Simon...shalom."

Simon nodded toward his box and scroll. "Are you finished?"

"For today." Caleb smiled, though for some reason the steward's scrutiny sent a chilly rivulet racing down his spine. "I am glad it's Sabbath."

"Oh? Did you have a bad week?" Simon's words and voice were sympathetic enough, but his eyes bored into Caleb's like daggers.

"Not one of my best," Caleb admitted with a small laugh, "but we all have weeks like this. It'll pass."

"Quite right," Simon agreed. "Have you heard from your son?" Caleb felt his face go hot with shame, and when he didn't answer right away, Simon said, "Don't worry, ben Lathan, he'll show up sooner or later. Boys always do." He fingered the iron keys that hung from his belt and gave Caleb a smile as warm as winter. "Oh, and how is your father doing?" Has he recovered?"

"He's better than he was," Caleb answered carefully. "But I doubt he'll ever fully recover."

"Pity." Simon's eyes gleamed in the twilight like a hungry cat's. "Good Sabbath."

At that moment the hoarse cry of the shofar sounded above them. Caleb swallowed and stammered, "Yes...yes, good Sabbath to you." He turned and hurried out of the Temple, feeling Simon's eyes follow him all the way to the gate.

When he was about half-way home, a thought struck him, and he stopped in his tracks. *Jacob was an obedient son. If he ran away from Simon, he must have had a good reason.* He turned and looked back toward the Temple, and though he couldn't see him, in his mind's eye he was certain the steward was still standing where he left him. The hairs on the back of his neck stood up. *Perhaps a very good reason.*

He turned again toward home, his steps slower now. *What did I know about Simon when I sent Jacob to him?* His feet faltered and stopped as his heart fell prostrate before the truth—*Nothing. I knew nothing, except that he was Caiaphas' steward. How could I let that happen? If I invest in some enterprise, do I not ask about the merchants and the landowners involved, whether they are honest? Dependable? Father taught me to be careful with my money, but I entrusted my son—my first born—to a man I knew nothing about. I just assumed, because of his station....* Numb with grief and shame, Caleb trudged home.

Prisca met him at the door when he came in. "Good Sabbath, Papa." She turned her face up to him for a kiss.

He obliged her and cupped her cheek with his free hand. "Good Sabbath, little one." His need drove him to his knees, and when he reached for her, Prisca fell into his arms with a glad sigh. Caleb held his daughter close to his heart, breathing in the scent of her hair. The comfort he got from her arms revived his naturally optimistic nature. *Jacob will be all right. He has the money I gave him, and he's a smart lad. He'll make a way for himself.*

When he released Prisca she said, "Mama's all excited today. She's going to a party!"

Caleb frowned. "A party?"

"It's a banquet," Diana corrected as she came in from the back of the house. She added in a breathless rush, "Oh, Caleb, I can't believe we've been invited. It's going to be the most important event of the year."

"Who is hosting it?"

"Caiaphas himself! Can you imagine?" At that moment, a hungry wail sounded from the baby, and Diana bounded up the stairs on feet so light, she might have been dancing.

Caiaphas invited us to his banquet. Caleb sat down in his chair and nodded thanks as one of the servants set a cup of wine on the table next to him. *I should be excited, too.* He twisted his father's signet ring on his finger, studied its engraved lamedh and ram's horn with unseeing eyes, and a sense of foreboding stole over him. *Simon is Caiaphas' steward—he's in charge of such things—but he didn't mention it to me. I wonder why?*

The following afternoon, he went upstairs and found the bed buried under a heap of Diana's clothing—dresses and veils of every hue and pattern under the sun. Diana stood near the window with a scarlet veil in her hands, inspecting it. Caleb fought down his irritation at her blatant disregard for the Sabbath, and with a laugh asked, "What's all this?"

"I need to decide what to wear to the banquet," she told him without looking up at him.

"Already? It's not for another two weeks."

"You don't understand. I need to wear something special—really special." She tossed the veil onto the bed as though it was a rag. With her hands on her hips she surveyed the pile of clothing. "None of this will do."

Alarmed, he envisioned the handful of coins huddling in the bottom of his box. They would not begin to cover the cost of another new dress—not the kind of dress he was certain Diana had in mind. He also knew from bitter experience that arguing with her would simply spur her to go and do as she pleased—at his expense.

If I can forestall her, even for a week.... Suddenly inspired to try a different tactic, he drew her into his arms and kissed her forehead. "Don't do anything rash, my love," he murmured in his most indulgent voice. "I may have a surprise for you."

She pulled back and searched his face, her eyes suspicious. "A surprise? What kind of surprise?"

He laughed and chucked her under her chin. "If I told you, it wouldn't be a surprise, now would it?" He kissed her again. "You'll be the most beautiful woman at the banquet. I promise."

"Hmmm." She stepped away from him and began refolding the clothes she had scattered on the bed. Her expression told him she was still unconvinced.

"This banquet is important to us both," he added, and gave her his best smile. "Trust me." He left the room and shut the door behind him. *Now there was a performance! How in the world can I back up my words? Deborah. I'll go see if Deborah can help me.*

*   *   *   *   *

"I'm sure I have something," she told him when he explained the situation at her house the next morning. "And I promise not to tell Diana." The bruise on the side of her head where Phineas hit her had faded to brown and yellow—a mere shadow of what it had been—but the cut from the shackles blazed an ugly scar across her temple that would never completely go away.

That fellow was Simon's creature. Caleb's heart constricted to think of his only sister lying bleeding on the floor. *I wonder if he's still looking for Jacob? If he hurts my son....*

Deborah broke into his thoughts. "Is something wrong, Brother?"

"Oh, no." He masked his anger with a smile. "I am glad to see you've recovered so quickly."

She touched at the wound with tentative fingers. "The physician finally let me get out of bed two days ago. Of course, I had to promise to let the servants handle all the work."

He put his arm around her and kissed her just below the bruise. "Make sure you keep that promise, little sister."

She smiled fondly and patted his cheek. "Come on, let's see what we can find for Diana."

Less than a half hour later, she said, "I think this is the one that will work best for her, and I'm sure she's never seen it." She held up a dress of fine, ivory linen, embroidered with gold leaves at the neck and hem.

Caleb nodded. "I think you're right." It pained him that his sister had far fewer clothes than his wife. "Are you sure you can spare this?"

Deborah laughed. "With another baby on the way, it'll be a long time before I go anywhere. Now," she added, "I have worn this a couple of times, but I can add something to the embroidery, and it'll look like new."

"Surely you won't need to do that," he protested.

"Oh, I'll enjoy it," she assured him. "This is about the only kind of work I can do these days. Just give me till the end of this week and I'll have it ready for you."

"You are an angel from Heaven," Caleb declared solemnly.

Now she laughed. "Funny, I don't remember you saying that when we were children!" Her smile faded, leaving her eyes troubled and searching. "Pray for me, Caleb. Pray for this baby. My time is coming soon, and I am worried...."

She didn't have to finish. They were all concerned about the effect of her fall on her unborn child. "I will," he assured her. "I will pray."

* * * * *

Jacob woke early the next morning hearing splashing sounds. He turned over on his mat and peered into the dimness. Joel stood across the room at a basin, washing his face. Jacob got up and went to stand behind him, making just enough noise to let him know he was there. "Are you going somewhere?" he whispered.

"I'm going to look for Mary's mother," his uncle answered without turning around. "And I need to try to find out where her brother is—not that he'll be any use. You stay here with Zerah and Gallus."

"Let me go with you," Jacob answered.

"No, it isn't safe," Joel kept his back to him.

He had known his uncle would refuse him, so he drew up his courage, leaned in closer and said, "No place is safe, is it? The past few weeks have taught me that. It's not good for you to go alone. What if you're arrested, too? Let me go with you. Then if something happens, I can come back here and get help." When he didn't answer, Jacob pressed, "You've done so much for me, Uncle Joel. Please let me do this for you."

Joel turned hollow, grief-filled eyes on him. "All right. You can come." Within seconds they were out the door. Joel knew the city well, and he led Jacob through Damascus' twisting streets without a pause. Most of the few people they encountered were legionaries, who merely eyed them as they passed. Finally his uncle said, "The prison is just ahead."

He gestured to a low building that sat like a mud-colored scowl against the eastern wall of the city. Jacob, who was expecting something more formidable remarked, "It's not very big."

"It's one of several," Joel replied. "Each district has its own." He didn't add that people rarely stayed in the prison for long.

Joel approached the sentries at the door. "I'm here to see a prisoner." He pulled two wrapped loaves of flat bread from under his tunic. "I've brought her food."

With an unpleasant smile, one of the guards said "Going to see your woman, huh? You want some company?"

The other broke in, "Stop it, Simius. You heard the commander's orders." To Joel he said, "We'll have to search you before you go in." Joel nodded and held out his arms so the sentry could check his clothing for hidden weapons. When he was finished, the guard looked at Jacob. "You going in, too?" He swallowed and nodded, and followed his uncle's example. When the sentry was satisfied they were unarmed, he stepped back. "Women's cells are on the right."

They stepped out of the dim morning into windowless darkness. Inside, the prison reeked of unwashed bodies, of filth and disease, and the stench hit Jacob like a slap in the face. Trying to shield himself from the nearly palpable reek, he covered his nose and mouth with a corner of his robe. Joel seemed oblivious, however, and stepped cautiously from cell to cell, calling, "Odelia?" Finally, four cells down, one of the women inside gasped and sat up. Joel stopped. "Odelia?" he said again.

"Joel?" She got to her feet, and with halting steps approached the iron bars that separated them. "Joel, is that you?"

"I'm here, Odelia." Jacob could barely see him, but he heard the tears that choked his uncle's voice. "I'm going to try to get you out."

She reached through the bars and grasped his hand. "Mary. Have you seen her? Is she all right?"

"Mary is fine. She's at home. Now I'm going to see what I can do to make them let you go." He started to pull away.

"No." Her grip on him tightened. "Don't worry about me. You have to go ahead and marry my girl. Do it today, and get her out of the city. Promise me."

His free hand covered hers. "If that is your wish, I will do it."

Odelia released him and took a step back. "They killed him, Joel. They have killed Amos."

"Who killed him?" His question was a dagger slicing though the dark. "Was it Onias?"

"Yes. He and the other leaders of the synagogue. They stoned him—right in front of my eyes." She sank to the dirt floor with a heart-tearing groan and covered her face.

Joel knelt down and reached through to her. "What happened to Jonas? Was he with you? Odelia, where is your son?"

When she looked up again, her eyes were blank and empty, void as a corpse's. "It was Jonas who betrayed us."

* * * * *

A more dismal wedding Jacob had never seen. Joel stood, his mouth set in grim lines, next to his teary-eyed bride as Zerah married them. There were no friends in attendance except themselves, and no family. There was no music, no wine but the little they had left, and no dancing—none of the things Jacob associated with a wedding. *There's so little to celebrate,* he thought sadly.

Zerah pronounced a blessing over them. When he had finished, the priest said, "Now Gallus and I will go and buy some food for our dinner." Gallus frowned at him and started to say something, but Zerah interrupted. "Come along. I need your help." And then they were gone, leaving Jacob alone in the house with the newly married couple.

Joel and Mary sat down on the cushions in the main room. Joel brought his head close to hers and whispered to her. She replied by nodding, or shaking her head, or occasionally by whispering back. Jacob felt he didn't belong there, and he tried to make himself unobtrusive. He even went to the door to go outside, but Joel stopped him. "Stay here with us, lad. I don't want you wandering out there alone."

So he stayed. And waited. After about two hours, he was pacing the floor. *What is keeping them? It doesn't take this long to buy food.* Unwelcome thoughts began to trouble him. *What if something happened to them? What if they've been arrested—or assaulted?*

Just when he made up his mind to go looking for them regardless of his uncle's bidding, he heard footsteps and voices. The door swung open, and Zerah strode in announcing, "I have a wedding present for you two." He put out a hand, and drew Odelia in after him.

"Mama!" Mary cried, jumping to her feet. In a heartbeat, the women were locked in embrace, laughing and crying at the same time.

Gallus edged around them, his arms full of bundles and baskets of food. "Now we can celebrate," he murmured, handing some of his burden to Jacob. "Help me with these, boy." Then he grinned. "I don't have enough hands."

A shout of surprised laughter erupted from Jacob. He clapped one hand over his mouth, and his face went hot. Zerah turned and smiled, "What?"

Jacob glanced at Gallus, who by now had turned away. "Nothing, sir. I'm just glad you're back."

Gripping the priest's arm, Joel asked, "How did you do it? How did you get her out?"

"Simple, my friend." Zerah rubbed his thumb against his forefingers in a gesture of greed. "I applied a little grease to the machinery."

Mary escorted her mother up the stairs so she could wash and change clothes. By the time they came down again, Gallus and Jacob had a small feast laid out, complete with honey cakes and wine. Jacob's stomach rumbled pleasantly at the sight and smell of the food.

Though the mood in the room lightened somewhat with Odelia's arrival, it remained subdued. *Mary's mother is free,* Jacob thought as they sat down to eat, *but her father is dead, and her brother was responsible for it.* He popped an olive in his mouth and chewed it slowly, savoring its dark richness. *How could he do that? I would never betray my father.* He took a sip of wine and picked up one of the sweets. All at once his heart sank, and the honey cake he held turned into something rotten, something vile. *I did betray my father. I ran away.* Waves of numbing shame swept over him. The dishes of food now sat forgotten, and the conversation at the table went on, grating in his ears until he couldn't stand it anymore. Excusing himself, he got up and went out.

He stopped just outside the door, gulping in the early evening air. A handful of people milled around in the street, going about their business. Jacob hardly noticed them, except for one—a boy about his own age, who hurried past on some errand. As he went by, their eyes met. But if Jacob expected to find an answer in the stranger's gaze, it eluded him. Hugging his robe around him, he started aimlessly up the street. He'd gone about halfway to the corner when he heard footsteps running up from behind. Fearing some kind of attack, he half turned, and raised one arm in defense.

It was Gallus. "Jacob, where are you going?"

He shrugged and stared at his feet. "Just walking."

Gallus nodded and turned his pale eyes to the clear evening sky. "It's a nice night for it. May I join you?" When Jacob nodded, he fell in beside him. "The past few weeks have been interesting, yes?"

He almost snorted at the legionary's mild assessment. "Very."

"My venerable master never ceases to amaze me," Gallus continued, tucking his arms into his sleeves. "He is old, and his appearance is soft, but he is one of the strongest men I have ever known."

Jacob remembered Zerah's labored attempts to keep up with Joel. "It was a long journey for him, but he made it."

"He did," Gallus agreed. "It was a long journey for all of us."

They walked in silence for a few steps before Jacob said. "They sent you out here to bring me back."

Gallus pursed his lips as if to suppress a smile. "I didn't make them any promises, except that I would stay with you."

His hands balled into fists. "I don't need a nursemaid."

Gallus' answer surprised him. "That is correct. You are nearly grown, and you have little need of a keeper. But perhaps you could use a friend."

A friend. Are you my friend? He decided to test Gallus' intentions. Expecting to be chastised for ingratitude, he said, "I think I made a mistake coming here. I should never have left Jerusalem."

"You miss your father."

Jacob swallowed. Gallus struck close, so close to the heart of what was bothering him. "I do miss him, yes. But it's more than that. I shamed him. I disgraced him by running away."

"You think you should have remained with Caiaphas' steward?"

The memory of the lash marks on his legs made him pause. Finally, "Yes, I should have." Gallus grunted, but did not comment. After a few more steps, Jacob asked, "Do you think I couldn't have done it?"

The legionary's voice turned harsh. "It has nothing to do with you." Then he softened. "In truth, if anyone could have held his own with Simon, you could." The two of them reached the corner, and Gallus stopped a moment to look. "Left or right?"

He shrugged. "Right, I suppose."

They turned the corner. "Zerah has been acquainted with Simon for many years." Gallus turned his gaze to Jacob's and held him there. "Simon abuses his boys—all of them. If what we have heard about him is true—and we have seen evidence that it is—then what he did to you was but a trifling thing."

He frowned. "Another boy from my school worked for Simon. He was dismissed him, but I don't remember seeing any lash marks on him, and he never spoke of being lashed."

Gallus looked away and said cryptically, "Some wounds do not mark the skin."

His manner restrained Jacob from asking what he meant, so he changed the subject. "Here we are, Gallus—we made it to Damascus. But now what? What do we do while we're here?"

"I have my work to do," he answered, "taking care of my master. You will also need to find work. It is not good to be idle."

"You're probably right," Jacob sighed.

"Someday you may be able to go home again."

Jacob noted that he didn't say 'you will be able', but only 'you may'. "Or I may be here for the rest of my life."

Gallus walked several more paces with him before answering. "An officer of mine used to have a saying whenever we were about to go on a mission, or into battle—'Vir diem tenet, et dies virum.'"

"What does that mean?"

"Translated, it says, 'A man holds the day, and the day holds a man.'" He glanced at Jacob. "What do you make of its meaning?"

"Well, I suppose it means that a man can do whatever he wills in the day." He paused and thought a while. "But only for that day?"

"That is correct," Gallus said. "A man cannot do anything about yesterday. It is done. And tomorrow is not within reach. Vir diem tenet, et dies virum. Today is enough for you to live. Let tomorrow worry about itself."

Jacob echoed the sentence thoughtfully, then said, "You would have made a good teacher, Gallus."

The soldier shook his head. "It does not profit me to think that way. What would have been is shadows and smoke. I am what I am."

* * * * *

Caleb's stylus hovered over the scroll. *What do I say to him?* He chewed on the inside of his cheek. *Why is this so hard?* Finally he shook himself. *Phillip is my friend, not my enemy.* He was startled that he still thought of Phillip that way after all this time, after the harsh words that passed between them, and with a pang, he realized most of the harsh words had been his own. Remembering Gedeon's counsel, he put stylus to paper and wrote:

"To Phillip, a true friend, I send you greetings...."

Chapter 7

Arin walked a few paces ahead of Lyssa along the seashore from Capernaum's well to their home, keeping one ear tuned to the languid lapping of the waves against the shore. Her steps gradually slowed to the water's rhythm. The jar she carried pressed down on her head and threatened to tip over, though she strode with her usual grace The damp sand underfoot pulled and dragged at her. Her home's security and comfort had been disrupted. She didn't want to be there.

Her grandparents had arrived three days before, and it was the first time she had ever met her grandmother. She had gone running down the beach to greet Gedeon, blind in her delight to the woman perched atop the camel he led. Gedeon caught her up in his arms, but when the camel knelt, and her grandmother got off...."*What kind of greeting is this? Where is my son?*"

Arin squeezed her eyes tight to shut out the memory. She had so looked forward to Gedeon's coming, but now.... *Grandmother Eunice is nothing like I imagined she'd be.* She reached up and adjusted the jar on her head. *Nothing like I hoped she'd be. She and Grandfather are not alike at all.*

She turned to look back. Lyssa lagged more than twenty paces behind her. "Come on," she called out. "We shouldn't dawdle. Mama needs us." Her words carried such a lack of conviction, Lyssa didn't bother picking up the pace. Arin waited a few seconds, then started forward again. *Neither of us wants to go home.* Then she remembered Papa and Grandfather Gedeon had gone off together somewhere that morning. *Mama and Salome are alone in the house with Grandmother.* That leant impetus to her feet. Looking back once more, she called, "Hurry, Lyssa!" Her new-found urgency prodded them on, and soon they were trailing up the path to the house.

Salome waited for her just inside the door, her thumb in her mouth. When Arin came in, Salome silently took her free hand, her natural exuberance melted away like candle wax in summer's heat. Arin stepped across the threshold. All was quiet—too quiet. "Where's Mama?" she whispered.

Salome popped her thumb out of her mouth and wordlessly pointed to the back door, which had been left open to let the sea breezes wash through. Arin set her jar down and went out, leading Salome. Her mother was bent over the lentil plants. Arin waited until she stood up before asking, "Where is she?"

Her question needed no explanation. "Still abed," Leah dusted off her hands, "and it's the third hour."

"Should one of us go in and see about her?"

Leah's mouth compressed into a thin line. "No, don't wake her. If she wishes to sleep, we will let her."

Arin looked back. Lyssa was just entering the house. She started inside with a warning to be quiet, but saw it wasn't necessary as her younger sister stole in, looking around furtively. *It's like we're all in a stranger's house and afraid of being caught.* She didn't stay inside for long. In moments she came out the back, too.

Leah straightened up, her hands on her hips, and surveyed her three daughters who now stood in a half-circle around her, watching her with solemn, questioning eyes. "Well, this will never do." She squinted toward the house. "I have too much work to do to be tiptoeing around." She started toward the door, rolling up her sleeves as she went. Arin, following two steps behind, heard her mutter, "I will not be held prisoner in my own house."

They went in, and Leah, no longer bothering to whisper, put the girls to work preparing for the noon meal. "Arin, pour some of that water into a basin for your grandmother, and get her a clean towel."

No sooner had she finished this task then she heard a stirring from the room where her father and mother normally slept. She carried the basin full of water across the room and stood at the curtain that served as a door, where she coughed to make her presence known. Moments later, her grandmother thrust the curtain aside and glared out, the lines at the corners of her mouth deepened in a frown.

"Good morning, Grandmother," she murmured, not expecting a reply. She held out the basin and towel. Without a word, the older woman snatched them from her hands, slopping about a third of the water onto the floor, and let the curtain fall back into place.

Arin ran for a rag to mop up the spill. When she was done, she turned to her mother, who gave her an encouraging smile, and a soft pat on the shoulder as she went by. "It's not you, love," she whispered. "You did well."

At that moment, Salome, who was struggling to bring her mother the heavy milling bowl and pestle, lost control of her burden, and the stone rolled out of the bowl and landed on top of her bare foot. Salome gasped with shock and pain. As Arin watched in horror, Salome's eyes squeezed shut, and a high-pitched wail started in the child's throat. Setting the bowl on the floor with a clatter, Salome ran to Arin's arms, muffling her screams against her sister's shoulder.

"Oh, Baby, your poor foot," Arin murmured into her hair.

Just then, Eunice swept out of the bedroom. "Leah, how do you hear yourself think with all this racket?"

Incensed, Arin bit her own tongue, and gathering her sister in her arms, trotted out the back door, pulling it shut behind her. Once outside, she eased herself onto the flat rock that served them for a bench, and rocked Salome, stroking her hair. *I wish that woman would go home. But when she does, Grandfather will have to go with her.* She tightened her arms around her sister in a fierce grip, holding on to comfort them both. In a little while, Salome's sobs subsided to whimpers, and Arin stood up and carried her to the shore, where she set her down.

"Let me have a look at that foot." Salome held the offended member out for inspection. Arin inhaled sharply, her breath hissed against her teeth. An ugly bruise, already purple with blood, was rising and spreading across the flat surface just next to her toes.

Seeing the injury to her own foot made Salome's eyes tear again. "It hurts, Arin," she moaned.

"I know it does," she said. "Sit down here. The water will help it feel better." Salome settled down and held both feet in the leading wash of the waves. Arin sat beside her and scooping up a handful of wet sand, packed it gently on top of the bruise. "There. Does that help?"

Salome sniffed and nodded. "It's cool."

"Wiggle your toes for me." The child complied, and Arin tried on a smile for her. "Your foot's not broken, just bruised."

"Do we have to go back?" Salome asked.

"Not right away," she replied, pulling off her own sandals and dipping her feet into the water. "We can sit here a little while."

Salome leaned her head against Arin's arm, comforting herself with her thumb as they both watched the tumbling tide. A few minutes later, she sat up and pointed to their right. "Look, a ship."

Arin shaded her eyes, and searched the waves before she finally spied the billowing sail gliding along the horizon. "You have good eyes," she smiled. "It's a Phoenician ship."

"F'nishin? What's that?"

Glad to have something to distract Salome's mind from her troubles, she said, "The Phoenicians live in cities north of here, and they sail all over the world. Papa says they go to far away places and bring back all sorts of things."

"Like what?"

"Well, just about anything you can think of. They trade in spices and pretty cloth, and different kinds of metal for making tools and jewelry. We trade our wheat and olive oil with them. Some places trade wine, or wool, or even animals."

"Why do the F'nishins trade?"

She smiled, "Papa says their country is small. It has so many mountains they can't grow enough food for their people, so they have learned to sail. That's how they get the food and other things they need. He says they're the best sailors in the world."

Salome leaned away from her and worked her fingers into the sand. Arin continued to watch the ship until it was almost out of sight. Presently, Salome patted her arm. "Here, Arin. Here's a shell for your box."

Arin took what looked like a lump of sand from her. "Let's see what this is." She immersed it in the water and shook it. As the sand began to fall away, she held her breath in amazement. *Can it be?* She held up the shell, its whorls dancing like a full skirt frozen forever in a joyful swirl. "Oh, Salome," she gasped, "I can't believe it. I've been looking for one of these for a long, long time."

"Is it a good one?"

"It's a very good one. This is the kind of sea snail that people grind up to make purple dye, the kind they use on rich people's clothes, like Herod's or Caesar's." Arin peered into the shell's chamber. The animal it once housed was dead and gone. "These are hard to find."

Salome screwed up her face. "Are you going to sell it to the F'nishins?"

She laughed, "No, never," and handed it back to her sister. "Here, you should keep it since you found it."

Salome inspected the treasure, ran her fingers along its ridges, and held it up to her ear. Finally she gave it back. "No, I want you to have it."

"Tell you what, I'll put it in my box," Arin said, "and we can share it." Salome nodded, satisfied with the arrangement. "We should go back now. Can you walk, or do you want me to carry you?"

With a whimper, Salome turned wide, sad eyes on her sister. "Will you please carry me?"

She smoothed the child's curls back from her face. "Of course I will. But let's pray for your foot before we go." She cupped Salome's heel in one hand. " Oh Lord, our Father who made the sky, and the sea, and everything that swims in the sea, please look down on your daughter Salome, and heal her of this injury. We ask it for the sake of your Son, Jesus. Amen."

"Amen," Salome echoed, "And please make Grandmother be nice to Mama."

"Amen," Arin murmured. Seconds later, Salome started singing a hymn that Lyssa had made up, a song about how the birds, and beasts, and the fish in the sea all give praise to the Creator. Arin closed her eyes to listen to Salome's piping voice, remembering that Papa smiled the first time he heard the song and said, "The animals grace this world simply by being what the Lord made them to be."

She listened until the notes trailed off over the splashing sea, sat quiet and still, her eyes closed, and then.... *Panic! Hundreds, no thousands of feet running.... A scream of terror....*

She gasped and her eyes flew open. *What was that?* The peace of their time on the shore was shattered, and suddenly she wanted very much to go home. With shaking hands she slipped on her sandals and stood up. "Do you want to ride on my back?" Salome nodded and held out her hands. Arin pulled her to her feet, and turning around, hoisted her up.

"Don't forget your shell, Arin."

The shell. With a grunt, she bent down and retrieved it from the sand. "Here," she handed it over her shoulder, "you carry it, since I'm carrying you."

She pondered what her mind had just seen. *Was that a prophecy? Where is it, and who are all those people? Is it going to happen to us?* She tried to put it out of her mind, but the trampling feet, and the screaming....

As they neared the house, Salome said, "Papa's home!"

Arin paused to look. Her father's walking staff leaned against the wall just outside the door. "In that case," she grinned, relieved to have something else to think about, "we should run." She took off at a gallop with Salome giggling and squealing as she bounced on her back. She stopped a few steps from the door and set her down. "No more fun, now. We must behave like proper ladies." Salome covered her mouth to muffle another giggle, and they went inside.

Phillip and Gedeon sat on the rug in the main room, sharing a cup of wine. Phillip looked up and smiled as Salome went to hug his neck. "There you are. Mama says you hurt your foot."

"The rock fell on it." Salome showed him her bruise.

"And Arin took you down to the water?"

Salome nodded solemnly. "It feels better now."

Arin glanced at Grandmother Eunice, who sat across from the men studying her reflection in a polished brass mirror. Phillip reached up for his daughter's hand. "Go help your mother, Beloved."

"Yes, Papa." She basked a moment in the warmth of his gaze before retreating to the cook fire.

In another hour, she and Lyssa set the bread, figs, and dishes of stew in front of the men. Leah brought out another decanter of wine and filled the cups. Phillip gave thanks and tore one of the fragrant loaves in two. He handed a piece to Gedeon, who said, "This smells good." He dipped into the stew and took a bite. "Wonderful," he announced.

"Well of course it's wonderful," Eunice said with the thinnest smile. "The meal is late. Everything tastes better when you're hungry."

Leah bit her lip, and Gedeon shot a warning look at his wife. "I wasn't aware that we were on a schedule, my dear." He took another bite and addressed Leah, "This was well worth waiting for, Daughter."

Leah flushed red and murmured, "Thank you, Papa." It didn't escape Arin that she used a more tender form of address for Gedeon, while still calling his wife "Mother Eunice".

Phillip paused, took in his family with his eyes, and said, "Our Jacob has run away from home."

Leah frowned, "He ran away? When?"

Gedeon answered, "Just after Passover. His grandfather fell ill, and Jacob disappeared several days later."

Puzzled, Arin asked, "Why did he run away? Did he love his grandfather so little?"

Gedeon shook his head. "Lathan's illness wasn't the problem. Jacob's father apprenticed him, and we think he may have been mistreated. Caleb says he's always been a good and obedient son." Eunice snorted at this, but said nothing.

Leah asked, "Does anyone know where he is?"

Gedeon answered, "I hoped he would be here, but if he came straight this way, he'd have arrived by now, since he left several days before we did."

"Where else might he have gone?"

Phillip said, "He could be with Joel in Damascus."

Gedeon took a sip from his cup. "Caleb thought he might also have headed for Antioch to look for his mother."

Now Arin was confused. *His mother? What is Aunt Diana doing in Antioch?*

"But if he did, he would have to come through here," Phillip said, "and we haven't seen him. Perhaps it's time we paid Joel a visit."

"Isn't Joel getting married this summer?" Leah asked.

"That's what he said last year when he was here," Phillip answered with a nod. He turned to Gedeon. "What route are you taking home?"

"Well...."

Eunice cut in firmly, "We are going no further on land. We shall sail home from here."

Gedeon sighed, "That is what I planned. If your mother wasn't with me, I'd probably go over to Damascus and see what I could find out."

Arin stole a furtive glance at her grandmother's scowling face. *Why is she so angry?*

Phillip said, "Then it's up to me. I cannot let the matter rest until I know whether he's safe with Joel or not."

"Oh really, Phillip," his mother smirked, "His own father isn't bothering to search for him. Why should you? The boy is not even related to you."

Arin's mouth fell open, and she blurted out, "Not related? But he's my cousin."

"You are mistaken," Eunice informed her with a sniff. "He is the son of Caleb and some little hussy he divorced years ago."

Gedeon growled, "Enough, wife. Phillip told me the whole story. That young woman was innocent, though Lathan led us to believe otherwise."

"He led *you* to believe otherwise." Eunice glared at him. "Are you saying Diana shouldn't have married Caleb?"

Gedeon shook his head. "I am saying that Caleb had no right to divorce his first wife, and if I had known what was really going on, I would never have given Diana to him."

Laying a hand on Phillip's arm, Leah asked, "What are you going to do?"

"I need to go to Damascus," he answered. "What remains to be decided is whether you and the girls go with me or not."

Lyssa asked, "How long will it take to get there?"

"If we all go, it will take a week," he answered. "If I go alone, I can go faster." Then he smiled, "But I'd rather have you with me."

"This is sheer foolishness," Eunice said. "The boy is not your nephew. He is not related to you. Even if you make the trip to Damascus, it is very likely that he isn't there, and your effort will be wasted."

Phillip shook his head. "No, Mother, not wasted. His uncle Joel is a good friend whom I seldom get to see. That alone makes the trip worthwhile. But even if it were not so, I'd still go looking for the boy. He isn't related by blood, but I love him as if he were, and he is Caleb's son. If I had a son," he gazed around the table, "or a daughter go missing, I'd hope my friends would step in and help me. I can do no less."

His mother scowled, but said nothing more, and when they finished eating, Leah and the girls cleared away the dishes. Eunice, however, remained sitting where she was, and picking up a vial of perfumed oil, poured some into her palm and began massaging it into her hands. The sweet, cloying fragrance, layered atop the lingering smells of food made Arin's head ache. "Mama, is it all right if I open one of the doors?"

Leah nodded. "The day is warm enough. Open them both."

No sooner had she done so when Eunice exclaimed, "Oh, shut those doors, child! That chilly air will make us all sick!"

Arin glanced at her mother, who sighed and nodded. Suppressing a deep sigh of her own, she shouldered the doors closed.

*   *   *   *   *

Two days later, Gedeon received word that the ship on which he had booked passage was ready to sail. "We leave in the morning," he announced, and the whole household threw itself into a flurry of packing. That night at dinner, he said, "I intended to sell our camel once I got here, but I think I'll leave him with you so you will have him for your trip." Salome had snuggled into his lap. He smoothed her hair with one hand, and smiled and winked at Arin. "And the girls can take turns riding."

The next morning, when they said their goodbyes, Gedeon embraced his son. "Send word as soon as you can." He stepped back, his eyes rimmed with unshed tears. "Let me know if you've found him."

"I will," Phillip promised, then turned and kissed his mother's cheek. "Safe journey, Mother. I am glad you could come."

"Consider well what I said about you chasing after that boy, son," she answered. "You know I am only thinking of you."

Phillip nodded without reply and stood back to let the others say their farewells. Arin threw her arms around her grandfather's neck. "I'll miss you, Papi."

"And I you." He kissed her and said, "You will be all grown up the next time I see you."

She offered her grandmother a kiss. Eunice replied by taking her hands and inspecting them. Clucking her tongue with reproach she said, "You must take better care of yourself, child, or no man will want you."

She spoke lightly, but her words cut Arin to the quick. She turned away and studied her hands—were they really so bad? Calluses lined her palms. Her nails and cuticles were clean, but ragged. Embarrassed, she crossed her arms to conceal them. As the family continued their farewells, she studied Grandmother's hands, the skin soft and pliant, her nails smooth and well-groomed. *And she didn't lift a single finger to help us the whole time she was here.* Arin glanced at her mother. Leah had the strong hands of a woman accustomed to hard work, hands that could hoe weeds one minute and dry a child's tears the next. Arin knew her own hands would look just like that someday. She thought about how those hands touched her, how they loved her, and she lifted her chin and uncrossed her arms.

* * * * *

Phineas pushed himself up off his mat, unable to completely bite back the groan of pain that followed, and stood panting and trembling in the middle of the room. He tried without success to swallow the sour taste that clung to his tongue. *At least they're not hovering this morning.* Joseph and his son, Josiah had kept watch over him day and night since they brought him to Sidon. He was ready for them to leave him alone and go about their business. Joseph's persistent good humor was beginning to grate on his nerves.

Using a table to steady himself, he lurched across the room to look out the window. *Just as I thought, an upper room.* He gazed a moment at the busy street below, then turned and picked up his clothing. His gray robe, which he expected to be torn and dirty after his fall, had been cleaned, and on closer inspection, he discovered a small tear that had been expertly mended. His tunic had also been laundered, and was folded neatly beside the robe.

"I'll wager they've robbed me blind," he growled, and snatched up his pack. For all Joseph's apparent kindness, Phineas didn't believe he was above helping himself to all or part of his money. There could be no other explanation for the merchant's cheerful lingering on Phineas' behalf. He dug into the pack and pulled out his purse. Leaning against the table, he shook the coins out into his hand, then frowned in puzzlement. "Nothing's missing," he grated between clenched teeth. "How can this be?" He had exactly the same amount now that he had when he rode to Sidon. Flustered, he raked one hand through his hair and grimaced at the oily residue that clung to his fingers. At the same time he caught a powerful whiff of rancid sweat mingled with sickness. Phineas braced himself against the table's edge and groaned with disgust. *I'm filthy.*

"Well, look at you!" Joseph came in bearing a steaming bowl of lentils and two loaves of barley bread, which he set on the table. "I'm glad to see you're rejoining the world of men. Come, sit down and eat with me."

"I just got up," Phineas muttered.

Joseph grinned, "So I see, but you need to eat to build up your strength." He noted the grimace on Phineas' face and asked, "Is something amiss?" Spotting the open pack where Phineas had let it fall to the floor, his voice lowered. "You haven't been robbed, have you?"

Phineas gave his head an impatient shake. "Everything's here."

Joseph exhaled through his teeth. "That's good news. Josiah and I tried to make sure your possessions weren't disturbed, but we couldn't be here every second."

"Oh really?" Phineas muttered under his breath.

If Joseph heard him, or if he took offense, he didn't show it. "What do you intend to do now?"

"To get out of here, but I'll have to make some arrangements, and I need to get cleaned up."

"Well, there's a bath house just down the street, a fairly new one. Why don't you sit down and have a bite to eat first, and I'll take you over there."

Phineas wanted to protest that he didn't need any more help, but he wasn't sure he could make it down the stairs unaided. And he didn't want to offend Joseph—not yet. He might still have need of him. So he sat down.

"Now, about that errand you were on," Joseph began after he had given thanks for the food, "I made some inquiries."

Phineas frowned. Too much time had lapsed while he lay helpless, and despite Joseph's honesty in the matter of his money, he didn't want him nosing around after the boy, while he himself remained ignorant of where matters stood. Trying to keep his tone casual he asked, "What did you find out?"

"Well, actually, your description of the two men struck a nerve with me while I sat here and watched over you, and I think I know who it is you seek—Jonathan, also called Barnabas, and Saul of Tarsus. Am I right?"

Phineas nodded. "Do you know them?"

"Not all that well," Joseph admitted, "but I have heard both of them speak. Barnabas is quite an orator. And Saul...." He made a see-sawing motion with one hand. "He's not as accomplished a speaker, but he has a way of cutting straight to the heart of a matter. The two of them together are formidable preachers."

Phineas, who had no interest in preaching, asked, "And the boy?"

"A friend of mine said they did have a young man with them, but that they left two or three days before we got here. He didn't know where they were going, but thought they might be headed to Antioch, or possibly to Cyprus."

"Cyprus?" Phineas scowled. "I had heard Antioch mentioned, but why Cyprus?"

"Barnabas is a Cypriot."

Phineas stared at the stew in his bowl. "I didn't know that." *Why didn't I know that?* He dipped his bread in the broth. "But if they were going to Cyprus, they would probably have sailed directly there from Joppa." Joseph grunted and nodded in assent. Then a thought struck Phineas, and his hand paused midway between the bowl and his mouth. "Did you say they had a young man with them? Just one?"

"That's what my friend said." Joseph sipped at his cup. "Is that not what you told me?"

Phineas pinched the bridge of his nose between his fingers. *Two boys. There have to be two, don't there? What is wrong with me? Why can't I think clearly? Did the snake's poison damage my mind? The boy named Jacob...and...and his best friend. That's right...I went to his mother's house to search.* "Two boys," he finally said aloud. "They should have had two boys with them."

Joseph grunted and took another mouthful of bread, chewing slowly. Finally he shook his head. "No, I am certain he said one boy. Could it be that the lad you seek somehow got word of his father's illness and turned back?"

"No." Phineas glanced at Joseph, sizing him up, then inched closer to the truth. "Actually, his father isn't sick."

The older man cocked his head, his eyes somber. "Oh?"

After several long seconds, Phineas said, "I confess that part was a ruse. The boy and his father had a misunderstanding, that's all, and the father is greatly desirous that the boy return. I feared the lad might be reluctant to go back, but if he thought the matter grave enough, he'd come willingly." He hung his head as if ashamed. "That was an error on my part."

Joseph laid a hand on his arm. "The truth suits you better. Now that we've finished our meal, let me go with you to the bath house." He stood and took a robe from where it hung on a peg near the door. "You can wear this over there and change into your own clothes when you've bathed."

Phineas slipped into the borrowed robe, wondering how long he could keep up the pretense of humble gratitude. He couldn't wait to shed the old man's clothes—and his company. The whole thing disgusted him as much as his unwashed body. *Perhaps in a few more hours I'll be finished with him.*

Phineas extracted one silver stater from his bag. "To pay for the bath." Joseph nodded, and held open the door, giving him his first glimpse of what lay outside his room, only a staircase leading down. His legs seemed to have a mind of their own as he attempted the narrow stairs, and he nearly stumbled once, but Joseph's presence—far more solid than his age made him appear—held him steady so that he didn't fall.

Once they gained the street, Phineas' legs remembered what they were made for, though his right leg was still swollen from the bite. Every step jarred his spine all the way to the base of his skull. By the time they reached the bath house, his teeth were set on edge, and he had to keep a tight hold on himself in order to not strike Joseph's smiling face. And somehow he knew Joseph was making it look like *he* was the one being supported by Phineas. Gratitude's demand only fueled his smoldering rage. By the time Joseph opened the door of the bath house, Phineas was nearly blind with anger and pain.

Phineas paid the attendant, who escorted him to a long table and helped him off with his clothing. He stretched out on his stomach on the table, and the attendant slathered warm olive oil on his back, saying, "I assume you will not be taking exercise this afternoon?"

"I think not," Phineas replied through clenched teeth.

"You had an accident, yes?" he asked. "Your leg—the bruises are terrible."

Joseph answered quietly, "A serpent bit him. Go easy on that leg."

"I will go ahead and clean you now so you can go straight to the caldarium. I recommend that you avoid the frigidarium today. The cold bath might revive you, but on the other hand, it could give you a chill." He picked up a strigil, a curved, blunt metal blade, and began to scrape the oil from Phineas' skin. "A massage after your bath will help the circulation," the attendant offered. "If you like, my lord, I will be happy to...."

"Yes, yes, give me the full treatment," Phineas interrupted with a growl, "but be silent about it."

A hand rested briefly on his right arm. Joseph's hand. "I will be in the caldaruim." And he was gone.

When he finished scraping him clean, the attendant said, "Now my lord, I will cleanse your hair, if you will move toward the end of the table." Phineas braced his arms and scooted himself to the end until his head rested in the attendant's hand.

The attendant picked up an ewer of warm water and poured it through Phineas' hair, then with a handful of sand, he began to scrub his scalp. The massage and the gritty sand made Phineas' head tingle, and when hot water was rinsed through his hair, he winced at the stinging, but he didn't complain. His head was clean. He had to admit this attendant knew what he was doing. He sat up and toweled off his hair, and put on the short robe he was given. "The caldarium is just out that door." Phineas thanked him and departed.

Three other men besides Joseph were in the caldarium, all of them seated across from him, dressed in short robes as Phineas was. The heated tile floor warmed the soles of Phineas' feet, and lessened the jolting shock of walking. Joseph sat scraping oil off his forearms with a strigil. He looked up and nodded, but said nothing. Phineas eased down beside him and took a deep breath of the steamy air. The three other men quietly argued among themselves in Greek about the relative merits of Egyptian wool, as opposed to Hebrew wool. Finding the conversation unbearably dull, he ignored them.

He and Joseph sat for a while in silence. At first, Phineas was pleased—he had grown weary of Joseph's garrulous company—but after the first few minutes, he began to wish the older man would say *something*. Finally he cleared his throat. "Now that I'm on my feet again, what are your plans? Where will you be going from here?"

Joseph answered, "I'll remain here a while...I enjoy being home."

Phineas frowned. "With your accent, I assumed you were from Jerusalem, or somewhere near there."

A slave came in bearing a tray of drinks. Each of them took one. Joseph sipped at his before setting it down and starting with the strigil on his legs. "I was born in Jerusalem, and grew up there. I left about twelve years ago, wandered around a while, then settled here. Of course, I only live here when I'm not trading. Most of the time I'm on the road between Sidon and Jerusalem, or between Sidon and Antioch."

Antioch. Keeping his tone casual, Phineas asked, "When do you go up to Antioch?"

"I'm waiting for a shipment of knives from Damascus," he replied. "They will probably be here in another week or two."

"And will you sail, or travel overland?"

"Oh, I'll go overland. I have the animals, and I'm not in a hurry."

Phineas nodded. *If I set sail in the next day or two, I should be able to avoid meeting him again.* The last thing he wanted was for Joseph to be there when he found the boy. If the old man interfered.... Presently he stood up. "I'm ready for the water now."

Joseph pushed himself to his feet. "I'm done scraping. I'll join you."

They passed into the adjoining room where six tubs full of steaming, fragrant water awaited them. Phineas lowered himself into one, sighing with pleasure.

Joseph let out a happy groan of his own as he climbed into the adjacent tub. He grinned at Phineas. "I always count it a good day when I can have a long, hot soaking bath."

Casting about for something to say, Phineas asked, "Why did you leave Jerusalem?"

Joseph splashed water onto his face. When he'd wiped most of the droplets off again, he answered, "I was thrown out of the synagogue."

Startled by the older man's naked honesty, Phineas sank down until the water was up to his chin, and asked with a short laugh, "What did you do to deserve that?" Silence met his query, forced him to sit up again. "Well?"

Joseph met his questioning stare and sighed. "I had the misfortune to be caught breaking the Sabbath, and the temerity to speak the truth to my accusers."

Now perhaps I'll have something I can use against you—if I ever need to. "How interesting. Please, go on."

Glancing around to ensure himself that they were still alone in the room, Joseph said, "You will find this difficult to believe, but I was born blind. You have perhaps heard of the Nazarene named Jesus, the one who was crucified fourteen years ago?"

So, Joseph had been touched by the one his followers called Christ! Phineas was pleased. Association with the traitorous Galilean continued to be dangerous for those involved. *I may never have to use this information—but who knows?* "Are you saying he healed you?"

Joseph nodded. "It was on a Sabbath. He put mud on my eyes and told me to wash off in Siloam. When I did, I could see. My neighbors insisted on taking me to the synagogue when they discovered my healing." He splashed his face again and scowled. "I tried to explain things to the leaders there, but they accused me of lying and cast me out." He paused, rubbing his brow, as if the memory pained him. "A few months later, I ended up in the company of another of the Nazarene's followers, a merchant. He taught me to trade, and I accompanied him until I was able to begin on my own."

"But you have a son, and he is far older than twelve," Phineas said. "Were you married while you were blind?"

"Oh, no. How can a beggar support a wife? No, I never married. Josiah used to be my guide—my eyes—in Jerusalem. He had no family, so I took him with me when I left, and eventually adopted him."

"I see." The corners of Phineas' mouth curled up. "A happy ending for both of you, then."

Joseph closed his eyes. "I have not really thought of it that way. There have been many difficulties. But yes, things are better for us now. Josiah is betrothed to a young lady. They will marry in the autumn." He glanced over and smiled at Phineas. "I am praying they will have many children."

"How nice for you. Tell me, are you still a follower of this Jesus?"

Joseph's voice went soft, but his words carried enough conviction to shatter stone. "He is the Messiah."

Phineas sank back down into the steaming water and out of Joseph's line of vision. He smiled broadly. He had all the information he needed—if he ever had occasion to use it.

*   *   *   *   *

Later, back in the unctarium, the attendant poured a lightly perfumed oil into his hands and began to work the muscles of Phineas' injured leg. Phineas gritted his teeth until they ached, but submitted to the pain, knowing the massage would speed his healing. *Tomorrow,* he told himself. *Tomorrow I will book passage on a ship sailing for Antioch, and as soon as I find that boy....*

Then he remembered what Joseph had said. Only one boy was seen with Barnabas and Saul. *But which one? And if that boy isn't Jacob, what then? The other boy will know. The two of them are friends. I will make him tell me.* He groaned as the attendant kneaded the site of the snake bite. *He **will** tell me.*

Chapter 8

The courtyard and main rooms of Caiaphas' palace blazed with light from dozens of lamps and torches on the night of the banquet. Diana stepped out of her litter, dressed in the borrowed ivory linen and adorned with all her best jewelry. Caleb was impressed with the work his sister had done on the embroidery—not that he normally paid much attention to such things. To him it looked like a different dress altogether. He hoped he could continue to conceal its true origin.

He had kept the household spending under tight control, and now it looked like he would recover from the losses of the past month. And though he still had misgivings about being invited to the banquet—anything Simon was involved in now seemed suspect—Caleb was determined to enjoy himself and promote himself as much as possible. He squared his shoulders as they crossed the courtyard. *I will prosper as my father did.*

He glanced over at his wife, her hair was done up Roman-style with what appeared to be dozens of elaborate braids. Caleb could only guess at the feat of structural engineering that held the plaits together. The whole concoction peeked out beneath a shimmering, nearly transparent golden veil. Caleb, freshly bathed, oiled, and trimmed, wore his best blue-striped robe. The two of them made a handsome pair, he knew. *It's too bad Father couldn't come with us. He would have enjoyed this.* He comforted himself with remembering the gratified smile on Lathan's face when he told him where they were going. He leaned toward Diana and murmured, "Did I not say you would be the most beautiful woman here?"

She laughed lightly. "How would you know? You haven't even seen any of the other women."

"I don't need to," he answered, eliciting a rare, fond smile from her.

They were greeted at the door by one of Caiaphas' servants, who directed Diana to the room where the women would hold their feast apart from the men. "Oh, look who's here!" one of the other women exclaimed when Diana went in. "You'll sing for us tonight, won't you, Diana?"

His wife's answer sounded like the tinkling of little bells. "Why, I'd be honored to, but I really don't have anything prepared." Caleb suppressed a grin as he turned away. Diana had been rehearsing for a solid week.

He accepted a cup of wine from another servant, and began to circulate among the men in the main room.

It did not escape him that he was not as warmly welcomed as his wife had been. *But then,* he thought wryly, *I can't sing.* He threaded among clusters of acquaintances and colleagues, exchanging greetings, light banter, and the usual gossip. But when he approached one of his investors.... *Did Thaddeus turn away from me?* Even as Caleb's stomach sank, he recovered and told himself, *He didn't see me, that's all, and he's talking to someone else. I'll greet him later when he's free.*

"Excuse me?" A man Caleb didn't know accosted him, and in a breathless rush, as if he'd been running, asked, "You are Caleb ben Lathan, are you not? I am Eli. My home is in Jericho. I spoke to Tobin, and he suggested I talk to you."

Caleb smiled, "How can I help you?"

"I have a piece of property I need to sell—a field with a small olive orchard on one end—that was turned over to me in payment of a debt. I am about to make a journey, and I need to sell the land quickly."

Making a mental note to thank Tobin later, Caleb answered, "I'd be pleased to assist you. Offhand, I can think of three or four men who might be interested in purchasing your field. Why don't you tell me more?"

"Well, on the south end, it's one thousand thirty-two cubits long. I measured it myself. On the west side...." Eli described the property—described it, and described it—from the appearance of its boundary stones to the placement of its smallest olive trees, astounding Caleb with his total recall of the most trivial details. He took a deep breath, and was about to launch into a protracted history of the field, when Caleb stopped him. "Why don't you meet with me this next week—say tomorrow afternoon?—you can take me there so I can see it myself."

"Oh yes, tomorrow will be perfect. Where do I find you?"

"Come to the Temple, and we'll go out to your property from there." When the man thanked him and turned away, Caleb spotted Tobin and crossed the room.

"Shalom, ben Lathan." Tobin held out a hand. "It's good to see you. I wondered if you'd be here tonight."

"How is your son?" Caleb asked. "I heard he was ill."

The older man smiled. "He has recovered. Thank you for asking. And your father?"

Caleb shook his head. "He was doing better for a while, but these past two days he's been worse."

Tobin shook his head soberly. "Shame to see a man as robust as your father fall into decline. Give him my regards."

"I will." Caleb took a sip of his wine and changed the subject. "I owe you thanks for sending Eli to me."

"Ah, yes, Eli. A bit effusive, isn't he?" When Caleb laughed in agreement, Tobin said, "I didn't have time to see to his property myself, but I thought you would probably be willing to take it on."

Caiaphas entered the room at that moment, announcing, "My friends, the steward informs me our dinner is ready. Come and eat with me." At the mention of the steward, Caleb searched the perimeter of the room for Simon's severe countenance, but did not see him. He knew enough not to feel relieved. *No doubt he'll sneak up on me later.* The men followed their host to the cushions and rugs spread out on the floor. When Caleb sat down, he found himself facing Thaddeus, the investor who had turned away from him earlier.

Thaddeus was a young man, not quite thirty, but already he was making his mark in Jerusalem. He had traveled all over the world, and his intimate knowledge of the Greek and Roman cultures and languages—and that of many other heathen nations—made him invaluable both to traders and to the powers in Jerusalem. He reminded Caleb of Phillip as he had once been. He recalled how Phillip had opened his eyes to the teachings of the Greek philosophers. *What was it Phillip said we were? Young rakes?* That memory made him smile. "Shalom, Thaddeus." Caleb reached across to hand him a loaf of bread.

Thaddeus nodded, but did not accept the loaf from him. Instead, he turned and spoke to his neighbor in a hushed voice.

Startled by his rudeness, Caleb thought, *Someone needs to teach that pup some manners!*

But he held his tongue. For most of the dinner he sat silent, listening to conversations around him. He tried a few times to engage the men on either side of him, but with little success. They seemed more interested in talking to others they already knew. Finally he decided to try again with Thaddeus, and asked him, "Are you planning any travel this year?"

"Why do you ask?" For all his worldly ways, Thaddeus didn't bother to hide the suspicion in his query.

Caleb chose to ignore this second spate of insolence, and managed to keep his voice even. "I was merely curious."

"I see," Thaddeus leaned forward and spoke in a near-whisper, "And who would you tell?"

Caleb almost laughed at the absurdity of the question until he saw Thaddeus' jaw bunch up as if he were clenching his teeth. That, coupled with a deadly anger in his eyes, made Caleb's stomach turn over. "Who would I tell? Why would I tell anyone?"

"How about your friend, Jonathan?"

Caleb frowned in confusion. "My friend Jonathan? I know several Jonathans. Of whom do you speak?"

Thaddeus' eyes bored into him. "Ben Hosa."

"Jonathan ben Hosa? The tax collector?" The conversations around them quieted at the mention of the tax collector's name. They were listening. Caleb swallowed. "I don't know him. Why would I tell him anything about you?"

Thaddeus' answering smile held no humor. "Why, indeed? Are you in some kind of financial difficulty, ben Lathan?"

"No...no, I am not," he stammered. "Exactly what are you saying?"

Thaddeus sipped at his cup, all the while keeping Caleb pinned with his stare. "Ben Hosa came to see me this afternoon. He's raising my taxes for the year by nearly thirty per cent."

Low whistles around the table all but drowned out Caleb's shocked exclamation. "That's terrible! But what has that to do with me?"

Thaddeus set his cup down, picked up the piece of bread Caleb had offered him and ripped it down the middle. "He says that you told him what my profits were last year."

Caleb sat bolt upright. "That's outrageous!" His denial exploded throughout the hall, and the rest of the table went silent. He felt his face go hot, but indignation made him bolder than he felt. "I did no such thing. It's a lie!"

Just then, Simon appeared over his right shoulder, startling him as he murmured. "More wine, sir?"

* * * * *

The rest of the evening did not go well. The man to Caleb's right clucked his tongue and said, "Tax collectors—filthy liars, the whole lot of them." Others murmured agreement, but after that, no one spoke to Caleb, and every time he looked up, he caught someone glancing quickly away, even Eli, and Caleb understood that his chance to sell that property was lost. Only Caiaphas met his eyes, and then but for a moment. When Caleb gave his head an involuntary shake—*I did not do this!*—the High Priest also averted his gaze.

Caleb lingered for what seemed an eternity until the first guests began to depart, and then excused himself. "Would you please summon my wife?" he asked the servant at the door to the women's room.

The servant went in to inquire, then came out and shook his head. "She has already gone, sir."

A new sense of dread overcame him. "Gone? When?"

"She left about a half hour ago, sir. She said she had a headache, and asked for her litter to be brought around."

A headache. Oh, no. She must have gotten wind of what Thaddeus said about me. He forced his feet to hurry home.

Diana met him at the door, her gray eyes blazing with rage. "How *dare* you?"

"My love," he began, "this is all a misunderstanding."

"This *dress*," she hissed, shaking a length of ivory linen in his face, and for the first time he noticed she had changed clothes. "You told me this was new. You told me you bought it just for me." She moved in closer, her breath hot and angry. "You lied to me. Two women at the banquet recognized it. It's your *sister's* dress." She spat out the word like a curse. "You made me look like a fool, like a cheap strumpet!" She flung the dress to the floor. "You have no regard for me, and no respect for yourself. Your father will be ashamed...."

All on its own—or so it seemed to him later—the back of his right hand flew out and struck her full in the face. Diana fell atop the discarded dress with a scream. "No," Caleb answered, his words harsh in his own ears. "You will not speak of it to him."

"Mama?" Prisca's voice, alarmed and fearful, dropped on his head from the stairway. Unable to look at his daughter, or to comfort his weeping wife, Caleb turned on his heel and walked out the door. Now he had two problems to deal with, but for the moment he chose to ignore what he had just done. Only once before had he struck a woman. Only once. His steps quickened, carried him away from his house. He spent the next several hours prowling Jerusalem's streets.

What would Father do about the lie? He wouldn't put up with it, and he certainly wouldn't ignore it. He'd get to the truth—whatever it took. Caleb frowned. *Thaddeus must have been telling the truth about what ben Hosa said, but why would ben Hosa lie about me? I don't even know the man. And I do not associate with tax collectors. Someone else is at the bottom of this. I have to find ben Hosa tomorrow, first thing in the morning. I must not let it go any longer, or I'll be ruined.*

He rehearsed his confrontation with the tax collector several times in his head before he went home. The house was dark and quiet when he came in, and Diana was not in their bed. This didn't particularly surprise him, and he didn't go looking for her. He was too tired for another fight. He slumped down on the bed, hiding his face in his hands. Finally, overcome by fatigue, he lay down without bothering to remove his robe. But tired as he was, sleep eluded him. He drifted off numerous times, only to snap back to dreary wakefulness as the evening's events circled his head like a flock of vultures. All that long, dark night he asked the questions that plagued him—asked and asked again, but the night offered no answer, and no rest. *Why the lie? Who is behind this? Who is doing this to me?*

* * * * *

"Papa was right," Arin remarked to Salome. "He said it would take a week to get to Damascus, and see—there it is!" She pointed to the distant walls of the citadel.

Salome shaded her eyes for a better look. "Is this where the F'nishins live?"

Arin chuckled and shook her head. Salome had been talking about the

"F'nishins" ever since they had seen the ship. "No, Baby, the Phoenicians live by the sea."

"Then who lives there?" Now it was Salome's turn to point to the mountainside city.

"We're going to visit a friend of Papa's. Do you remember Joel? He came to our house last summer. He had that baby goat with him." Salome didn't reply, but nodded vaguely, leaving Arin to doubt that she remembered Joel after all. *I wonder if Jacob is really here?* Her papa had made a point of praying for him every day, several times a day. *If he is here, he probably doesn't remember me. I gave him my favorite shell from my collection, but I doubt he remembers that, either. We were just little children—younger than Salome.* She remembered her amazement when Jacob told her he had never seen the sea. To her five-year-old mind, everyone knew about the great waters. After all, the rhythm of the tides had been a constant for her from the cradle, and everyone she knew lived at its edge. *I wonder if he's seen it yet?*

The sun had dipped into the western hills by the time they skirted the city and arrived at Joel's house. "According to that fellow down the road, this should be the place," Phillip remarked as he pulled the camel after him up the path. Lyssa was riding now. Arin walked alongside her father, with Mother and Salome following just behind. "See?" he pointed to a wooden enclosure ahead and to their right. "There's the goat pen. I can hear them."

Arin, too, heard the bleating. *But lots of people keep goats.* Though she knew Joel well, she felt suddenly shy about approaching a strange house. Suppose they had the wrong place after all?

"Peace to this house!" Phillip called out.

Moments later, the front door swung open, and Joel stuck his head out. "Who is there?" His eyes widened when he saw them, and he let out a whoop. "Phillip!" He bounded down the path. Phillip held his arms out, and with a hearty laugh kissed his friend on both cheeks and hugged him, pounding on his back. Joel was laughing, too, though Arin saw tears on his face. "I can't believe it," he was saying. "I didn't think you'd come until summer." He stepped back, "And you brought your whole family!" He turned back toward the house and bellowed, "Mary! Come out here and meet my friends!"

A young woman came to the door, wiping her hands on a rag. She smiled as she stepped out and started down the path toward them. "You have already married?" Leah asked Joel.

He nodded, his broad smile slightly dimmed. "We had to settle for an early wedding when Mary's father died."

"How sad," Leah murmured, then brightened as Mary neared. "I am so happy to meet Joel's bride." Mary blushed and murmured her thanks as Leah began to introduce her to the girls.

Phillip gripped Joel's arm. "Is Jacob here?"

Joel's smile faded completely. "Did his father send you?"

"You know I haven't spoken to Caleb in years." Phillip's face settled into lines of weary grief. "Why do you ask me this?"

"I'm sorry, Phillip," Joel sighed. "I'll explain everything when we're inside."

The men made the camel kneel and helped Lyssa dismount. "Have you eaten?" Mary asked.

"We bought provisions in Damascus," Leah answered. "Enough for us all." She threaded her arm into Mary's, and the two of them turned toward the house. "I am sorry to hear the news about your father." Mary murmured her thanks as they started up the path with Lyssa and Salome close behind.

Arin hung back with the men, hoping to hear more. She accepted one of the bundles her father unloaded. Each of the men shouldered a pack, and she followed them to the front door, still hoping Joel would say something else about Jacob, but apparently he intended to talk inside, and her father asked no more questions.

After they had eaten and had their fill of conversation about their trip, and about mutual acquaintances and the latest news from Jerusalem, Phillip said, "Now tell me about Jacob."

"Jacob has gone to Damascus." Joel picked up his cup. "He is living there with Zerah."

Phillip leaned forward. "Zerah? Our Zerah the priest?"

"Our Zerah the priest," Joel affirmed. "He came up with me after Passover. His manservant is also with him."

"Why did Zerah leave Jerusalem? His family has been there for generations. I thought he'd never live anywhere else."

Joel's voice went quiet. "He was forced to leave. But that's another story, and one better told by him. We brought Jacob with us because...well, it was necessary."

"My father came to us in Caesarea a couple of weeks ago saying Jacob ran away," Phillip said. "Father was deeply worried about him, and he didn't know why the boy left, though I think he had some suspicions."

Joel grimaced. "Well, if he was talking to Caleb, I am certain he didn't get the whole story."

"Do you know what happened?"

"According to what Jacob told us, Lathan ordered Caleb to send Jacob away."

Arin gasped, and covered her mouth. *How could he do that? How could any father do that?*

"Lathan made some pious speech about Caleb's infant son being a son of promise, and compared Jacob to Ishmael." Joel's face flushed with anger. "Jacob was standing just outside the door. He heard the whole thing."

Arin watched her father's hands curl into fists as he said, "Surely Caleb didn't agree to it. Please tell me he stood up for his son."

"I wish I could." Joel shook his head. "He did agree, and he sent Jacob to apprentice with Caiaphas' steward."

"But that would keep him in Jerusalem, yes? Where Caleb could at least keep an eye on him?"

"I don't doubt that was Caleb's reasoning, but he didn't know anything about the steward. I didn't either, until Zerah told me...." Joel stopped himself with a glance around the table. "It is not seemly to say. We had to get him out of there."

Phillip's face darkened like a summer storm. "Was he hurt?"

"Only lashed on his legs," Joel answered. "The marks have already healed. No great harm done."

Only lashed? No great harm? Arin tried to swallow, but her mouth had gone suddenly dry. *What could be worse than lashing? Did that awful steward intend to kill him?*

"Jacob is doing well now," Joel continued. "He's living with Zerah in the city, and he's found work for a glass merchant. We're hoping he'll be content to remain here a while. The longer he stays away from Jerusalem, the better."

Phillip raked his fingers through his hair and blew out a long breath. "You'll have to continue to be cautious. There was a stranger asking about him in Caesarea just before my father arrived. He apparently thought Jacob was in the company of Barnabas, and Saul of Tarsus."

Joel frowned. "Why would he think that?"

"Jacob's best friend is with them. I suppose he reasoned that if Jacob wasn't in Jerusalem, he'd be with his friend. After all, he didn't know you were in the city for the Feast, since you didn't show yourself to Caleb."

Joel nodded, "I see. So Caleb sent a man to look for Jacob? What does the fellow look like?"

"Caleb didn't send him. The steward did, and Joel—he is the worst sort. He assaulted Caleb's sister—yes, Deborah—even though she was with child. He knocked her to the floor. She is all right, but they won't know about the child until it comes."

Joel went silent. No one at the table spoke. Arin bowed her head. *Was that the same man, the same **thing** that was after Sheliel?* A tremor of fear tore through her. That man was following Saul. She sent up a desperate plea, *Oh Lord, keep Saul from this evil man. Preserve him—and Jacob, too.* In her mind's eye she saw a man stumbling, his arms outstretched, groping to find his way. Remembering a bit of old prophecy, she felt emboldened to add, *Strike the bad man blind for his sin* *against you, Lord. Stop up his ears.* All around her she heard the others also murmuring prayers.

Father, I thank you that my cousin is all right, that he made it safely here with Uncle Joel. She still thought of Jacob as her cousin, and had always called Joel her uncle, though he wasn't related. She gave thanks for their own safe journey, and a plea for the little one yet unborn in Jerusalem.

Lost in prayer and worship, Arin was unaware of any mark of time. She finally raised her head when Joel said to Phillip, "I'll take you to Jacob tomorrow. He'll be glad to see you."

*   *   *   *   *

Overjoyed was more like it. When they got to Damascus the next day, and Jacob spotted Phillip, he shouted with delight and hurled himself at his uncle, nearly bowling him over. Phillip laughed and held him close, "It's good to see you, too, lad." Kissing the top of his shorn head, he murmured, "And you're safe.... You're safe...."

Arin watched the two of them. The love and relief on her father's face made her eyes smart with tears. Her vision blurred, and she closed her eyes for a moment.... *feet running, pounding at the stone pavement. Screams of terror. A cry, 'Where are you?' harsh with tragic urgency, 'Where are you?'....* She shuddered in the hot afternoon. The skin on her face and neck crawled with gooseflesh. She opened her eyes to the sun, welcomed its glare as an astringent antidote to darkness.

"You remember Arin, don't you?" Hearing her name on her father's lips shook her back to the present.

Jacob was just pulling away from her mother's arms. He turned to her, studied her features as if to compare them with his memory. "I do remember you." He gave her a brotherly peck on the cheek. "But you were a lot smaller then."

Arin blushed to the roots of her hair, and blurted out, "So were you."

Jacob laughed and answered, "So I was." He greeted Lyssa and finally Salome, his eyes wistfully lingering on the littlest sister, who returned his gaze with a sunny, uncomplicated smile.

To Arin's relief—and disappointment—Jacob now turned his attention back to her father. "How long can you stay?"

"I planned on a week," Phillip replied, encircling his shoulder with one arm. "We'll have plenty of time to visit and get caught up on the last few years. We have much to discuss." He glanced toward the door of the merchant's shop, smiled and nodded at the heavy-set figure observing them from the step. Instead of returning

Phillip's friendly gesture, the merchant folded his arms across his wide chest. "I think your master wants you to go back to work. We'll see you tonight at Zerah's."

Jacob trotted back to the shop as they turned to go, but he paused on the step and looked back, meeting Arin's eyes for the briefest moment before lifting his chin in salute and disappearing inside.

* * * * *

He set to his afternoon tasks with a will. At first, he worried that his master, a big block of a man named Attalus, would punish him for the time he spent talking to Phillip and his family. Simon would have, and so would Grandfather. But as the day wore on, and Attalus said nothing about it, Jacob's joy at seeing his uncle again won out over his fear.

He set the bags of lime in order, and double-checked the smaller bags of additives that the blowers used to color the glass. Sometimes Attalus let him watch the blowers work, and the results of their craft fascinated him, how sand, ash and lime could be cooked, and the resulting hot liquid made into something both durable and fragile. And so beautiful. The colors were amazing. He repeated what the glass blowers taught him as he lined the additives up on their shelf. *Copper for light blue, or for red, depending on the amount added. Antimony for opaque yellow or white. Iron for green or amber, or even for black.*

Attalus understandably kept the silver and gold dust—for yellow and red glass, respectively—locked away. The vases and perfume bottles produced with gold and silver were made only in small quantities, and sold to the wealthiest clients. *I wonder if Attalus will ever let me go with him on one of his trips to Phoenicia?* Now that he had come all the way to Damascus, he had grown curious about what lay beyond, about the places he'd heard of—Egypt, and Greece, and Rome.

When he had straightened up the supplies and put the tools in order, he double-checked the deliveries of wood and fine sand for the next day's work. That done, he swept the shop, whistling a cheerful tune lightly between his teeth as he worked, and only when he was nearly finished did he notice his master watching.

Attalus remarked in Greek, "Seeing your friends has made you happy, yes?"

Jacob swallowed. "Yes, sir, it has."

"You have not seen them in a long time, I think." Attalus picked up a tall ewer and packed it carefully into a wooden crate lined with straw.

He turned his attention back to his sweeping. "It has been about three years since I last saw my uncle."

"Ah, he is your uncle." Attalus fitted the lid on the box and tied it down with the first of several leather straps. "Three years. That is forever to a boy your age."

Jacob did not reply, but his master was right. The last three years had seemed like an eternity. He counted back over them in his mind. In that time, Joel quit working for Lathan, and soon left Jerusalem altogether. Then Phillip no longer came for Passover. But those years were over now, Jerusalem was far away, and what had seemed an age was behind him. One by one, he was recovering the threads of his life he once thought were lost. Two threads remained, and Joel had told him that he sent a message to Jacob's mother. *Will she come? Will she bring my brother with her?*

"Go home, boy."

His master's command jolted him out of his thoughts. It was at least another hour until sunset. And Attalus had a shipment to go out in two days. "But, sir...."

"Go home, boy," he repeated, more softly now. "Spend time with your family. "But, he held up one finger, and his black brows knit together in a show of stern severity, be ready to work all the harder tomorrow morning."

Jacob grinned, "Thank you, sir. I will."

Blessing his good fortune, he hurried off down the street to the house he shared with Zerah and Gallus. When he got there, the evening meal was nearly ready. He let out a quiet sigh of happiness—Mary's mother was doing the cooking. Phillip and Joel were ensconced in one corner, deep in conversation with Zerah. Phillip looked up as Jacob came in and gestured to him to come and join them. At the same moment, Salome ran up and took his right hand, beaming at him with her father's smile. His longing for his father and for Prisca pierced him, and Jacob bent down and hefted the little girl into his arms and held her close, burying his face in her shoulder.

When he set her down, Salome put her thumb in her mouth and went to Arin, who pulled her into her lap and met Jacob's eyes. For the first time he noticed how much both girls looked like their father, while Lyssa favored his aunt Leah. *They're about Prisca's age. It's a shame she doesn't know them. I'll have to remember everything I can about them so I can tell her when I see her again.* His gaze returned to Arin. She had been watching him, but now she looked away quickly, and in the dim light he thought he saw her face color as though she were embarrassed. He felt his own face grow hot, and he turned toward the men.

At dinner Jacob sat across from Gallus, who remarked curtly, "You came home early today."

Jacob dipped his bread into the stew. "Attalus let me go." He took a bite and closed his eyes with pleasure. Gallus was a decent enough cook, but Mary's mother had a rare talent with seasonings that put the Roman to shame.

Phillip asked Zerah, "Any word of your son?"

The priest shook his head. "The last I heard, he was in Alexandria. I sent word to a friend there, telling him that I had moved to Damascus, so perhaps I will hear from Justus before long...." His voice trailed off, and he took a sip from his cup. "I do not pray for his safety, but for his strength and courage." He cleared his throat. "He is my only son...." His voice faltered again and fell silent. Then he glanced at Jacob, and a smile lifted the sadness in his face. "But here I have a son of my heart, and he keeps me busy."

Phillip smiled, "I can see that." To Jacob he said, "Zerah tells me you've found work here."

"I am working for a glass merchant," he answered.

"Tell him how you were hired," Joel prodded.

He ducked his head, somewhat abashed at being the center of attention. "Well, I inquired in the marketplace, and one of the fishmongers told me Attalus might need an apprentice. When I found him, he was in the middle of an argument with one of his glass blowers, and didn't want to talk to me, but just as I started to leave, he yelled, 'Boy—you there—where did you say you were from?'" Jacob did his best imitation of Attalus' booming manner, eliciting laughter around the table. "When I told him, he asked if I could read Hebrew. Attalus can only read Greek and Latin, and he had just gotten a letter in Hebrew from a client in Jericho. So I translated it for him." Jacob shrugged, "He was so happy not to have to pay someone else to translate the letter, he asked me to come back the next day. I've been working for him ever since."

"That's brilliant!" Phillip exclaimed, clapping his hands. "The Lord has made a way for you. Your father would be proud."

He bit his lip. Proud? How could his father ever be proud of him again?

Phillip leaned toward him. "I sent word to your father to let him know I found you, and that you are safe."

Jacob lowered his eyes and continued to chew on the inside of his lip. *What if Father comes here? What will I say to him? Or worse—what if he doesn't come? What if he never comes?* His reply came in a hoarse whisper. "Did you tell him where I am?"

"No," Phillip answered, "We dare not." To his puzzled frown, he added, "Zerah and your Uncle Joel were right to get you out of the city. For now, it isn't safe to let anyone there know where you are."

Gallus muttered, "Just as I thought." His ice-blue eyes lingered on Jacob, measuring him.

In the face of his friend's scrutiny, Jacob pulled up his courage and asked, "Will you tell me?"

Phillip and Zerah exchanged a knowing look before Zerah answered, "You are being pursued. Not by Simon, but by an agent of his."

"How...how do you know this?"

Phillip said, "He came to Caesarea looking for you."

Jacob frowned. "Caesarea? Why would he go there?"

"Apparently he thought that you were with your friend Mark."

He sat quiet, pondering this news, then nodded. "I can see why he might think that. But by now he must know I'm not with them."

"We don't know what he knows," Joel said. "That's the point, and that's why your father can't know where you are."

"Your apprenticeship to Simon is binding," Phillip explained. "He could legally demand you be returned to him. If your father remains ignorant of your whereabouts, he can't be forced to give you up."

"I see." He nodded, but his heart was still weighted by guilt and remorse. "So I'll have to remain here."

"For the time being, yes," Phillip rested a reassuring hand on his shoulder. "But remember this, you are surrounded by friends, and at least your father will know you are all right."

Gallus cut in, "Your father also has guessed at the reason why you left."

His head snapped up. "He has? How could he know?"

Phillip began, "Your grandfather came to see me..." At Jacob's exclamation of alarmed disbelief, he corrected himself, "I mean my father, lad, your grandfather Gedeon. He was in Caesarea after Passover. Caleb asked him to send word if he found you, and I received a letter from Caleb a few days after my father was gone. He asked me to assure you—if I found you—that he does not blame you for running away. He feels he acted in haste by sending you to Simon, and he knows it was a mistake."

"Do you think my father will ever come here?"

"Who can tell?" Phillip smiled. "Perhaps he will."

Zerah said gently, "I think it is more likely, Jacob, that you will have to wait. Perhaps in a few years Simon will lose interest, and then you can go home."

In a few years.... The future loomed like an impossibility. Then he remembered what Gallus had told him just after they arrived in Damascus. *"'Vir diem tenet, et dies virum'. Today is enough for you to live, Jacob. Let tomorrow worry about itself."* He raised his eyes to Gallus' and repeated, "Vir diem tenet, et dies virum." Gallus nodded, and lifted his cup in salute.

Chapter 9

"What do you mean, I've just missed them?"

"I am sorry, my lord, but the men you speak of boarded a ship bound for Cyprus two days ago." The wharf master had dealt with Phineas before, and was now taking some pleasure from his discomfiture. "As a matter of fact, the ship you came in on yesterday left for the island this morning. A shame you didn't know that. You could have gone with them."

Phineas ground his teeth in frustration. So far, this journey had been a disaster—one set-back after another. Taking a deep breath, he gathered his thoughts and reminded himself, *I am closing in on them. I know where they are. They will not elude me again.* But even this self-reassurance rang hollow, because he knew Jacob was not traveling with Barnabas and Saul. The wharf master had confirmed it, and had described the boy. One young man only, and that young man had to be John Mark. *Jacob is not with them. But the other boy—he knows. He is Jacob's best friend. He knows where he is. Of course, I'll have to be more careful than ever. Cyprus is Barnabas' home territory.* For all the complications, however, Phineas was still determined to see his mission through, and felt confident he would get the information he needed.

He asked, "When is the next ship going to Cyprus?"

The wharf master shrugged. "None today that I know of. The *Phoenix* is sailing tomorrow for Crete. I don't know whether Demos planned to stop at Cyprus on the way, but even if he didn't, your purse might persuade him." He grinned, and rubbed his thumb against his forefingers.

This wretch sees me weak, or he would not dare his insolence. Phineas' battle with the viper's poison left him gaunt, with prominent purple shadows pooled around his eyes. To make matters worse, he was still so unsteady on his feet that he was forced to resort to a walking stick. *But this shall pass,* he vowed to himself. *And I will be back.* His lips curled up in a humorless smile that made the wharf master swallow and look away. "Where is this *Phoenix*?"

"She is the fourth ship down from this one, my lord. Her hull is black, and you'll see the carved phoenix on her prow. Ask for Demos."

Phineas detected a certain satisfying edginess in the wharf master's answer. *He is eager to be rid of me, no doubt.* "I'll be sure to tell him you sent me," he replied smoothly. He reached into his purse and pulled out a *mina,* which he casually tossed to the ground at the wharf master's feet. Pretending not to notice the insulted glower that followed him, Phineas set off to find the captain of the *Phoenix*.

Phineas found the ship the dock master had described, a large merchant galley with ten oars on each side. A brightly-painted bird, which he presumed to be a phoenix, erupted from the prow in flaming orange and red, its wings furled back, its open beak lifted toward the sky in a frozen cry of agony. Phineas paused and stared at the figure, entranced and repelled at the same time. The bird was watching him, its glossy black eyes following his movements.

Jerking his eyes away from the disturbing image, he continued to the foot of the gangplank. Sailors were coming on and off the ship steadily, unloading and loading for the next voyage. Pulling himself together, he held out a hand to stop a disembarking seaman. The fellow was huge, a full head taller than Phineas, his forearms corded with muscle. He carried a bundle the size of a full-grown pig slung carelessly over one shoulder. Phineas said, "This is the *Phoenix,* is it not? I wish to speak to your captain."

The sailor gestured with his chin over his laden shoulder. "On the main deck." And he strode off without offering any further information.

Phineas eyed the gangplank dubiously. A few weeks before, he would have boarded without a second thought. But though the ship was anchored and secured to the wharf by several thick ropes, it still bobbed in the water, just enough to make him doubly aware of the unsteadiness of his weakened legs. *If I fall.... No, he will have to come to me.* Grinding his teeth for the second time that morning, he counseled himself to patience.

While he waited, he fished a silver coin from his purse and studied the men on the ship's deck to discern which was Demos. After just a few moments, he had the captain singled out, a barrel-chested man wearing a brown-striped robe belted closely to his waist. Fringes of gray marked his hair at the temples and the sides of his beard. He carried an open scroll in one hand, and was issuing orders to the others as they carried the ship's lading below deck. Phineas waited at the bottom of the gangplank until another seaman began to traverse it. Holding up the coin, he said, "I wish to speak to your captain."

Without a word, the sailor plucked the silver from his fingers and strode back up onto the ship. He spoke to the captain, who turned and studied Phineas with a frown. After handing the scroll to another, he came to the head of the gangplank, and halted there, his hands on his hips. "You wanted to see me?"

Sensing intimidation would not work with this one, Phineas made his most courteous bow. "The wharf master sent me to you. I understand you are sailing for Crete. Do you intend to stop at Cyprus?"

"Just came from there," Demos answered with a shake of his head. He gestured toward Phineas' stick. "You don't look like you're fit for a voyage."

He gave a self-depreciating laugh. "I look worse than I feel. Actually, I just sailed up from Sidon the day before yesterday." Pulling his face into lines that leant gravity to his words, he added, "My business in Cyprus is a pressing matter. I will make the stop worth your while." He lightly jingled the purse at his waist.

"In whose name are you going there?"

Without the merest hesitation, he answered, "It is my own business." If he had been in Joppa or another of Palestine's cities, or even in Tyre or Sidon, he would have used Caiaphas' name, but here he was far away from the High Priest's influence. Here that name could just as easily work against him as for him.

The captain eyed him doubtfully, then started down the gangplank. "Let me see the color of your money, friend."

Phineas shook out one of his gold talents. "Will this do?"

To his surprise—*What? Does he think I'll offer more than this?*—the captain hesitated, rubbing at his chin. Finally he said, "Very well. I will take you to Cyprus. But on my ship, you are on your own. If you can't fend for yourself...."

He couldn't control the flush of anger that rose to his face. "As I said, I have just disembarked from Sidon."

"Yes, but that is easy sailing, all close to the shoreline. You get on my ship, we'll be out in the deep."

"I can handle myself," Phineas retorted.

Demos nodded once. "You'll have to. Be here at first light." With that, he turned on his heel and strode back onto the deck of the *Phoenix*.

Growling low in his throat, Phineas stumped back toward the inn where he was lodging. But for all his prowess, for all his pride in his powers of observation, he failed to notice a pair of piercing black eyes watching him from the shadow of a nearby building, eyes that had tracked his every step. When he was gone, a figure stepped out from between a stack of crates and hurried to the ship. Demos spotted him as he boarded and called out, "Joseph!" After a strong embrace, he asked, "What in the world brings you to Antioch, my old friend?"

"Actually, it's not 'what', but 'who'," Joseph replied. "The fellow you were talking to a few minutes ago, the one with the walking stick."

Demos nodded and narrowed his eyes. "He wants passage to Cyprus. I agreed to it, though I don't like the look of him. You know him?"

"I tended him while he was ill," Joseph answered. "He said he was looking for a boy traveling with Jonathan and Saul, two preachers of The Way from Jerusalem."

"Does he intend some kind of mischief?"

Joseph sighed, "I cannot be sure, but I'm afraid so. While he was in my care, I asked around about the men he was seeking. When I realized who he was after, the Spirit sounded a strong warning in my heart. So I began to ask about *him*. He's from Jerusalem, and he's somehow connected to Caiaphas."

"The former High Priest? That can't be good news."

"Assuredly not. Caiaphas has proven himself to be exactly the man his father-in-law, Annas, groomed him to be. This fellow you just spoke to—his name is Phineas, by the way—once he was on his feet again, I decided to follow him. I wanted to find out what he was really up to, and stop him if I could, or at least slow him down."

Demos folded his arms across his broad chest. "This is a dangerous game you play, Joseph."

Joseph pulled a scroll from his sleeve and gave it to the captain. "That's why I need your help, my friend. Obviously, I cannot follow him once he boards your ship. But if you'll find Jonathan, the one who is also called Barnabas, and give him this message, they will at least be warned."

"You're sure they're on Cyprus?"

"One of the believers here says they set sail the day before yesterday."

"What about the boy that's with them?"

Joseph shook his head. "I think that's a ruse. They do have a young man traveling with them, but I doubt he can be the true object of Phineas' search. My feeling is that he intends to bring Jerusalem's persecution northward, and try to halt the spread of The Way."

Demos' expression lowered like a thunderstorm as he hefted the scroll in his hand. "How will I know to find Barnabas?"

"Cyprus is Barnabas' home. He's well-known there. And he's not hard to spot." Joseph ran his fingers through his beard. "He's tall, I'd say a half a head taller than you are, strongly built and well-favored. If they're still on Cyprus, and if they're preaching, you should be able to locate them quickly."

Demos cracked a smile, but his eyes still flared with anger. "Why don't I just dump this Phineas overboard and be done with it?"

Joseph chuckled, "I entertained that thought myself. But I've prayed about what to do, and I think he's supposed to be allowed to go on his way."

Demos stuffed the scroll into his sleeve. "I'll have to do some praying myself, then, to resist the temptation."

"I will pray for you and your crew," Joseph promised.

"With that fellow on my ship," Demos answered, "we'll need it."

* * * * *

The following morning, Phineas returned to the *Phoenix* well before daybreak. He avoided the agonized stare of the bird on the prow, and stood for several minutes studying the gangplank as a man might peruse his enemy before a battle. Finally he took himself in hand. *The water is as calm as it's going to be. And if I fall on the way up, there are fewer people about at this hour to see.* Taking a deep breath, he stepped onto the ramp and began his slow progress up to the ship. Though the walk was no more than a dozen short steps, by the time he gained the deck, sweat dripped from his brow, and his knuckles had turned white from grasping his stick. Once on board, he lowered himself onto a crate to catch his breath.

He wiped the moisture from his brow and took long, deep gulps of the salty air. *Tonight I'll be on the island. By tomorrow or the next day, I will have found them.* In his mind, he rehearsed what he would say to Jacob's friend—a variation on the story he had told Joseph. *The boy will believe it, he has no reason not to. He'll want to help his friend.* The day before, seeing the reactions he got from both the wharf master and the captain of the *Phoenix,* Phineas dismissed the thought of using force to get his information. He was in no condition himself, and though he considered finding whatever synagogue might be on the island and stirring up trouble for the traveling preachers from that quarter, he didn't want to risk it. *It could end up causing me trouble, depending on how well the Cypriots think of their Barnabas. Though, if they bear him no particular love, that might be fun to do just before I leave.*

As he sat in the cool morning breeze, a ship next to the Phoenix began unloading its cargo. About a dozen slaves, chained together at the ankles shuffled down the gangplank, heads down, shoulders bowed. Phineas eyed each one, as he always did, particularly the women, his eyes aware and searching. When the last slave had disembarked, he shook himself. *She's dead by now—she has to be.*

His father had been cold and severe, his mother cold and stubborn. She would not submit, would not be the devoted wife and mother. By the time Phineas was ten years old, she had contrived to leave home a half-dozen times, despite his father's keeping an ever tighter rein on her. When she ran away, his father went after her, sometimes pursuing her himself, other times hiring someone to do the chasing for him. The beatings he gave her when she was brought back grew harsher each time, but they were never harsh enough to stop her from trying again.

Finally, in his twelfth year, she ran for the last time. His father went after her, leaving Phineas alone with a servant. Early one morning, about a week later, his father came home without her. "Did you not find her?" Phineas asked, having long since ceased referring to her as "my mother".

"I found her all right," he growled, "but I'm done with her. She's gone."

"Gone?" Phineas, who had received from her all the affection and attention she'd have given a stray dog in the road, felt no grief, only curiosity.

"I sold her." His father poured a cup of wine and emptied it in one long gulp. "She said I treated her like a slave. Well, now she'll see how good she had it. We're better off without her." And that was that. Neither of them spoke of her again. Phineas busied himself growing up, and seldom thought of her, but every time he saw a consignment of slaves, he compared the women to his memory of her. And every time he was hired to look for someone's slave, he watched for her out of the corner of his eye.

* * * * *

Within the hour, the ship's crew were boarding and getting ready to sail. A few of them nodded at him, but otherwise left him to himself. Just as the rosy glow in the east brightened and the sun peeked over the horizon to spill its first light across the water, Demos came on board. He stopped and asked Phineas, "You rather sit above deck, or below?"

"I'd rather stay on top."

"Sit here, then." Demos indicated the crates Phineas had used earlier. "Keep out of the crew's way. If the sea gets rough, you go below. No arguments."

He sketched a short bow, though inside he was seething. "I understand."

At that, Demos turned his back on him and began calling out orders to his crew. Minutes later, all the securing ropes and anchors were hauled in. The oarsmen took their places and dipped the huge paddles into the waves. The ship backed away from her moorings and at the captain's command, the oarsmen on Phineas' side of the ship lifted their oars out of the water, while those on the other side continued to pull until the ship was turned. Then both rows of oarsmen began a chant to keep time to their work as they glided the ship away from the wharf.

The *Phoenix* was underway. Once she was fully out of the dock, with her prow pointed west, a call from above made Phineas look up. Almost directly overhead, a sailor hanging aloft in the rigging unfurled one end of the mainsail. As the canvas fell loose, he sang out the first line of a plainsong, which the oarsmen on deck answered with a following line and a firm slap of their oars. A second sailor on the other end of the mast called out the third line and dropped the canvas so that the sail fully billowed out and took up the wind. The oarsmen answered again with another mighty slap. Their muscles bunched as they hauled at the water.

A third seaman perched atop the smaller foremast sang out as he unfurled the sail there. The song carried from mast to deck and back again until both sails were engaged and full of the wind's breath. As the ship picked up speed, the oarsmen shipped their oars as one man, now relying on the power of the wind to take them out to sea. Phineas watched the coastline behind them recede into the distance until all but the highest ground was swallowed up into the horizon. Gulls wheeled and screamed overhead.

Phineas rarely had occasion to sail, and since this type of travel was something of a novelty, he was content to sit and watch the crew at work, and to feel the play of the ship on the water. He had suffered no sickness on his voyage from Sidon, and did not now expect to be bothered by the rolling motion of the deck. The captain and crew left him alone—and this he preferred to the cloying, solicitous care he'd received from the captain of the ship that brought him from Sidon. Such over-concern only served to remind him of his weakness. *But that is behind me now. Sidon is behind me. That merchant Joseph is behind me. I am getting stronger each day.* He turned his face toward the bracing wind as if to draw its vitality into himself.

"The day is fair, and the wind is with us." Phineas looked up to see Demos standing just behind his left shoulder. At this rate, we will put in at Salamis by nightfall."

Annoyed at having his thoughts interrupted, he had to work at it to keep his voice cheerful. "Thank you for telling me."

"Do you intend to stay long on Cyprus?"

Wondering at the captain's sudden interest, he answered, "No more than a day or two, I hope. Why do you ask?"

Demos shrugged. "No reason, just curious, I suppose. I know people on the island."

"I'm looking for a couple of men...friends of mine," Phineas answered. "I have an urgent message to deliver."

"Who are they? Perhaps I know them."

Desiring to deflect further questions, he shook his head. "They don't live on the island. They are only visitors there."

"I see." The captain stepped around Phineas' seat on the crates and started toward the back of the ship. "Let me know if I can assist you." He went to the stern and stopped to speak to the steersman at the tiller.

Before nightfall. Inwardly, he cursed himself for offering a whole talent for the short voyage. *Cyprus isn't that far out of his way. I should have haggled with him. If I were closer to home—and if I had my strength—I could do something about it. But not now.* He took another look round at Demos' able-bodied crew and winced. *I'll have to pay as agreed. Well,* he consoled himself, *with Simon footing the bill, it hardly matters. Not that I'll turn the boy over to him when I get him back to Jerusalem. There's going to be some bidding. And Simon is going to have to answer a great many questions.*

* * * * *

The *Phoenix* pulled into the port city of Salamis on the island of Cyprus late in the afternoon. "Demos!" the wharf master there called out as they secured the first line to the dock. "What are you doing back again so soon?"

Demos waved at him and answered, "I have a passenger. And since I'm here anyway, I have a bit of business to see to."

Phineas pricked up his ears at that. *What business could he possibly have? But, of course, he'll still take my money for landing me here!* He hoisted himself to his feet and held onto the railing until the ship was fully secure. Then slowly he picked his way across the deck to the gangplank. He started down, but to his horror, his right foot slipped on the wet wood, and he started to fall. He cried out, expecting the impact of his head and back against the plank....

"Got you," Demos grunted as he caught him under his arms and set him right. "Good thing I was just behind you. Hang on to me till you get across."

"Thank you," Phineas rasped between gritted teeth, though inside he railed, *Don't touch me!*

When he reached the dock, he fumbled with his purse, and with shaking hands—he couldn't stop their trembling, and how he hated it!—tried to hand over the gold talent he promised for his passage. Demos, however, refused. "That's far more than any passenger would have to pay for this voyage."

Nonplussed—*Can this devil read my mind?*—he said, "You made the stop for me. I hired you to bring me here."

"It's not out of my way," Demos answered. "Two staters will be enough." When Phineas gave him the silver coins, the captain said to the wharf master, "This man is looking for someone on the island. Perhaps you can help him."

"Maybe, if they've come in recently. Who are you looking for?"

Phineas glanced at Demos, who was moving away and appeared not to be listening. "I have an urgent message for a young man who is with two older men—preachers, I believe. One of them is from here. His name is Jonathan...."

"Say no more," he held up one hand with a smile. "I know exactly who you're talking about. They spent about a week here in Salamis teaching about the Galilean Jesus, the one they call the Christ. Interesting story, though I'm not convinced...."

Unwilling to give ear to the wharf master's views on spiritual matters Phineas interrupted him,. "Do you know where they are now?"

"They headed for the interior a couple of days ago," he answered. "They're probably working their way to Paphos, on the other end of the island. You can hire a horse, if you're fit to ride, or I know several people who have wagons who can take you. Of course, you'll have to wait till morning if you go by wagon. There's a passable inn just around that corner there where the boys are mending the nets."

I could leave tonight. He glanced off to the west. The sun was now just the thinnest sliver of fire on the horizon. Feeling unduly tired from the voyage and his near-fall, he reluctantly decided to wait until the next day. *Tomorrow will be soon enough.* He thanked the wharf master, and turned toward Demos to find that he was already aboard his ship again. He hesitated, wondering what Demos' business on the island was, and how soon the *Phoenix* would sail again. *I should stay and find out.* But, suddenly aware that he was aching all the way to his bones, he decided to go on. *Looks like they're getting ready to sail right away. And the captain has no* more interest in what I do. Well and good. Fewer questions.* With that, he set off to find the inn.

Demos watched him from the corner of his eye, then said to the steersman, "I'm leaving now, Zeno. If I'm not back by first light, go ahead and take her alee of the island around to Paphos. I'll meet you on that end."

* * * * *

"They left here this morning, headed for Paphos," the innkeeper told Demos. The captain had stopped briefly in one of the seaside villages to eat before continuing his quest to find Barnabas and Saul. "They received a message from Sergius Paulus himself. The governor wants to hear what they have to say."

"They probably wouldn't be in Paphos yet, then," Demos mused aloud.

"Oh, I shouldn't think so," the innkeeper agreed. "Jonathan will be busy talking to his friends and relatives. He didn't seem to be in a hurry, governor's summons or no."

"How far is the next village?"

The innkeeper frowned, "No more than an hour's ride by day, sir. But the dark will slow you down. Are you sure you don't want to stay the night here and leave in the morning?"

Demos smiled, "I thank you, but no. The moon is nearly full tonight. Her light is enough to travel by, and I have need of haste."

"Then can I get you some provisions to take along?"

Demos gave him a few coins. "If you'll refill my wineskin and bring a couple of loaves of bread—maybe some cured fish, too—that will be enough." The innkeeper bowed and hurried to gather food for his guest. While he was gone, Demos closed his eyes. *Lord, my desire is to do your bidding. Make the way before me plain. Let all who work against You be confounded; let them become as nothing. Send your word to the very ends of the earth, so that all may hear, and know your might and glory.*

Once he had his provisions and bade the innkeeper goodbye, Demos mounted his hired horse and set out westward again, keeping the sea to his left. The moon favored him with her silver smile and lit the road until the rocks gleamed like argent treasure. Riding horseback was not Demos' favorite mode of travel, but his mount was well-behaved and sure-footed, and in just over an hour he skirted a hillside and came upon a village. The innkeeper had instructed him to look for a house with a large stone well set in a walled-in garden. This was where a kinsman of Barnabas' was supposed to live, and where the preachers would be most likely to stop. Demos found a good-sized dwelling near the center of town that fit the description.

"This must be it," he murmured as he reigned in and dismounted. Lamplight scattered yellow beams through the latticed windows, and as he tied the horse to a nearby tree, he heard laughter and snatches of conversation. He picked his way up the path and knocked on the heavy, planked door.

Moments later, the latch turned. The door opened, and an elderly man stuck out his head. His eyes glimmered under a thatch of white hair that shone radiant in the moonlight. "Who is there?"

"Peace to your house, Grandfather. My name is Demos."

The door cracked open wider, and the old man peered into the captain's face. "How can I help you, Demos?"

"I am looking for three men who are traveling across the island. I have been given a message for them." The old man did not reply, but continued staring at him. Demos wondered, *Does he not understand me?* He shifted his feet and added, "Their names are Jonathan—he is also called Barnabas—Saul of the city of Tarsus, and John Mark, who is from Jerusalem. Have they come through here?"

The old man studied him a minute longer, just long enough to make him think he'd knocked on the wrong door after all. Then he grunted, as if he'd made up his mind. "They haven't come *through* here, friend. They are inside."

Thank you, Lord! Demos pulled Joseph's scroll from his sleeve. "Then may I speak to one of them?"

"You may speak to all of them." He swung the door wider and beckoned with his hand. "Come in, come in."

He ducked his head to step across the threshold and into the light. There he stopped and gazed around him, his eyes wide with surprise. There had to be thirty or more people seated on the floor. One man stood in the middle of them. He had been talking, but stopped when Demos came in. *That isn't Jonathan,* he thought. *He's not big enough.* He cleared his throat and addressed the man in the center of the room. "I am Demos, captain of the *Phoenix*. I have a message for Jonathan called Barnabas, and Saul of Tarsus."

"I am Saul," he replied. "This is Jonathan." He indicated a man sitting to his right. "What is your message?"

He handed over the scroll. "There is a fellow on this island who comes from Caiaphas looking for you. It's possible that he means to do you harm."

Saul unrolled the scroll, and after he read its contents, passed it to Barnabas. "Where is he?"

"In Salamis," Demos answered. "I brought him in on my ship this evening."

Barnabas' eyebrows shot up, his handsome face perplexed. "*You* brought him? Then why the warning?"

Demos hung his head. How to explain? "I would have preferred—*greatly* preferred—not to bring him, but the man who gave me that message believed that this Phineas should come to Cyprus."

Saul's eyes gleamed in the lamplight. "Perhaps the Lord means him to find us." His expression softened. "You are weary, brother Demos. Sit down and join us."

He chewed his lip in a moment's indecision. *I should get back to my ship. But I did tell Zeno to wait for me in Paphos tomorrow.* It had been a long day, and now that his mission was done, fatigue answered for him as he lowered himself to the floor.

*   *   *   *   *

Phineas pried himself out of bed the next morning, every bone and joint in his body aching. Ignoring his discomfort, he hurried to dress and arrange his day. After a quick, unsatisfying breakfast, he walked as quickly as his legs would carry him back to the docks. Several minutes of searching brought him to the wharf master. Phineas announced, "I need to hire a horse."

"Ah, yes. Good morning, sir," the other replied. "So it's a horse you want? No offense, sir, but are you sure you're strong enough to ride?"

"No offense taken," he answered, though his cold tone belied his words. "It will be good for me to ride again. It will strengthen my legs."

"That could be," the wharf master agreed, nodding soberly. "Well then, wait here, and I will fetch one for you."

When he walked away, Phineas looked around him, noticing that the *Phoenix* was no longer tied to the wharf. The bird with the uncanny eyes had flown away. *So they've gone.* His sense of relief surprised him. *They mean nothing to me.* But there had been something, hadn't there? Something about the captain that set his teeth on edge, the same way Joseph had done. Irritating—both of them—though now as he thought about it, the two men were very different. Where Joseph was talkative, driving him nearly to distraction with his amiable chatter, Demos was taciturn, almost unresponsive.

He could not remember anyone in all his adult years that he had genuinely liked. People either bored or amused him, and he was able to tolerate both—up to a point. Beyond that point, he managed to stay in control, whether by intimidation or manipulation. Joseph was different, but Phineas had chalked up his dislike of the merchant to his own physical weakness, a memory that now irked him nearly as much as Joseph's garrulous presence had done. *So what is it about Demos? And why does he make me think of Joseph?*

Suddenly aware of the passing time, he growled low in his throat. "Where is he?" The wharf master was not back yet, and it seemed to Phineas that he'd been waiting too long. He paced back and forth, searched the docks with his eyes in the direction the wharf master had gone, debated the wisdom of going after him—tracking him down. *If he's not here soon, I'll find a horse on my own. If I have to do that, I'll also make him regret it.* A few seconds later, Phineas spotted him coming his way, leading a decrepit nag by a worn rope.

"I know he doesn't look like much," the wharf master sang out cheerfully as he came within earshot, "but I've ridden him myself. He's a worthy animal." He handed the lead over to Phineas. "He's a steady one, and he's got a lot of stamina, for all his rough looks."

"Rough?" Phineas let out an incredulous snort. "He looks half dead. You don't expect me to believe...."

The wharf master held up a hand in a gesture of peace. "I'll tell you what. You give him a try. If he doesn't suit, when you bring him back, you don't have to pay his hire."

He weighed his need for haste against his still-uncertain condition. "Very well," he finally answered. "But if he fails on the road, you'll be seeing me again." His lips stretched into a thin smile. "Pray that you don't." With that, he led the horse to a crate, and refusing any help, climbed atop it and mounted from there. He wheeled his mount around, and without another look at the wharf master, set off toward the western road.

The wharf master watched him go with a cold smile of his own, a satisfied smirk. Hadn't Demos told him yesterday to slow the fellow down?

* * * * *

After the first hour's riding, Phineas began to think perhaps he had taken on more than he could handle, even at his horse's plodding gait. His thighs ached with steadily-increasing heat, and the bite wound, still not fully healed, sent exquisite stabs slicing repeatedly through his right leg. He passed the first village without stopping, thinking, *If I stop now, I may never get on this nag again.* After about half an hour, he came upon a second village, and realizing he'd reached the end of his endurance for the time being, located the inn.

A burly man came bustling out the door to meet him when he reined in. "Let me help you down from there, sir."

Since he had already begun a slow slide from the beast's back, Phineas had little choice but to accept the innkeeper's assistance. Once his feet touched solid ground, he leaned heavily on his stick to keep himself from swaying as the innkeeper led the horse away. *I didn't fall,* he said to himself with some satisfaction. *That, at least, is something.*

A little later, over a lunch of roasted fish, he said, "I am looking for someone on the island. I need to deliver a message."

The innkeeper filled his cup. "Oh? Who is it you seek?"

"Two men, and a lad with them. They are preachers. Their names are Jonathan and Saul.... What is funny?"

The innkeeper shook his head. "You are the second man in as many days to ask after them. A fellow came through here last night. Seaman, I think, or maybe a fisherman. You could smell the salt on him."

Phineas set his cup on the table. "That's very interesting. What did the fellow look like?"

"The seaman? He was about your height, maybe a bit taller. Dark hair with gray streaks at the temples and in his beard."

"Brown-striped robe?"

The innkeeper nodded. "That's the one. You know him?"

Phineas smiled. "I do. Where did he go from here?"

"Toward Paphos. The preachers went that way yesterday morning. Your friend went after them last night." He shrugged. "For all I know, they could be there by now, though I doubt it. Can I get you anything else?"

He shook his head. "Just bring my horse around when I'm done." He finished his lunch in silence. *So Demos went ahead of me. Why? How did he know who I was looking for? What business does he have with the preachers? He told me before I boarded that he'd just come from here, that he didn't intend to land here.* A slow, unpleasant smile spread across his face. *He's telling them I'm coming. Warning them. He knows about the boy.* He drummed his fingers, slowly, thoughtfully against the base of his cup as he stared at the wall with unseeing eyes. *But how? How does he know?* Finding no ready answer to the enigma, he took up his stick and stood, announcing. "I have to go now." He tossed a few coins on the table.

By the time he was outside again, the innkeeper had brought his horse. When he had given Phineas a leg up, he said, "I told the other fellow to ask in the next village. There's a house there, a large one, two stories, with a stone well sitting inside an enclosed garden. You should have no trouble finding it. The man who lives there is Jonathan's cousin. No doubt you'll find your friends as well."

Phineas grinned. "Oh, I'll find them. You have been most helpful."

* * * * *

It took him nearly two hours to reach the next village. He had to hold his horse to a slow walk—not that the plodding beast seemed to mind. By this time, his muscles, tendons and joints all ached with smoldering heat. His back hurt, his knees were screaming, his hips felt like they were coming out of their sockets. *When this is over,* he promised himself, *when I have done what I came to do, I'll hire a cart or wagon to take me back to Salamis. No more riding. And maybe I'll have this animal made into glue while I'm at it.* Though he doubted he'd really bother anymore with the horse, the thought made him feel better.

Near the center of the village, he found the house the innkeeper described—a two-story surrounded by a waist-high wall of stone, and in the yard between the wall and the house, a ring of stones that he presumed to be the top of a well. "Perhaps now I finish this," he muttered, but he knew his words were far from true. He'd had all his journey to plan his strategy, and plan after plan had fallen apart. This was not the end of his seeking—far from it. With a groan, he swung his leg up over the horse's back and dropped to the ground. His legs buckled, and he would have fallen, but his desperate grip on the bridle kept him upright. Trembling, he leaned his head against the horse's shoulder. The nag chuffed and shook his head, but otherwise remained still, allowing him to gather his strength.

After several long minutes, he raised his head and stepped back, gazing at the house with narrowed eyes. Then he turned and led the horse away across the road into the shade of a stand of trees. He found a grassy spot and eased himself down to wait. Somehow he was going to have to cull the young man away from his companions. He knew enough about Saul of Tarsus to believe he'd have trouble deceiving him. The same was probably true of Jonathan, or Barnabas, or whatever he called himself.

After about ten minutes, a child about nine or ten years old came running out of the house and started up the road. Phineas seized the opportunity, and called out, "Young man!"

The boy stopped and turned toward him. "Yes, sir?"

"You look like a smart lad. Would you like to earn a little money?"

The child's face lit up, and he trotted over to Phineas on long, coltish legs. He slowed as he reached the edge of the road, and passing the horse, ran a gentle hand along its flank. "Is this your horse?"

Phineas gave him his warmest smile. "I hired him, so I suppose he's mine, at least for today. Tell me, do you live in that house?" The boy nodded, and Phineas said. "You've had visitors, haven't you?"

"Grandfather's cousin and his friends. They're still here," he answered, scratching at one grubby knee. "Grandfather asked them to stay another day."

"I am so glad to hear that. I was afraid they might have already gone. One of them is younger than the others, yes? His name is John Mark?"

The boy nodded eagerly. "Do you know him?"

"I'm a friend of his," Phineas answered. "I need to talk to him, but...." He drew his face into sorrowful lines. "...my legs aren't working very well." He leaned forward like a conspirator and added, "A snake bit me."

The boy's gasp of horror was music to Phineas' ears. "Was it a poisonous one? Do you need a doctor?"

"It was poisonous, and I was very sick, but I'm better now. I don't need a doctor, but I do need you to do something for me." He held out his smallest silver coin. "But it has to be a surprise. Will you to go into the house and tell John Mark to come out here?"

The boy's eyes were fixed on the coin in Phineas' hand. "What is your name, sir, so I can tell him?"

"Never mind that," he answered. "This is a surprise, remember? And don't tell anyone else in the house that I'm here, all right?"

"It's a secret?"

"The best kind of secret," he replied, and pressed the coin into the child's waiting palm. "You think you can do this?"

"Yes, sir." A white, even grin flashed in his sun-browned face just before he leapt up and scurried back to the house.

Perhaps my luck will hold this time, Phineas told himself.

* * * * *

Within the hour, he was lounging in a farmer's wagon on his way back to Salamis. The fragrant hay beneath him offered a cushion against the jolting and bumping of the wagon's wheels on the stone road. He sighed and glanced back at his hired horse, now trudging dutifully along behind the wagon. *At least I'm not riding* **that** *anymore. I'll be in Salamis before nightfall. Tomorrow I'll find a ship to take me off this accursed island.*

He rubbed at his aching leg and rehearsed the information John Mark had so willingly, so *eagerly* given him. And what a wealth of information it was! Phineas had taken a risk coming here when he knew Jacob wasn't with the preachers. But he had cast the lots anyway, and this time the lots favored him.

He has to be with his uncle in Damascus. His uncle Joel. Joel was in Jerusalem for Passover. The boy didn't leave with his friend, as I surmised. He left with his uncle, and the uncle spirited him away from old Simon's clutches, which shows he must have some intelligence at least, to have gotten the boy away.

Damascus. That's where the boy is, unless....

Unless the uncle took him to his mother. But that's not likely. After such a long journey to the Holy City, a man has to return to his own. He has things to take care of. And Antioch is a long way from Damascus—farther even than Jerusalem. He leaned back in the hay and allowed himself a smile. *The boy's mother and brother live in Antioch. Her name is Miriam, and the brother's name is Jonathan.*

Chapter 10

Over the course of the week that Phillip's family spent visiting in Damascus, Jacob and Arin rekindled the friendship that began when they were small. In the evenings after dinner, they talked—tentatively at first—Arin telling him about Caesarea, and Jacob answering with stories of Jerusalem. As the days passed and their time together grew more comfortable, he told her about his journey to Damascus, and the events leading up to it—as much of the tale as he could bear to repeat. Zerah had a spacious house, but with so many people, someone else was always close by, listening to the story, adding questions or comments, but it was Arin, with her quiet demeanor and steady gaze, who was his audience. She rarely said anything, but he found telling her relieved some of the burden he'd been carrying.

The day before their last evening was a Sabbath, and since he didn't have to work, Jacob had some time alone with her while Leah and Mary were chatting upstairs and the men were away. Lyssa had gone outside, while Salome, who climbed into his lap earlier, had now fallen fast asleep.

"She's too old to be doing that," Arin murmured. "Isn't she heavy for you? We could lay her down on a pallet."

Jacob smiled. "I can still feel my legs. I enjoy holding her, Arin. She reminds me of my sister. Prisca used to sit in my lap all the time."

"But Prisca's older than Salome, isn't she?"

"She's closer to Lyssa's age," he nodded, kissing the top of the child's head. "But Salome is more like her." He grew quiet as he smoothed the raven curls back from her forehead.

Arin didn't speak, and he was grateful she didn't feel the need to. Somehow she understood that it was enough to sit with him and share his silence. He felt comfortable enough in Damascus, and he enjoyed his work, but Jacob missed his sister and his father. He was homesick, more now than when he first stepped through the city's wide gates. His longing to go home tore at him—some days until he could hardly stand it. But having Arin there and holding Salome in his lap soothed the ache in his heart.

"Oh, I nearly forgot. I have something I want to show you." He had waited all week, and now was the right time. But his arms were occupied. He nodded toward Salome's slumbering form and said, "Do you think you could pull my purse out from under her? I can't manage it with one hand."

Arin had to move in close to him to get to the cord that held the purse to his belt. He felt his face redden as she worked the pouch out from underneath her sleeping sister, and for a moment he regretted asking her to do it. *I should have waited till later. And why does everything have to make me blush?*

But when she pulled away from him, Arin's cheeks were flaming, too. "Here....I have it now."

"Open it," he told her. "There's something inside I want you to see."

A small, hard object rested in the bottom of the bag. "Is it a rock?" She glanced at him once before opening the mouth of the purse and reaching in. Her fingertips found the cool, smooth object. She pulled it out and gasped, "The shell!" Her eyes widened with surprise, and her hand shook so badly, she nearly dropped it. "I can't believe it, Jacob" she breathed. "You kept the shell I gave you. All this time...."

"All this time," he nodded. What he didn't—and couldn't—tell her was that the shell had been a sort of talisman. When his grandmother Abigail died, when Joel left Jerusalem and Phillip stayed away, when his grandfather's abuse had been its worst, Jacob often slept with it in his right hand. It reminded him that there were people who loved him, even if they were absent. He pulled Salome in closer and said, "I want you to have it now."

Arin locked eyes with him, studied him. He could hardly bear her searching gaze, but neither could he tear his eyes away from those clear, gray depths. Finally Arin broke the silence. "No." She dropped the shell back into his purse and closed it up. The merest hint of a smile flickered across her face. "No, you still haven't seen the sea."

* * * * *

They're leaving in the morning. On that last day, Jacob raced from the glass shop toward Zerah's. His feet felt so light, they hardly seemed to touch the ground, and for a moment he almost thought he'd take wing and fly, but then....

"Hey! Watch where you're going!" He had tried to dodge a man carrying a brace of baskets across his shoulders on a yoke, but his elbow caught one of the baskets, and scattered dried dates into the road.

"Oh, I am so sorry, sir," Jacob panted.

He stopped to gather the fallen fruit, and managed to get it all before it was trampled by careless feet. But when he tried to return them to the basket, the man shook his head. "Oh, no you don't. Those are ruined. You'll have to pay for them."

"Ruined...?" He stared ruefully at the dates. He didn't have much money, but his time was even more precious, and he didn't want to spend any of it arguing. So he piled the dates in one hand, balancing them there while he fished a coin out of his purse with the other. "Is this enough?" Without a word, the date vendor snatched the coin from his fingers and went on his way.

Now what am I going to do with these dates? I don't want them, and I can't run anymore—unless I toss them in the street. When he came to the corner, he spied a blind beggar sitting across the way. Jacob approached him and said, "Peace to you, father. How would you like some dates?"

The beggar's face turned toward him and wrinkled his nose, as if to try to catch Jacob's scent. "Are they fresh?"

Nonplussed, Jacob rolled the fruit around in his hands, peering at them in the fading afternoon light. "I think so. They look fresh to me. Here, try them and see what you think." With that, he unloaded his sticky burden into the blind man's lap.

"They smell good." The beggar bit into one, rolled the bite around on his tongue, then smiled. "Yes, they are fresh and sweet. Heaven bless you, son...."

Jacob didn't wait around for the remainder of his benediction. He took off for Zerah's again—still running, but at a more reasonable pace. He didn't want to have another mishap to slow him down again. He had only one more evening to visit with Phillip. A few more hours to spend with Arin. *With my cousins,* he corrected himself.

He turned the last corner on his way home, and not wanting to burst into the house breathless and panting, slowed to a walk and wiped his brow. He paused outside the door to straighten his robes, and without thinking, ran his hands through his hair. His short locks reminded his fingers of the uselessness of that gesture, but even at fifteen, lifelong habits are hard to break. He shook his head and smiled ruefully as he turned the latch to go in.

"Jacob, you're home!" Salome ran to him when he crossed the threshold and took his hand, as she had done every evening when he came in. "Will you tell me the story about the camel tonight?"

"Salome," her mother gently scolded, "Jacob just got here. Give him a chance to catch his breath."

"I don't mind, Aunt Leah," he answered. "Truly I don't." *Because you're leaving tomorrow.* To Salome he said, "I have something for you. Come over here and sit with me." He glanced at Arin and noted the smile that played at the corners of her mouth as she watched him settle onto the floor with her little sister. From the pouch that hung at his belt, he pulled a loop of bright blue cord. Dangling from it was a single bead of glass that shimmered ice-blue in the lamplight, like a clear winter sky.

Salome gasped in delight. "A necklace! It's so pretty. See Arin?"

Arin's smile broadened. "It is very pretty. Try it on."

"Put it on me, please, Jacob." Salome's eyes sparkled brighter than the bit of glass as he slipped the cord over her head. Entranced, she held the bead up by its cord, which she twirled between her fingers, making the glass wink and glimmer. Then she leaned toward Jacob and planted a wet kiss on his cheek.

"You're welcome," he chuckled as she got up to show off her treasure. She went to where the men sat together, and they in turn exclaimed over the glass as if it were a precious gem. Jacob had to bite his tongue to suppress a smile when Salome approached Gallus. The former solder, who had seen his share of bloodshed in battle, looked over at him with something akin to helpless terror when Salome said, "See what Jacob gave me?"

"Ah...." His throat bobbed once, and he stammered, "Yes...it's...it's a blue bead, isn't it?"

"It looks like your eyes," Salome answered, holding the bead close to Gallus' face for comparison.

"Does it, now?"

"Yes." She stared at him for a long moment. "You have pretty eyes—for a man. But you should smile more."

Jacob gleefully noted a sheen of sweat on Gallus' forehead when the little girl skipped away. *He's going to have my head for this!*

By the time everyone in the house had made some gratifying exclamation over Salome's necklace, dinner was laid out and ready to eat. "That's a pretty trinket you gave Salome," Phillip remarked. "Did the glass come from Attalus' shop?"

Jacob nodded. "Sometimes when they're making a batch of glass for a dish, or pitcher, or whatever, a little will be left behind in the oven. This week Attalus has been showing me how to take those leftover bits and make them into beads. I drop them onto a flat stone and bore a hole into each one while the glass is still soft, and let them cool and harden. That bead Salome has is the first one I did."

Joel asked, "Where did you get the cord?"

"From one of the dyers. Attalus sent me over there on market day, and I bought several lengths, colors that I thought would go with the glass I had." He gestured to Salome. "Let me see your necklace a moment." Once Arin helped her take the cord from her neck, Salome brought it to him and laid it reverently in his palm. He held it up. "See? The bead is flat on this side, from where it cooled on the stone. It took me a few tries to figure out how to string the cord through so that the bead would lie correctly when it was worn."

Phillip examined it. "I see. You had to push a loop of cord through the hole, not just one end."

"Yes, and that made it a bit harder, because I had to bore the hole a little wider, but then I could put the ends through the loop." He slipped the cord back around Salome's neck.

"I am curious." Gallus helped himself to a few olives from the bowl. "What does Attalus want you to do with the beads—besides giving them away?"

Jacob took a gulp of wine and grinned. "I had a feeling you'd ask me that. Attalus says he first started working with beads when he learned the trade. When he saw the ones I made, he told me that he would let me have whatever leftover glass I can glean. I drop them there, and bore the holes while they're hot, but I have to string the necklaces at home on my own time, and buy my own cord. He says I can sell them myself in the marketplace for whatever price I can get, as long as he gets one-third, and I tell everyone who buys a necklace where the bead came from, and encourage them to go to him for glass."

Zerah smiled and raised his cup in salute. "Sounds like a fair bargain. Congratulations, lad. You've taken your first steps as a businessman."

"Actually," Jacob leaned forward and addressed the end of the table where the women were sitting. "I have necklaces for all of you." He opened his pouch again, and extracting a cluster of cords and beads from it, began to separate them. The women got up from their places and came to stand over his shoulder, like a flock of gentle doves, murmuring their admiration and softly giggling as he pulled the cords apart and gave them each his gift. "Here you are, Aunt Leah. Mary, this one is yours. Mother Odelia...." Mary's mother insisted Jacob call her 'mother', and he complied, though he felt shy about doing so.

"This one is clear," she murmured in a tone of wonder, holding it up to the light. "It has no color at all."

"Colorless glass sounds like it should be easy, but the truth is, it's more difficult to make than the colored kind," he told her. "If they don't put any colorant in it, it comes out pale green. Attalus has been working on colorless glass for years. That bead is from the last batch. He says it's the closest he's come."

"It looks like a tear drop." Odelia's eyes were moist as she leaned down to kiss the top of his head. "Thank you, Jacob."

Lyssa got a drop of emerald green, the green of high summer—on a cord of saffron yellow. "Look how that lights up her eyes," Leah observed with a smile.

When he had given all but the last one away, he stood up, saying, "And this one's for Arin." He draped a cord of purple over her head. The drop suspended from it was deep, brilliant blue. "The color made me think of the sea."

It was all the explanation he needed to give. Arin, flushed with pleasure, rose up on her tiptoes and kissed his cheek. "Thank you."

* * * * *

After dinner, the family had a final time of prayer together. Arin sat in one corner, a little behind her mother, and directly across from Jacob. Her eyes kept straying to him, even as she tried to focus her attention on what her father was saying. Judging from the way she kept catching his glances, he was having the same difficulty.

"We'll be going first thing in the morning," Phillip told them. "The Lord has been good to us. We made it safely here with no loss, and we found Jacob alive and well." He paused a moment to rest a hand on Jacob's head. "For that, we are most thankful." Then he smiled, "As if that weren't blessing enough, we discover that our rowdy Joel has gotten himself married." Everyone laughed, except Mary, who turned scarlet. "And we come away from this journey with new friends. Gallus, I didn't have the pleasure of meeting you on my last trip to Jerusalem. It does my heart a world of good to know that you're keeping an eye on my old friend here." He clapped a hand on Zerah's shoulder.

The priest harrumphed at that. "Keeping an eye on me, is it? He's as much a trouble-maker as I ever thought to be."

Phillip laughed. "You two deserve each other. And Odelia, all of us have greatly benefited from your company." He patted his stomach. "Another week of this, and even the camel couldn't carry me home."

"Amen," Zerah intoned, closing his eyes and suppressing a belch.

Over the laughter that followed, Joel said, "Let us pray for you, for your journey home, and for continued peace in Caesarea." He lifted his hands and closed his eyes. "Our Father in Heaven, You who made the earth and the sea, and all that dwell in the earth, we come to You in the name of your Son...."

Arin bent her head and closed her eyes. *Lord, I know we have to go home, but I don't want to leave.* She shifted uneasily on her cushion. *What kind of a prayer is that?* With a sigh she forced her thoughts along a more disciplined path for a while, then stopped to listen. Odelia sat to her right, and she wept and entreated the Lord for her wayward son, still absent. No one had seen him for weeks. Touched by her grief, she joined her heart to Odelia's pleas. *Father, pursue him. Show him the riches of your Son's love. Open his eyes to the truth, and bring him home to his family, and to You....*

Voices rose and fell in worship and petition for the better part of an hour. Finally Mary's voice, sweet and high, rose above the others with a hymn. "I lift up mine eyes unto the hills, from whence shall come my help. My help is from the Lord God, Maker of Heaven and of earth...." Several joined her song, but Arin remained silent, content to sit still and listen. She took in a deep breath, and then... *the raging thunder of feet, thousands of them...running and stumbling... screams of terror... of agony...and still the feet keep running...pounding at the stone pavement....* Arin clutched her arms close, held herself still. *At last, the screams subside to weeping... moaning.... And a man's voice calls out in desperate fear, "Where are you? Where* **are** *you?"*

And it was over. But Arin, still lost in the dark moment, lost in the despair of that final cry, continued to hold herself while tears dropped unheeded from her face. *I know who it is.* She opened her eyes and briefly met Jacob's quizzical, concerned look before closing them again. *I have to tell him. But how?*

As I am Known

* * * * *

Her answer came later that evening. Jacob sought her out while she was mending a hole in her father's robe. "Arin, are you all right?"

"I'm all right." She gave him a tenuous smile.

What happened while...while everyone was praying?" He briefly covered one of her hands with his own. "I saw you crying. You looked so upset. Won't you tell me?" When she bit her lip, he pressed, "Please let me be your friend."

With that, she put down her sewing. *Will you still be my friend after this? Or will you hate me? Oh, Lord in Heaven, I have always thought of Jacob as my friend—even all the years we were apart. I don't want to lose this... Help me tell him.* She sighed and remembered Saul's gentle admonition. *God, You are good. I will trust You.* "It's hard to explain," she began, and took a long, shaking breath. "Sometimes I see things."

He frowned. "You see things? Well, of course...."

"Not with my eyes, Jacob. I see things in here." She touched her head. "Usually when I *close* my eyes."

He swallowed hard as he struggled to understand. "You mean, visions?"

"I...I don't know. I guess so. Maybe that's what they are." She pressed her fingertips to her forehead. "I've always told my father about them, but not this one."

"Why not?"

"I tried to tell him once, but the Spirit stopped me. I think it wasn't the right time yet."

Jacob felt the blood drain from his face. "You have these visions regularly? Are you saying you're a prophetess?"

She regarded him with her gray eyes. "I keep forgetting—you aren't a follower of the Lord Jesus, are you?"

"No... no," he stammered, and for the first time, such an admission left him feeling bereft. "I'm not."

"My father says the Spirit was poured out on all his followers shortly after the Lord's resurrection—and continues to be. My sisters prophesy, too."

"What?" He clapped a hand over his mouth, half-afraid he had shouted. He glanced around, and seeing no one was paying attention to him, realized the shout had remained caged in his mind. In a whisper he asked, "Even Salome?"

"Even Salome, but she's only spoken prophesy once."

Jacob bent his head and stared at his hands, not knowing what to think. He knew what his grandfather would have thought—oh, yes he did! He could hear the old man's railing. *"They're demonized! It's the work of Beelzebub! The whole family is cursed!"* A sudden light came on in his head. *That's one reason why Phillip no longer goes to Jerusalem.*

He turned his attention back to Arin. He sensed she was telling him the truth. And there was no possible way she was demonized. Not Arin, and not either of her sisters. They were just normal, ordinary girls, like Prisca. Could their belief that the Nazarene was Messiah be true? Unwilling to step off into that void, he asked, "You said you couldn't tell your father what your vision was. Can you tell me?"

"Strangely enough, I believe the Spirit is saying I'm *supposed* to tell you." She bit her lip. "And my father does need to hear it, too. It's time. Would you get him to come over here? I don't want the others—just him."

Jacob did as he was asked. He went to Phillip and lightly touched his shoulder. "Uncle Phillip? Arin needs to speak with you."

He had been listening to one of Zerah's stories and laughing, but when he turned to meet his daughter's eyes, his face sobered. "I'll be right there."

Moments after Jacob had seated himself again next to Arin, Phillip joined them. "What's this about, daughter?"

"I've had a vision, Papa. In fact, I've had it several times over the past few weeks. But tonight, I understand more. It concerns Jacob."

Phillip nodded, as if visions and prophesies were commonplace events in his life. "Tell us what you've seen."

Jacob felt his stomach drop, and his heart thudded in deep rhythms behind his ribs like a blacksmith's hammer at the forge. *This prophecy concerns me. If it's true....* He could just imagine what the Lord of Heaven thought of his running away. *Arin may hate me after this. Perhaps it's right that she should do so....* He braced himself for the worst.

Arin said, "The way the vision always starts, I hear—and then I see—feet running. Hundreds of them, Papa, maybe thousands. And there's screaming and crying, and finally I hear a voice calling out, 'Where are you? Where are you?' It's a man's voice."

Jacob waited for the rest. When he realized there was no more, he asked, "Is that all?" He rubbed at the side of his face with one hand. "You mean, you don't know where it is, or who you're hearing?"

"I'm pretty sure it's in a city, because I see walls and a stone street. I assume the city is Jerusalem."

Phillip's brows drew together in a studious frown. "Why so?"

"The man's voice at the end...." Her cheeks flamed red, and she glanced once at Jacob before turning her attention fully to her father. "I know whose voice it is." He didn't ask, but sat quietly and waited for her to say. "It's Caleb, Papa. It's Jacob's father."

Jacob stared agape, stared at Arin, then stared through her into nothing. *My father. There's some kind of trouble. And...and he's looking for me.* Suddenly aware his mouth was hanging open, he snapped it shut. "Uncle Phillip...." His words came out hoarse and unsteady.

The muscles in Phillip's face tightened. "Are you certain, Arin?" When she nodded in reply, he said, "Jacob, you and I have to talk. It's a pleasant evening. Let's go up on the roof." Before he stood, he bent over and kissed his daughter's face. "Well done, beloved."

Jacob got up like a man in a dream and followed him out the door and up the outside stairs that led to the roof. He pushed himself up the stairs, one by one—lifted each foot and pushed hard. He sometimes had nightmares that something was chasing him, something monstrous, and he was trying to run, but his limbs were too heavy and slow to obey. They felt that way now. If the night was pleasant—as Phillip said it was—he didn't know it, his sight and hearing were as dulled as the rest of him. Once they gained the roof, he stopped and looked around, blinking, unable remember why he was there.

"Come—sit here with me." Phillip's invitation fell on near-deaf ears, but Jacob did manage to obey. He settled down facing his uncle and waited. Phillip regarded him for a long moment. "Jacob, you...."

"I have to go home," he cut in.

Phillip's lips pressed together. He wiped at his forehead with one sleeve and sighed. "Tell me why you think so."

"My father is looking for me. He needs me."

"I sent a message to your father the day I found you," Phillip told him. "I sent it on a ship sailing south to Joppa. That was almost a week ago. For all I know, he has it by now. He knows you're safe, or soon will."

"He needs me. I have to go home." His vision cleared somewhat, and he leveled his gaze at his uncle. "Do you believe what Arin said was true?"

"If you're asking if I believe she faithfully reported what she saw, I do."

He did hear well enough to catch the hesitation in Phillip's answer. "But?"

"Prophesy is not always as straightforward as it appears on the surface. You have to be careful of your assumptions."

Jacob frowned. "What assumptions?"

"Arin assumes the city she saw is Jerusalem, and so do you."

"My father never leaves Jerusalem—or almost never," he answered. "The farthest I can remember him going was to Jericho. That was a couple of years ago. And he came back the very next day."

"A compelling argument for Jerusalem," Phillip nodded. "But, Jacob, what if he gets my message and decides to break old habits and come here? The city she saw could just as well be Damascus."

"You really don't think that." Despite his love for his uncle, he let the challenge in his words stand. He felt he had aged a decade in the past five minutes, and any courtesy he owed his uncle lay buried in the moment's need.

Phillip sighed and closed his eyes. "No, you're right. My feeling is that it's Jerusalem."

His honest admission loosened the grip of shock on Jacob's senses. He inhaled deeply, as if he had finally reached the surface of some deep and suffocating well. He turned his eyes to the stars overhead. "Arin says her sisters prophesy, too."

Phillip nodded. "Each of them has done so, yes."

In all his schooling in the scriptures, Jacob couldn't remember a precedent for such a thing. *One prophetess, yes. Deborah, the great judge of old, prophesied. But three girls? They aren't even women yet. And all in one family? How can such a thing be?* He shook off the shrill, scolding voice of his grandfather that still echoed somewhere in the back rooms of his mind. He wanted no part of that kind of thinking. But nothing in his experience leant perspective to this night's events. How was he supposed to make sense of it? At last he turned, pleading, to his uncle. "Help me understand this."

Phillip leaned forward, and putting one hand around the back of Jacob's neck, pulled him toward himself until their foreheads touched. His gentle grip tightened. "I will do my best." When he had released him and sat back, he added, "And to do that, I need to tell you a story."

I met your father on the way to Jerusalem for Passover. This was the same spring you were born. In fact, I think I remember your father telling me later that you were born while he was away. My father had taken me and my sister—your stepmother—down for the Feast. Father is Greek, as you know, but he worships the Lord. Caleb and I fell in together on the way down, and became friends. We had many hours to talk and get acquainted." Phillip stopped and chuckled, "Actually, I think I did most of the talking. I was proud of my grasp of Greek philosophy, and your poor father needed a friend, so he was willing to listen to my prattle. When we came to the city, your grandfather invited us to dinner for the last day of the Feast. I think that was when the trouble started—when Lathan met my father and saw my sister."

After the Feast, we went back north, up to Antioch. Diana went on home to Ephesus with a cousin, but my father had a villa in Antioch, and we stayed there through the summer. He managed the family's holdings, and I kept myself busy trying not to get into too much trouble. Late that summer he received a message from Lathan. Your grandfather was sick, and he wanted to meet with my father, so we sailed down to Joppa and made it back to Jerusalem just in time for Tabernacles."

Lathan was dying of some kind of wasting disease. I didn't see him myself, but my father said he already looked like a corpse. I spent part of that feast with Caleb, trying to just be his friend. I didn't know how else to comfort him. We went to synagogue on the Sabbath, and on our way back to the house, we ran into Jesus of Nazareth coming out of the Temple. Your father had already told me that your mother was healed by him, and that day we saw him touch a blind beggar. Actually, he smeared mud on the fellow's eyes and told him to go wash off. So your father and I followed him—followed the beggar, that is—to see what would happen."

"Was he healed?" Jacob asked.

Phillip nodded. "He was. But I think the turning point for me was when Jesus knelt down to talk to the man. He put himself on the beggar's level, something no priest would ever do."

"What happened after that?"

"Your mother was fairly well acquainted with Jesus, and as your grandfather lay dying, she went and found him, and brought him into the house. He laid hands on Lathan and healed him." Jacob, who had heard this part of the story from Zerah, only nodded. Phillip went on, "Your grandfather was enraged. He insisted that he recovered on his own. And he sent yet another message to my father—a message that he was ready to finalize a marriage contract between Diana and your father."

Jacob ran his fingers through his shorn hair and spluttered, "But...but Father was still married to my mother."

"He was. That didn't matter to Lathan. He had already cooked up a story about your mother, telling my father that she was an unfit wife, and that Caleb was about to divorce her. He was one smooth talker, your grandfather. So before Caleb put your mother away, his next wife was already on her way to him."

Though he was unaware of it, Jacob had been holding his breath, and now it exploded out of his chest. And the force of that explosion blew the door shut on his grandfather's voice and bolted it. That voice would never control him again.

"I saw your mother only once," Phillip said. "She was there when Jesus was crucified. I was there, too—with Lathan and Caleb. We passed her when we started down off the hill, and I knew who she was from the way she looked at your father. She was in distress. Her time had come to deliver your brother right there on that awful hill. I tried to make Caleb stop, but he wouldn't, so I went and got a litter for her, and her friends took her away."

"After that, I stayed in Jerusalem, and when Jesus was resurrected, I became his follower."

"And after *that,* Grandfather hated you."

The lines around Phillip's eyes deepened. "In some ways, your grandfather is a remarkable man. You are right—he hated me—for my faith, and because of the influence I had with your father. I think Lathan was afraid that I would muddy his carefully orchestrated plans. And believe me," he added darkly, "if I had fully understood what he was up to, I would have. But Lathan tolerated me for a long time, much longer than he wanted to, I think, because of my father and my sister."

"But he was patient, and over the years, he planted seeds in Caleb's mind to make him doubt me—never anything big—just hints and suggestions. His favorite tactic was to say something critical or unflattering to Caleb, and make it sound as if I had said it to Lathan, or even to Diana, in confidence. He did the same thing with her, until my own sister would barely speak to me. I lost my best friend and my sister at the same time."

"Uncle Phillip," Jacob had bowed his head, and now sat staring at his fingers, "You say Jesus of Nazareth was resurrected, that he came back from the dead. But I was taught that his disciples stole his body from the tomb and hid it."

Phillip nodded. "I've heard that story, too, but it leaks like a sieve. The tomb was guarded. Have you ever seen a Roman guard asleep at his post?"

Jacob shrugged. "No, I haven't, but I suppose it happens."

"It could happen, yes. But do you think a whole squad of them would fall asleep at the same time?"

His mental picture of that made Jacob smile. "No, I guess not. They'd be in a world of trouble if they did."

"They certainly would," Phillip agreed. "But the thing that finally convinced me was watching Jesus' disciples—the ones that were closest to him. When he was crucified, they ran away. I did see one of them on the hill, but the others were afraid to come that close."

"Why were they afraid?" Jacob asked, though he thought he knew the answer.

"Ever seen someone crucified?" Phillip's eyes cut into him, and he had to look away. "You have, and you know what it does to a man. They were afraid they'd be caught and executed the same way. But after the tomb was found empty, they were different—fearless as lions. They are all in danger of crucifixion, or imprisonment, or whatever persecution the powers that be may devise against them, but that doesn't stop them."

"So their courage convinced you?"

Phillip rested a hand on Jacob's shoulder. "Would you die for a lie?"

"Would I..." Jacob began, and then he understood the question. "No, not if I knew it was a lie."

"Would you be willing to suffer crucifixion for something if there was even a doubt of its truth in your mind?"

He shook his head. "No."

"So you see, Jesus' followers had no doubt. They saw him after he was raised from the dead. I've heard their stories. They have no doubt who Jesus is, and they are willing to die—they are willing to suffer—for him. A good friend of mine was stoned to death in Jerusalem for his faith. His name was Stephen. Your Uncle Nicanor and I helped bury him."

Jacob's heart tested the truth of Phillip's words—gingerly—the way a man tests the planks of a bridge with one foot before stepping across the chasm. Would it bear up? Would it hold him? He chewed on his lip, and then said, "If I become a follower of Jesus, my father might reject me."

"He might," Phillip agreed.

He pulled his arms in close to himself, as if he felt a chill in the toasted summer night. "But you are a follower, and Joel is...."

"And your mother and brother, and your Grandmother Abigail was."

His head came up. "She was?"

Phillip smiled. "She took some convincing, but yes. You know, there is another possibility. Your father may not reject you. He could come to faith in the Christ himself."

He pondered Phillip's story. *Jesus healed my mother, and my grandfather, and Uncle Phillip saw him—he saw him!—heal a blind man.* The next thought was more difficult. *My father saw it, too. His own wife and father were both healed. How could he not believe?*

The faces of those Jacob loved who were Jesus' followers paraded before his eyes—Phillip and Arin, Joel and Mary, Mary's mother, John Mark, Zerah, Grandmother Abigail. And there was something about them all he admired, something he wanted to emulate. Something about them—something about Phillip's story—resonated deep inside, sang and echoed like a trumpet call. He knew it was true.

Messiah! The word sent a tremor racing down his spine. "I believe. I want to be part of it."

For a moment he was unaware that he had spoken aloud, but Phillip reached out to him and gripped his arms. "Oh, lad, you won't regret it!" His eyes brimmed with tears. "I have prayed for you every day of your life since I accepted this faith."

For the second time that night, Jacob's heart thudded painfully in his chest, but this time not from fear. He felt like he was standing on the brink of high adventure. He was about to become part of something far bigger, far grander than himself. "Tell me what to do."

Phillip released him and sat up straight. "Let's pray."

* * * * *

Later that evening, Jacob stepped out of one of Damascus' pools where Phillip had just baptized him. He shook the water from his dripping hair and accepted the towel his Aunt Leah offered. With a grin, Phillip clapped his shoulder and started back toward Zerah's house. The rest of the family followed, leaving him alone with his uncle Joel, who held his robe and a dry tunic. A stray breeze raised the flesh across his back, and he shivered and quickly shucked off his wet tunic.

Joel said, "I want you to know what joy it has given me to have you with me these past months. And now that you belong to the Christ, you're my brother, as well as my nephew."

Jacob nodded, but he couldn't yet bring himself to meet Joel's eyes. He took the dry tunic and threw it on over his head. "It has been a joy to me as well." Joel held the robe for him as he shrugged into it. "Uncle Joel...." he hesitated. A new rash of gooseflesh raced across his shoulders and down his back, though the evening was warm.

"What is it, Jacob?"

"My father isn't here, and I wondered if you'd stand in his place for me."

Joel cocked his head in curiosity. "About what?"

He suddenly felt a catch in his throat, and tried a couple of times to clear it. Finally he said, "It's early to ask this, but I...." Now his face flushed hot.

Joel laid a hand on his shoulder. "Is it about Arin?"

He nodded. "Would you approach Uncle Phillip for me?"

"You are both young," Joel answered. "You'll have to agree to a long betrothal."

"I understand, and I expected to. I have a lot to learn before I'm ready to marry. But she is the one." He raised his eyes. "Will you speak to him?"

Joel smiled. "I will."

*   *   *   *   *

Phillip's family left just before daybreak. Jacob kept trying to swallow the lump in his throat, but each swallow seemed to just make it bigger. His Aunt Leah hugged and kissed him, and Lyssa did the same. He caught Salome up in his arms briefly and squeezed her until she squealed. Arin was last. *Careful, now,* a new voice inside counseled him. Phillip had told him to listen for it—the Spirit of God. He glanced at Phillip before leading Arin a few steps away. They exchanged a chaste kiss, and instead of hugging her, he took her hand. "I'll miss you, Beloved." A quiet thrill raced through him when he used the endearment.

Arin swallowed, her own eyes bright with tears. "And I you. Come to us when you can."

He nodded. "When I can."

Phillip said, "We're not so far out of the way if you are going to Jerusalem." He embraced Jacob and added, "I think it will not be long before you can go home, lad. In any rate, come to Caesarea."

"I will," Jacob promised.

When they were gone, when they turned the corner and were out of sight, he sat down heavily on the step and let his tears fall. He made no sound, but covered his eyes with his hands and squeezed them shut until it was over. Then he wiped his face and nose on the hem of his robe, and stood up. He drew in a deep breath, took another swipe at his face with his sleeve, and started off down the street to the shop. *How is it possible,* he wondered, *to feel so wretched and so good at the same time?*

Chapter 11

Caleb hadn't set foot inside the barn in years. There had been no reason for him to. His uncle Simon had kept goats, and for a while Lathan had done the same, but as the animals died, he neglected to replace them, and so the goats were all gone now, though a faint tang of them still lingered in the early autumn air.

He paused just inside the door, letting his eyes adjust to the dim light. Sunlight penetrated a few cracks in the walls, and dust motes rose and fell in the bright shafts. *I really should tear this old thing down. It serves no purpose.* He took a few steps farther into the darkness. Some small animal, a mouse probably, rustled beneath a pile of straw banked up against one corner. Pigeons cooed from the rafters overhead. Otherwise, all was quiet. *But then, it would serve no purpose to tear it down.* He ran his hand along the top rail of what used to be a goat pen.

This is as good a place as any to lose what's left of my mind,

The thought of losing his mind, of letting go, letting himself sink into oblivion, had a certain appeal. *How did life turn out to be so complicated?* It hadn't seemed that way in the beginning. "A man works," he murmured. "He works and makes his living. He marries and has children. He makes his devotions to God." Simple.

So where did I go wrong? He sank down onto the pile of straw, unaware that he was sitting in the exact spot Jacob occupied the night of Andrew's banquet, just before he ran off to John Mark's. *When something went awry Linus used to say. 'Let's take this apart and look at it.'* Caleb sighed. *He was here at Passover. I wish he was here now—I need to talk to someone. The year I worked for him in Capernaum was one of the best years of my life.*

"All right," he muttered as he lay back in the straw, for once not caring whether he dirtied his robe. "I'll take it apart and look at it, starting with my business. I did not report anyone to ben Hosa, or any other tax collector." Saying it aloud made him grind his teeth with disgust. "I would never sink so low. I have not lied to anyone, and I have not cheated anyone." He winced when a twinge of conscience nipped at him, and added, "Well, if I skimmed a little extra on a man's investments, it was only to cover added expenses, never to fatten my purse. Father did the same thing, and so do the other money lenders—everyone knows that. Otherwise, my dealings have been sound. Father may have been harsh at times, but he was a good businessman, and a good teacher. Still, I need some counsel. Father is far too sick. Perhaps I should talk to Tobin—see if he can advise me. That's what I'll do. I'll go see him."

"How about my family?" Caleb gnawed at the side of one thumbnail. "I guess that isn't going so well, but it's not my fault. Diana is difficult. Phillip warned me she would be, and he was right. No matter what I say to her, I cannot make her see reason. Of course, she's a woman, and women are not logical. But even when a woman doesn't understand, she still should be obedient. Father would probably tell me I need to take a firmer hand with her. I guess I'll have to. I can't go on like this, having her flout my wishes at every turn."

"And the children? The baby is too young to be any trouble. He's growing so fast. He seems different every day. By next Passover, he'll probably be walking a little. Prisca? Her nightmares have all but gone away—it's been at least a week since her last one—Heaven be thanked for that. How old is she now? Ten? She's growing up." Caleb muttered, "I'm going to have to start looking for a husband for her. No sense in putting it off till the last minute." He plucked up a piece of straw and toyed with it. "Finding her a decent marriage prospect in Jerusalem is going to be difficult if I don't clear my name—and soon."

Jacob. Caleb fell silent, unable to speak his first-born's name aloud. *Would that I knew where you were, son. I haven't heard yet from Gedeon, or from Phillip. Not a word, for good or ill. If I knew where to find you, I'd come and get you and bring you home—contract or no contract.* A single tear coursed across his face and dropped into the straw. *Father would tell me to leave it be, to let him go.* He sighed deeply. *There's nothing I can do anyway. I don't know where he's gone, and I can't leave Jerusalem to go looking. Not now. Not with the way things are.*

"I'll go pay Tobin a visit." But for a while he remained where he was. *Jacob used to come here often, even when he wasn't being punished. Sometimes I wondered why.* Caleb looked around him. All was peaceful in the dim light. All was quiet. He closed his eyes. *Now I think I understand.*

* * * * *

About an hour later, having thoroughly dusted the residue of his straw resting place off his robe, Caleb knocked at Tobin's door. "I am Caleb ben Lathan," he announced to the servant who answered. "I would like a word with your master, if he is home."

"He is. Please wait one moment, sir." Instead of ushering him in, the servant left him standing on the step. Caleb took the time to review something Lathan had said years before. *'If you ever find yourself in a desperate situation, you must take the greatest caution never to* appear *desperate. Keep yourself calm. Watch what you do with your hands, and control your voice as well as your words. Keep your wits about you. Don't go unkempt—wear your best clothing and anoint your head. This city is full of wolves, all of them sniffing about, and if you're not careful, they* will scent your fear. Above all, do not beg anyone for anything. Better to be devoured than pitied.'

Caleb took a deep breath, and when the door opened, he lifted his chin. "Shalom, Tobin. May I have a word with you?"

"Shalom, ben Lathan." He smiled. "Of course you may. Anything for the son of an old friend."

Tobin's greeting was warm enough, but Caleb couldn't help but notice that the older man stuck his head out the door, and looked right and left before shutting it again. *Am I already such a pariah that he's worried about who may have seen me come here?*

He followed his host through the main room to a table in one corner. Tobin called for wine, and gestured toward the cushions. "Make yourself comfortable." They sat down together and engaged in customary small talk until the servant filled their cups and left. Tobin leaned back on one elbow and asked, "Now what can I do for you?"

Caleb cleared his throat. *Keep yourself calm.* "I'm looking for counsel, sir. My father has always spoken well of you. I thought perhaps you might guide me."

"That's very flattering," Tobin replied with a nod. "I hope I can live up to your expectations."

He allowed himself a chuckle. "No doubt you will. I came to ask your advice on the matter of the accusation that was made against me several weeks ago at Caiaphas' banquet." When Tobin nodded without reply, he added, "The accusation was false. I am looking for a way to prove it, and to clear my name."

"What have you done so far?"

"Thaddeus said Jonathan ben Hosa told him that I gave ben Hosa information about Thaddeus' assets. The first thing I did was go to ben Hosa and confront him."

"And what did he say?"

"He denied everything, said he never talked to Thaddeus at all." *Which is a bald-faced lie,* he wanted to add, but refrained. *I must be careful of my words.* "When I went to see him a second time, he was no longer there."

This made Tobin sit up. "No longer there? What do you mean?"

"I mean he was gone—disappeared. I asked around, but no one would tell me anything. It was as though he never existed."

Tobin grunted and took a swallow of wine. "Interesting. Does Thaddeus know this? Were you able to make any headway with him?"

"None at all." Caleb casually lifted one shoulder, continuing his act. "But he's neither here nor there. I don't need his custom. What I do need is to put an end to these rumors so that I can go about my business."

"Yes, yes...quite right. Has anyone else accused you?"

You would know the answer to that, you old fox. "Not to my face."

As I am Known

"All right. I'll tell you what I know, and what I surmise. Your father did me a favor once. I owe you that much." Caleb understood what Tobin did not say—that this was the only favor he could expect from him. "After Thaddeus accused you at the banquet, I made some inquiries of my own. Thaddeus' star is rising these days, and I couldn't believe he'd make a baseless accusation against you, but neither could I believe that you were so foolish as to do what he claimed."

Caleb colored at that. *Thaddeus is a rising star, and I am only not 'so foolish'?* "Thank you for your confidence, sir. What did you find out?"

"Ben Hosa got himself into a bit of a scrape with his employers last year. One of the many disadvantages of collecting taxes for Caesar is that Caesar has eyes and ears everywhere. Ben Hosa apparently forgot that. He was caught with his hand in the jar, and arrested. They would probably have nailed him up, but someone stepped in and intervened. Whatever money he owed Caesar was paid—you know it had to be no small sum—and ben Hosa was set free."

Caleb frowned into his cup. "Who intervened? Did you find out?"

"I did. It was Simon, Caiaphas' steward."

Suddenly light-headed, Caleb set his cup down carefully and stared at it. "Simon." He raised his eyes. "Did he do it under Caiaphas' orders, or on his own?"

Tobin swirled the wine in his cup with a lazy motion. "What do you think?"

"I won't banter words with you, Tobin. I have no love for Simon, for reasons of my own. If you told me he sacrificed a pig at every full moon, I'd believe you. If you think he used ben Hosa to try to ruin me, I believe that. What I don't understand is why. I have never done anything to him, at least not to my knowledge."

Tobin peered at him over the rim of his cup. "Perhaps *you* didn't...."

Caleb narrowed his gaze on his host. "If I didn't, then who did?"

Tobin tugged at his beard and stared at the wall somewhere over Caleb's head. "How old were you when your family came to Jerusalem?"

"Oh, five or six, I guess. I really don't remember."

"So you don't remember that much about the first years of your father's work as a money changer?"

"No. At that age, he didn't talk to me about his work, and I was going to synagogue school, and trying to make friends, all of that. Why do you ask?"

"Well, you know Lathan took over your uncle Simon's table after he died. The table, the house you live in, all the furnishings, Simon's reputation, *everything* was handed down to your father with Annas' blessing. Your father was set up for life, and he learned the business quickly. He appeared at first to be no more than an uneducated farm boy, but he surprised all of us with his acumen. Soon after Simon died, one of the other money lenders, a relative of Annas'—his name was Ezra—tried to step in and control the rest of us by telling us how much we could charge, and forcing us to pay him part of our profits."

Caleb gaped at him in open-mouthed astonishment. "Surely he didn't get away with it?"

"He did, briefly. I think old Annas would have yanked him up sooner or later, but someone else beat him to it. Your father."

Caleb was stunned. After a brief struggle to control his reaction, he managed a smile. "I can imagine how infuriated Father would have been, but what could he do in a situation like that?"

Tobin shrugged. "I never learned exactly what he did, or how he pulled it off, but your father somehow started a rumor that Ezra was over-charging his clients. I think, at the same time, he brought his own rates down. This happened during Tabernacles."

"A busy time," Caleb observed.

"Exactly. By the time Ezra figured out something was wrong, it was too late for him to do anything about it. A few days later, Annas sent him away—away out of Jerusalem, Caleb. He never came back, and he never recovered. Your father ruined him."

"I didn't know any of that," he said, and a gray shadow of dread stole over him. "But what has that to do with Simon?"

Tobin steepled his fingers together. His eyes drilled into Caleb's. "Simon is Ezra's son."

* * * * *

It was almost time for Tabernacles again. Caleb walked over to the Temple before going home. He went into the Outer Court, all but deserted now that it was past sundown, and paused on the step where his table was normally located. *If I do well during the feast, I can make enough to carry us through the winter. Ben Hosa is gone, so I don't have to worry about any more rumors starting with him. But what can I do about Simon?* Direct confrontation would likely do him no good. Simon was far too slippery to be caught in that net.

And I put my son—my Jacob into his hands. At that thought, his knees gave way, and he slipped to the pavement and knelt there like a supplicant, his head bowed. "Jacob," he whispered. "Son, if you come home, if you come back to me, I promise I will never let you go again." The words of another promise he made not so long ago now shamed him. "Father, you set a little stone in motion, and now that stone's become an avalanche that will bury the rest of us. I should have refused you. You are wrong about Jacob."

He raised his eyes to the gate of the Inner Court, now veiled in deepening shadow. *I will come back tomorrow and make a sacrifice,* he told himself, *for Jacob's safety and return.* He got to his feet, and though he felt inexpressibly weary, he made himself walk home with the step of a man who hadn't a care in the world. After all, one never knew who might be watching.

Prisca met him at the door. All but one of their servants had been dismissed, and now his daughter took it upon herself to welcome him in and bring him refreshment every evening. "Shalom, Papa." She turned her face up to him for a kiss. "Did you have a good day?"

"I did," he lied with a smile. "How about you?"

"Tamar came over for a while." She handed him his cup as he sat down. "We shelled some almonds and helped Mila make bread."

He took a sip of the wine, and kissed the top of Prisca's head when she leaned it against his shoulder. "Is everything all right, little one?"

She sighed, and he had the impression that her eyes were closed, though he couldn't see them. "Everything is all right," she murmured. A few seconds later, she pushed away from him and wandered off.

A pang shot through him at her solemn demeanor—it was so unlike her. *Prisca is much quieter than she used to be,* he mused. *I suppose it's because she's growing up.*

Diana came down the stairs with Andrew in her arms. "Prisca," she called, "can you come and take your brother?" When she handed the baby over, she sat on the cushions next to Caleb. "You're late tonight."

Is this an accusation, or a simple observation? Greatly desiring to avoid a quarrel with her, he conceded in his gentlest manner, "You're right, my love, it is late. I had to go talk to someone."

She nodded and pulled a scroll from inside her robe. "A message came for you today. The handwriting looks like Phillip's."

He took the scroll and examined it. "It does," he murmured. *Perhaps he's had news of Jacob.* He offered Diana a smile as he broke open the seal. "We haven't heard from him in a long time."

She turned her eyes on him, brimming with worry. "You don't suppose it's bad news, do you? What if something's happened to Mother, or to Father?"

Caleb, eagerly scanning the message hardly heard her. "He's found Jacob."

"Alive?" When he shot her a questioning look, she stammered, "I...I mean, is he all right?"

He lowered the scroll to his lap. "Yes. Heaven be praised."

"Oh, well...if that's all it is...." Diana got up and called out. "Mila, we're ready to eat now. Prisca, come along."

There was more to the message, but he would have to leave it for later. In the meantime, he felt a burden lift from his shoulders. *Jacob is alive and safe. I didn't notice where Phillip said he is, but I'll read the whole message after dinner. And maybe in the spring, after Passover, I will go to him.*

He ate his meal in silence. As it turned out, Andrew was the only one who contributed conversation of any kind. He squealed and cooed on his pallet, while the rest of the family remained largely unresponsive. When dinner was over, and Prisca and Mila had cleared the dishes away, Caleb took the scroll in hand again and unrolled it.

To my friend and brother, Caleb,

I know the matter that is closest to your heart, and I want to tell you first of all that I have found Jacob. He is safe and well, and except for missing his home and family, he appears to be happy. I feel at this time it's best not to tell you where he is, but ask you to trust that he is in good hands.

I received your message. I am sorry to hear of Lathan's illness. I pray that Heaven will give you comfort and strength. As to the rest, if there were harsh words between us, I have put them out of my mind. You have been my friend for many years, and that friendship is no less dear to me now than it ever was. I hope you will come to see us in Caesarea.

Give my sister my loving greetings, and tell her that Leah and I share your joy in the birth of your new son. Mother and Father set sail for Ephesus over a week ago. I think Mother was relieved to travel some other way than by camel! Tell Prisca my daughters send her their love, and they hope your family will come and pay us a visit.

Joel and Zerah both send their greetings. Our love and prayers are with you always. Phillip

Caleb put the scroll down and rubbed hard at both eyes. *Maybe things aren't so bad as I thought.* He was well aware that Phillip's letter changed little, but the words of love and assurance acted like a tonic on his battered heart.

"You have a letter, Papa." Prisca dropped down on the cushion beside him. "What does it say?"

He smiled and pulled her close to his side. "It's a letter from your Uncle Phillip. Do you remember him?" When she shook her head, his smile dimmed a little. "That's my fault, daughter, and I will remedy it. We'll go to see them—perhaps after Passover."

"Does he have children?" Prisca asked.

"He has three daughters," Caleb told her. "One is older, there is another just your age, and the youngest one is a few years younger. The letter says they send you their love and hope you'll come to visit them."

"They don't live here, do they?"

"No, love. They live in a city called Caesarea. It's north of here." *I also want you to know that your brother is all right. No one has hurt him.* This last he didn't say out loud. Later he would wonder why.

* * * * *

The next day was reasonably profitable. Caleb's table stayed busy most of the day, and he even acquired a new investor, a Roman named Titus Albans, physician to the procurator and to other Roman officials. Caleb decided, after some internal debate, to take the bull by the horns with his new client. "I will tell you from the outset, sir," he began, trying to emulate what he recalled of his father's demeanor, "There has been a rumor circulating in this city that I am in league with a tax collector. It isn't true, but you are likely to hear it from one quarter or another."

"I've been the target of a few baseless rumors myself," Titus informed him with a thin smile. "I will make my own decisions based on your performance, not on words flying in the wind."

"Excellent." Caleb shook his hand. "I am pleased to do business with you, sir."

At the end of the day, he put his money and scrolls away and prepared to go home. *I haven't seen Simon lately,* he mused. *Not a trace of him. Did he disappear with ben Hosa?* Caleb shook his head ruefully. *I should be so lucky!*

He picked up his box and started for the gate, when a familiar figure stepped out from the shadow of Solomon's portico and stopped him. "Sir? I need to talk to you." It was John Mark.

Caleb nearly dropped his box. He stared at the young man for a full minute before he finally found his voice. "This is about Jacob." The youth nodded, and Caleb said, "We shouldn't talk here."

John Mark glanced around him, his expression wary, uneasy. "No, I think somewhere else."

"Very well. Come with me." On the way back to his house, he asked, "How long have you been home?"

"The ship I was on docked at Joppa last night, sir, and I rode in from there this afternoon."

More questions surfaced on the way, though he didn't speak them aloud. *Was Jacob with you? Do you know where he is now? Is he all right?* When they reached his house, he said, "Follow me." He led John Mark down a narrow alley to the back of his property. "In the barn. No one will hear us there."

Once they were inside, Caleb set his box down and turned to his visitor. "Now tell me about my son."

"Do you know where Jacob is, sir?"

He leaned against the rail of the goat pen, his arms crossed. "To be honest, I was hoping you'd tell me. I thought he ran off with you. Did he not?"

"No, sir. I didn't even know he left Jerusalem until recently." John Mark removed his turban and wiped his forehead with his sleeve. "I was on Cyprus—we had sailed there from Antioch, you see—and this man, a sea captain, came to us with a message that another man, sent from Caiaphas, was looking for us."

At the mention of the former High Priest's name, the short hairs on the back of Caleb's neck stood to frozen attention. "The man from Caiaphas—did you actually see him?"

"Yes, I did," John Mark admitted.

"What did he look like?"

"He looked ill, sir. He was thin, shadows under his eyes."

Caleb interrupted him. "Never mind that. What was the color of his hair? What was he wearing?"

"Gray." John Mark spoke slowly, remembering. "His hair, his robe—I think even his eyes might have been gray."

Simon's creature. Caleb shuddered. *He is still looking for my son. And if Simon's bent on revenge, he will never give up.* "You say you saw him. Did he talk to you?"

"Yes. We all thought he meant to stir up trouble for us, for the message we were preaching. But when he found us, he only wanted to see me. He wasn't interested in the others at all...." There John Mark faltered, and his eyes dropped to the floor. "He...he made certain threats against Saul and Barnabas, and against the family we were staying with if I didn't tell him...."

In one swift movement, Caleb surged forward and grasped John Mark's shoulders. "Tell him what?" He gave the youth a shake. "What did you tell him, boy?"

"He wanted information about Jacob." Tears started to spill down John Mark's face. "He wanted to know where he was. I didn't know for sure, and I said so, but I did tell him where Jacob's mother and uncle live." He covered his face and sobbed. "I...I had to. I'm sorry. He would have had them all killed."

Caleb staggered back as if floor was giving way under him. "How long ago was this?"

"Ah...." John Mark rubbed at his eyes while he collected himself. "I guess it would be about three weeks now. I didn't leave Saul and Barnabas until we got to Meletus. I sailed straight home from there."

"Three weeks... three weeks...." He began to pace back and forth, trying to gather his scattered thoughts.

"I'm sorry, sir. I should have come sooner."

He stopped his pacing. With his back turned to John Mark he said, "Tell me where they are—Jacob's mother, and his uncle Joel. Tell me what you told him."

"Jacob's mother is in Antioch. I actually met her while we were there—and Jonathan, Jacob's brother."

Caleb had spent the years after he divorced Miriam disregarding any thought of the child she bore when he sent her away. He had always thought of it as a child of adultery. *Jonathan. So she had another boy. Is it possible I have a son I've never even seen?* Aloud he said, "And his uncle Joel? Where is he?"

"Damascus."

Without turning around, he said, "I should probably tell you that the same man you spoke to hunted for Jacob here in Jerusalem first. He went to your mother's house."

John Mark's horrified echo was barely more than a whisper. "He went to my mother's house?"

Caleb nodded. "He didn't hurt her. I think she wasn't even home when he came." He sighed like a man giving up his last breath. "You'd probably better go to her now."

John Mark started for the door, but stopped. "Sir, I want to help you...."

He cut him off. "I will call for you if I need help."

When the youth was gone, Caleb remembered the final line from Phillip's letter. *'Joel and Zerah both send their greetings.' Damascus. That's where they are, and that's where Jacob is. Phillip wrote that to let me know who Jacob was with, without telling me where he was. Joel must have been here for the feast. He left afterward, and Zerah went with him, and they took Jacob. But why did Zerah leave Jerusalem? I still don't understand that.*

Phineas is after my son. A new thought occurred to him, making him tremble there in the shadows. *And if I have another son—and he finds him.... I have to go. I don't have enough money, but if I sold the house... if I sold everything I have.... Father will never understand, but I will have to try to make him understand. How can I honor my father, and still be responsible for my son? And what about Father's care? I'll have to go talk to Deborah.*

* * * * *

When he told her what he wanted, Deborah swept the tears from her face with trembling hands and gave him a smile. "I am proud of you, Brother."

He had expected disbelief from her, and host of questions. Her simple declaration stunned him. "Proud of me? Why do you say so?"

"You have finally learned what is most important. Your house here, and your business—those are all good things, admirable things. But Caleb, that boy is more important than the rest combined." She moved in closer. "And I will finally tell you another thing, because I think now you are ready to hear it."

He colored and looked away. "What is it?"

She reached out and gently turned his face to hers again. "Miriam's other child, the one she gave birth to just after you sent her away, he *is* your son. I saw him, Caleb. He could hardly look more like you."

He sank into a chair, and Deborah drew another up close and sat down. "Perhaps," he cleared his throat. "perhaps you'd better tell me everything. I don't want to go dashing off in ignorance."

Deborah took one of his hands in hers. "Father was wrong about Miriam. She was never untrue to you. She loved you, and—Heaven bless her—she loved Father, too. That was why she brought Jesus of Nazareth into the house that day. And Caleb," she pressed his hand more tightly, "Jesus did heal Father. I think you know that, deep inside. He healed your wife, he healed your father, and he healed Reuel."

He frowned, "Reuel was healed? Father never told me that."

"Would you have expected him to?"

Those words, spoken in Deborah's gentle voice, fell like a hammer blow. He leaned forward with his face in his hands. "So what you're saying is that my putting Miriam away and marrying Diana was—what? All due to scheming on Father's part? Why? Why would he do such a thing?"

"Caleb, *think!* Who did Father hate above all others? Jesus of Nazareth. Was Father the kind of man who would ever be bound by gratitude to someone he hated? Who brought Jesus into the house? And when Father found out about Miriam's healing, and who healed her—well...."

With a pang, he remembered his own reluctance to tell his father that Miriam had been healed. Even then he knew—he had to have known, hadn't he?—how Lathan would react. "He had me put her away just because of the Nazarene?" After all these years, Caleb could still not bring himself to speak the healer's name.

"Well, there was that." Deborah studied her hands, now folded in her lap and added, "but he also thought Diana was more suitable for you—higher socially, better educated, moneyed family. He told me so in one of his more...unguarded moments."

Miriam was innocent. I wronged her. That day I handed her the writ and sent her away.... He groaned at the memory, "Deborah, I can't stand this."

"But you have to, Only Brother. Our father is not the saint you've created in your mind. He is a man, with a man's sins and frailties. You have to know it, and you have to stand it, for Jacob's sake, and for your own."

He murmured, "And for Jonathan's."

Her eyes widened at this. "What? What did you say?"

He blinked back his gathering tears. "The other child—Miriam named him Jonathan, didn't she?"

"Yes, she did. But how did you know that?"

"I had a conversation with John Mark—you know him, don't you? He's back in Jerusalem, and he said he met Miriam and Jonathan when he was in Antioch."

He sat up and faced her. "You've known about Jonathan all along, Deborah. I am curious—why did you keep it from me?"

"Do you blame me? I did what I thought was right. Remember what you did with Jacob when you sent Miriam away?"

The day he divorced Miriam came back to him with full force—her quiet dignity, even when her son was torn from her arms. "You thought I'd take him from her—the way I took Jacob."

Her eyes on him were full of understanding and pity. "Would you have?"

The truth of his own answer threatened to choke him. "I might have. I...I don't know, Deborah."

She nodded, "At first I kept quiet because Jonathan was so tiny, and I knew he was better off with his mother than with us. It was going to be hard enough to raise Jacob without her." She sighed, "I know we could have handled a newborn, though it would have been difficult, but frankly, I couldn't do that to Miriam. And I knew Reuel well enough to know he'd be a good father to him."

Here was another piece of new information. Caleb suddenly found it hard to swallow. "Miriam married Reuel?"

Deborah nodded. "Later on, when I saw how Father was with Jacob, how he treated him, I knew I was right to leave Jonathan with Miriam. Abigail and I talked about it a number of times. She believed the day would eventually come when you would need the truth. That day has come—though she didn't live to see it." After a moment, she asked, "What is John Mark doing back in Jerusalem?"

The man who was hunting Jacob found John Mark on Cyprus." Over her horrified gasp, he added, "He now knows where Miriam is, and where Jacob is."

Deborah went white and grasped his hand. "Oh, Caleb, if he has Jacob...."

"I know," he answered. "And now I have another son to think about as well, which is why I have to go right away." With that, he stood up, and pulling her to her feet, he embraced her. "How is your baby?"

"He's fine," she answered into his shoulder. "The physician says his left hand will never develop properly where...where I fell on it, but I'm choosing to disbelieve him." She stepped back with a tremulous smile. "I massage it with oil every day and pray. Otherwise, he's as healthy and robust as any little boy."

"I will find Jacob," he promised her. "And if I can, while I'm at it, I'll take care of that Phineas fellow, too."

"No, Caleb, vengeance will not serve you well. Leave that to the Lord. Just find our boy and see to it that he's safe."

He noticed that she didn't say, *"and bring him home"*. And where was home now? He was leaving the only home he remembered. *Will Jerusalem ever be home again after this?* He cupped her cheek with one hand and touched his forehead to hers. "You'll keep a room open for us for the Feast, won't you?"

Deborah covered his hand with her own. "Of course I will. You're always welcome here. You know that. And don't worry about Father. I will take care of him."

He nodded and released her. "I will send a message when I have found Jacob."

"Are Diana and Prisca going with you?"

"They will go to Caesarea with me. We're stopping off to see Phillip. But from there, I plan to send them on to Ephesus, to Diana's father. I don't want them in harm's way—should it come to that."

Deborah murmured, "Yes, that is wise. There is no point in giving that man another target."

"One more thing. I am leaving some money for you with Tobin ben Simeon. It should cover any expenses you have with Father's care. In fact, there will be enough for you to hire someone to help you with him." He took her hand and squeezed it. "Please do it. I don't want you wearing yourself out."

"All right, Caleb. I will." She walked with him to the door, and when he had opened it, she kissed his cheek. "Go under the Lord's mercy, Brother. I will be praying for you."

"Thank you, my sister." He returned her kiss. "Thank you for everything."

*　　*　　*　　*　　*

A little later, he sat down beside Lathan's bed. "Father, I need to talk to you."

Lathan cracked one eye open. "What is it?"

"It's about Jacob," he answered.

Now Lathan's head turned toward him. "Is he alive?"

Caleb frowned. Diana had asked the same question. "Yes, Father, but he is in danger, and I have to go to him right away."

"No," Lathan growled. "You will do no such thing. You swore to send him away, and it is better so. He's old enough to look out for himself." He coughed, and his next words came out in a rattle. "If he's in some kind of trouble, it's his own doing. Let him suffer the consequences."

He felt his face flush with anger. "No, Father. The danger he's in was not of his own making. You had a hand in it."

Lathan's eyes widened with alarm, showing the sclera, yellowed with disease. "How... how did you know? Did she tell you?"

"Deborah? She told me some things. And I have recently learned things from others as well. Did you know that Caiaphas' steward, Simon, is the son of the moneychanger you ruined all those years ago? He's out for revenge now, Father. He's trying to ruin me, and he wants to destroy Jacob. You started this."

Lathan grunted and looked toward the ceiling. "Lies," he whispered.

"Is your good friend Tobin a liar? Is your own daughter a liar?"

Lathan shook his head. "You have a son here...."

Caleb leaned toward the bed and cut him off. "I have *three* sons, Father. Three. One of them is in danger, and the second may be. I will see to it that Andrew is safe, but I have to go."

"Your work...."

"My work will keep. Or not."

Laughter erupted from Lathan's ruined chest, but ended in a coughing spasm. "Foolish!"

"Perhaps I am foolish. But if I am, it will be for the right reasons. Now, this is how it will be. You will go to Deborah's. She will take care of you. I am sending Diana and the children to Ephesus, to Gedeon. And I am selling the house."

"You will do no such thing!" Lathan spluttered.

Caleb stood up. "You gave Diana money I couldn't afford for her to take. I have recovered from it, just barely. You've forced me to sell the house in order to save my son."

* * * * *

Selling the house was easier than he thought it would be. Titus Albans, the physician, was looking for a house. "I am leaving Jerusalem on a family matter," Caleb told him, "and I may not be coming back. I have a good-sized house in Upper Jerusalem. Why don't you come and have a look at it—see if it's what you want?"

"Will tomorrow evening be convenient for you?" Titus asked him.

Caleb agreed, and sensing Lathan might try to throw water on his plans, packed him up and took him to Deborah. When he told Diana what he was about to do, she was understandably furious that he was selling out without consulting her—turning their world upside down!—and she spent the evening with a friend, leaving Andrew in Mila's care, and Prisca to attend on her father. He was initially embarrassed by Diana's absence, but Prisca saved the day for him.

"Shalom," she greeted Titus at the door. "Are you my father's friend?"

He smiled and gave her a courteous bow. "I hope so, little girl. Is your father at home?"

"He is having a cup of wine," she answered, taking his hand and leading him in. "Would you like some?"

"Why, thank you. I believe I would." He gazed all around him, and when he settled across from Caleb, he said, "This is a nice house. But I think, as your investor, you should explain to me why you are leaving."

He waited until Prisca had filled his guest's cup before replying. "What I said earlier is true. It is a family matter." When Prisca had retreated out of earshot, he added, "I have a son who is in some trouble. I have to go and find him."

"Ah. Now that I understand." Titus' eyes gleamed as he took a sip. "Good wine, ben Lathan. I was a son like that. Turned my father's hair white. But why would you not bring him home once you've found him?"

Caleb shook his head. "It's not what you think. Jacob is a good boy, and none of this trouble is his fault." He narrowed his eyes on his visitor, trying to gauge how much he could safely tell him. Then, for no reason he could put his finger on, he said, "I apprenticed him to Caiaphas' steward, Simon. He mistreated Jacob, and Jacob ran away from him. Simon believes he has a bone to pick with me because..." he swallowed before he could finish, "...because of something my father did to his father."

"I see," Titus nodded. "Revenge. And you must not have known about it."

"That is correct. Simon is also the author of the rumors I told you about earlier. He appears bent on destroying me."

"Well, you can't let that happen. Not without a fight. I understand why you're going, but of course, I have to ask you—what about my investments?"

"There is another money lender in Jerusalem that I've known for years—Tobin ben Simeon. I have already spoken to him about you, and he's agreed to take over for me. In fact, I'm leaving some of my own money behind with him. He's a shrewd businessman and trustworthy. He will give your account the same care that I would."

Titus studied him a moment before nodding. "Very well. Why don't you show me the rest of the house?"

Caleb took him through the house and property. Prisca showed up again once they were outside. "This is our garden," she told him. "We have figs and almonds."

"And do you have flowers in the summer?" he asked her.

"Mostly in the spring," she answered, and began telling him about the different kinds, and where they were planted.

Their conversation surfaced a host of old memories in Caleb. His mother had loved the garden. So had Miriam. Many of the plantings here were hers, and continued to thrive after all this time. He picked up a stone in the path, studied it a moment, and let it fall from his fingers. He could still see her grubbing in the dirt—and smiling.

Chapter 12

"You're going to hurt your eyes, Jacob, squinting in the dark like that," Odelia fussed. "Let me light another lamp and bring it over to you."

He suppressed a smile and didn't bother to discourage her. He had learned not to—she would bring him a lamp, regardless. He held a bead as red as heart's blood pinched between the thumb and forefinger of his left hand, and was about to push a crimson loop of cord through it when his light brightened. "Thank you, Mother Odelia," he murmured when she set the lamp on the table. "That's much better."

"Well of course it is. Nobody can see in the dark. Are you hungry?"

Now he almost laughed. *I can't remember the last time I was hungry! Now how can I refuse more food without hurting her feelings?*

Fortunately, Zerah came to his rescue. "Wife!" he called out, "Come over here and talk to me. I'm the one who wants your company. Leave that poor boy alone."

"Pssht. Poor boy, indeed!" Odelia huffed, but she obeyed Zerah's request, and soon was ensconced in the corner with him.

Zerah and Odelia had quietly married in the fall. Since her husband's death, she had no way to adequately support herself, and no relative in the city to take her in. Joel started adding a room for her onto his house, but Zerah had other ideas, and when he offered marriage, she accepted without batting an eye. "I'm sure it was my sterling good looks and smooth talk that won her over," he later boasted.

"No doubt," Gallus nodded without cracking a smile. "That and the honey cakes you keep stuffing her with."

Jacob privately thought Zerah getting her out of prison in the first place was a deciding factor, that and the fact that they had both recently lost spouses. But whatever Odelia's reasons for marrying the priest, they all benefited from the arrangement. Gallus, no longer having to wait on Zerah, was able to find work. Jacob had someone to mother him. Odelia had the security of Zerah's support, while she cooked, and cleaned and fussed over everyone. Zerah in turns teased her, and showered her with little gifts. It made for a happy home.

We are the oddest family, Jacob couldn't help thinking as Zerah chuckled at something Odelia said. *The four of us thrown together, like patches on an old garment. None of us are cut from the same cloth. None of us matches. But somehow it works.*

Gallus came in a little later, carrying three scrolls in his arms. "What do you have there?" Zerah asked him.

"Poetry." Gallus spat the word out as if it tasted bad. "You have me in over my head, and now I have to read this poetry."

Jacob raised his head from his work just long enough to catch the gleam in

Zerah's eyes as he spoke. "Over your head? Nonsense. Who better than you to tutor Ananias' children?"

Gallus laid the scrolls down on the table. "You know as well as I that most of my Latin is military, and much of that is...unsuitable."

Jacob put his head down to his work again. He didn't want Gallus to catch him grinning, since he was partly to blame for the Roman's discomfiture. He had recited the bit of Latin he learned to Zerah, and hinted that Gallus had the inherent qualities of a teacher. Zerah saw to the rest, and found him work teaching the children of the synagogue's leader. The soldier and the priest had already had this argument—more than once.

"So you're going to have to read a little poetry and polish yourself up. It won't hurt you a bit." Zerah said.

"I feel like a hypocrite, like an actor on a stage. If those children ever get wind of how little I really know...."

"Nonsense," Zerah repeated. "I've done my share of teaching. It's all a matter of staying two steps ahead of your students. In a way, it is like acting, and there's nothing wrong with that. Everyone acts at one time or another." He gestured toward Gallus. "Even soldiers. *Especially* soldiers."

Gallus' countenance lowered like a thunderstorm. "Soldiers are not actors."

"Why, of course they are. When you went into battle, even though you were afraid, didn't you try to make yourself *appear* fearless?" When Gallus didn't answer, he said, "There, you see? It's all the same. It's acting, only this way, no one loses a limb."

"You are hungry. aren't you?" Odelia asked Gallus as she stood up. "Let me get you some dinner."

Gallus blinked once, still unused to having someone else wait on him. "I am, thank you."

"Besides," Zerah continued, as if he'd never been interrupted, "tutoring will enable you to save some money and buy your little friend free."

Gallus had nothing more to say. That last argument trumped all the others. Gallus had a sweetheart in Jerusalem, a slave in Caiaphas' household. This was all Jacob knew. He hadn't pressed for details, and the close-lipped soldier hadn't volunteered any, but Jacob did wonder how long it would take to save enough to free her. *Will he have enough by spring? He might.* None of them had talked about going down for the next Passover. *I'm sure we won't go, or at least, I won't. It isn't safe for me.* A pang of sadness caused his hands to falter just as he was passing a loop through another bead. *It'll be my first Passover away from home, my first without my father.*

He aimed again and got the cord through this time. He wanted to make and sell as many necklaces as he could. He smiled as he worked. *If I'm going to take a wife,*

I need to provide for her. Maybe in a couple of years, I'll be blowing glass, and I can make her something really nice for a wedding present. The thought caused a pleasant flush to rise to his face.

Gallus sat down across from Jacob and watched him work for a while. He moved the scrolls aside and thanked Odelia when she set his food in front of him.

"Where did you get the scrolls?" Jacob asked him.

"A friend of Ananias' lent them to me."

"And what kind of poems are they?"

"Epics." He heard a glower when Gallus added, "They are *not* love poems."

Jacob glanced up and said mildly, "I wasn't trying to insinuate that they were." He knew tutoring made Gallus feel like a fish out of water. "Maybe," he suggested, "as an exercise, you can translate some of the Psalms into Latin. The children will be familiar with those."

"Jacob, that's brilliant!" Zerah exclaimed. He jumped up and hurried over to rummage in a chest at one end of the room, muttering, "I know they're in here somewhere. Ah, yes, I have found them." He emerged holding up a roll of blank paper and a stylus. "All we need to do is mix up some ink."

Clearly alarmed now, Gallus looked from Jacob to Zerah and back again. "I can't do that. I don't know your psalms well enough...."

"I do," Jacob said. "My hands are working, but my mind isn't occupied. I will say them for you. You translate them and write them down."

Zerah sat next to him, huffing a little in his excitement. "Actually, I was thinking you should recite some of the prophets—perhaps Isaiah. But start with the psalm that begins, "My God, my God, why hast thou forsaken me?"

Puzzled, he put his beads and cords down. With a frown Jacob asked, "Why that one?"

"Go ahead and recite it," the priest urged, "You will see what I mean."

He closed his eyes a moment to gather his memory before he began,

"My God, my God, why hast Thou forsaken me, and art so far from saving me,
    from heeding my groans?
    Oh my God, I cry in the daytime, but Thou dost not answer,
    In the night I cry, but get no respite...."

The room went silent as a tomb. Even Odelia had stopped her bustling and stood quiet to listen. He went on, wondering why Zerah chose such a heart-rending psalm.

"My strength drains away like water, and all my bones are loose.
    My heart has turned to wax, and melts within me.
    My mouth is dry as a potsherd, and my tongue sticks to my jaw...."

Gallus stood up suddenly, jarring the table. "Crucifixion," he muttered. "You speak of crucifixion."

Jacob felt the blood drain from his face. He turned to Zerah, who nodded. "I wasn't there when Jesus was crucified, but my friends who were told me that the Lord spoke those very words, 'My God, my God, why hast thou forsaken me?' while he was hanging on the cross." Zerah paused to let his words sink in. "The psalm is also prophecy." He looked up at Gallus. "Many of your countrymen will turn to the Lord and be saved. Don't you think they should have the prophecies to read for themselves?"

Gallus sank down again, this time to his knees. "Sir, I am not adequate...."

"Of course you aren't," Zerah replied brusquely. "The three of us together are not adequate. But are you willing?" When Gallus did not reply, he added, "I believe someday the Word of God will be for all people everywhere. Men of every nation will read for themselves, in their own language, and know what a sacrifice has been made for them." His voice trailed off, "Not soon, but someday."

He heaved himself to his feet again, and going to the fire, scooped a handful of ashes into a bowl and adding a few drops of water, mixed some ink. This he set in front of Gallus. "See what you can do." With that, he retired to his corner again.

Jacob watched Gallus with interest. The former soldier had told him that he once helped to draw maps for his officers. *But writing is more precise. Will he be able to write with his left hand?*

Gallus picked up the stylus, and dipped it into the ink with one smooth motion. "Say the first line to me again." When Jacob had repeated it, he set the stylus to paper, and—to Jacob's astonishment—began to write without hesitation.

When he had finished the first line, Jacob said, "You write very well with your left hand."

Without looking up at him, Gallus replied, "I am left-handed. Now what is the next line?"

* * * * *

Jacob wove in and out through the throngs in the streets the next morning, trying to hurry, but unable to suppress several huge yawns that threatened to crack his jaw. He and Gallus had stayed up—at Gallus' insistence—until the entire psalm was translated onto paper in Latin. He didn't know what hour he finally fell into bed, but it was far later than he was used to, and this morning he could hardly pry his eyes open.

I wonder if Zerah is right, that the scriptures will someday be translated into every tongue on the earth. He shook his head, recalling the work it took just to do one psalm. The two of them had recited, and talked, and questioned, and argued far into the night. *What a daunting task translating all the scriptures will be! Why, it will take hundreds of scribes—thousands. And then there will have to be copies made.* Even as his head swam with the enormity of the task, he smiled. *But we did a bit. We started. I wonder what Arin would think of all this?*

His uncle Joel found him at mid-day, sitting on the step of the shop eating his lunch. "Tomorrow is Sabbath," he said. "Mary and I want you to come out to the house and spend it with us."

"Do you want us to come tonight?" Jacob asked.

Joel said, "I meant just you this time—by yourself. And yes, I think it would be a good idea if you'd go ahead and come right after work. I'll stop in at Zerah's and let him know."

Jacob puzzled over the strange invitation. Always before, they had all shared the Sabbath rest together, whether at Joel's house, or in Damascus at Zerah's. *Why do they want me there, and not the others? Odelia is Mary's mother. Why did they not invite her?*

Attalus didn't give him much time to think about it. "Jacob," he called minutes later. "Come back inside. We have to finish this order."

"Yes, sir." He dutifully got to his feet.

The rest of the afternoon passed quickly, as Attalus kept him busy running from one task to the next. Just before sundown, he handed him his pay. "Good work, boy. I will see you the day after tomorrow."

Jacob slipped the coins into his purse. "Thank you, sir. Good Sabbath!"

Attalus grinned. He wasn't Jewish, but one day of rest in seven had always made sense to him, so he closed shop along with his Jewish neighbors. "Good Sabbath to you as well."

Jacob hurried north through the city, stopping just long enough to purchase a few extra loaves of bread, and emerged from the northern gate at the moment the sun's torch lit the rim of the western mountains, setting the clouds ablaze with flaming tongues of orange and rose-pink. He trotted most of the way to his uncle's house. The fiery clouds had cooled to shades of purple by the time he arrived at the path leading to the door. There he stopped for a minute to catch his breath.

Joel must have been watching for him, because he opened the door and started down the path to meet him. "That was quick! Did you run all the way, lad?"

Jacob grinned, "Just about. Since I was by myself, I didn't want to be out here after dark."

Joel took the bread from him and slipped an arm around his shoulder. "Good thinking." He led him to the door and stopped just before he opened it. "I know you're wondering why I asked you to come, and not the others." When Jacob nodded, he said, "There is someone here who wants to see you." With that, he pushed the door open.

Jacob's first thought was, *Father!* but when the door opened he saw another boy, someone about his own age. Even though he had never met him, one look at his face told Jacob who he was. Mary was facing him, and between them stood another woman with her back to him. When he crossed the threshold, Mary whispered to this other woman, and she turned around, her dark eyes wide with hopeful apprehension. He took a step toward her without knowing it.

Her hands went to her throat. "Jacob," he heard her whisper. "Jacob, my son."

"Mama." Moments later, for the first time in fourteen years, he was in her arms.

* * * * *

Diana was unusually quiet on the journey from Jerusalem to Caesarea. She sat perched high atop a camel in a covered litter, occasionally complaining of the cold, taking little interest in where they were going. Caleb had tried several times, unsuccessfully, to draw her out. Finally he decided to leave her alone to sulk. *This is how it has to be,* he told himself.

"I don't see why you're hiring a camel for me instead of a horse," she had complained the day before they set out. "I would prefer a horse."

"I'm sure you would," Caleb answered. "But how would you carry Andrew?"

"Prisca can carry him."

"Really?" *A feral dog has better maternal instincts than my wife does!* Caleb shook his head. "You cannot expect Prisca to carry him all the way to Caesarea."

"You help her, then," Diana retorted. "You can take turns."

Caleb raised one eyebrow. "And what happens when he wants to nurse?"

"Then we will stop long enough to let him...."

He held up a hand to indicate he'd heard enough. "I bought the nicest litter I could find for you, and you will ride the camel. With Andrew." Hence the pouting.

Prisca, on the other hand, had never set foot outside Jerusalem, and the journey was a grand adventure for her. She walked alongside her father, taking a child's natural delight in everything the countryside had to offer. "What are those men doing over there, Papa?"

"They're sowing wheat for next year," he answered. "And they're a little late getting to it. But it rained all last week, and I suppose that delayed them."

"Do we buy our wheat from them?"

Caleb smiled. "We buy it from the market in Jerusalem, and the market sellers buy it from the farmers. It's possible that we've eaten some of their wheat."

"You said we're going north," she remarked a little later.

"We're going west first. When we get to the Great Sea, we'll turn north. Caesarea is north and west of Jerusalem."

"So this way is west?" She pointed ahead.

"That's right, and sometime tomorrow we'll be at the Great Sea."

"What's that way?" Prisca pointed behind them.

"The Jordan river, and beyond that, there is a great desert."

"So we are between the Great Sea and the Great Desert?"

Caleb laughed. "So we are—caught between two extremes."

She watched her feet take the next few steps. "I'm glad we're going to the sea, and not to the desert."

"Are you? Why is that?"

"The sea is better," she declared solemnly. "There's no water in the desert."

"Well, there is water," he told her. "It's just hard to find. You have to know where to look. But I think I like the sea better, too. You want to lead the camel a while?" He handed the lead rope to her, and she took it with both hands, glancing back over her shoulder now and then, apparently mystified that the enormous beast was under her control.

* * * * *

It was Salome who spotted them first. "Mama!" she called, jumping up and down in her excitement, "Papa! They're here! They're coming!"

Leah grinned, "Calm down, Salome. They won't get here any faster just because you're yelling."

Phillip look his youngest by the hand. "We'll go out to meet them." Lyssa jumped up and went with them. Arin stayed in the house, helping their mother get dinner ready. She was glad for the excuse not to go out. Ever since Papa received the message that they were coming, she had been floundering in mixed emotions about the visit. She had never met Prisca, and was curious to see whether she was like Jacob at all. On the other hand, she wondered how she would ever be able to welcome Jacob's father—even though he was her future father-in-law. *He sent his own son away. How could he do that? How could any father do that?*

"Men make mistakes," Phillip told her when she broached the subject with him. "I think Caleb knows now that sending Jacob away was a mistake. Don't take offense at him, Arin. He will have to pay the consequences of his decisions."

And there was the matter of her vision. Would Papa tell him about it, and would she have to repeat what she saw to Jacob's father? She hoped not. Once she had told it to Jacob, she stopped seeing it, and she had no desire to visit that horror again.

"Arin, is the bread ready to bake now?"

Leah's question drew her out of her reverie. "Almost. I just have to shape them." She stopped kneading and divided the dough into balls. As she finished pounding them into flat circles, she heard voices at the door. Phillip came in first, and a chill wind hurried past him into the house. Arin shivered. *Winter comes early this year.* Jacob's father came in next, carrying his baby boy in his arms. He was followed by Diana, whose tight-lipped expression mimicked Grandmother Eunice perfectly. *I could have met her anywhere,* Arin thought, *and even if I didn't know her, I'd know whose daughter she is.* Prisca followed close behind, flanked by Salome and Lyssa. The three of them were holding hands, and Arin smiled. Prisca, at least, would feel no lack of welcome.

Leah went to Diana and kissed her cheek. "Welcome to our home." She clasped Diana's hands between her own. "But you're so cold! I've made a broth for you. It's nice and hot. Let me get you some." On her way back to the fire, she chucked Andrew under the chin and laughed when he ducked his head and giggled. Arin had already dished up a cup of the broth, and she handed it to her mother, who took it to Diana. "Here, wrap your hands around this. It'll warm you up."

Diana sniffed at it suspiciously. "What's in it?"

Leah's smile faltered. "It's lamb, and I stewed it with lentils and barley, a few vegetables, and some spices."

It was Arin's favorite soup, and she had helped Leah begin it the day before, washing and soaking the lentils, and roasting and cutting the meat. She had drawn water the first thing this morning, and they'd cut the vegetables and started the soup cooking. It had bubbled on the fire for hours, and the whole house was full of its fragrance.

Diana took a sip, and gave Leah a wan smile. "At least it's warm." Ignoring her husband's glower, she sat herself down on a cushion at the table. She sipped at the soup and looked around her with an expression of dismay, as if to say, "Am I really going to have to spend the night here?"

All Arin could think of was the cooking and cleaning they had done to get ready for their visitors. *How dare she? How dare she treat my mother that way?*

Her face must have reflected her indignation, for the next thing she knew, her mother's arms were around her. Leah whispered into her ear. "Don't be angry on my account, daughter. I knew Diana would be this way. In truth, I'd have been surprised if she acted differently." She pulled back, studied Arin's face, and said, "We'll talk later. For now, I need your help. Concentrate on making our guests feel welcome."

"Yes, Mama," Arin murmured. She started setting dishes of food out on the table, stepping gingerly around Diana as she went.

When they sat down to eat, the girls settled at one end of the table, and the men at the other, with the two women in between. Arin kept one ear on the chatter of Prisca and her sisters, while she watched the exchanges between the adults. Leah tried several times to start a conversation with Diana, but she retreated into one-word answers and indifferent shrugs of her shoulders.

"Tell me about Jacob," she heard Caleb ask her father, and her attention turned fully to the other end of the table.

"Yes," Diana said. "Tell us about Jacob." When Caleb gave her a puzzled frown, she said, "We were in such a hurry to leave Jerusalem, we didn't have much time to talk." She arched her brows at her husband. "He is the reason we're here, is he not?"

Phillip's eyes were full of sympathy for his friend as he said, "We all went to see him in the summer."

"He isn't here, then?" Diana asked.

"No, he's...elsewhere." Phillip smiled at Caleb. "You would be proud of him. He's working for a glass maker, learning that trade, and by all accounts doing very well."

Diana toyed with the bread in her hands. "Why will you not tell us where he is? Caleb will have to know, after all, if he's going to find Jacob and save him from..." she waved the bread vaguely in the air, "...whoever it is that's looking for him."

Caleb's eyes narrowed on her. "Did I say someone was looking for him?"

She lifted her shoulders. "I suppose not. I just assumed...."

"All I said," he cut in with a growl "was that I wanted to go and find him and bring him home."

"Bring him home to what? You sold the house."

Arin felt a stirring in her spirit, a warning. Something was terribly wrong. Her own parents argued at times, but always privately, and never in someone else's home. This man and his wife—she had a hard time thinking of them as her uncle and aunt—were starting a fight, openly, and as guests in her parents' house. But there was something else, something about Diana that bothered her far beyond the woman's rudeness and disregard. It was as if everyone at the table was sitting in the light, except Diana. Some shadow, some darkness hovered over her, an umbra that mere light did not penetrate. *I've never sensed anything like this.* She glanced at her father, and was surprised to see grief etched in the lines of his face. *Does he see it, too? I'll have to ask him later.*

All conversation at the table ceased. Even the little girls quieted their chatter, reflecting the tension that radiated from the opposite end of the table. Finally Phillip said, "We will talk of this another time. Caleb, how is your sister?"

The muscles in Caleb's face visibly relaxed. "She is doing well, and she sends you her greetings. She had her baby late in the summer. He is healthy and strong, but his left hand is damaged."

"Oh, the poor little thing!" Leah exclaimed. "Was it because of Deborah's fall?"

"The physician thinks so," Caleb nodded. "Deborah is still holding out hope that it will mend with time."

Phillip smiled, and the whole room seemed to warm with the light of it. "We will pray that it will. Your sister is one of the kindest people I've ever known." He chuckled, "I even asked her one time if she'd adopt me and make me her brother, too."

Arin heard a sharp intake of breath and looked at Diana. Her face had gone white, except for two spots of high color on her cheeks. Phillip quickly added, "I meant no insult to you, dear one. You were still far away in Ephesus at the time. I guess I missed your company." He got on his knees and leaned across the table to kiss her.

She accepted his peace offering without comment, and then folded her hands in her lap and refused to eat any more, even when Leah brought out a bowl of honeyed dates. The other adults abandoned their efforts to include her in the fellowship. Leah took Andrew from Caleb and played with him, chattering and cooing—"What a wonderful boy you are! What a blessing!"—and laughed when he tried to put his fingers in her mouth. Finally, worn out from the attention, he laid his head on her shoulder, and she stroked his back and hummed to him under her breath until he fell asleep. Arin didn't miss the look of sad longing in Caleb's eyes when he glanced her mother's way.

"How long can you stay with us?" Phillip asked.

"Not long, but I hope to come back through here once I've found Jacob," Caleb answered. "I intend to go as soon as I can book passage to Ephesus for Diana and the children."

Phillip nodded. "I'll go with you tomorrow and help you find a ship. You'll want to get them away quickly, before winter sets in."

"It's been so long since I traveled, I appreciate any help you can give me," Caleb answered.

"I am getting a headache," Diana announced. "Where do you want us to sleep tonight? On the roof?" She spoke lightly, as if in jest, but her smile sent a shiver up Arin's back.

Leah chose to accept it with good humor. "Oh no, we'd never do that to you, Diana—not in this weather. The men can sleep up there, and we women will take the house."

Phillip laughed, "That will be refreshing! Actually, we want you and Caleb to have our room, and we'll sleep out here with the children tonight."

"How cozy." Diana murmured. "Caleb, did you bring our things in?" With that, she excused herself, and retreating to the other room, drew the curtain closed.

Phillip let out a long sigh. Caleb cleared his throat. "I apologize for my wife's behavior. She's been like this since I told her we were leaving Jerusalem."

"I'm sure she feels uprooted..." Leah began.

"It's no excuse," he answered. "Well, I suppose she'll be happier when she gets to Ephesus."

Phillip shook his head. "No, my sister carries her miseries and offenses like a standard—holding them high and waving them proudly. And once she gets home, our mother will pet and coddle her, and give those offenses plenty of room to flourish."

"What can I do?" Caleb asked. He rubbed at his brow as if trying to erase the lines of worry and fatigue that had settled there. "I couldn't leave her alone in Jerusalem. Frankly, even if I had the money to do that, I don't trust her. And there's no one I know well enough to look after her except Deborah, and Deborah has more than enough to handle, between seeing to her family and to Father."

"You could leave Diana here," Leah offered.

Caleb barked out a laugh of disbelief. "What? After the way she's treated you tonight? If it were me, she'd be about as welcome as a toothache."

"Perhaps after a few days she'll warm up to us. Truly, Caleb, I wouldn't mind."

Caleb turned to Phillip. "You are most fortunate in your wife, my friend." Then he shook his head. "But I think it will be best if I send her on. When I have found Jacob, I'll take him with me, and we'll go up to Ephesus. I have never been there, and I'd like to see it. And Jacob and Gedeon have a certain fondness for each other."

Phillip laid a hand on his shoulder. "You, Caleb, are most fortunate in your son. We'll talk more about him tomorrow. There are some things I want to tell you."

* * * * *

Phillip and Leah bedded down with the girls in the main room. Phillip only had to tell them to stop giggling a few times before they drifted, one by one, into sleep. Arin stayed awake the longest. The cold wind out of the north had scrubbed the clouds from the sky, and the half-moon sent a timid ray or two of light peeking in through the shuttered windows.

Jacob's parents must fight like that all the time. Why do they do that? Can they not hear how they sound? And Jacob grew up listening to them. The murmuring voices of her mother and father across the room, quiet and low, touched and caressed her, soothed her troubled heart until it fell still. *I am most fortunate in my parents. Thank you, Lord,* she thought as sleep overtook her.

* * * * *

Jacob and Jonathan spent the first hour of that Sabbath in a kind of slow dance, each one eyeing the other, sizing the other up, the way Roman athletes did before they wrestled. After his initial embrace of his mother, he wanted to hold her at arm's length, too—to study her. But Miriam would not permit it. She held his hand and would not let it go, as if to reassure herself he was really there. Jacob didn't have the heart to push her away, and when Mary set dinner on the table—a feast of lamb, cooked eggs, dates and olives, and the loaves of bread Jacob had bought—Miriam sat down next to him.

"Tell me about yourself, son. I want to know what you have been doing." She tore a loaf in half, laid it in front of him, and lightly touched his hand.

Where do I begin? The present seemed reasonably safe. "I am working for a glass maker, a Damascene named Attalus, and learning the trade," he said. "I live with a priest who came with Joel from Jerusalem."

"You're a glass maker." Miriam smiled him, and then at Jonathan. "That is something new for our family."

Glancing over at Mary, Jacob noted she was wearing the necklace he made for her. *I wish I had one of those with me now to give to my mother. I'll go get one when Sabbath is over—the red one, I think.* "You have a vineyard, don't you?"

Miriam nodded and smiled at Jonathan, encouraging him to answer. "The whole family works it," he said.

Jacob glanced at Miriam, but asked Jonathan, "You have other brothers and sisters?"

Jonathan broke open a cooked egg. "One brother and one little sister. We all help Papa with the vines."

"I have a little sister, too," Jacob said, "and a baby brother...." He stopped and colored when he realized what he was saying—and to whom.

"It's all right, Jacob," Joel said. "Your mother knows."

Miriam patted his shoulder. "It's good that your father has other children. I would grieve for him if he didn't. I truly hope he's as happy with his family as I am with mine." She offered him a tender smile. "Tell me about your sister."

"Her name is Prisca. She's nine years old." He stopped, walled in by all the things he wanted to say, but couldn't.

"She loves you," Miriam finished for him. "You are her protector." He nodded and ducked his head. "As Jonathan is for our little Abigail."

He wiped his eyes on his sleeve. "You named her for Grandmother."

"We did, yes." Perhaps sensing Jacob's growing emotional distress, Miriam changed the subject. "Tell me about your glass blowing."

"Well, I don't actually do the blowing myself," he began, but her dark eyes on him were encouraging, she seemed eager to hear whatever he had to say, to know everything about him. More than that, she made him feel as if he was better than he really was, that his life was somehow bigger, and grander than he thought of it himself. The way she listened to him reminded him of Arin. He described his work, all the while thinking, *I can see why Father married her.*

Later that evening, Jacob and Jonathan bedded down at one end of Joel's one-room house. Jonathan whispered, "You're fifteen, aren't you?"

"I'll be sixteen in the spring," he answered, turning on his side to face his brother.

"You're only a year older than I am."

Jacob frowned, "Were you born after...?"

Jonathan's face hardened. "Yes, after he divorced her."

"Did you know about me—before now?"

"Mother told me about you several years ago." Jonathan raised up on one elbow and propped his head on his hand. "Did you know about me?"

"Not until a few days before I left Jerusalem. Uncle Joel told me."

"You mean *he* never told you? Your father?"

Now Jacob raised up and mirrored his brother's position. "He is your father, too, you know."

Jonathan shook his head in denial. "Reuel is my father. He raised me."

Jacob could not think of a retort to that, and he lay back down and stared at the ceiling.

"What is he like?"

He turned over again. "What is Father like?" Jonathan didn't answer, but he didn't need to. Jacob searched his heart before answering, "He's a good man. He really is, Jonathan. What he did to our mother was wrong, but I think he was deceived. He's been a good father to me. I miss him."

Now Jonathan turned on his stomach and raised himself on both elbows. He leaned toward Jacob and whispered. "I can't think of him as my father because he doesn't think of me as his son."

"He was deceived," Jacob repeated. "If he had known, he would have...." His voice trailed off to follow his thoughts, and when he caught hold of the truth, breathed, "Oh...."

"He would have what?"

Jacob's eyes turned back to his brother. "He would have taken you away from her. He would have raised you in Jerusalem and sent her away by herself." A new thought made him raise up again. This time, his face was only inches away from Jonathan's. "Maybe he left you with her on purpose. Because he didn't want Mother to be alone."

"I cannot believe that." When Jacob started to protest, he added, "Look, maybe he is a good man, as you say. Maybe he was deceived. All I know is that our mother was innocent, and he sent her away." Jonathan's face closed, hard as a fist. "He sent me away."

Jacob swallowed and he lay down again. How could he defend their father? *He sent me away, too.*

"Maybe you could come with us when we go back to Antioch."

Jacob turned and stared at his brother in stunned silence. "You want me to go with you?"

A glimmer of humor touched the edges of Jonathan's eyes. "I believe that's what I just said."

Lacing his fingers behind his head, Jacob said, "It's a long way to Antioch, isn't it?"

"It took us nearly two weeks to get here," he replied, "and the weather was with us."

"I...I'd like to," he admitted, "but I need to think about it—and pray about it."

Now Jonathan did smile. "I hope you will. Good night, Jacob."

"Good night, Jonathan."

Jacob lay awake for a long time that night, listening to his brother's breathing as it deepened to the steady rhythm of sleep. Silently, he got up onto his knees and bowed his head. *Lord, should I go? What do I have holding me here? Zerah and Gallus are my friends. Joel is my uncle. Would any of them miss me if I left? I have work, but there are probably a hundred boys my age in Damascus who could do what I do. I have a mother and a brother. Should I not go with them? Don't I truly belong with them? What do You want me to do?* With a pang, he reminded himself, *It would put me much farther away from Arin. And from my father.* Tears filled his eyes, and he covered his mouth to suppress a sob. *Lord, what about my father?*

* * * * *

On the first day of the week, Jacob hurried back into the city even before the sun rose from its barren bed in the eastern desert. He went to Zerah's first and retrieved the necklace he wanted to give his mother.

Zerah tried to stop him. "Jacob, tell me how your visit with your mother went."

He paused at the door, one hand on the latch. "It was good, sir. I need to get to work now. I'll tell you all about it at noon."

Zerah laughed and waved him off. "Go on then." Jacob heard him say to Odelia as he closed the door behind him, "I'm glad I don't have to rush around like that anymore!"

When he got to Attalus' shop, he said, "Sir, I need to talk to you."

"Talk while we work," his master answered. He pointed to a missive lying on the table that served him for a desk. "Here's a letter I want you to translate. But go ahead and bring the sand around to the back for me."

As they got ready to begin the day, Jacob told him about his mother and brother.

"And you haven't seen them in all these years?" Attalus' eyes were round with disbelief.

Jacob set a bag of sand down near the oven. "That's right." He sighed, "That's a story too long to tell. But they have invited me to go with them to Antioch."

Attalus' hands went to his hips. "Antioch." He turned away and opened a bag of antimony. "That's a long way."

"Yes, sir. It is a long way." He bit his lip. "I'll go get a load of wood."

"Jacob, wait." The big man sat heavily on a bench and studied his apprentice for a long moment. Finally he smiled, though his eyes remained serious. "It just so happens I have a relative in Antioch—a cousin. He isn't a glass blower, but he trades in glass. Remember that shipment we sent out three weeks ago?"

"The one with all the blue glass?" Attalus nodded, and Jacob asked, "That went to your cousin?"

"It did." His eyes narrowed. "For years I have been paying caravans to take my glass up there, but caravans are not as reliable as an agent would be—someone who understood my business and worked directly for me. Perhaps it's time I hired an agent."

Jacob had been untying the cords on the bag of sand. Now his fingers stilled on their own. "Do you mean you want me...?"

"I think you can do it. It's a big responsibility for a young man. But you have been faithful in your work. You can travel between here and there, see your mother and brother, see your friends and family here."

Jacob could hardly believe his good fortune. "How often do you send glass that way, sir?"

Attalus shrugged. "About once every two months. You take the glass there, deliver it to my cousin. He pays you, and you bring the money to me. Sometimes there will be other things for you to bring back, other merchandise."

Seeing this as an answer to his prayer, Jacob said, "This is far better than I hoped for, sir. I really didn't want to quit working for you."

"But you felt you had to. I understand." Attalus stood up. "Let's get back to work. We'll hammer out the details this afternoon."

At midday he ran to Zerah's again, stayed just long enough to bolt down some lunch and tell about his Sabbath with his mother and brother. He couldn't yet bear to talk to the priest about leaving. *I'll do that tonight,* he decided.

On his way back to the shop, a young man a little older than himself stopped him. "Are you Jacob, son of Miriam?"

"I am," he answered. "What do you want?"

"Your mother is here in the city," the youth answered. "She needs to speak to you right now. It's a matter of some urgency."

"Where is she?"

But the stranger had already turned away, leaving Jacob to follow. He looked back over his shoulder once and called, "This way. Hurry!"

He led Jacob down an unfamiliar side street, and before he knew it, he was lost in the ancient maze of old Damascus. The stranger stopped at the door of an unkempt house, and drew aside a stained curtain that served as a front door. "She's in here, and she's hurt."

"She's hurt?" Jacob stepped in, and before he had time to wonder where Jonathan was, or to even peer into the darkened room, a sharp blow to the back of his head sent stars careening across his vision and rendered him senseless before he hit the floor.

Chapter 13

Caleb left Caesarea with a heavy heart. Diana was gone with Andrew to Ephesus, and Prisca remained behind with Phillip's family. *It didn't turn out the way I intended.*

Two days before, he and Phillip had gone down to the wharf to book passage on a ship to take Diana and the children to Gedeon's home in Ephesus. They talked to several captains before finding the one they wanted. When they came back to the house Phillip said, "We have a ship for you, Diana. It's leaving the day after tomorrow."

Caleb added, "And there will be another family on board, so you and the children will have company."

"Were there no ships leaving sooner?" Diana asked.

"One was," Caleb answered. "What was its name, Phillip? The Eagle? It's leaving with the tide tomorrow, but it's a smaller vessel. You'll be far more comfortable on this other ship."

Diana lifted one shoulder in her characteristic shrug. "As you wish."

Later, in the deepest hours of the night, Prisca roused them all with a shriek. Caleb jumped out of bed and hurried to comfort her, but when he reached her, she was already surrounded by the loving arms of Phillip's girls. They cradled and petted her, soothing her with gentle words.

Caleb knelt down beside them. "Did you have another bad dream, love?"

"Yes, Papa." Her voice caught with a sob. "The bad man got Jacob."

He started to tell her that Jacob was all right, that the bad man didn't have him, when he was interrupted. "Oh, not again!" Diana's impatient sigh behind him was like vinegar in his teeth. "Prisca, you really must get hold of yourself. You can't be doing this to me all the way to Ephesus."

Prisca wiped her eyes with a sniff, and avoiding her mother's eyes, leaned forward and whispered, "Papa, I don't want to go to Ephesus."

Caleb sat down on the floor and pulled her into his lap. "Don't you want to see your Papi?"

"I want to stay here." She laid her head against his shoulder.

"Oh really, Prisca," Diana broke in with a snort, "you can't mean that." When Caleb looked up at her with a frown, she changed to a cajoling tone. "Don't you want to go stay in the nice, big house in Ephesus?"

Without a word, Prisca shook her head. He held her for a while, until his wife's footsteps told him she had given up and retreated to the bedroom. "Are you feeling better now?"

"Yes, Papa." Another of the long sighs he'd begun to hear from her.

He kissed the top of her head. *She sounds like she carries the weight of the world on her little shoulders.* "We'll talk about it tomorrow," he promised her. "Go back to sleep now." He released her and watched her climb back into the tangle of girls on the floor before he stood up.

"Caleb." Phillip sat up and motioned to him, so he crossed the room and sat on his heels next to his brother-in-law. "You know you can leave Prisca here. We'd be happy to keep her, for as long as you need."

Caleb nodded and ran his fingers through his hair. "Let me think about it. I suspect she'd be happier here."

The next day, he and Phillip went out again, this time to have a visit with Sheliel the tanner. "I don't know if he will remember anything about Simon's man hunter that will help you, but he may."

The visit turned out to be fruitless. Sheliel had already told all he knew, and by this time had forgotten much of what he had said. When they got back to the house, Leah met them, her eyes red with tears. "Caleb, I'm sorry. I tried to stop her."

Caleb rushed into the house, demanding, "What has she done?"

"She's gone." Leah stood there, wringing one end of her veil in her hands. "She took Andrew and left just after you did."

"Did she say where she was going?"

"All she said was, 'I'm going home.' I assume she meant to Ephesus."

Caleb and Phillip exchanged a look. Phillip said, "She must be taking the earlier ship."

The two of them raced to the wharf in time to see the ship bound for Ephesus disappear over the horizon. Caleb stood, his hands limp at his sides in defeat, watching the top of the sail until it was swallowed up by the sea.

"How could she do that?" Phillip murmured. "How could she leave her own daughter?"

Startled, Caleb asked, "What do you mean? Did she leave Prisca here?"

Phillip nodded. "I saw Prisca just before we ran out of the house. Diana took Andrew, but not Prisca."

Caleb's eyes wandered back out to the now-empty sea. He pulled his purse from beneath his robe and opened it. "Looks like she took about half of my money. She must have done it last night. Well, that will be plenty to get her home." He turned to Phillip with a sigh. "I'll have to accept your offer to keep Prisca until I get back with Jacob."

"Excuse me?" A short, stout man approached them, waving a scroll. Caleb recognized him as Caesarea's wharf master. "Is one of you the husband of the lady who just left? Elegant lady with a baby?"

"I am her husband," Caleb replied.

"She gave me a message for you, sir." He handed over the scroll, and added helpfully, "I can arrange for another ship to go out and intercept her."

Caleb unrolled the paper and scanned the message. It was scrawled in Diana's childish hand, and full of misspellings. *"Caleb, I am taking the babby and going home to my mother. Do not try to come after me, sinse you don't want us. I will not go back to Jerusallum. If you expet to see us agan, you will have to come to us. Diana."* He sighed and shook his head. "That won't be necessary." He rolled the scroll up, and slapped at the side of his leg with it. To Phillip's questioning look he said, "She's already on her way. Let her go."

The next morning, he kissed Prisca goodbye. "I'll be back as soon as I can. You be a good girl, and mind your aunt and uncle."

Her dark eyes, troubled and anxious, searched his. "I want to go, too, Papa. Why can't I go with you, ?"

"Because I need to hurry, my love. But I'll be back," he smiled and added, "and I might have a surprise for you." She returned his smile, threw her arms around his neck in a fierce hug, then wheeled around and ran back into the house.

Leah watched her go. "Have no worry on Prisca's account. We'll take good care of her. We won't spoil her—much."

He laughed and kissed his sister-in-law on the cheek. "Just treat her like one of your own."

He turned to embrace Phillip, who said, "Give our love to Jacob. You remember the directions to Zerah's?"

Caleb nodded. "If all is well, I'll see you soon."

* * * * *

Jacob came to suddenly, the way light bursts into a room when the shutters are flung open to the sun. But when he opened his eyes, all he could see was sackcloth. Someone had pulled a bag over his head, and the same rough cloth bound his mouth. He tried to spit it out, then to force it out with his tongue, but it wouldn't budge. He lay on his right side on planks of wood. The steady clopping of an animal's hooves on stone pavement, and the way the rough boards pummeled his ribs with every bump and lurch told him he was in some kind of conveyance. When he tried to move, to shift himself, he discovered that his hands were tightly bound behind him, so tightly that the ropes cut into his wrists. He turned his head, stirring up dust from beneath him. It filled his nose, and he sneezed.

"So you're awake," came a voice from somewhere above him. "If you value your life, you will keep still and quiet."

In desperate confusion he ignored the warning and tried his feet, but they, too were bound. *What is happening? Where am I?* He turned his head again, now wincing at the dull throb in the back of his skull. *Did somebody hit me?* Then he remembered. *That stranger. I followed him...he said Mother was hurt....* Blinking at the blur swimming in front of his eyes, Jacob tried to collect his scattered reason. *That had to be a ruse. But what if it wasn't? How did he know about her?* The cart continued to creak and jolt along the road. *How long have I been out? Have they missed me yet? Are they looking for me?* Finally accepting the futility of his struggle against his bonds, he lay still, and his thoughts turned heavenward. *Lord, You see me. Give me strength and wisdom. Deliver me from my enemies.*

After about another hour, the movement of the wagon slowed, and then stopped. The voice above him said, "I am going to unwrap you now. If you fight me, you will regret it. Nod if you understand."

When Jacob nodded, he felt a hand grasp the cloth of his mask from the side, and he was hauled into a sitting position. His aching head swam with the sudden movement, and the resulting dizziness was like a demon child that kept trying to push him over on his other side. He finally won the struggle to sip upright, and in the next moment, his mask was whipped away, and he found himself face to face with a man in a gray robe.

He is from Simon. Jacob didn't know how he knew, but he was certain.

"Now I will remove the gag, and I expect some answers." The man in gray untied the knot of the gag—none too gently—and stood back.

Answers? What kind of answers does he expect from me?

"You are Jacob ben Caleb." This was not a question. "You ran away from your master, from Simon. Why? And why did he send me to look for you?"

Remembering the sting of Simon's lash against his legs brought the old anger back. The heat of it filled him and gave him strength. It felt so much better than fear. Jacob held onto it and clamped his mouth shut.

The man in gray smiled, "You will tell me." Without changing expression, he backhanded him across the face.

A coppery taste of blood filled Jacob's mouth. He leaned over the edge of the cart and spat red onto the ground. Still holding on to his rage, he answered, "I ran away for my own reasons. I don't know why he sent you after me. Why don't you ask him?"

Another backhand to the other side of his face, and this time two gray men swam across his vision instead of one. He shook his head to clear it. Already he could feel his face swelling from the blows. For another moment, his anger sustained him, but when a chill wind cut through his clothing, he shivered and looked down. "No." he moaned aloud in horror. *This is a slave's tunic. Where is my robe? Where is my turban?*

The man in gray grinned at him. "Oh, it's not as bad as all that. I merely took the liberty of changing your clothing for something more useful. Think of it as a costume."

"Who are you?"

"You can call me Nimrod." The man's grin widened. "I am a hunter of great renown."

"A hunter?" Fear was back, making Jacob's voice sound small in his own ears.

"Instead of tracking animals, I track men and women. Runaways. Runaway slaves, runaway wives, runaway apprentices—such as your esteemed self. I find them and return them where they belong." The man began to pace back and forth as he spoke. "I have been looking for you for a long time. You have given me more trouble than three other runaways put together." As if he read Jacob's thoughts, he added, "Before you rejoice too much at that, you should understand that all this trouble makes me angry and impatient. Simon wants you back alive, but I don't think he'll mourn too deeply if I hand him your corpse instead."

He continued to pace, and stroked his chin, as if pondering some unanswerable cosmic enigma. "Another matter concerns me. Or perhaps I should say my curiosity is piqued." He stopped and faced Jacob with an expectant smile, his hands clasped behind his back in an awful parody of a schoolmaster. "Can you tell me why your own family wants you...shall we say...out of the way?"

Out of the way? The man in gray might as well have been speaking another language. Jacob's ears refused to process the words. His answer, spoken between swollen lips, "What do you mean?" came out in an almost unintelligible mumble.

The man's smile brightened until it was nearly radiant. "Members of your family have paid me to see to it that you never come back."

Jacob's stomach heaved with shock. If the man in gray had punched him, it would not have been more painful. He took a deep breath to fight his rising nausea. "You lie."

"Lie? Oh no. The truth is too much fun." He resumed his pacing. "I received money from one of your family members."

Jacob refused to believe it. "From who?"

"You'd like to know that, wouldn't you?" He leaned in close, as if to tell a secret, and his smile faded beneath his cold, gray eyes. "I am the one asking the questions. So far, your answers haven't been satisfactory."

The flame of Jacob's anger still flickered, and he drew on it, fanned it higher. He glared sullenly at "Nimrod" and clamped his aching jaw shut. His captor whipped his hand out again, this time in a fist, and knocked him back against the side of the cart. A trickle of blood snaked down his face from his forehead. *He is going to kill me.* Amazed to discover that this didn't frighten him, he struggled back to a sitting position.

"No slave looks at his master that way," the man in gray said smoothly, as if instructing a room full of students. "The ones who show anger and hatred are the ones who die first."

"I am not a slave."

"I could kill you for that," the man shook a finger at him, and grinned, "but it's true. You aren't a slave—yet. However, here is what is going to happen, and I advise you to pay attention if you want to reach Jerusalem alive."

Jerusalem! I got away once. I can do it again. Lord, help me find a way! He kept his eyes lowered, so that his captor couldn't see his thoughts.

"We are about an hour from an inn I know about. We will stop there for the night, but you will be bound for the entire journey. Simon told me how you got away from him the first time. Clever, but don't expect it to happen again—at least, not with me. If you start screeching for help, or if I find you've said anything to anyone—*anything*, do you understand?—I will gag you again. And if you persist in giving me difficulty, I will kill you."

Jacob shivered and nodded, his eyes averted. He had spent years tamping down and concealing feelings of anger toward his grandfather. *This is not so different,* he told himself. *I can do this. And I will get away, sooner or later.*

* * * * *

Caleb stepped through Damascus' massive gates that same afternoon. *Three days,* he told himself. *I made it in three days.* He hadn't eaten anything since the morning before, and felt a little light-headed after his climb up the road into the city, but for the sake of finishing the journey he ignored his stomach's rumbling and pushed on. Using the directions Phillip gave him, he wound through its streets until he came to the lane where Phillip said he would find Zerah's house. And there he stopped. Joel stood just outside the door—Caleb recognized him at once, though he hadn't seen him in several years—arguing with a man who appeared from the back to be Zerah's servant.

Neither man noticed him, and as he neared them, Joel said, "Zerah has no business going, and you know it. You come with me if you want, but we have to hurry if we're going to catch up with them." He stopped speaking when he saw Caleb, and his jaw dropped. As Gallus turned, Joel said, "You're too late. He's gone."

Caleb halted in his steps, and the bag he was carrying fell unheeded to the pavement. "He was taken?"

"We assume so, yes. His master came an hour ago to tell us that Jacob didn't come back to work this afternoon." He took a step toward Caleb. "Do you know who hunts him?"

Caleb nodded, burned by the glare in Gallus' pale eyes. "Phineas. Simon sent him. I came because of Jacob's friend, John Mark. He was on a journey, and

Phineas trailed him to Cyprus, thinking Jacob had gone with him. John Mark knew you were here, Joel. That's how the man was able to track him down."

To Caleb's relief, Gallus turned his silent scrutiny away from him and back to Joel. "We must leave immediately. If we hurry, we may reach Jerusalem before the man-hunter does."

"Or overtake him on the road," Joel turned to Caleb. "You have seen this Phineas? You know what he looks like?"

"I will know him if I see him."

Gallus started inside. "Let me put some things together, and we'll be away."

Caleb started to follow, but Joel caught his arm. "Wait. You may not want to go in. Miriam is in there."

Miriam. So the sting of my sins catches up to me at last. Caleb lowered his eyes and sighed deeply. "I have wounded too many innocent people, Joel. Now I will have to answer for it." He looked up. "But I thought she was in Antioch."

Joel's grip on his arm softened. "She came down the day before Sabbath. I had sent her a message to let her know Jacob was here."

"She got to see him—to have some time with him?" When Joel nodded, Caleb said, "I'm glad for that."

Joel had never released Caleb's arm, and now he gave it a tug. "Come. I think you should go inside after all."

He resisted the pull. "Won't it upset her?"

"She's already upset," Joel reminded him. "Perhaps seeing that you are looking for him will reassure her."

Without a word, he allowed himself to be led inside. Zerah was head-to-head with Gallus in quiet and urgent discussion on one end of the room. And Miriam—there she was, and she looked the same as he remembered, except for a touch of silver that swept through the raven waves at her temples. *This was my wife. How did I ever justify sending her away?* His heart almost stopped when she turned toward him, her dark eyes swollen with tears and shadowed by worry. *If Father hadn't interfered....* Caleb clenched his teeth with frustration. *But I allowed him to interfere. It was my fault.* He took a deep breath and went to her. He wanted to take her hand, but reminded himself, *It is not proper. She belongs to another now.* His hands knotted into fists at his side, and his throat closed up. He swallowed to clear it, without success, and when he spoke, his voice sounded harsh in the quiet room. "I did you a great injustice. The blame is mine alone. I hope someday you will forgive me."

A single tear tracked down Miriam's face. "I forgave you long ago, Caleb." She lifted her chin. "Now our boy needs you."

He nodded, his heart hammering painfully against his ribs. "I will find him, Miriam. Whatever it takes, I will bring him back to you."

A new voice broke in behind him. "I am going with you."

He turned, and felt all his blood drain from his face. *Jacob! No, not Jacob. This is his brother. This is my son.* Caleb's knees gave out, and he sank to the floor, gasping for breath.

"Caleb!" Dimly he heard cries from the others in the room, but his ears were inexplicably full of water, and the forms that hovered over him darkened and blurred to obscure shades. He felt a hand against the back of his neck, pushing him toward the floor, and he had no strength to resist. Moments after his forehead touched the cold stone, his hearing and vision started to clear. "Keep his head down!" he heard Gallus say. "Odelia, bring water." Caleb lifted one hand. *How is it so heavy?* A few seconds more, and he was able to sit up. He stammered, "I...I'm all right."

"Here, drink this." A cup was put to his lips. He sipped the cold water, swallowed, and felt the shock of it drop into his empty belly. He hauled in a deep breath and took another drink. "I'm all right," he repeated, shamed by his weakness. He couldn't raise his eyes. The boy was there, watching. *What must he think of me?*

Miriam sank down on her heels beside him. "When was the last time you ate?"

"Yesterday morning," he answered dully.

"Well, no wonder." He raised his eyes to hers. "I'll get you some of Odelia's stew. You can eat it while the others prepare to go." She stood up and moved away, leaving him to face his son.

Jonathan's eyes never left him, and the silence between them quickly became oppressive. Caleb felt exposed, naked. He hugged his arms to himself and cleared his throat. "You are named Jonathan." When the boy didn't answer, he added, "That is a good, strong name." More silence, and he had nothing else to say. To his enormous relief, Miriam came back and placed a bowl and a piece of bread into his trembling hands. He dipped the bread into the soup and asked, "Did you get to talk to your brother?"

"We talked last night," Jonathan answered.

Even his voice was similar to Jacob's. Caleb briefly closed his eyes. *Jacob. I was so close! If I had gotten here just a little sooner....*

"I am going with you," the boy repeated.

Caleb met his gaze before looking away. "It is not for me to say." He fell silent, struggling with this new pain. Finally he said, "I'm sorry, Jonathan."

* * * * *

In less than an hour, the four of them were on the road heading south out of Damascus with Gallus and Joel leading, and Caleb following with Jonathan at his side. None of them spoke much until after they crossed the river, and Caleb gathered the courage to ask Jonathan, "I am curious. Why did you want to come with us? You hardly know Jacob."

"He is my brother," Jonathan answered. And that was it. Apparently he felt no further need for explanation.

Caleb chewed on his lower lip. *Reuel fathered you well,* he thought. *Perhaps better than I would have done.* Aloud he said, "I am glad your mother and your uncle permitted it."

Jonathan shot him a questioning glance, but did not reply. Caleb spent the next hour sneaking looks at the boy, fascinated by this other son of his, but trying not to stare outright. Jonathan and Jacob were unquestionably brothers. They had the same unruly mop of curls, and their faces were cast from one mold, though Jonathan's eyes, a few shades lighter than his brother's, looked out above a generous scattering of freckles that Jacob didn't have. The biggest difference Caleb discerned was in the boys' build. Both were tall, but Jonathan looked somewhat stockier than his older brother. *Perhaps,* Caleb thought, *it is because he's worked more with his muscles, while Jacob has worked with his head.*

We're coming for you, Jacob. I wish you could see us. Surely it would strengthen your heart. I wish there was a way to let you know.

*   *   *   *   *

Jacob flexed his fingers, somewhat reassured that he still could, and that his hands still hurt. *At least I can feel them.* His feet were another matter. He had lost sensation in them sometime during the interminable night. *That was the longest night of my life,* he thought. *And perhaps one of the last.* In the darkest hours he came face to face with the reality that he might not live to see Jerusalem again. *What do You have in mind for me, Lord?*

Simon would not hesitate to kill him, he knew, and that he thought he could bear. But he also guessed torture would come first, though he still didn't understand Simon's need to hunt him down. *All I did was run away, but it doesn't matter, does it? Once he has me, he'll do whatever he wants, with no one to stop him. Just a few choice words to the authorities, and he can have me crucified.*

He thought about the crucifixions he had seen, and how his father always tried to shield his eyes from the horror. It was the worst kind of punishment he could imagine. *I don't know how I'd be able to stand it. But Uncle Phillip said the Lord Jesus went willingly to the cross. To save me from my sins. Grandfather never understood—never tried to understand. Lord, hide me in the shadow of your wing. You are my rock and my fortress. I will trust You. If You can use this—if You can use my suffering to bring my father to You, I gladly submit to your will. Glorify Yourself in me.*

The morning came slowly, but it did come. Jacob managed to doze off, and when he woke, Phineas stood over him, prodding him with his foot. (Jacob knew his captor's name now. The innkeeper had greeted him with it when they arrived.) "Sit up," he commanded. He did as he was told, and Phineas untied his hands. Moments later, he heard the clanking of cold iron. "Hold your hands out in front." Jacob did so. The deep gashes and livid purple bruises circling his wrists shocked, but did not surprise him. *It's probably a good thing I can't see my face, the way the son of a pig knocked me around yesterday.* Phineas clucked his tongue with feigned sympathy as he clapped iron manacles on him in place of the ropes. "You shouldn't fight your bonds so. You've hurt yourself."

He lowered his head to keep himself from spitting in Phineas' face. *Avenge me, my Lord!*

"I've had a lovely breakfast," Phineas told him as he secured another set of irons around his ankles. Jacob hardly felt the metal against his skin. His feet had gone numb. But he did feel the ache in his empty stomach. He had been given nothing the night before. "Fresh bread, and some nicely smoked fish, dried figs." He looked at Jacob with a smile. "You're hungry, aren't you, boy? Thirsty too, I'll wager. Well, too bad." With that, he hauled him to his feet. "It's time to go. Come along."

Jacob took one step after him, stumbled and fell to his knees. "I can't feel my feet," he panted.

With a growl, Phineas yanked him up again. "You'll walk under your own power, slave. If I have to carry you, it'll be because you're dead."

He took one uncertain step, and another. He had to watch himself walk, to concentrate on putting down the blocks of wood that his feet had become, and picking them up. In that way he made it out to the cart.

Phineas pushed him up into it. "We will be in Caesarea before nightfall," he said, and then grinned at the sudden surge of hope in Jacob's eyes. "Not that Caesarea. You *do* have friends there, don't you? I suspected as much. No, we're going to Caesarea Phillippi. We'll be nowhere near your friends."

Jacob tried to feign indifference, but he was crushed. And Phineas dashed his hopes even further when he added a chain that attached the manacles on his hands to the ones on his feet. "Just so you don't get any ideas about garroting me," he grinned. "Now lie down and be still. If you're cold, cover yourself with that canvas. Otherwise, be silent." With that, Phineas climbed onto the cart and flicked a lash at the donkey harnessed to it.

Jacob suppressed a groan as he lay down. It took some doing, but he wrestled with the length of heavy material until he was covered. By pulling his knees up and hugging his arms, he was nearly warm. But there was nothing to put under his head, and the movement of the cart kept jolting him, so he finally gave in and pillowed his head on one arm, trading warmth for the smallest measure of comfort.

A hawk screamed overhead, sending new shivers through him, and he tried in vain to burrow deeper beneath the cover. Finally, worn out with hunger and fatigue, he closed his eyes. *Lord, watch over my mother and brother to keep them safe. Thank You for letting me meet them.* One tear pushed out of his eye and trickled down his face. He thought of Arin, and had to cover his mouth to stifle a sob. *Lord, I know You speak to her. Will You not tell her where I am?* Several minutes of silent weeping followed, until he wiped his eyes on his sleeve, and lay his head down again, now utterly spent.

In the next moment, a deep, heavy warmth stole over him. A bit of a Psalm sang in his heart, gentle as a lullaby, *"You hem me in—behind and before; You have laid your hand upon me."* Along with the warmth came peace. Sheltered under the hand of God, Jacob sighed like a little child and fell asleep.

* * * * *

The old priest stood looking out the doorway of his home, heedless of the cold air swirling around his head, lifting the ends of his prayer shawl, and chilling the room behind him. Miriam watched him for a long time, and the way he held himself his shoulders stiff and hunched, along with an occasional sniff told her he was grieving. The thought of approaching him had her chewing her lower lip. She knew who he was. She remembered. And yet....

He loves my son. In the end, that enabled her to overcome her reluctance. "Sir?" She gave his shoulder the lightest touch. He turned, and she clearly saw her reflection in his glistening eyes. "I...I wonder if you would be willing to help me with something."

A spasm of pain briefly seized his face. A moment later, his features relaxed. "Sweet lady," he answered, "whatever I can do for you, I will."

"Do you have paper? I want to send a message."

"I have some," he turned inside and closed the door behind him. "Who do you want to send a message to?"

"My husband and I have an old friend who runs a caravan from Sidon to Jerusalem. He will probably be home this time of year—in Sidon, that is. He would be another pair of eyes to look for Jacob."

Zerah opened the lid of his trunk, then he paused and turned with a puzzled frown. "If he's home in Sidon, and the man-hunter is on his way to Jerusalem, how will sending him a message help you?"

Miriam ducked her head and toyed with the ends of her shawl. "I thought that he—the hunter, that is—might not go directly south. He might head for the coast instead, and take a ship south."

Zerah stared at the door, stroking his beard, "And if he does, Joel and Caleb will miss him completely."

Miriam nodded. "This friend of ours knows many people in the coastal area—traders, merchants, sea captains. If he puts the word out, it may be that someone will spot them. And even if they don't," she took a deep breath and let it out slowly, "it is still worth it to me to pay for the message." She wiped at the corner of one eye with trembling fingers. "Anything to find my boy."

"It is a good idea," he answered, pulling a short length of paper and stylus from the chest. He laid them on the table. "Now for ink." When he had mixed it up, he set it alongside the paper and looked at her. "I think I want some wine. Would you like some?" When she protested that she should get the wine for him, he chuckled, "I lived as a bachelor for a long time, and I'm still content to serve myself—and you, too."

While he had his back turned, Miriam sat down at the table, picked up the stylus, and dipped it in the ink. *How should I begin?* "To our friend and brother," she wrote. She paused there and looked up to see Zerah watching her with an expression of astonishment. "Is something wrong?" she asked him.

"You can read and write?" He set the wine down and sat across from her. "You may be the only daughter of Abraham I've ever met who could."

Miriam felt a blush rise to her face. "Caleb taught me how when I was deaf."

"Did he?" Zerah folded his arms on the table and leaned toward her. "Tell me about it—if you don't mind."

Odelia, who all this time had been tending to dinner over the cook fire now came and sat next to her husband, her eyes avid. "I want to hear this, too."

Zerah laughed, "Now don't you get any ideas!" He pulled her toward him and gave her a loud smacking kiss on the cheek. She pushed him away, but giggled like a newlywed at his attention.

Miriam smiled. "I don't know for sure why Caleb thought it was important to teach me—perhaps so he would have a way to talk to me. Whatever the reason, he was a good teacher. In the end, I was able to read and write without any problems, though by that time, I could hear."

"The Lord Jesus healed you."

She nodded. "We had a servant—though she was more like a mother to me than anything else. She took me to Jesus, and after he healed me, she and I went out often and listened to his teaching."

Zerah stroked his beard again and gazed at the ceiling. "I'm guessing that was during the time you lived in Capernaum."

"Yes. It probably wouldn't have happened if we'd stayed in Jerusalem."

Zerah's face colored in the pale winter light. "No doubt. No one in Lathan's household would have dared such a thing." He picked up his cup and drained it in one motion.

"Yet you were his friend."

He grunted. "Friendship with Lathan is a risky thing. Any proximity to him is dangerous." He met her eyes squarely. "You aren't the only person he drove out of Jerusalem—not even the first."

"Is he the reason you left and came here?"

Zerah nodded. "He discredited me." Then he shrugged, and with a rueful smile added, "But I saw it coming, and by that time I cared little what he might try to do. The biggest problem I had was shielding my wife, my Ruth, from the trouble." He turned his gaze to Odelia and patted her hand. "That was when she was ill—just before she died."

Miriam bowed her head. *Too many old memories, too many old hurts. For all of us.* She took a deep breath and straightening in the chair, picked up the stylus again to finish the greeting. "To our friend and brother, Joseph...."

* * * * *

Jacob didn't know what jerked him out of his slumber, but he was aware that the cart's movement had stopped. He lowered the canvas from his face. Phineas was not in the seat. His heart lurched, and started pounding. *Has he gone?* He swallowed and lay still, listening, but all he heard was the wind, and occasional creak from the donkey's harness. *No, he has to be here somewhere. And I can't get away—not with these chains.* But he sat up anyway, every nerve alert for the presence of his captor.

The cart was off the road, and the donkey's head lowered to the sparse grass at its feet. Jacob craned his neck one way, then the other, but Phineas was nowhere in sight. He shivered in the cold air, all the while looking around him. A cluster of boulders to his right offered the only hiding place he could see. *That's where he has to be—behind those rocks. How far would I get, I wonder, if I climbed into the seat and just drove away?* The thought was too tempting. As quietly as he could, he started toward the front of the cart. The reins were right there, tied to the seat. He stood to sit on the raised seat, and started to swing his legs over.

"I wouldn't do that if I were you," the mocking voice reached him from the boulders. Phineas stuck his head out and grinned at him. "Even if you succeed in turning the cart around and getting away, remember your chains. You are a slave, and no one will believe otherwise, no matter what you tell them. No one will help you."

Confused and weakened with hunger, he froze in indecision. Phineas spoke the truth. Who would dare help a runaway slave? He gazed around him. He didn't even know where he was. Now the hunter sauntered out from behind the rocks and started toward him, closing the gap between the boulders and the cart. Jacob ground his teeth in frustration with himself. *Why didn't I get away when I had the chance? What is wrong with me?* From deep within his spirit came a word of quiet counsel. *Be still.*

"I need to relieve myself," he muttered as Phineas approached the cart.

"Then get down and go do it," the man in gray replied. He offered no help, and Jacob had to figure out how to get down in his chains. He turned one way, and then another, and it quickly became apparent that he was going to fall no matter what he did. "Hurry up," Phineas growled.

Clenching his jaw against the cold, he half-dropped, half-fell out, landing on his left side. The rocks bruised his bare feet and his hip, but he didn't turn an ankle, or otherwise hurt himself. He pushed up off the ground and stumbled off to the relative privacy of the boulders.

"Watch out for snakes!" Phineas called out, and inexplicably laughed.

When he was done, Jacob leaned his head against one of the rocks. *Lord, I know You are with me—even here. I give myself over to You, my life, my future, everything. Do with me as You will.* He straightened up. Grandfather would scoff at such a prayer. But he could still sense the bidding in his spirit to be still. He took a deep, shaking breath and started back to the cart.

In another hour, Phineas said. "There it is—Caesarea Philippi—your home for the next few months."

Puzzled, Jacob said, "I thought you were taking me to Jerusalem."

"Oh, I am," Phineas assured him. "Just not right away. The timing of these things is vital." He gave no further explanation, and Jacob asked no more questions. He didn't want to hear any more. The man's voice was poison in his ears.

Caesarea Philippi, named by Phillip the Tetrarch in honor of the emperor and himself, perched on a triangular plateau under the watchful gaze of Mount Hermon to the northwest. Jacob had passed this mountain on the way to Damascus with Joel and Zerah, but now its three peaks were completely hidden under a heavy blanket of snow. The enormous height of the mountain had awed him in the spring. Now weight of all that stone loomed against the sky like a crushing threat.

He turned his attention to the city as they entered. They passed elaborate pagan temples of gleaming white marble that stood in sharp contrast with the red variegated stone of the cliffs behind them. Impressive palaces lined the broad street, much grander than anything he'd ever seen, but their lofty columns and wide porticoes only made him feel more alone, more of a stranger. All around him he heard snatches of Latin and Greek, and other languages he could not identify. Only rarely did he hear Hebrew or Aramaic. His heart sank. *I am farther from home here than*

I ever was in Damascus. As the cart rattled and bumped its way through the streets, he saw only a handful of people who looked or dressed like Jews. And fewer still noticed him in his thin tunic and chains. After all, what was one more slave among so many?

Phineas turned the cart onto a side street, and the buildings gradually became less ornate, and more utilitarian. Finally, he pulled back on the reins and stopped. When Jacob saw where they were, he thought he might faint. *A prison. He's going to put me in there and leave me. They'll never find me. They'll never even think to look for me here.*

Phineas got down and motioned to one of the sentries at the door. "Get him out of the cart, would you?" He tossed the soldier a silver coin.

The burly legionary came around to the back of the cart, reached in and grabbed Jacob's ankle chains, and with one powerful pull, hauled him out and set him on his feet. Without a word, he nodded to Phineas and took up his station again at the door.

While Jacob stood swaying, dazed and dismayed, Phineas looked over the building's edifice and smiled. "Home at last." He turned with an impatient gesture. "Come on. In you go."

Like a dumb animal being led to the slaughter, Jacob put his head down and followed his captor inside. He half-hoped the interior would be warmer than outside, but was disappointed to find it only darker—and reeking. *Just like the prison in Damascus,* he told himself. But here there would be no Joel to bring him bread, no Zerah to set him free.

"Is Tertius here?" Phineas asked the guard who met him inside.

"He's out, but he'll be back before nightfall." The guard shifted his uncurious gaze to Jacob.

"I need a cell for this one," Phineas said, handing over what looked like a much-used scroll. "Solitary. I don't want him to have any interaction with the other prisoners."

The guard scanned the missive and ran a thoughtful thumb along his jaw line. "I can arrange that. You want him fed?"

Phineas smirked. "Keep him alive."

"How long are you going to leave him here?"

"For the winter, I think. If I change my mind, I'll come and fetch him."

"What about his chains? You want them to stay on, or do I take them off?"

Phineas began fishing more coins out of his purse. "Once you lock him up, you can take the chains off his hands. Leave the ones on his feet."

The guard nodded. "You want to come and see the cell yourself?"

Phineas shook his head. "I'm sure you'll handle it correctly. Besides, I'm starving. It's past my dinner time." He glanced at Jacob and grinned. "The trip has made me hungry."

Moments later he was gone. The guard picked up a truncheon and eyed his new prisoner dubiously. "You aren't going to give me trouble, are you?"

Jacob shook his head sadly. "No sir."

The guard pointed toward a door with his club. "That way."

With his chains clanking against the cold floor, he stepped farther into the nightmare. The corridor, lined with iron-barred cells on either side, stank of filth and decay. Dark forms crouched on the floor. Some stood at the bars, their eyes gleaming at him in their dirt-crusted faces. The guard behind him carried a torch that cast Jacob's shadow into the cells as he passed.

"All right. Stop there." He halted at one of the doors and watched the guard raise the heavy bar that bolted it shut. The door swung open, and he stood blinking at the cramped, dirty cell inside. "Well, what are you waiting for?" A nudge on his back from the truncheon propelled him in. Seconds later came the echoing boom as the door shut behind him, and another as the bolt fell into place.

Chapter 14

I returned sooner than I imagined, Caleb thought as he began his ascent toward Jerusalem's southernmost gate. Their group had split up when they were within sight of the city, in hopes their arrival wouldn't be noticed. Jonathan and Joel went in through the Damascus gate, while Gallus circled around to the west and went in by the aqueduct. Caleb turned east, and taking the road toward Bethany, doubled back and crossed the Hinnom valley. Normally, he would not have chosen to go that way. Few did, except to haul their refuse out and throw it into the perpetual fires that burned in the belly of the valley. The stench of sewage and of burning, rotting carcasses made his eyes sting and water.

He passed a group of lepers huddled like a flock of vultures over—what? He didn't want to know. As he hurried by, one of them raised up to stare at him, and laid what was left of an ulcerated hand over the lower half of his face, rasping, "Unclean!" Caleb covered his own nose and mouth with a corner of his robe, and gasping for air, began the climb toward the gate. Even so, the irony didn't escape him that he was safer entering here than he would have been going through the Temple Gate. Gallus had made him shave off his beard, and cut his hair to look like a Roman, and he was wearing an old, threadbare robe he bought off a camel driver in Perea, but that was the extent of his disguise. He didn't want Simon to know he was back. Not yet.

Once inside the gate, he went straight to the Siloam pool and splashed generous handfuls of water onto his face, scrubbing at his skin with his fingertips to rid himself of the odor he'd picked up coming across the Hinnom. Then he sat on some nearby steps to wait. The others were going to meet him there.

He looked around him. A few women tended to laundry at the pool, but no one he recognized. He sat forward with his elbows on his knees, laced his fingers and lowered his head. He thought about going to Deborah's, but knew he didn't dare. *If Simon is watching for me, that's one of the places he'll look. As long as he thinks I'm out in the world somewhere looking for Jacob, he may keep him alive. Once he knows I'm here....* He clenched his jaw and pushed that thought away.

A hand laid on his shoulder caused his head to jerk up. It was Gallus. "I've found a room for us. Come."

* * * * *

Five paces by four paces. My world is reduced to five paces by four. In chains. If my feet were free, it would be fewer. The square on the door where I can see out is two hand lengths high and wide. They bring bread and water twice a day. Jacob leaned against the back wall of his cell, staring at the barred square.

'*But your spirit is free.*'

Jacob's bruised lips curled in a smile. *Yes, it is,* he answered the thought as if speaking to a close friend. *Uncle Phillip said it would be.* He gazed around the dark cell, and now that his eyes had adjusted, was able to make out every stone and joint of mortar, every scratch on the wall, every bit of straw on the floor. He murmured, "Thy word is a lamp to guide my feet, and a light on my path."

That single scripture brought back the memory of helping Gallus with translations. He said aloud, "Rescue me from my enemies, O my God, be my tower of strength against all who assail me, rescue me from evildoers, deliver me from men of blood. Savage men lie in wait for me, they lie in ambush ready to attack me; for no fault or guilt of mine, O Lord, innocent as I am, they run to take post against me. But thou, Lord God of Hosts, Israel's God, do thou bestir thyself at my call...."

By the time he'd finished reciting, "O thou my strength, I will raise a psalm to thee; for thou, O God art my strong tower," he felt encouraged. *Rabbi Sameas told us, 'In the day of trouble, recite the Scriptures so that the light of Heaven may shine on you.'* "You were right, Rabbi."

Jacob closed his eyes. "I lift up mine eyes unto the hills, from whence shall come my help. My help is from the Lord God, Maker of Heaven and of earth...." Without realizing it, he sang the words aloud.

"Shut up with that noise!" came a yell in Greek from down the corridor. One of the other prisoners.

Instead of being cowed, he thought of another psalm and translated it into Greek in his head. When he was sure he had it right, with an impish smile, he went right up to the door and started to sing—louder this time, "How good and pleasant it is when brothers live together in unity...." His singing wasn't so good this time, the translated words didn't quite fit the tune. But when the same voice started yelling again, another hushed him. "Shut up, fool. Leave the boy alone."

When he was finished, that voice called out, "Sing us another."

"They are written in Hebrew," he answered. "and I can't make the Greek fit the music."

A short silence followed. "Just speak them, then. You are not that good a singer anyway."

Jacob laughed. "All right." He thought for a minute, and began, "O Lord, you have searched me and you know me. You know when I sit and when I rise...."

In the middle of that psalm, he heard footsteps. One of the guards was coming down the corridor. *Should I stop?* Before he could decide, the steps halted, just short of his cell. The guard was listening. A tremor shook him to his bones, but the quaking was not fear. A rare boldness seized him, and when he finished the psalm, he remembered a passage from Isaiah that Zerah loved to quote concerning the Messiah. He took a deep breath and called out, "Who could have believed what we have heard, and to whom has the power of the Lord been revealed? He grew up before the Lord like a young plant whose roots are in parched ground. He had no beauty, no majesty to draw our eyes, no grace to make us delight in him...."

Something happened to Jacob then that he didn't expect. As he continued to recite, the walls of his prison fell away and disappeared. The guard and the prisoners faded with them. He was alone—yet he had an audience, and that One was listening. He saw his words rise like sweet incense, redolent with worship, toward a bright throne. He fell to his knees. "After all his pains he shall be bathed in light, after his disgrace, he shall be vindicated; so shall he my servant vindicate many, himself bearing the penalty of their guilt. Therefore I will allot him a portion with the great, and he shall share the spoil with the mighty, because he exposed himself to face death, and was reckoned among the transgressors, because he bore the sin of many, and interceded for their transgressions."

Unaware of any passage of time in the throne room, Jacob remained on his knees. *Lord, you were unfairly imprisoned, too.* Gradually his surroundings came back to him, and he sank to a sitting position. Out of the quiet that had enveloped the corridor, a voice called out, "Who is this you're talking about?"

*   *   *   *   *

"He hasn't come back. He's not in Jerusalem." Gallus sat down in the room's single chair and rubbed his face until his skin reddened. "I got to talk to Mina, and she says Simon is beside himself—anxious and irritable. He's become so unreasonable with the servants and the slaves in Caiaphas' household that Caiaphas himself pulled him aside to ask what was wrong with him. She says Simon's settled down since then, but not much." He raised his eyes to meet Joel's. "A man like Phineas won't be able to sneak into the city. Simon has eyes everywhere."

"So where is he?" Caleb asked. "We didn't pass him on the road. That must mean he took a different way back."

"Or," Gallus added, "he decided to hole up somewhere."

Joel frowned. "Why would he do that?"

"To throw us off the scent." Gallus stood up and went to pour himself a cup of water. "Phineas is a hunter. He thinks like a hunter, and so must we if we expect to find him."

"Then let's think this through." Caleb started pacing. "If he took a different road, he'd either have gone south through Samaria, or along the coast. He could have even found a ship to make the short voyage from, say...Sidon or Tyre."

"But in that case, he'd be here already," Joel said. "Assuming the ship didn't sink." He glanced at Caleb, and added, "Sorry."

Jonathan broke in, "I think he's waiting."

Caleb turned. The boy seldom spoke, but his economy of words tended to conceal a thoughtful heart. Caleb had learned to listen to him. "Waiting for what, Jonathan?"

The youth's eyes shifted to Gallus. "You said he was a hunter. I have hunted in the wilderness outside of Antioch, and I've seen wild dogs that were stalking another animal suddenly sit down and act like they weren't interested—until they were ready to make a kill. Sometimes a lion plays with its prey before it feeds. He's waiting. It's part of a game."

Caleb said, "So you're saying he's the lion, and we're...what? The mice?"

Gallus nodded. "He thinks we are—we and Simon."

"Are we so small in his eyes?" Caleb's mouth tightened into grim lines. "Does he think we cannot do him harm?"

Gallus' blue eyes glittered cold in the afternoon light. "There is a saying among our sages, 'A small serpent kills a large bull with a bite.' Let him think we are small. In the end he will find that we aren't mice."

*   *   *   *   *

Over the next several days, Jacob spent most of his time standing at the bars of his cell door preaching what he knew of the Christ to the other prisoners. His initial anxiety—*I am inadequate. What do I know?*—was struck down by his memory of Zerah's simple admonition to Gallus. *"The three of us together are inadequate, but are you willing?"*

Lord, he pleaded at the start, *I have no one to help me but You. Give me the words for these people.* With that, he shared everything he knew, suddenly thankful for all those Greek lessons he suffered through as a child. He recited scriptures that pointed to Messiah and explained them, telling the prisoners everything he could remember that Phillip or Joel had said about Jesus of Nazareth. Jacob preached and preached until his voice gave out.

And through those days, and through his words, and through the quiet invitation of God, some prisoners believed, though he couldn't tell how many. Instead of constant arguing and cursing from the other cells, he now heard scattered prayer and praise. Each time he did, he found strength. *Lord, only you could bring Heaven into this Hell! Now I understand why You brought me here.*

But a few nights later, a bitter wind blew down from the north, and the temperature in the prison plummeted. Jacob gathered his meager pile of straw into one small heap and stood on it to protect his bare feet from the frigid floor. It was all he could do. He had no cloak or blanket, not even another person in the cell with him to share body heat. His breath puffed out in wisps of vapor between his chattering teeth. He had eaten nothing but coarse bread and water for days, and weakness and fatigue pressed on him like a millstone. *If I could just sleep....* But he knew that if he stretched out on the floor, he would never wake up.

He crouched down, and sitting on his heels, pulled his tunic over his knees. That helped a little, and he stared blankly at the wall, willing himself to stay awake. The stone wall stared back until it filled his vision, and all at once he had an idea. Standing up, he shuffled his pile of straw over until it was next to the wall. That done, he squatted on his heels again, pulling his tunic over his knees. He tucked his arms down inside the tunic and leaned forward until his forehead rested against the stone. In that way, with the wall to balance him, Jacob was able to sleep.

* * * * *

"Nicanor is here," Joel said. "He is going to recruit some men to help us watch for Phineas."

Caleb greeted his brother-in-law, then grabbed Joel by the arm and pulled him aside. "You weren't supposed to go to him. He's family, and that means he's being watched."

If Nicanor took offense, he didn't show it. "No one has been paying any attention to me, Caleb. And no one here remembers Joel. Your secret is safe—not even Deborah knows you're here. My friends and I can help you."

"How many men do you think you'll have?" Joel asked.

Nicanor gazed up toward the ceiling, and silently started ticking off his fingers, mouthing their names as he went. Finally he said, "Twenty easily, maybe more if we are pressed." He faced Caleb. "Phineas is no stranger. They know what he did to Deborah, and are well aware of what he looks like. I will post men at each of the gates. They will watch for him."

"Don't these men have to work?" Caleb asked.

"Well, of course they do," Nicanor answered mildly. "But with so many, we can spread the duty out among them, so no one will suffer unduly. "

Gallus said, "Thank you, Nicanor. Your help is greatly appreciated."

He smiled and clasped Gallus' left hand. "Our women are involved as well. They are praying for Jacob's safe return."

After he left, Caleb said, "I still don't think this is a good idea. I don't know these people he's recruited."

Joel faced him, his eyes hurt and angry. "What about the people you do know?" He held up a finger in Caleb's face. "Can you name one—even *one* among them you'd trust to help look for your son?" He hung his head. Joel pressed, "And why do you not know Nicanor's friends? You don't know them because you've been too busy currying favor with untrustworthy men.... Where are you going?"

Caleb had reached the door, and without looking back, he said, "Out." Once he stepped into the winter night, he jammed his turban down on his shorn head and pulled his cloak tight around him. A mist fell from the sky—too light to be called rain, but enough to chill him, nonetheless. *This is crazy. Now I have strangers looking for my boy. I should be out there looking for him, but I'm stuck in the city. This is foolishness.* Joel's words still stung. *Is there anyone here besides my sister and her husband I can trust? Surely there is someone.* He went through his list of friends and acquaintances, dismayed to discover that it was a short list after all, and concluded that Joel might be right.

Whether he was right or wrong, it was not a good night to be out wandering the streets. *This weather is nasty.* The next thought cut him to the heart. *What if Jacob is out in it?* He turned his face to the sky and blinked at the falling mist. *Please, no. Please let him be safe inside somewhere.*

* * * * *

The next morning dawned somewhere outside, but no ray of sunlight penetrated the stone prison. The only way Jacob knew it was morning was that the guard brought him his ration of bread and water. He looked up and peered at it with bleary eyes, then put his forehead against the wall again. Even in the dark he saw the rime of ice already growing around the edge of the bowl. He licked at his parched lips. He needed water, but thirsty as he was, the very thought of drinking something that cold sent a quaking shudder through his body. When it subsided, he dozed off again.

A sudden clanging against the iron bars of his cell jerked him awake. The guard was standing just outside the door. "You have a visitor."

Jacob's heart sank. He wasn't prepared to face Phineas this morning. Releasing a deep sigh that wreathed his face in vapor, he stood up.

The door swung open, and a hooded, cloaked figure stepped into the cell. "Bring a brazier," the visitor said to the guard, "and I'll want a chair." Jacob decided he had to be dreaming, or hallucinating. The voice belonged to a woman.

He stared agape while she pulled the hood back and faced him. Her silver hair, swept up Roman-fashion, told him she was probably older than Mother Odelia. But only a few tell-tale lines around her mouth and amber-colored eyes marred her otherwise supple skin. "I am Helena," she addressed him in Greek. When he hesitated, she smiled at his dazed expression and prompted, "And you are...?"

He caught hold of himself and answered, "Please forgive me, lady. My name is Jacob."

"You are a Jew?" He nodded. Seconds later, the guard opened the door again and placed a chair inside for the visitor to sit on, along with a metal brazier, which he lit with his torch. "Bring this boy a blanket," Helena ordered.

"But my lady..." he began.

The timbre of her voice never rose above a murmur. "Do not argue with me. Go find him a blanket—a nice, thick one. I will pay for it." The guard bowed and backed out. The woman named Helena regarded Jacob for a full minute with her amber eyes. "You are innocent."

Those three words stabbed him to the heart. He bit down hard on his tongue and clapped a hand over his mouth to forestall a sob. It didn't help. He bent over at the waist, and covered his face to hide his tears, but the cry of pure agony that erupted from deep in his chest echoed in the bare room. *How does she know, Lord? And why is she here?* He labored against the onslaught for several eternal minutes, eyes squeezed shut, jaw clamped down against the heaving sobs, and his hands knotted into fists. His fingernails dug into his palms until they bled, and this new pain was enough to distract him. At last the tears subsided.

"I am sorry. I did not mean to cause you distress." She waited a while, then asked, "Will you not speak to me?"

He gradually got his breathing under control, swallowed against the thickness in his throat, "There is...." He wiped one side of his face against his shoulder. "...there is danger in it, lady. I was told to speak to no one." He sucked at the seeping wound on the heel of his palm.

"Yet I hear you've been preaching to the other prisoners." She arched her eyebrows. "Is that not so?"

He nodded, momentarily transfixed by the fire in the brazier, but not daring to move closer to it. Preaching was different. Wasn't it? Gathering his courage, he raised his eyes. "If I have hurt anyone by speaking, I will take responsibility."

She stood up and began pacing the short length of his cell. "My son, Tertius, is the commander of this prison. He tells me that since you came, the number of fights among prisoners has sharply declined." A smile played at one corner of her mouth. "Imagine that. He also told me who brought you here. Is this Phineas the one who ordered you not to speak?" Jacob nodded again, and she said, "I do not fear his kind any more than I do a scorpion on the floor. If he stings, you see, I will crush him."

She turned and sat down again. "Now, tell me why you're here."

"It is a long story," he answered.

She gestured at the walls of the cell. "Do you have some other pressing matter to attend to? I want to hear your long story. All of it."

* * * * *

Another week passed, with no sign of Jacob or of Phineas. The four men sat down to dinner on the first day of the week. "How long will we have to wait?" Caleb ripped his loaf in half and stabbed it into the sauce.

Gallus shrugged. "There is no way to know."

Joel picked up his cup. "Maybe he's waiting until spring."

"Passover." Jonathan stopped chewing when he realized the others were staring at him. "I would wait till then, if it was up to me. Big crowds. A man can slip in easily without being noticed."

Gallus nodded and gestured with his bread. "And he'll come in through one of the southern gates, not the Damascus gate or the Temple Gate."

"In order to avoid running into anyone connected with Caiaphas or Simon," Joel agreed.

"I can't just sit here and wait," Caleb complained. "There has to be something else we can do—something we haven't thought of."

"But what would that be?" Joel asked. "We've talked to everyone in the city we trust, and we've posted ourselves and our friends at the gates and around Caiaphas' palace." Then he grinned at Caleb, "By the way, you make a very convincing beggar."

Caleb grimaced. It galled him to pretend to be crippled and sit across from the palace every day, his face and clothing smeared with dirt. "Not convincing enough. I only got a few minas today. If I had to do this for a living, I don't think I would live long."

"Well, you're not in the best spot," Joel laughed. "I did better up at the Temple."

Caleb grunted. "I'm going to confess to you—and please don't be offended—I don't have a lot of confidence in your friends."

Joel's scarred eyebrow went up. "Why not?"

"Aside from Nicanor, what is their stake in this? Why should they put themselves out to look for a boy they don't even know?"

Joel laced his fingers together and studied him. Finally he said, "Jacob is their brother."

Caleb's eyes shot over to Jonathan, who seemed unperturbed. "What do you mean 'their brother'? None of them is any relation to him that I know of."

"Jacob is a follower of the Way. So are they. That makes him their brother."

"The way?" He felt a slow flush working its heated way up his face. "You mean the Nazarene sect?"

Joel said, "It's time you faced some things. Jacob and Jonathan's mother was healed by the Nazarene. So was your father. Jesus of Nazareth *is* the Messiah. He is the savior of the world."

"And my son believes this?"

"Your *sons* believe it," Jonathan said.

Gallus leaned toward Caleb, his eyes full of unyielding compassion. "We are all of this faith."

Jacob, what have you done? Caleb lost his appetite, so he reached for his wine, finishing the contents of his cup in a single swift swallow. He poured himself another. "Brothers." He gestured to each of them with the cup. "So you three are brothers. Joel, and Jonathan, though you're actually uncle and nephew, and you, Gallus—a Roman. Brothers."

"I am not Roman by birth," he answered, "I am from Gaul. But yes, we are brothers."

Caleb turned to Jonathan. "Do you agree with this?" When he assented, Caleb prodded him, "What does it mean to you, then, to say you are Jacob's brother? If he's brother to all of these, doesn't that make your relation to him less? Doesn't it dilute it?"

"It enhances it," Jonathan answered.

Caleb took another drink to rinse the sour taste out of his mouth. "On the way down here, I asked why you wanted to come with us, and you said it was because Jacob was your brother. Which did you mean? That he was your brother by blood, or your brother by this... this faith?"

"Both."

He saw the knowing look that passed between Gallus and Joel. Irritated, and feeling left out, he tossed down the rest of his wine and poured yet another cup. At this, Joel took the pitcher and placed it out of his reach. It only annoyed Caleb further. "So if I became one of you, I guess that would make me Jacob's brother, too. Ridiculous!"

Joel said, "I don't understand why you scoff. We Jews have always called ourselves brothers. Our doing so now that we believe Jesus is Messiah is no different."

"It is different," he argued, suppressing a belch. "When *we* call each other 'brother', it means we come from a common ancestor. Abraham is our father, so in that sense we are brothers. But you who follow the Nazarene can be of any race," he gestured toward Gallus, "from any nation on earth, correct? If some Nubian slave shared your faith, would he be your brother as well? Or some *Samaritan*?" He spat this last word out as if it were foul in his mouth.

Gallus shook his head. "By my life, I do not understand it—the contempt you have for the Samaritans—though Zerah tried to explain it to me. They are your fellow countrymen, and they also share your common ancestor."

"They are half-breeds and idolators," Caleb growled.

"And you are a wealthy, full-blooded Jew... how? By accident of birth. And just so you know, we do have a brother in Damascus who is a Nubian slave."

Caleb snorted, "Whatever you say." He stood up from the table, and grabbing the wine pitcher by the neck, carried it to his pallet. He sat down with his back to the others and took a long drink. He hardly tasted the wine at all, and drinking it wasn't that pleasant, but he went to it like a man with a mission. The winter nights had been too long, and too uneasy. He intended to finish what was in the pitcher, and get himself some more, if he had to. *I'm going to drink until I pass out. And if I'm sick in the morning, I'm sick. Some miseries are better than others.*

Before long, he heard the others whispering among themselves. "You don't need to whisper," he announced, his voice beginning to slur. "I don't care what you're saying. I won't remember it in the morning anyway."

Gallus answered, "As you wish."

In the next moment, the three of them raised their voices in prayer. "Our Father in Heaven, we bless your holy name. You who made the earth and the seas, and all that live within them, we praise You and give You all glory and honor...."

Caleb ground his teeth. *They are doing this on purpose. They're trying to shame me.* His fingers dug into his scalp, and would have pulled his hair out, but it was shorn too close to give them purchase. The wall he was facing was beginning to bow in the middle, and the floor undulated gently beneath him. He raised the pitcher to his lips, only to find it empty. With a groan, he put it down and stretched out on his pallet, pulling his blanket up over his face, and draping one arm over his head to muffle the voices. *My sons believe in the Nazarene. You win, Miriam. They are your boys after all.*

* * * * *

Jacob finished his breakfast, which now included a boiled egg, in addition to his ration of bread. He suspected he had Helena to thank, though he hadn't seen her since their initial meeting three days before. He nibbled slowly at the egg, savoring every bite. There had also been a small smoked fish included with every evening meal. Neither the egg nor the fish was enough to satisfy his appetite, but they helped assuage the hollow-chested hunger he had suffered since his capture. And then there was the pile of straw he was now sitting on, brought in by four slaves. Fresh straw, and deep enough to burrow into at night. When he did, he could almost imagine himself sleeping in the barn at home, though the smells here were definitely human, and not animal.

He continued to preach and recite scripture every day, and now he sometimes heard the other prisoners sharing his message with newcomers. *I wish I could tell Uncle Phillip about this. I wish I could tell Arin. Once I get to Jerusalem and get away, I will go back to Caesarea and see them.* And yet.... He closed his eyes. Deep in his gut he knew he might not get away again. *I may not even live to see the city.*

His thoughts were interrupted by the guard at his door. "Visitor," he announced.

Jacob stood up as Helena swept into the cell. The guard followed her in with a chair and brazier, as before. She sat down and took her time scrutinizing him in the fire's light before she said, "You have improved. You looked half-dead the last time I was here."

His blanket still wrapped around his shoulders, Jacob made a polite bow. "I thank you, lady. You have saved my life."

She waved this off with a negligent gesture. "I did nothing to speak of." She folded her hands in her lap and said, "Now, you and I have things to talk about. I've made some inquiries—primarily about Phineas and his doings." Her mouth pursed in an expression of distaste. "I hardly think it's possible for anyone to disgust me more than he. However, that is not why I came." Her focus narrowed on him. "Your Greek is good. Do you read and write as well?"

"Yes, lady. I was schooled in Greek as a boy."

She pulled a scroll from her sleeve. "Read that aloud to me."

He unrolled the paper, and holding it up to the firelight, began to read. The scroll turned out to be a contract for the sale of a plot of land somewhere in Phrygia. He stumbled once over an unfamiliar word, but otherwise read it through without a flaw. She took the scroll back and asked, "Do you write as well as you read?" When he said he did, she asked, "What about Latin?"

"I only know one sentence in Latin," he answered. "A friend taught it to me."

She raised her delicate eyebrows. "And what would that be?"

"Vir diem tenet, et dies virum."

Now she rewarded him with a smile. "A wise saying, Jacob. You have no doubt found it to be true." She stood up and began to pace. "I have given much thought and prayer to what you said to me the last time I was here." She met his surprised expression with an amused look of her own. "I didn't tell you then, but I, too am a follower of Jesus of Nazareth. When my son told me you were preaching, and what you were saying, I naturally took interest." She paused and faced him. "I don't have to tell you that the situation in which you now find yourself will likely end in your death."

Jacob hung his head and sighed. "I have reason to believe so."

"I greatly desire to prevent that," she said, and sitting down, folded her hands in her lap once again. "Therefore, I have a proposition. Sit down and let me tell you what I have in mind."

* * * * *

Phineas took a last bite of bread and chased it down with a swallow of the inn's passable wine. He was in a pleasant mood. That morning he woke up with no noticeable pain anywhere in his body. All that remained of his illness was a purple scar on his leg—and even that was fading. *One more month,* he told himself. *I'll let Simon stew that long before I take the boy to Jerusalem. I'll slip him into the city through the Hinnom gate. If we go in just before nightfall, no one will see us. Then I can tuck the boy away and dangle the scent of him under Simon's nose.*

His musings were interrupted by a man who appeared at his elbow. "Excuse me, sir. Are you Phineas of Jerusalem?"

Phineas pushed back from the table. "I am. Who are you?" Out of the corner of his eye, he noticed that the innkeeper had paused to listen.

"I am a messenger, sir, sent by the lady Helena of Berea. She wishes a meeting with you."

"Does she?" Phineas' stare bored into the messenger, as if he could ascertain the meaning behind the request. "When and where does she want to meet?"

"This afternoon at her villa, if you are not otherwise engaged."

He grunted. "Very well. Tell the lady I will be honored to meet with her. I'll be there within the hour." When the messenger had given him directions to the villa and departed, he turned his attention to the innkeeper, who had suddenly made himself busy. "So what you know about her, Jonas?"

"About who, my lord?" The innkeeper's stout, ruddy face was a picture of innocence.

Phineas smiled indulgently. "Oh, come now. You heard every word. What do you know about the lady Helena? She's related to Caesar, isn't she?"

Jonas' head bobbed up and down. "Yes, a cousin of some sort. On her mother's side, I believe. Other than that, I can't say as I know much, except that she's rich, and widowed, and she has...." he squinted up at the ceiling, "... maybe four children—all grown, of course."

"Does she live here year-round?"

"No, she's one of those that's in and out, if you know what I mean. Comes this way in the winter time and heads north again when the weather warms."

"I see. What do you suppose a woman like that wants with someone like me?"

"Oh, I couldn't say, sir. Perhaps she's had a slave run away, and she wants you to go after him."

"Have you heard that she's lost a slave, or are you just guessing?"

Jonas shrugged. "In a big city like this, runaways are not usually news. I don't know."

Phineas took a final swallow of the wine and left. Once out of doors, he traversed the city with purposeful steps, and before long was striding up the broad lane that led to Helena's winter villa. The beauty and order of the well-kept grounds—even in mid-winter—did nothing to arouse either admiration or envy in him, nor did the wide, white marble portico supported by graceful columns. He cared nothing for such trappings. What interested him was what lay behind a person's eyes, and how he could manipulate it. *Fear and greed. From the lowest slave to the highest-born noble, fear and greed drive the human story. Everyone is afraid of something, and everyone can be bought. I'll be interested to see what drives the lady Helena.*

He mounted the steps and rapped at the front door. "I am Phineas," he announced to the burly Greek who answered.

"Yes, sir. You are expected." The servant's black eyes, flat and devoid of emotion, looked him up and down before he stepped aside to usher him in. "Please follow me."

He led Phineas to a spacious room to the left of the main hall. Helena was seated at a table piled with scrolls. She glanced up as he entered. "Phineas, I presume?" She gestured to a chair across from her. "Please be seated. Can I offer you refreshment?"

He bowed and sat down. "Thank you, lady, but no. I have just eaten." He glanced at the servant, who had taken up a position just behind Helena's right shoulder.

"Very well. We will dispense with formalities." She folded her hands across the paper that lay open in front of her, obscuring his view of it, and she did it so naturally, he almost believed it was of no import. "I have made some inquiries about you, and I understand you are a man hunter."

"I search for runaways," he answered, settling more comfortably into his chair, now that he knew what she wanted him for.

"You must be good at it, if the reports I hear are true."

"Let the reports speak for themselves," he answered with a casual wave of his hand. "I do not wish to boast."

"Then I hope you will do business with me."

"I will be honored to be of whatever service you have in mind, lady."

She smiled. "You have remanded a boy to Caesarea's prison. I wish to buy him from you."

Phineas found his tongue suddenly stuck to the roof of his mouth. When he managed to move it again, he said, "You want to do what?"

"You heard me," she answered. "I will buy the boy from you. Forty silver pieces. It's more than a fair price."

Frantic for some way to slow the conversation down, to give himself time to think, he said, "You don't want him, lady. He's violent."

Her eyes widened, as if startled. "Violent?"

"Yes. He started a number of fights, and on top of that, he's a perpetual runaway. If you buy him, you won't have him for long. This is the third time I've gone after him."

Helena said nothing, but just watched him. The tiny lines at the corners of her eyes deepened, and Phineas recognized her expression. *She knows I'm lying. How does she know about the boy? Why does she want him?* The Greek bodyguard's stare was aimed at the wall somewhere over Phineas' head, but he had no doubt that he was reading him as well. *He's probably quicker than he looks.* A thin sheen of sweat broke out on his forehead. "My lady, I have orders to take him to his master in Jerusalem."

"Perhaps you do, but I will not take no for an answer." Her amber eyes drilled into his, and she turned the paper on the table around so he could see it. "This is the bill of sale. There are two copies. You will sign both, and I will give you one to take, along with the money, to the boy's master."

Phineas licked at his lips. "But how can I tell him that I sold the boy? He is greatly desirous that he be returned."

"I can't imagine why." Her smile held no trace of humor. "You said yourself the boy is violent, and a perpetual runaway. I should think his master will be glad to be rid of him."

Phineas was caught. *I have to get away from here and take that brat back to Jerusalem. And I will make him pay for this!* Rising from his chair, he said, "Very well, just let me go and fetch the boy, and I'll bring him to you."

"There is no need," she answered. "I will take care of that matter myself. Sign here, please."

He took the stylus from her and dipped it into the waiting bowl of ink. For one moment, he considered spilling the ink onto the documents. They'd have to be written all over again. But her eyes were on him, watching and challenging, and there was her massive bodyguard standing an arm's length away. In the end he didn't dare. *I'll run back to the prison and get him out, and be gone before anyone can stop me.* He signed both papers with an angry flourish.

Helena handed him a leather purse, along with one copy of the bill of sale. "It's been a pleasure."

He shook his head, as if in deep regret. "I don't know what I will say to his master."

She plucked one of the other scrolls from the table and turned her attention to it, dismissing him. "I'm sure you'll think of something."

* * * * *

Phineas ran as fast as his feet would carry him all the way back to the prison. By the time he got there, his chest was tight and aching with the unaccustomed exercise. He hurried past the sentries, and once inside, said to the commander, "Tertius, I wish to take my prisoner out of here now."

"Which prisoner is that?"

"The boy Jacob. I brought him in several weeks ago. A matter has come up, and I need to be on my way to Jerusalem."

Tertius shook his head in refusal. "You'll have to be on your way without him. He was removed this morning."

It took a few seconds for the commander's words to sink in. "Removed?" Phineas exploded, "How could that happen? Who took him?"

Tertius' right hand strayed to the hilt of his sword. "The lady Helena."

"With no bill of sale?" he raged. "He didn't belong to her. He belongs to me."

The Roman stood his ground. "No longer. You have sold him to her. She said this morning that she was buying him from you, and she wanted him released."

"And just like that," Phineas snapped his fingers, "you let him go." He moved in closer and snarled, "I'll have your head for this."

One corner of Tertius' mouth curled up. "No, I don't think you will."

The Roman's arrogance was astonishing. *But he's just a low-level officer,* Phineas told himself. *I've dealt with his kind before.* "Who do you think you are?"

The commander's chin lifted, and his eyes bored into Phineas'—his amber-colored eyes. "I am the lady Helena's son." Phineas staggered back as if he'd been slapped. Tertius matched him step for step until Phineas' back was to the door. "Go to your inn and gather your things. I want you out of the city by nightfall." He stopped, and with a leisurely motion drew his *gladius,* hefting the short-bladed weapon in his hand as if testing its weight. "And don't do anything foolish. We will be watching."

Phineas turned on his heel and stalked out of the prison. *Jonas didn't tell me that Tertius was her son. I will kill him for that.* His rage grew with every step he took toward the inn. As if in answer to the inflammation of his mind, his leg began to ache again. Cursing under his breath, he rounded the last corner, and reaching the inn, pulled a knife from his belt. He intended to slit Jonas' throat with it, just before he noticed the heavy tramping of footsteps behind him, and he whirled around and found himself facing two armed legionaries. Only then did he remember Tertius' parting words.

Growling low in his throat, he put the knife away, and hurried to his room, where he snatched up his belongings, his mind groping for a way to revenge this insulting morning. Coming up empty, he strode through the main room on his way out. "Are you away, then, sir?" Jonas called after him. "You still owe for this past week.... Sir?"

Phineas tried to barrel his way out of the door, but the soldiers blocked his way. "This man says you owe him money," one of them said.

"He's the best innkeeper in town," the other added, running an absent finger along a scar that ran from his ear to his chin. "And he's our friend. We don't like it when people cheat our friends."

Phineas yanked his purse open and fished out three silver coins. He tossed them to the ground at Jonas' feet. "That enough?"

"Oh no you don't," the first soldier said. "You pick that money up and hand it to him proper."

He took a long, deep breath in an effort to cool his rage. He did as the soldier ordered, and gave Jonas his money. "Thank you, sir," Jonas said cheerfully. "Pleasure having you."

He tried again to leave, but the soldiers still blocked his way. They had no reason to stop him now, he knew. They were toying with him. Gritting his teeth, he shouldered his way between them. As he started off down the street, he heard Jonas say, "You boys come in and have some wine on the house."

And one of them answered, "Thanks, Jonas. We'll be back for it later. We have to follow this son of a snake first—see to it that he's out of the city." Hearing that, Phineas picked up his steps. He couldn't leave Caesarea Philippi fast enough.

Chapter 15

Somewhere far to the east, in a nameless place unmarked by time or man, a puff of wind kicked up on the desert floor, scooping into its vortex tiny grains of swirling sand that gave it a color, a shape, and a visible presence. Alone, it would have soon collapsed and died, but aided by a stronger gust out of the north, it instead grew to twice the height of a man, and increased in strength as it moved south, continuing to pick up sand and debris as it went. In a flat, barren land, with no mountains or hills to barricade it, the boiling cloud swelled and gained speed. The hum of the wind escalated to a roar. The cloud, engorged with wind and sand, became a mighty wall, higher than any tower, wider than any city. With the howl of a conquering army, the titan tide swept across the desert, turning the sky black and blotting out the sun, killing and burying both man and beast, engulfing and overwhelming all that stood in its path.

* * * * *

Jacob fingered the texture of his finely-woven wool tunic and shook his head in bemusement over the ups and downs of his fortunes in the last several months. *My life seemed so dull and quiet until...until that day.* Because of his father's rash oath, he had been tumbled in fortune's capricious wind. Some of it, he had to admit, had been very good. The faces of his new-found friends and family paraded one by one through his mind—Zerah and Gallus, his mother, Jonathan.... And Arin. Her solemn, gray eyes lingered until his right hand lifted on its own, reached out as if to touch the image.

I may never see her again. I may never see any of them again. He squeezed his eyes shut against the bitterness of his thoughts. He rubbed at his face vigorously, and sniffed. *No tears,* he told himself. *Not today. I am safe from Phineas and Simon, and I am out of prison.* Then he smiled. *But prison wasn't all bad—mostly, but not all. I guess I learned how to preach.* He fingered the gold loop dangling from his right ear and winced. The piercing was going to sting for a few days. *I wonder what will happen to me now?*

At that moment, Nikos, the massive, swarthy Greek who served as the lady Helena's bodyguard, put his head in the door. "She wants you."

Jacob followed him to the front of the villa, scrutinizing the Greek's gait and build as they went. Nikos' bulky muscles forced his arms to swing out, instead of dropping straight down to the side as most other people's did. Jacob found himself almost copying the bodyguard's confident stride, then stopped when he realized it might look like mockery if Nikos suddenly turned around. *I don't want to make this fellow my enemy!*

Helena still sat at the table where she had conducted her earlier meeting with Phineas. She looked up and announced, "Oh, yes—much better. He does need a haircut, Nikos. See to that this afternoon." To Jacob she said, "The tunic suits you. Did you get enough to eat?"

His face flushed with embarrassment, remembering how he had attacked the food offered him, and devoured it all. Now he felt a little queasy from his overloaded stomach, and realized, *It must have been this way for Mary when we found her alone in Damascus.* "Yes, lady. Thank you."

Helen stood and turned away, as if he were no longer of any consequence. "There is no need to thank me, Jacob. Understand—you are not my guest. You are my responsibility."

He swallowed and murmured, "My apologies, lady."

She turned back, her expression softened. "I have work for you this afternoon, work that cannot be done on an empty stomach. I hired a Latin tutor. You will take lessons with him each day until we leave in the spring."

He offered her a short bow. "I will do my best."

"I'm sure you will." She regarded him for a long moment. "Now about the other matter we discussed. I have decided to trust you. You may send one message to whomever you wish, so that your family will know you are alive and well."

He sighed, as if a massive burden had fallen from his shoulders. "I don't know how to thank you, lady. It will mean the world to me to be able to reassure them."

Helena nodded. "I suppose you've wondered if I will keep my word to you, to release you before I die."

His chest went tight with apprehension. That one fear had nagged at him all morning, ever since her visit in the prison. He could end up being a slave for the rest of his life. Yet, what choice did he have? If he remained in the prison, sooner or later Phineas would come for him. *Even if I managed to escape again, Phineas would never give up and leave me alone. He won't leave my family alone either. He would haunt us all. To have that...that devil coming after Arin....* No, that he could not bear. Unable to find words of courage, he only nodded.

Helena gathered several of the scrolls on the table and handed them over to Nikos. "I have decided to trust you. You must also trust me."

*   *   *   *   *

"It's a beautiful day," Leah told Arin about a week later. "So warm for winter. Why don't you take Prisca and your sisters down to the beach for a little while? You've been cooped up in the house too long."

Arin kissed her mother's cheek. "I'll find you a pretty shell. I'm sure you need another one."

Leah laughed and gestured toward the shelves and window sills. Every spare bit of space had a shell of some kind tucked into it. "And where will I put it?"

"Tell Papa to add another room to the house."

Still laughing, Leah prodded her toward the door. "Go on, now. Out with you!"

Arin gathered the others, and they followed her like a row of baby ducks down to the water's edge. Once there, Prisca and Salome found sticks and busied themselves drawing pictures in the sand and laughing with glee when the waves washed them away. Lyssa wandered off to the north a little way, humming under her breath, then sat down a few yards up from the water and proceeded to bury her feet in the cool sand.

Arin closed her eyes and turned her face to the sun's warmth, drinking it in. *Maybe spring will come early this year.* She hugged her arms to herself and stepped back when a wave lapped at her feet. It was warmer than usual, but hardly warm enough to get wet. Her eyes searched the rolling sea. Only one sail showed itself, billowing in the wind far to the south. *Not many ships out this time of year.* Except for Lyssa, the beach to the north was empty, and though Caesarea lay close to the south, she saw no one coming from that direction.

Ever since they'd gotten the message that Jacob was missing from Damascus, she held onto the hope that she'd see him. He would come trotting up the beach, and everything would be all right. She closed her eyes again. *Lord, do You tire of hearing me plead for him? Keep him safe and well. Heal whatever wounds exist between him and his father. Strengthen Jacob with your joy in this time of testing. Give him power and boldness in your Spirit.* Arin's throat ached with unshed tears. *Return him to us, if it is your will for him. As for me, Lord, I will trust You.*

A cool hand touched her wrist. Arin opened her eyes. Prisca was watching her, her expression solemn. "Are you all right, Arin?"

She smiled and took her cousin's hand. "I was just praying. Have you and Salome found anything interesting?"

Prisca lifted one shoulder in a gesture that mirrored her mother's. "Not much. Are you praying about my brother?" She fingered the ice-blue bead at her throat—Salome's necklace. Salome had told her that Jacob made the bead, and when the little girl realized Prisca had no necklace of her own, had given it to her.

Arin pulled Prisca to her side. Her question needed no answer. Presently, she asked another. "Why didn't my father tell me about Jacob?" Prisca knew now that Jacob had run away, and that her father was looking for him. She didn't know about the latest message, sent more than a month ago from Zerah in Damascus. Phillip and Leah had told Arin, but kept the news from the younger girls. "There's no point in frightening them," Phillip said. "Especially Prisca."

"I don't know," Arin replied. "Sometimes grown-ups do things that we don't understand."

Salome called out, "Look! Somebody's at the house."

Arin turned around. A man she had never seen before was standing at the door. As she watched, he handed her mother something that looked like a scroll. *Maybe it's word about Jacob.* Tempted as she was to run back inside, she knew it would do no good. Mama couldn't read, and Papa was away in town, and wouldn't be home until after dark. *I can read a little, but Mama won't open the scroll. She'll want to wait for Papa to read it first.*

Curiosity chewed at the edges of her thoughts for the next hour. Then she looked up and spotted her father coming up the beach toward them. He was home early. "Papa's here," she called out to the others. They all jumped up and descended on him in a squealing, giggling mass.

Laughing, "Here are my girls!" Phillip greeted each of them with a kiss.

Arin returned his kiss, and taking his hand, she leaned in close and murmured, "I think there's a message for you at home."

His expression sobered, and with a glance at Prisca, he nodded. "Let us hope it's good news." When they reached the house, he sat down first and let Leah give him a cup of wine. Once the younger girls were out of earshot, he said, "Arin tells me a message came today."

Leah nodded. "It's in our room."

A few minutes later, he stood up and disappeared into the adjoining room. Arin watched him go, her heart pounding painful rhythms in her chest. *Please, Lord,* she pleaded silently. *Please let him be all right.* She couldn't tear her eyes away from the curtained doorway. *Papa's face will tell. When he comes out, we'll know if the news is good or bad.*

Finally, the curtain was pulled aside, and Phillip emerged, his brow furrowed in puzzlement. Leah and Arin both waited in one corner, and he came to them and said, "He's alive." But when he looked at Arin, his eyes were full of pity. "I'll tell you the rest later."

Leah, who was standing just behind Arin, put her hands on her daughter's shoulders and said in an urgent whisper, "Have mercy on the girl, Phillip. Take her outside to tell her if you must, but don't leave her wondering."

"Very well." He glanced around. Lyssa was combing out Prisca's glossy, black hair, while Salome looked on in apparent fascination. None of them paid the slightest attention to the adults. He turned back to Arin. "The message is from Jacob himself. He is alive and well, though he was in prison."

"Prison?" Her fingertips found her glass bead, touched it for reassurance. "Why was he in prison? How did he get out?"

As I am Known

"The fellow who hunted him found him and put him there for a time. Jacob's out because someone helped him."

The grief in her father's eyes seemed to tell another story. "But that's good, isn't it, Papa?" she pleaded. "If he's alive and he's free...."

"He isn't exactly free," Phillip answered. "Jacob has been made a slave."

A sudden roaring, like the sound of a mighty waterfall, crashed down on Arin's head. The room went black, and silent, and she didn't hear her mother's cry of alarm when she hit the floor.

* * * * *

Gedeon arrived in Caesarea a few days later. "I feel like I've run all over the world," he sighed as he sat down. "But," his face brightened, "my girls are here." The younger ones crowded around him, and he petted and fussed over them until Arin brought him a cup of wine. "I'll play with you later, I promise," he told them. "Let me talk to your father a while."

They ran out the back door, but Arin stayed where she was. Gedeon glanced over at her, and Phillip said, "If it's about Jacob, you can speak. Arin is his betrothed."

"Is she?" Gedeon gave her a tender smile and cupped her face with one hand. "Now that's a match I wouldn't have thought of—yet it suits." He turned to Phillip. "I started for Damascus just after Diana landed in Ephesus." He shook his head. "There is more about that than I can tell you now." He took a swallow of wine. "Perhaps I'll have the heart for it later. In any event, by the time I reached Damascus, Jacob was already gone. I found the priest you told me of, and Jacob's mother was also there with him. He said he had sent word to you of the boy's disappearance."

When he told me what had happened, I hurried to Jerusalem. Since I was on horseback, the trip only took a few days. But, as Caleb may have told you, he has sold his house, and I didn't know where to begin to look for him. Finally, he saw *me*." Gedeon shook his head. "I would never have recognized him. He was disguised as a beggar, and when he accosted me, I nearly hit him. I thought he was trying to rob me."

To make a long story short, he asked me to come here, to check on Prisca, and to tell you that he, along with the boy's uncle and brother, and Zerah's servant are all in Jerusalem waiting and watching for the man hunter."

Phillip said, "We received a message from Jacob earlier this week. He won't be going to Jerusalem."

Gedeon's brows shot up in astonishment. "Is he all right then?"

"He is safe," Phillip replied, "but at a cost."

Arin felt her father's searching eyes on her. She held herself still, willed herself not to cry.

"Jacob allowed himself to be sold as a slave." When Gedeon groaned in distress, Phillip added, "His message says that his mistress is a follower of Christ—as he is also—and that she treats him well. He also said he would be able to write to us from time to time to let us know how he is doing."

"Who has bought him?"

"His letter didn't say, nor did he say where he is now."

"I would buy his freedom if I knew...."

"No, Father. Jacob specifically asked that we not try to do that. She bought him to protect him, and I suspect he feels he is protecting us by remaining with her. The rumors I am beginning to hear about Caiaphas' steward lead me to believe Jacob may be doing the right thing."

"Then there's nothing more we can do." Gedeon turned to Arin, and with a moan of empathy, pulled her to him. "I am so sorry, little one."

The tears would wait no longer. She put her arms around his neck, and laying her head on his shoulder, let them fall.

*   *   *   *   *

Caleb spotted Phineas first. He had grown weary of sitting across from Caiaphas' palace every day, and on that morning had almost decided to try his luck elsewhere. *One more day,* he finally told himself. *If nothing happens today, I'll move.* All through the morning, he watched with one eye and waited. A filthy rag covered his left eye to make him appear half-blind and to partly cover his face. He held out his alms bowl, and whenever someone ventured by, begged for coins in a high, whining voice.

Late that afternoon, just about the time he was ready to get up and go back to the room, he noticed a gray-robed man coming toward the palace from lower Jerusalem. Caleb followed him with his one uncovered eye. *Is that him? No,* he decided, *Phineas didn't walk with a limp, and that fellow is definitely limping. And Phineas was not so thin as that one.* Still, he waited, uncertain. *I only saw him that one time. Perhaps my memory is playing tricks on me.* But when the man in gray passed right in front of him, Caleb had to stifle a gasp. *That is the man!* Phineas stopped at the courtyard gate and spoke to the servant there, and it was all Caleb could do not to jump up and run to find the others. *But I must not call attention to myself. The main thing is to find Jacob. I have to wait here till he comes out again and follow him.*

So he waited, hoping and praying Phineas wouldn't linger in the palace. He also hoped either Joel or Gallus would happen by so he wouldn't have to trail him alone. He got his first wish. Phineas spent less than an hour inside before coming out and going up the street the opposite way from which he came. Caleb waited until he was about twenty paces ahead before he stood up to follow, his alms bowl forgotten where he left it.

By this time it was nearly dusk, and people were packed almost shoulder to shoulder out on the street, many heading away from the Temple. Tomorrow was the day of Preparation for Passover. At first, Caleb was glad for the traffic—Phineas would be less likely to notice him among so many. As they progressed, however, he began to have a hard time keeping up with the man in gray, who despite his limp, moved through the crowd with surprising speed. Once, a tall, muscular man carrying a large basket on one shoulder came between them. Caleb lost sight of the back of Phineas' head, and with a mild oath tore the bandage from his face and crumpled it in his fist.

There he is. Caleb found a small gap in the crowd and trotted the next few paces to get a little closer. Just as he did, Phineas turned abruptly and ducked into a house. Panting from exertion after sitting still for so long, he fought through the crowd to cross to the other side of the street. There he surveyed the house, looking for something unusual about it that would seal it in his memory, but it was no different than all the others. *I need some way to mark it.* Then he remembered the rag he still carried in his hand. He tore off a long strip, and crossing the street again, tied it to the lattice of one of the lower windows. He stood back, looking left and right. No one took any notice or interest in what he had just done. The strip of cloth, though visible, was not enough to arouse anyone's curiosity. *It will have to do,* he told himself, and took off to find Gallus.

All three men were in the room when he burst in the door. "He's here," he announced. "I just saw him, and I know where he's staying. Come."

Without a word, they followed him until he came to the house he had marked. "That's it," he muttered. "The one with the bit of cloth hanging from the window."

"Keep walking," Gallus ordered. "Don't stop here in the street. Go down to that corner."

Once they were out of the immediate vicinity of the house, Gallus stopped and turned to study it at a distance. After a few minutes, he said, "Jacob's not in there."

"How can you be so sure?" Caleb asked.

"It's too easy," he answered. "Phineas knows Jacob escaped from Caiaphas' palace, and that was from a locked room, with a sentry in the courtyard. If I were Phineas, I would put him somewhere secure, like a prison, and maybe not even in Jerusalem. Maybe in Joppa, or in Jericho."

"Is that him leaving?" Jonathan asked, nodding toward the house.

They all looked back, and a gray-robed man stepped out and started back toward the Temple. "That's him, all right," Caleb said. "See how he limps?"

The four of them followed. "Did he always walk with a limp?" Joel asked. "I don't remember you telling me that."

"He didn't," Caleb answered. "Something must have happened to him."

"Too bad it didn't finish him off," Joel muttered, "whatever it was."

The deepening sky made it difficult for them to track him, but between them they managed to keep him in sight. "Where is he going now?" Caleb asked aloud when Phineas passed by Caiaphas' palace. "I assumed he was coming here again."

A few more streets and a turn, and Phineas stopped and knocked at a door. He gave the answering servant a slip of paper. Caleb's mouth fell open, and he stepped back, groping for a wall, for anything to hold him up.

"What's the matter?" Gallus asked him.

"That is my sister's house."

Joel frowned. "Phineas hurt your sister. What would she have to do with him?"

"I don't know," Caleb answered, swallowing the bitter bile that had risen to his throat.

"Let us watch and see," Gallus said. "Perhaps we will find out."

Caleb said, "I want to get closer. There's a space there where that wall juts out. He won't see me." Without waiting for anyone to reply, he crept off. He had just reached his new vantage point when the door of Deborah's house opened again. He peered around his corner, and felt his knees almost buckle under him when his father stepped into the street.

"What news?" he heard Lathan say.

"The boy is out of the way," Phineas replied. "Now pay what you owe me."

"You killed him?"

"You didn't hire me to kill him. All your message said was that you wanted him out of the way, and he is. He's a slave in the household of a Greek woman. He won't be coming back."

Lathan shook his head. "Not good enough. You understood exactly what I meant when I sent you that message. You will not be paid."

Phineas leaned in closer to Lathan, and though he lowered his voice, Caleb could still hear every horrible word. "Remember what I did the last time I was here? You have other grandchildren. It would be such a shame if one of them had an accident, or Heaven forbid, if anything happened to their mother. Don't you think so?"

Lathan's querulous protest grated in Caleb's ears. "You wouldn't dare!" When Phineas didn't back down, he growled, "All right. Here's your money." He pulled a leather purse from his sleeve and thrust it at the gray-shadowed man.

Phineas bowed, and with a mocking chuckle said, "It's been a pleasure. And believe me, you got what you paid for."

Lathan went back inside, slamming the door behind him, and Phineas walked away, still chuckling. Caleb watched Gallus and the others retreat into the deep shadow between two houses just before he passed. Phineas never saw any of them. Once the man in gray was out of sight, Caleb leaned into the street and vomited.

* * * * *

Early the next morning, after a restless night haunted by harried, unsettling dreams, he was picking at his breakfast when a knock sounded on the door, and Gedeon came in, leading Prisca by the hand. When she saw Caleb, she exclaimed, "Papa!" and ran to his arms. He gathered her into his lap and held her close, stroking her hair, and kissing the top of her head. *I have all but destroyed my family through my ignorance and inattention.* He closed his eyes and turned his face upward. *Please don't let me do further harm to this little one.*

After several quiet minutes, Prisca said, "See my necklace, Papa? Jacob made it himself."

"Jacob made it?" he echoed, mystified.

"Well, he made it for Salome," she answered, "and Salome gave it to me. Arin and Lyssa have one, too."

Caleb lifted the bead from her neck and examined it. "That was nice of Salome, but are you sure Jacob made this? Perhaps he bought it for her."

"He did make it," Gallus broke in. "He was working for a glass blower, and he had just learned how to make the beads before...." Catching Caleb's warning glance, he finished, "...before I left Damascus."

"I see." *Jacob was building a new life for himself.* Caleb hung his head. *He didn't need me after all.*

He heard a sharp little intake of breath from Prisca. Before he could stop her, she got out of his lap and went to stand beside Jonathan. Caleb, reading the curiosity on her face, thought, *She knows he's not Jacob. But they look so much alike. What will she think of him?* He held his breath and watched as Jonathan turned his face to her, and the two of them studied each other for several silent seconds. Finally, Prisca touched his shoulder. "Are you my brother, too?"

Caleb's heart shattered. He covered his face, bent forward until his head touched the floor, and wept. "I'm sorry.... I'm so sorry.... Please forgive me," he choked out between great, wracking sobs. To whom was he pleading? To Prisca, or to Jonathan? To Jacob? Or maybe to Miriam? He hardly knew. To all of Heaven and earth, perhaps. His whole life, it now seemed, was nothing more than one long story of error, mistake, weakness, and poor judgment.

Gedeon sat beside him and put an arm around his shoulders. "Phillip has news of Jacob," he whispered in his ear. "He's been enslaved. You will have to decide what to do."

Gedeon's words took hold of him and sat him up. He wiped his face on his sleeve. Prisca regarded him with wide, solemn eyes from her place, now in Jonathan's lap. He took a deep breath, and blew it out. "The first thing I must do is to confront my father. Jonathan, if you are willing, I want you to go with me."

Jonathan nodded once. "I am willing."

Caleb stood up and turned to Gallus. "There is no more need for disguise, is there?"

"I think not," he answered.

"I am going with you," Gedeon announced. "I have something to say to Lathan as well."

Gallus said, "We'll all go."

A few minutes later they were starting up the street, with Prisca clinging to Jonathan's hand. "We'll leave her with Deborah," he said to Gedeon, "and I'll have my conversation with my father elsewhere." His face felt like it was aflame. "I'll drag him outside, if needs be."

As it turned out, they saw Lathan entering the Temple as they passed by on the way to Deborah's, and turned aside to follow him. "Are you sure you want to do this here?" Gedeon asked, "With all these people?"

Caleb snorted, "And wound his dignity?"

He caught up with his father just inside the gate, and took him firmly by the arm. Lathan gasped in surprise. "Caleb! I didn't expect to see you back so soon. What happened to your hair—and your beard?"

The dull, yellow hue of Lathan's skin had not improved in Caleb's absence, but his father's illness did nothing to move him. "I have to talk to you, Father." With that, he started back out of the Temple gate, pulling Lathan after him.

"Here now, what's this all about?" the older man protested. "What is the matter with you, son? Why...?" The final question fell to the pavement as Lathan came face to face with Jonathan. "What are *you* doing here?" he finally rasped. "I thought...."

"You thought what, Father?" Caleb gave him a shake. "You thought Jacob was *out of the way,* didn't you? Those were your words, remember? You paid that man to kill my son."

"No, oh no...no." Lathan wagged his head in denial. "It wasn't me. It was all *her* idea."

"What are you talking about? Whose idea?" All at once he knew, and he thought he might retch again.

Gedeon passed a trembling hand across his brow. "Caleb, I haven't told you. I'm sorry. I haven't been able to speak of this to anyone but Phillip." He paused. "I am so ashamed of my daughter...."

"You ought to be." Lathan shook an accusing finger at Gedeon. "It was all her idea."

Gedeon's dark eyes blazed with wrath as stepped forward and spat at Lathan's feet. "Her idea or yours, what does it matter, you old fool? Both of you deserve to die for this."

A cry of outrage erupted from the Temple. They turned as one toward the sound. "Men of Jerusalem!" a man shouted as he ran past them. "God is blasphemed on our holy day!"

Gallus caught another man as he hurried past. "What's going on?"

Gasping and pale with shock, he answered, "One of the guards—a Roman, not a Temple guard...." He covered his face and shook his head.

"What happened?" Gedeon insisted. "What did he do?"

"He exposed himself." The stranger glanced down at Prisca, and his face flushed with embarrassment. Refusing to say more, he wrenched his arm free and fled.

His confrontation with his father momentarily forgotten, Caleb stood and waited to see what would happen. "They've gone to Cumanus," he heard someone say. "Surely the procurator will punish this man." But that hope proved futile. After what seemed an interminable wait, word came back, "Cumanus makes light of it!" Someone else shouted, "It's the procurator's doing! He incited the guard to profane our Temple and insult our God!"

"This grows more monstrous by the minute." Caleb turned to his father. "I will deal with you later. You take Prisca and go to Deborah's." He gave his arm one final shake. "And make haste. Get her there safely, do you hear me?" To Prisca he said, "I want you to go to Aunt Deborah's, my love. Hurry, now." Prisca reluctantly took her grandfather's hand. As they walked off, it was hard to tell who was leading whom.

Though Caleb and the others remained just outside the Temple gate, it was clear that the crowd inside was growing more and more agitated with each passing minute. In less than a half hour, a contingency of Pharisees stormed out, dust frosting their heads, their robes rent to the waist. "They have profaned the house of the Lord!" one of them cried, flinging his hands heavenward. Caleb's stomach did a slow roll. More than two dozen Jews surrounded one Roman guard a few feet away, all of them shaking their fists and shouting into the legionary's stony face.

Caleb turned to the others. "We should get out of here." He looked in the direction he had sent Prisca and Lathan, and his heart shot up into his throat. In all that time, they had gone less than a stone's throw, and there was his father, arguing with someone—he had stopped to argue!—still holding Prisca's hand. Caleb almost started after them, when Prisca tugged at her grandfather's hand, pulling him away.

"At least my daughter has some sense," he muttered, and kept his eyes on her blue dress as they worked their way through the crowd and away from the Temple.

Just then, Jonathan gripped his arm. "Do you hear that?"

Caleb listened, and below the growing roar of voices in the Temple came another sound, ominous, like the growl of thunder that precedes a storm. "Do you hear that? What is it?"

"Feet." Jonathan whirled around to look behind him. "Marching feet."

Caleb's eyes met Gallus', and he saw his own horror mirrored there. "Soldiers. Cumanus is sending soldiers from the Antonia!"

"We have to get out of here now!" Joel shouted.

In a panic, Caleb tried to go up the street toward Prisca, tried to muscle his way into the throng, but the crowd had grown so dense, he couldn't get through.

"No, Caleb!" Joel called to him. "You won't get through to them. Is there another way? Can we go around?"

Go around. We could get there by going south and cutting back. "This way," he urged them over the rising, rhythmic thudding of the approaching Romans, and he started toward the house he'd recently sold. *At least I know that area,* he reasoned. *And if Prisca keeps my father moving, they'll be all right. We'll get to them.*

But they hadn't taken six steps when someone screamed. Caleb looked back once over his shoulder. The leading edge of the army was just appearing around the corner from the Antonia. More screams followed, and the mass of humanity surged toward them. Caleb shouted, "Run!"

And they did run, pushing past doomed bystanders who hadn't yet grasped the peril of their situation. Caleb ran alongside his son, with Joel two steps behind. And just behind him the thunderous noise of fleeing feet escalated, punctuated by screams of terror and pain. *We aren't going to make it. They're going to run us down and trample us.* Still he ran, with his lungs on fire, and his heart ready to burst in his chest. He turned up the street where he once lived.... *But I don't live here anymore. There is no refuge here.* Then he remembered. *Maybe there is.* "Around back!" he shouted.

Just then, the front door opened, and Titus Albans stepped out. His mouth fell open with horror at the raging tide of humanity rushing down the street toward him. When he saw Caleb he called out. "Ben Lathan! In here, quickly!" As Jonathan turned toward him, Titus caught his arm and pulled him to safety. Caleb grabbed Joel and hauled him inside with him, and Titus slammed the door shut.

"Where is Gallus?" Joel asked. "And your father-in-law?"

"They were right behind us," Jonathan said.

After taking two deep breaths, Caleb headed for the back door. "Where are you going?" Joel demanded.

"My little girl is out there," Caleb answered, without breaking stride. "I am going to find her." But there was no way out. When he got to the back door, he couldn't open it, and he heard shuffling and groans just beyond the door's solid planks. The crowd was packed in against every opening. All of Jerusalem seemed to be one solid mass of bodies. Without concern for Titus, Caleb ran upstairs to his old room, which was thankfully vacant, and hurried to the window. What had been a garden just an hour earlier was now a scene from the bowels of Sheol itself. People were packed in, shoulder to shoulder, until it seemed they were no longer individual bodies, but merely a mass of pulsing, groaning flesh. No one had room to breathe, much less to move. The crying and wailing from below sounded like the torment of the damned. And if Prisca didn't make it to Deborah's.... Somehow Caleb knew she hadn't. She was out there in the struggling, roiling, dying crowd.

I can't get out. I can't get to her. Caleb dropped to his knees. "My little girl—Lord, I have no right to ask anything of You." An image of Jesus of Nazareth kneeling in the street before the blind beggar filled his mind. "If You really are who Phillip says You are, show yourself mighty on behalf of my child. Not for my sake—do with me as you will—but for the sake of my sons. They believe in You."

* * * * *

Prisca heard them coming before her grandfather did. They were still a long way from Deborah's house—too long a way. She turned back to look when she heard the footsteps thundering behind her. A wall of bodies rushed headlong toward them, and they were going to run her down. She wouldn't be able to outrun them on her own—and her grandfather was sick and slower than she was. Instinct, fused with her brother's teaching, took over. She headed for the niche of the nearest door, pulling at Lathan's arm as she went. "This way, Grandfather!"

"What are you doing, foolish child?" he snapped, tearing himself loose from her grasp. "This is not our house."

Prisca's momentum carried her into the niche, and she watched with horror as Lathan turned just in time to face the first man who ran into him. He managed to stay on his feet for a few more seconds, but the heedless stampede would not, could not stop. "Grandfather!" Prisca screamed as he was knocked onto his back. She heard his sharp cry of agony as he went down. Unable to bear the sight of him being trampled, she turned away, covering her face and hiding it in the shallow corner where the door met the wall.

Seconds later, she could no longer look back, even if she had wanted to. Other bodies pressed in on her, squeezing her hard into the tiny space she occupied until she could not turn her head—or move at all. Only the fact that she had her arms in front of her gave her any room to breathe. The bodies around hers continued to press, until she was certain they would crush her alive. Her forehead and face ached from being forced against the unyielding door and wall, but she was helpless to ease the pressure. In the next moment, she heard one of her ribs snap just before the pain sliced through her like a hot knife, but she couldn't draw enough breath to scream, or even to weep. Her heart sent up a final, desperate cry of its own. *Papa... Jacob... where are you? Where **are** you?* And the tiny bit of world left to her went mercifully black.

* * * * *

Out in the street, the stampede began to spend itself. When it finally became clear that the Roman army was not going to mow them down with their double-edged swords, those who could still stand upright gazed about them in dismay at the carnage they themselves had wrought—far, far worse than anything Rome might have done.

On another street, not far from where Lathan's mangled body lay, at the bottom of a pile of ruined and broken flesh, the edge of a gray robe lifted briefly in a passing breeze, fell back to the pavement, and lay still.

Little by little, across the city the screaming stopped.

Then the wailing started.

Chapter 16

Titus' footfalls as he came downstairs sounded heavy as one who carried the world on his shoulders. Going to Caleb, who sat with his head in his hands, the physician touched his shoulder. "The crowd is leaving the garden. It's probably safe for you to go out now."

Caleb raised his head. His eyes looked like bruises in his face. "I don't know how to thank you, Titus Albans. Your opening the door to us saved our lives."

"I am glad I could help," the Roman answered. "When you find your daughter, if she needs medical attention, bring her to me."

"I suspect you'll have your hands full for a while," Caleb answered, unwilling to say what he really thought, that Prisca was probably beyond help.

"Nevertheless," Titus said, "bring her here."

Nodding wordlessly, Caleb stood up, and he and the others went to the door. But though they pushed on it, it refused to budge. No one wanted to speak of what surely lay piled against it. "Let's go out the back," Jonathan suggested. "We cannot wait for all those..." he swallowed, and his face paled, "...all those people to be gone."

They were able to open the back door. The garden was in shambles, the flowers and small trees lay broken and trampled in the mud. An old man stood against the wall near the door, weeping and clutching his wrist. Caleb turned back toward the house and called out, "Titus, someone out here needs you."

Apparently, no one else who had been in the garden was injured. The last of those refugees were filing out the back gate. Caleb followed them, unwilling to stop to survey the ruin that had once been a green and blooming haven. Nor did he spare a thought for his father.

He was bent on finding his daughter.

Once they gained the street, they came into full view of the extent of the tragedy. Survivors, weeping and groaning, pulled the dead and the dying away from the walls of the city, and laid them out in silent rows on the street. "So many," Joel murmured, stepping around a human barricade. "So many have died."

Jonathan wiped his eyes on the back of his sleeve. "I've never seen anything like this."

Caleb slammed the door of his heart shut and bolted it. "This way." He turned right at the next corner.

Joel followed at his heels. "Is it possible that they could have made it to Deborah's? Don't you think we should check there first?"

Caleb shook his head. "Father didn't listen to me. I told him to hurry, to get her out of there, and the old fool stopped to have words with someone in the street. No, I don't think they made it to Deborah's, unless by some miracle."

"And what about Gedeon and Gallus?"

"We just have to hope they're all right. If Gallus is with Gedeon, he'll help him." *They have to be all right. Prisca needs me.*

All around, suffering survivors held out their hands toward them, wailing and pleading for help. One, a man about Lathan's age, clutched at the hem of Caleb's robe as he passed. "Have mercy, son. Help me." Caleb pulled away without a glance and continued on his course. He turned a deaf ear to the pleas, a blind eye to the trouble. He would spare no compassion for anyone until he knew what became of Prisca.

Finally, he turned another corner and stopped, muttering, "This is the street. Somewhere in here." He gestured to a chest-high heap of bodies that clogged the junction. "But there's no way around this."

Joel let out a low whistle. "I didn't think it was possible."

"What?" Caleb bent over to tug on one of the bodies and said, "You'll have to help me move them—unless we're going to climb over them." When Joel moved in closer to help, Caleb said, "What didn't you think was possible?"

"That anything could be worse than what we've already seen." With a grunt, he heaved at the corpse on top, a young woman who appeared to be pregnant, and moved it to one side. "Did you? But this is worse. I wonder if we'll even be able to walk down the street."

Caleb shook his head. "It is worse, but we will get down there. We have to."

"Let me through," Jonathan said. "I'll work from the other side." Caleb started to protest, *What other side?* when Jonathan hiked up the skirt of his robe, tucked it under his belt, and climbed over the bodies that blocked their way. He looked up once at them, at their shocked expressions, and shrugged. "They can't feel it." Once on the outside of the heap, he began pulling the bodies off one by one—a middle-aged man, a boy in his teens, an older woman—like so many bags of grain, and carrying them away. Soon Caleb and Joel were able to step over and pick their way up the street.

"The last time I saw her," Caleb said, "She was just there." He pointed to a spot where the street wound down and away to the right. "So we should find her somewhere past that."

They didn't search long before Caleb spotted a swollen, yellow foot jutting out at an odd angle underneath another body. "Over here!" he yelled. Joel and Jonathan removed the bodies that lay atop Lathan's. But Prisca wasn't there. Caleb went to his knees and studied the wreck that had been his father. "What have you done?" he muttered. In an agony of grief and anger, he lifted Lathan's torso and shook it. Lathan's head lolled back, his eyes wide and blind. "Where is she, you

As I am Known

old fool? What did you do with her? Was I your enemy, that you set out to destroy me?" He gave the body another fierce shake, shouting, "Where is she?"

Joel stopped him, pulled Lathan from his hands. "It's over, brother. It's over. Let him go."

"Prisca!" he shouted. "Where are you? Where are you?" There was no reply but the moans of the dying. Caleb raised his face to the clear blue sky, so pure and indifferent, and taking a deep breath, he howled like a wounded animal.

* * * * *

When the riot started, and Caleb took off running with Joel and Jonathan, Gedeon knew he would never be able to keep up with them. Gallus remained behind with him, and grasping his arm said, "I have an idea, sir. Come with me." Gedeon followed Gallus' broad-shouldered form as he turned the corner of the Temple wall and headed north in a trot.

No one else was going that way. They were all fleeing in the opposite direction. "Where are we going?" he called out.

Gallus shouted over the screams of the panicked crowd. "To the Antonia."

A couple of men running past them nearly knocked Gedeon off his feet, but Gallus reached back and steadied him. "You all right?"

Gedeon nodded, and panting, added, "Go... hurry."

After what seemed an age, they reached the fortress overlooking the Temple. Gallus fished around inside his collar, and pulled out a round metal token hanging on a leather strap around his neck. This he showed to the sentry, who nodded and stood aside to let them in. "Come with me," Gallus said, "I want to see what's happening." He started to mount the steps leading up into the tower.

Gedeon clutched a handful of his robe, stopping him. "What about my granddaughter?"

"Caleb sent her away before the riot started," Gallus answered. "She should have had plenty of time to reach her aunt's house." His blue eyes, rimmed red with unshed tears, told Gedeon his hope was nowhere as sure as his words. Quietly he added, "We cannot get to her, if she's out there in it."

Gedeon leaned back against the tower wall, put his head back and closed his eyes. "You go up. I'll wait here."

"As you wish," came the answer. "I won't be long."

Gedeon sighed deeply under the weight of his helplessness. *So much of this is my fault. If I had paid more attention, if I had investigated the matter of Caleb's divorce before I agreed to give Diana to him.... It was wrong—the whole thing was wrong—and I didn't have the eyes to see it. Now an innocent young man's life is* ruined, and Prisca...." The screaming from outside the walls pierced him to the core. He covered his eyes with one hand and wept. *Heaven has judged me.*

Several minutes later—"You there, what is your business?" A balding legionary with two day's growth of beard punched at his shoulder.

"I'm here with him," Gedeon wiped his eyes and pointed vaguely up the stairs. "With Gallus."

"That so?" the other snarled.

"It is so." Gallus broke in, returning down the steps. He showed the soldier his token. "He is with me." The legionary left them, muttering something under his breath about breaches of security.

When he was gone, Gallus said, "We'll be able to leave soon, sir. It looks like the worst of it is almost over." Gedeon nodded without reply, and he added, "It is a good thing Zerah is not here to witness this. It would break his heart."

With an effort, Gedeon pulled himself together and dried his eyes. "Tell me, if you will, how did you come to be his servant? Weren't you once a soldier?"

"Yes," Gallus said. "I was in the Eighteenth Auxilius. About fifteen years ago, I was part of a detachment ordered to stand watch at a tomb."

"At a tomb?" Gedeon frowned.

"At the tomb of a man who had been crucified two days before."

Suddenly he understood. "Ah, Jesus of Nazareth. I've heard all manner of rumors concerning that. But you were there. Will you enlighten me?"

"At the beginning, we passed the time jesting about the man we guarded. None of us knew anything about him except that he'd been executed for claiming to be a king. We joked that we were bodyguards for a dead emperor. I think we all felt insulted to have to stand watch over a corpse, and joking was our way of shrugging it off. The stone was rolled into place over the entrance of the tomb and sealed; no one was going to get in. In fact, it would have been difficult even if we hadn't been guarding it—the stone was that big, and that heavy."

Early in the morning, just before dawn, a giant warrior—half again as tall as any of us—appeared in shining robes." Gallus paused and shook his head. "Shining isn't the right word. *Blazing.* His robes blazed like the center of the sun. That's all I remember of him. In the next second, I was asleep. So were the others."

He pushed away from the wall. "I'm going upstairs to have another look. I'll be right back."

Gedeon waited, trying to picture the scene in his mind. *It was just at this time of year, I believe—right around Passover. And Phillip was at the execution. He told me he saw the man die. They put the body in the tomb, and rolled the stone over the door. I've never heard of guards being posted at a tomb. What would be the point, unless he was buried with treasure, the way the Egyptians do? A giant man in blazing robes? Is he saying they saw an angel?*

His thoughts were interrupted when Gallus returned, his face tight with tension. "I think we can go now. The running has stopped. Now we will have to face what has happened here."

"Tell me the rest of your story," Gedeon urged him as they left the Antonia.

"When we woke up, the stone was rolled away, and the body gone. Of course, we had to go and report it. If we had been guarding a living prisoner who escaped, we would be executed for dereliction of duty." Gallus' voice turned thoughtful. "I'm still surprised they didn't have us executed. We reported what happened, and they sent us out of the room while they debated what to do with us. I did not imagine they would do what they did."

"What did they do?"

"They paid us! They called us back in and gave us each a generous purse, telling us to say that Jesus' followers had stolen his body away in the night while we slept. They paid us to lie. Some of the guard justified it by saying we didn't know what had happened to the body, and that one story was as good as another."

"But you didn't think so," Gedeon said.

"As we were leaving, I saw a priest standing off to himself. Tears were streaming down his face, and as I passed, he tore his robes and prostrated himself on the floor. That frightened me, raised the hairs on the back of my neck. Once they paid us, our commander said we were off duty for the rest of the day, so I stood outside the Temple, hoping to see that priest again. I didn't understand what was going on, and I wanted to know why a bunch of holy men would pay us to spread a lie."

"About a half hour later I saw him leave, and followed him. He went to a couple of houses, and stayed in the second one for a long time. But at the end of the day, he went home. I marked where he lived and went back the next morning. We had a long talk."

"Zerah was the man you followed."

At this point in his story, Gallus and Gedeon rounded the corner of the Temple. Both of them stopped and gazed about them in shock. "It looked bad from above, in the tower," Gallus murmured, "But nothing like this. I've been in battles." He pressed the fingers of his left hand to his eyes and repeated, "Nothing like this."

Gedeon drew a deep breath, willing himself to look beyond the heaps of dead and dying, to shut his ears to the moans and crying all around them. "We have to find the others. We have to find my granddaughter." One more shuddering breath, and he stepped into the chaos.

* * * * *

When Caleb's howling ceased and he came to himself, he looked up to find Gallus and Gedeon flanking him, staring at Lathan's corpse lying prone in the street. Gedeon said, "And what of Prisca?" Where is she?" His voice came out in a rasping whisper.

"We haven't found her yet," Joel answered.

Gallus nodded toward Jonathan, who had busied himself pulling crushed bodies away from walls and lining them up on the pavement. "I'll go help him."

Caleb struggled to his feet. "We'll all help." He wiped at his face with an impatient hand. "I can do nothing for him." Without another glance at his father, he started pulling bodies away from the walls on the opposite side of the street from Gallus and Jonathan. Joel helped him, and Gedeon—well past the strength of his youth—arranged the corpses decently, straightened their clothing, and closed their eyes.

After about ten minutes, Jonathan cried, "Here she is! I found her!"

Caleb and Joel rushed to him, and together they pulled the last of the smothering bodies away from Prisca. Jonathan lifted her in his arms and carried her to the middle of the street. Purple bruises covered her face where she'd been pressed into the door. The evidence of Prisca's suffering sent a wrenching pain through Caleb's gut. "Is she breathing?"

Jonathan shook his head, and his voice caught. "I don't think so."

"Give her to me," Gallus demanded. He took her limp form and laid her down in the street. Bending over her, he put an ear against her chest. "She lives," he announced, "But barely." He looked around him, then stood up, surveying the street. "Jonathan, help me put her over my shoulder."

"We should get her to Titus Albans," Caleb said. "He's a physician."

"There's no time," Gallus panted as he and Jonathan hoisted her up. "We have to get her breathing now." Soon they had the little girl draped over his right shoulder with her head behind him. Gallus wrapped his right arm across her legs and grasped her ankles with his left hand. Without explanation, he started running up the street with her.

"Where are you going?" Caleb shouted. "That's no way to carry her. You'll hurt her!"

To his surprise, Gallus turned and trotted back, and just as he reached them, Prisca cried out. He lifted her off his shoulder and cradled her in his arms, patting her face gently. "Wake up, little one. Come on, wake up."

Prisca opened her eyes. Caleb heard a rush of breath from Gedeon. "You saved her. How did you know what to do?"

"We sometimes did this in the army," Gallus answered, "but we used horses— we'd drape the injured man over the horse's back and make the animal trot. It didn't always work, but often enough."

Caleb went to his daughter, and stroked tendrils of black hair away from her bruised face. "We have you now, love." She reached her arms out to him, and he took her from Gallus, his tears dropping onto her face and neck. "You're going to be all right."

Prisca turned her head toward Jonathan, her glazed eyes unnaturally bright in her swollen, discolored face. "I found a door, Jacob, just like you taught me. I got into a door."

Jonathan's fingers brushed her cheek. "You couldn't have done any better, little sister. I'm proud of you."

She turned back to Caleb with a moan. "My side hurts, Papa."

"We'll get you to a doctor, my heart," Caleb answered. "He'll take care of you." He started off, then turned and glanced back at Lathan's body.

Joel said, "You go on with her. Jonathan and I will take care of him."

Caleb nodded, but then stopped and handed Prisca back to Gallus. Wrenching the signet ring from his own hand, he took Lathan's, and jammed it onto the swollen fifth finger, saying, "You are no longer my father." Standing up again, with Gallus and Gedeon following, he went to find Titus.

* * * * *

This funeral was nothing like he would have expected. Caleb heaved a deep sigh as the stone was rolled over the tomb's entrance. Only family was present—Deborah and Nicanor, with their children, and he with Jonathan and Prisca, along with Gallus, Joel and Gedeon. And that was it. No friends, no hired mourners, no extra pallbearers to carry the bier, no flowery eulogies. Everyone in the city was too busy—busy burying their own loved ones, busy burying the bodies of their brethren from every corner of the world. *At least he's in a tomb. He wasn't put into one of those trenches.*

Only a precious few of the dead were sent home to relatives. Most were either laid to rest in long trenches in the fields away from the city, or they were tossed over the city wall into the Hinnom valley and left to burn. "Heaven have mercy on us," was an often-heard remark in those dreadful days when the pall of smoke hung like a filthy cloak over Jerusalem. "It's all we can do." No one was sure exactly how many died. The last Caleb heard, the number had topped twenty thousand. *And more will probably follow.* He hung his head. *So many were injured.*

Prisca interrupted his thoughts by tugging at his sleeve. He bent down. "What is it, love?"

"Papa," she whispered, her eyes haunted and fearful, " why is that man is staring at us?"

Caleb turned. Simon stood about twenty feet away, his arms folded across his chest. With a smirk of satisfaction, he said, "Shalom, *ben Lathan.*"

Caleb's jaw clenched with barely suppressed rage. He pulled Prisca closer to his side. "What do you want now, Simon? The man who ruined your father is dead." He started to add, *and my son is enslaved,* but stopped himself. Jonathan was standing right there. *Does Simon know who he is?*

The steward stepped forward a couple of paces. "Yet your children live. And I see Phineas told the truth—you do have another son. How convenient."

At this, Gallus pushed out from behind Caleb and ambled over until he was nearly within arm's length of Simon. Sneering with undisguised contempt, he looked him up and down, then turned to Caleb. "He came alone. How *convenient.*" He circled around behind him, and stopped. "Shall I take care of him for you, sir? I'll make it look like he was trampled, and toss him in the Hinnom. No one will ever know the difference. No one will miss him."

With a cry of alarm, Simon bolted away from Gallus. He shouted over his shoulder as he ran away, "It's not over yet, ben Lathan. I'm not finished with you!"

When he was gone, Nicanor laid a hand on Caleb's shoulder. " You know he was not in jest."

Caleb nodded. "I know. He'll never stop until we're all dead or ruined."

"Deborah and I have talked about leaving Jerusalem," Nicanor remarked. "We have friends in Antioch. Perhaps we'll pack up and go."

"I think I won't be coming back here to live," Caleb said. "My memories of this place are hardly happy. And I still want to find my son."

* * * * *

Evil tidings flew swift, mounted on eagles' wings until they covered the whole country. Within days, every family in Palestine, and many beyond its borders, began the heart-rending process of mourning for their loved ones.

In Caesarea Philippi, Helen called Jacob in to her. He had been packing the dozens of scrolls she intended to take with her back to Berea. The whole household bustled with its annual preparations to leave. "I just received word from a courier," she said. "There has been an incident in Jerusalem. Since you have family there, you should know."

Jacob frowned. "What kind of incident?"

"A riot," she answered, "and it was very bad." She paused, then standing up, began to pace as she often did. "Many people were killed—thousands. A friend of mine was among them."

"I'm sorry for your friend." Jacob turned away, and rubbed at his temples. *A riot.* Then he remembered. *Arin's vision! The running feet, the screams—her vision was about the riot. But in the vision, Father was looking for someone, and he knows I'm not there. Who then? Grandfather?* A sudden explosion of breath rammed into his chest, and he grabbed at the edge of the table as his knees began to buckle. *Prisca!*

"Jacob? What is it?"

Reluctantly he turned to face her. "I told you of my uncle who lives in Caesarea Maritime...."

"Yes. The one to whom you sent the message."

Jacob nodded. "Actually, we aren't related by blood. He is my stepmother's brother." He paused, panting from anxiety. "His oldest daughter...." He swallowed hard, "Arin is a prophetess, and during the winter she had a vision of the riot. In fact, she saw the same vision over a period of months before she told me about it." He raised his eyes to meet Helena's. "I have reason to believe my little sister was caught up in that riot."

"But you have no way of knowing for sure."

"No, lady. I do not."

"Will your uncle know?"

Jacob nodded, "I imagine he does."

Helena took her seat again. "Then perhaps it will help you to know that we are on our way to Caesarea Maritime." She smiled at his startled expression. "We have a brother in the Lord who is a sea captain, and he ferries me to and from Greece every year—from Caesarea. You have so far proven yourself trustworthy. I will allow you to see your uncle while we are there, so that you may know how your family fares."

Jacob might have rejoiced in being blessed with an understanding mistress, but he couldn't get Prisca out of his mind. *Lord, is she alive, or is she... with You? What did Jesus teach about the resurrection? He himself was raised from the dead, but what does that mean for the rest of us? Will we be raised, too?*

* * * * *

"You never finished your story." Gedeon said to Gallus that night after dinner. He and Joel and Gallus were alone in the room. Caleb had taken Jonathan and Prisca over to Deborah's, where they planned to stay the night.

Gallus answered, "How far did I get? Where did I leave off?"

Gedeon stared at the ceiling and rubbed his jaw. "I believe you said you followed Zerah home, and the next day you and he had a long talk."

Gallus took a last swallow of wine and nodded. "Zerah told me what he knew about Jesus of Nazareth. The trial, he said, was illegal by Jewish standards. That alone angered and sickened him. The day before—the day I followed Zerah—he went to see some colleagues of his. After talking to them, he believed that Jesus was the Messiah, the son of God that the Jews have been waiting for."

I spent most of the day with him, and he showed me many of the old prophesies, and how they were fulfilled with Jesus' crucifixion and resurrection. Then he asked me what I believed happened. 'You were there at the tomb,' he said. 'What did you see?'"

I told him about the bright warrior that appeared to us, and how we fell asleep. 'So what do you think about that?' he asked me. I told him I didn't know, but that what we were paid to say was a lie. His followers couldn't have gotten past us if we'd been awake, and they couldn't have made all of us fall asleep at the same time. We weren't drinking, and we were well-rested when we took up the post. Then there was the warrior. He wasn't a dream or a vision—he was *there*. Each of us saw him. I offered the money to Zerah, told him I didn't want it. It was dirty money—blood money. 'Give it to the poor,' he said."

Then I asked him what he thought happened to the body. He looked straight at me and said, 'He was raised from the dead.'" Gallus paused before adding, "That didn't surprise me as much as it should have. I think in the back of my mind I had already come to the same conclusion."

"And then you became one of them," Gedeon said.

"Not right away," Gallus answered. "For a while I assumed Christ was a god for the Jews only. But I continued to see Zerah whenever I could, and he convinced me otherwise, again by using prophecy. When I confessed my faith and joined the Way, I knew my days in the Legion were numbered. Rome does not tolerate divided allegiance from its soldiers, so I went to talk to my centurion. He had been in charge of the crucifixion. He said he understood my dilemma, that he himself was still struggling with all he saw the day Jesus died. But he also said there was only one honorable way out of the army—and that was to be disabled."

Gallus held up the stump of his right arm. "So he did this."

The shock forced Gedeon to put his head down and close his eyes to stop the room from spinning. "As a punishment?"

"No, I asked him to."

Joel broke in with a gasp, "I didn't know that, Gallus. You never told me." The soldier answered with a noncommittal shrug, as if the loss of his hand was but a small thing.

Gedeon said, "So you gave your right hand to become a follower of the Nazarene. Why your right hand? Could he not have taken the left?"

"He had to take the sword hand. Otherwise, I might have been deemed still fit for combat." One corner of his mouth curled up. "I didn't bother to remind him that I am left-handed."

"What did you do after that?"

"I went to Zerah the day I received my discharge and offered to be his servant. He has taught me much, and I have never regretted it."

A long silence followed. Finally Gedeon spoke. "My son Phillip also believes in Jesus of Nazareth. He has risked everything—our family inheritance, his mother's regard, my respect, even at times his own safety, his own life. I have not always agreed with him, but he is a man of courage and conviction. If the story you tell is true, if Jesus was raised from the dead, Phillip's risk-taking makes sense."

"And if Phillip is a man of sense," Gallus countered, "he wouldn't risk so much for a lie."

Gedeon raised his eyebrows and nodded. "Well said. I have long believed in the God of the Jews, and have worshipped Him, forsaking the gods of my fathers." He stared into his empty cup. "My son is right. I don't know how I know this, but I *know* it." He looked up at Gallus and Joel. "You have a wonderful and courageous faith. I want to be part of it."

Later that night, just before the three men surrendered to sleep, Gedeon said, "Gallus, you saved my little girl. I am in your debt."

"I only did what I was trained to do," he replied.

"Perhaps. But is there something I can do for you? Is there some way I can repay you?"

After a pause, Gallus answered. "There is a slave in Caiaphas' household, a girl named Mina...."

* * * * *

"Nikos." Jacob, who had grown weary of reciting Latin declensions under his breath as he walked, trotted to the front of Helena's curtained litter and fell into step with the bodyguard. "You've been on this journey before, haven't you?"

The Greek nodded. "Many times."

"How long does it take to get to the other Caesarea from here?"

Nikos pursed his lips. "We should make Bethsaida tonight. Tomorrow, we will sail across the lake to Tiberias." He lowered his voice, "That is, if the lady doesn't dawdle."

"I heard that, Nikos," came Helena's unruffled voice from inside her litter. "Visiting old acquaintances is not dawdling."

"And from there," he resumed, as if he had not been interrupted, "we go west to Sepphoris, then south and west to Caesarea Maritime. About five days' journey altogether."

"I see. And how long do we stay in Caesarea before we sail?"

"That is for Demos to say."

"Demos?"

"The captain of the ship we will take to Greece. We sail when he says we sail. Maybe a day, maybe a few hours, maybe a week."

"I see." Jacob watched his feet carry him the next few steps. "I know nothing about sailing. I've never even been on a boat."

"Is that so?" Nikos eyed him as if he were some new species of animal he'd never seen before.

"I've never been to the sea at all, though I'm from Jerusalem, and the Great Sea isn't that far away. But I have been to Damascus."

"Damascus," Nikos nodded. "Interesting city. We went there... I believe it was five years ago."

"It was four years ago, Nikos," the lady Helena corrected him.

Nikos didn't smile, but his eyes shone with amusement, and Jacob knew the Greek remembered exactly how long ago their trip to Damascus had been. He misspoke on purpose so Helena would react.

Nikos gave him another sidelong glance. "You are a scribe."

Am I? He had written and sent dozens of messages for Helena in the past few weeks. Jacob nodded thoughtfully. "Yes, I suppose I am."

"If I wished to send a message to someone, will you write it for me?"

"If the lady Helena permits," he answered, "I will be happy to."

A few minutes later, Nikos asked, "The matter of reading and writing—is it difficult?"

Jacob hesitated. *He is asking me if he can learn. And he probably can, though I've known some who had a hard time with it.* Finally, he said, "It is sometimes difficult, but if a man perseveres, it can be done."

"We will have idle time on the journey, especially on the voyage. If the lady permits, will you teach me?"

Again Helena's voice floated out to them from the litter. "Please do, Jacob. It'll keep him out of my hair."

He ducked his head to suppress a smile. "I will be honored to teach you, Nikos." *It will also keep my mind occupied, and off—other things.* He could hardly wait to get to Caesarea, but at the same time, he dreaded it. He dreaded what he was going to have to do. Taking a deep breath, he said, "I can teach you the Greek alphabet as we walk, and later I'll show you what the letters look like."

Nikos nodded, "That is acceptable."

"I will say the letters, and you say them after me. Alpha... beta... gamma... delta...."

* * * * *

That night, in one of Bethsaida's inns, Jacob brought a cup of fresh goat's milk to Nikos as he sat guard outside Helena's door. He knew Nikos would stretch out and sleep there. The bodyguard took the cup and thanked him, then said, "I was not in favor of the lady Helena buying you."

Jacob sat down, hugging his knees. "Why not?"

"You were a stranger, and I don't like strangers so close to her. It was obvious from the start that she was going to treat you with greater favor than most slaves. I thought you'd take advantage of her good grace."

Jacob nodded. "I can understand that, but I am curious—did you actually *tell* her you were against it?" When Nikos nodded, he said, "She shows you great favor, then. I don't know of many slaves who are allowed to advise their masters."

"I am not a slave."

Jacob felt the color rise to his face. "Are you not? My apologies, Nikos. I assumed...."

The Greek shrugged. "Most people do. I let them think what they will. But I am her hired servant. My family has served hers for generations."

Jacob sat and digested this. He had been raised to ignore other people's servants. But knowing Gallus and Nikos—and now being a slave himself—had opened his eyes to a new reality. *We are all alike in many ways, regardless of station.* "Do you have a family?"

"My wife and children are in Berea," Nikos answered. "I get to spend the warm months with them."

They talked quietly about Nikos' family for a while, and the Greek asked, "How about you? I know you have someone in Caesarea."

Jacob nodded and cleared his throat, unsure if he'd be able to keep his voice steady. "My father and sister are in Jerusalem. I have an aunt and uncle, and cousins there as well. My mother and brother are in Antioch." He looked up, and caught the puzzlement on Nikos' face. "It's a long story. I also have an uncle and aunt by marriage, in Caesarea, and...." He trailed off, unable to finish.

"You have a sweetheart."

Jacob pressed his eyes with the fingers of his right hand. "Arin. We are... were betrothed, before...before all *this* happened."

"You have broken your betrothal?"

"I will do that when we get to Caesarea. I won't hold her to a promise I can no longer keep."

*   *   *   *   *

The journey from one Caesarea to the other was fairly easy and uneventful, except for the unnatural quiet of the cities. People passed each other on the streets with barely a glance. Everywhere Jacob looked, he saw someone weeping. He felt like weeping himself, but he held on to hope that his fears for Prisca were wrong.

They had walked a gentle down-hill grade from the heights of Caesarea Philippi, on its elevated plateau, to the coastal city of Caesarea Maritime. When they came into view of their destination, with the wide, blue sea beyond, Jacob's heart swelled at the sight of the expansive water, then closed like a fist with anxiety. *Lord, I don't know how I can do this. It hurts to even think of it. And I don't want to hurt her. Give me the right words to say.*

Once they reached the city, Helena sent Jacob with Nikos to the docks to look for Demos. They found him on the deck of his black-hulled ship, shouting orders to a knot of sailors on the wharf. When he caught sight of the burly Greek, his sun-bronzed face lit up with a grin. "Nikos, you're here at last! Come aboard, my friend!"

Jacob followed him up the ramp onto the ship. He felt the deck bob gently under his feet—just enough to remind him that he wasn't standing on solid ground. He tried not to stare at the bustling seamen around him, or the soaring masts above. Nikos and Demos embraced, slapping each other on the back. Demos said, "And who is this with you?"

Nikos turned. "This is Jacob. He is scribe to the lady Helena."

Demos' enormous hands swallowed Jacob's. "Welcome aboard, Jacob. You ever sailed before?"

"No sir," Jacob answered.

Demos grinned. "I thought you had that look about you. We'll make a seaman of you in no time." To Nikos he said, "You'll have to cool your heels a few days before we set sail. I'm waiting on another passenger from Jerusalem."

"From Jerusalem? What's the latest word from there?"

Demos' smile faded. "It's the worst I've ever heard. Two of my men were there. Both survived, Heaven be thanked, but thousands are dead. They say the whole country is mourning."

"It is," Nikos answered. "Everywhere we've been. Jacob has family in Jerusalem."

Demos' black eyes, full of concern, met Jacob's. " And have you had news of them?"

"Not yet, sir. I am hoping to find out something while we're here."

Demos nodded and laid a hand on Jacob's shoulder. "I will pray for you, that the news will be good." To Nikos, he said, "You're staying in the usual place? I will send for you when my other passenger arrives—assuming the weather holds."

As they left the ship, Nikos said, "The lady Helena instructed me, that if we weren't sailing right away, to give you the afternoon to visit with your family. You'll probably want to have a meal with them, so return to the inn two hours after sundown."

Jacob nodded. "I will."

As I am Known

He started to turn away, when Nikos said, "All may yet be well, Jacob. Don't let fear strangle you."

Jacob watched him stride away down the wharf, and with a sigh, he folded his arms and faced the water. *I'm here, Arin. I finally made it to the sea.* With a start, he remembered that he'd have to ask directions to Phillip's house. *And time is short. I only have this afternoon.*

A short, muscular man approached him. "You look lost, lad. Is there something I can help you with?"

"I am looking for someone who lives here," Jacob answered. "His name is Phillip."

"Well, I know a few Phillips." He rubbed at his scruffy beard. "There is a Phillip who is a tax collector... not that one? And there's a tent maker named Phillip. He has one leg."

"No, that wouldn't be him either," Jacob said. "This Phillip is a preacher...."

"Oh, *that* one. He comes down here at least once a week and preaches, talks to the men. Everyone likes him." When Jacob nodded, the wharf master pointed north. "That way, about a mile up the beach. Little, two-room house."

Jacob thanked him and trotted off. Soon he was in sight of the house. *That has to be it.* His steps slowed, and he licked at his lips and wiped his forehead. Absently, he toyed with the earring that marked his station. *Will they understand?* Running his fingers through his hair, and straightening his robes, he started toward the door.

He hadn't gone a dozen steps when it swung open, and Prisca stepped out, staring at him open-mouthed. Without a word, she ran down the path toward him, limping and clutching at her side. His heart constricted with anguish at the purple stains on her face. *She's been hurt.* Jacob ran to meet her, wrapped her up in his arms and held her close. "Baby girl," he murmured over her, kissing the top of her head. "You're alive."

"Oh, Jacob," she sighed. "I knew you'd come."

He closed his eyes and let the tears fall. "I was worried about you, little sister. So worried."

"I found a door, Jacob," she answered into his robe. "Just like you told me to. I got into a door."

When he opened his eyes again, he saw his father tearing down the path toward them, shouting his name. And there was Arin, standing in the doorway, waiting.

Chapter 17

"I am ready for my dinner now, Simon." Caiaphas lowered himself onto the cushions with ponderous dignity. "What does the cook have for me this evening?"

"Doves with onions, sir, stewed in wine and spices." Simon poured his master's wine into a silver cup embellished with elaborate twinings of grape vines and pomegranates. He took a sip of the wine and set the cup before Caiaphas. "I will bring it in."

He carried the platter in from the kitchen, enough food to serve three hungry men, and laid it on the table. Without bothering to look up, Caiaphas asked, "Have you tasted it?"

"I haven't, my lord. My apologies." He dipped into the dish and sampled a mouthful of the meat. "It appears to be safe, and if I may say so, it is delicious."

Caiaphas heaved a sigh and drew a long face. "I do hope so. All this fasting has made me hungry."

Simon kept his expression carefully neutral, but he thought, *You old bag of wind, you haven't been on a real fast in my lifetime.*

"I tell you, Simon, the city faces a terrible dilemma."

"Does it, my lord?"

"We have buried the dead, and cleaned up the streets, but the stench of the riot continues. The people go about grumbling. No one is happy. And I understand that they are mourning. I myself lost a nephew and a brother-in-law."

"So what do you suppose makes them unhappy?" Though he was obligated to keep the conversation afloat, Simon was growing bored with Caiaphas' posturing.

"They feel helpless," he answered. "A great evil was done to them, and they have no recourse. No doubt Caesar will replace Cumanus soon. And the swine of a soldier who started it has been beheaded, but that is not enough."

"What *would* be enough?" Simon asked. "With so many dead...."

"Precisely my point," Caiaphas gestured at the air with a flopping piece of a dove's carcass. "With so many dead, how can there be any hope of restitution?"

Simon didn't bother to remind him that the Romans had killed no one, that the riot was largely a result of sheer panic on the part of Cumanus, as well as on the part of the crowd in and around the Temple precinct.

"If only there were someone we could *blame,*" he continued, "someone who could be publicly punished."

Simon's ears pricked up at this, his boredom suddenly forgotten. "You are looking for a scapegoat."

Caiaphas paused in mid-bite and frowned. "A scapegoat?"

"Of course, my lord. The sins of the people laid upon one creature, that creature sent into the wilderness...."

"To be torn apart by wild animals," the High Priest nodded. "An interesting thought. Justice would be satisfied."

"And Rome also," Simon offered.

Caiaphas coughed, and took a drink of his wine. "Well, at least I could tell Caesar I had done *something*."

"It just so happens, my lord, I know of a man who is suspect in the incident."

Caiaphas turned his head, his gaze on Simon as casual as a coiled snake. "Do you? Who is it?"

"Caleb ben Lathan."

Caiaphas snorted. Moments later his ample belly shook with laughter. "Surely you can do better than that! Ben Lathan's a bungler, not a man of intrigue."

But Simon would not be put off, not when the prize he sought lay so close at hand. "I wouldn't be so sure of that, my lord. Remember, he was in league with tax collectors."

"Well, that was the rumor, of course, but it was never proven."

"Pardon me if I speak frankly, my lord. In my experience, rumors usually have some basis in fact."

"Go on." Caiaphas stuffed another mouthful down. "I'm listening."

Simon fought his rising nausea. Really, it was almost too much—that this disgusting dog should be in power, while he himself was forced to beg for crumbs! "Ben Lathan sold his house and left the city not long after that, and the tax collector in question has also disappeared. That should be evidence enough of their collusion."

"All right, I take your point. But what has that to do with the riot?"

"Ben Lathan was in the city again when it happened." He didn't bother to mention the obvious—that more than two million others were there as well. "If he is a collaborator with the Romans, and we know he was, and if he was ruined when he was discovered, which he was, then wouldn't he want revenge? How better to avenge himself than by inciting an incident with Rome?"

"There are too many holes in your case, Simon. Ben Lathan is a decent enough man. Why would he want all those people to die?"

Simon shrugged. "He probably didn't. He couldn't have foreseen that his actions would fly out of control as they did. However, ignorance that does not make him innocent."

"Hm-m-m." Simon waited, compelled himself not to fidget while Caiaphas mulled it over. "I assume he survived the riot."

"Yes, sir. His father was killed, but he himself survived."

"So Lathan has died. That's too bad." Caiaphas lifted his cup in salute. "Now there was a man with some skill."

Simon's rage ground like shards of glass between his teeth. *Lathan wasn't nearly as skilled as I am. After all these years of waiting and planning, my time has finally come.*

"Very well, Simon. Tell me what you have in mind."

The next morning, Simon set out from Jerusalem on horseback, with a scroll signed by the High Priest himself, accusing Caleb ben Lathan of blasphemy, and authorizing Simon to bring him to justice. There would be no trial. "Just let me take care of it," Simon had said. "That way, you can stand clear of the dirty work and still say you saw justice done."

"And you're sure he's in Caesarea?"

"I had him followed, my lord. As of yesterday he was still there."

"Fortuitous that the procurator should be there also," Caiaphas mused.

"Indeed. Very convenient."

"Take care of it then, and report it to Cumanus as I have instructed. Then return here with all speed and report to me."

Simon made a low bow, happy to have a way to hide his triumphant smile. That smile surfaced again as he rode out of the Damascus gate. *Now I begin to understand what Phineas loved about his work. Pity he was trampled.* His thoughts turned to Caleb. *Pity his firstborn is under that woman's protection. I can't get to him. But there is always the other boy—and ben Lathan himself is in my hands.* **My hands!**

* * * * *

Jacob's fears concerning his family's welcome were swept away within the first minutes of his appearance, and he was astonished at how many of his loved ones were packed into his uncle's house. Aside from Phillip's family, and his father and sister, there was Gedeon, his Uncle Joel and Gallus, with Gallus' new bride, Mina. Jacob let out a whoop of joy when he spotted Jonathan in the throng, and gave him a hearty embrace. Only Zerah, Odelia, and Mary were missing—and his mother.

"How long can you be with us?" Caleb asked him.

"I was given this afternoon until two hours past sundown," he answered, "but we may be in Caesarea a few more days. Perhaps... perhaps I can get permission to come back." The hesitation of his answer dropped into a silent room, making him painfully aware of the restrictions of his status. "She really is a kind woman...." he began.

Caleb embraced him, his eyes wet and shining. "Son, we understand what you did, and why. You are not to blame."

"Speaking of that," Phillip said, "I sent word to Zerah and your mother, telling them what happened. I wanted them to know you were safe." He crossed to a shelf in one corner, picked up a small scroll, and handed it to Jacob. "This is a reply from your mother. She hoped I'd be able to get it to you somehow."

Jacob took the message and tucked it into the purse at his belt to read later. He turned to his father. "I want to explain why I sent word to Uncle Phillip, and not to you." His hands clenched together, his knuckles knotted and taut. "When Phineas kidnapped me, he told me that someone in my family paid him to kill me." The misery of uncertainty made his voice rough. "I believed him. I knew you didn't do it, but since I didn't know who did, I couldn't safely send a message to you."

Caleb answered, "You acted wisely. Your grandfather and stepmother agreed to this evil. And I was no longer in Jerusalem. If the message had ended up with Deborah, it's likely your grandfather would have heard about it. I am sorry, Jacob. I didn't see the damage he was doing to the rest of us until it was almost too late."

"Does Grandfather know what's happened to me?"

Caleb shook his head. "Your grandfather was killed in the riot."

A whimper just behind him made him turn around. Prisca buried her face in her hands and started to cry. Jacob went down on his knees and pulled her to him. "What is it, Prisca? What's wrong?"

"I tried," she sobbed. "I tried to help him, to pull him into the door with me. But he wouldn't come."

"Oh, little one," he murmured and held her to him. "It wasn't your fault, Prisca. Please don't blame yourself." Then he saw a familiar cord around her neck. "Well, what's this? What do you have here?"

She sniffed and dried her eyes. "Salome gave it to me. She said you made it."

Jacob looked around him and found Salome, her eyes brimming with tears. Recalling her delight when he gave her the necklace, and keeping one arm around Prisca, he beckoned to her with his free hand. He drew her into their little huddle and kissed her forehead. "You helped my sister," he said. "Thank you, Salome." She nodded and wiped at her own eyes, and Jacob whispered, "I still had some necklaces left in Damascus. If you'd like another, I'll get my friend Gallus to send it to you."

Salome's happy gasp told him he'd said the right thing. She whispered back, "Do you have another blue bead?"

"It's hard to remember for sure, but I think there was a blue one. If not," he kissed her again, "I'll have him pick out the prettiest one and send it."

At that, the two girls joined hands and scampered off. Jacob stood up. He smiled at Gallus. "You heard?"

The Roman nodded. "You had them in that little wooden box on the shelf, didn't you?"

"Send Salome the blue one—I'm almost certain I had another of that color left—and pick out a pretty one for Mina. Oh, and would you see to it that my mother gets one? Take the rest back to Attalus with my thanks." His face clouded over. "I will miss him." He sighed, "I want to write to Zerah...." Jacob shook his head, unable to say more.

"If you are unable," Gallus answered, "I will take him word of your love. He is fond of you, Jacob. When you were stolen, I was afraid for him, afraid what the strain might do to him, but he's held up well and said in his last message that he prayed for you every day."

"The Lord heard his prayers," Jacob said, "be sure to tell him that." His eyes went to Arin.

Gallus followed his gaze. "Go on, lad. She needs to have you to herself."

Jacob approached Leah and kissed her cheek. "May I borrow your daughter for a little while?"

"Of course you may," she answered with a tremulous smile. "Take as long as you need."

Jacob held out a hand to Arin, who had been watching with wide, gray eyes. She took it, and he led her outside and toward the shore. His heart was a lump of lead pounding dully in his chest, and all the way down the path he searched for the right words, for something—anything—he could say that would make breaking their betrothal easier. When they reached the edge of the water, they stood and watched the waves wash the sand at their feet. Finally, Jacob said, "I made it to the sea, Arin."

"What do you think of it?" she asked him.

"It's far bigger, far grander, than any words can tell," he said, cherishing the feel of her hand in his. "And in another day or two I'll be on it, sailing in a ship."

Arin nodded and looked away. Her free hand strayed up to wipe at her face. Jacob's throat locked in helpless desperation. *I have to do this. Lord, help me.* He swallowed several times until he was sure he could speak, and even then it came weak as a whisper. "Beloved, I am releasing you."

Arin didn't answer right away. Thinking she had accepted his words, he tried to let go, but she held onto him. "Why?" she asked, and her grip tightened. "Why are you doing this?"

"Because I can't keep my promise to you. The lady Helena owns me until she dies, or until she sees fit to release me. I don't know when that will be, but it may be years." He bowed his head. "It will *probably* be years."

Arin's voice when she answered was edged with iron. "I do not release you." She turned to him, her eyes dark as a storm, and repeated, "I *do not* release you."

She gazed into his eyes, and her expression softened. "Jacob, I have loved you ever since we were little children. And you have loved me." She spoke no more than the truth, and he nodded. "The Lord bound us together long ago, and the cords that hold us cannot be broken by time, or distance... or even death. Solomon's song says so, remember?"

"'Love is stronger than death,'" he quoted.

"I will wait for you."

He started to protest, but she laid a finger against his lips. "You want me to be happy, and you think releasing me will make this parting easier, but Jacob, I am happy with you. I am happy to have you in my heart. I will wait, however long it takes, and I will entrust you to the Lord."

Groaning in agony, he pulled her to him, and resting his face atop her head, anointed her hair with his tears. "I can't stand this."

Arin was crying too, her halting reply muffled against his robe. "You have to stand it, Jacob. We both have to."

He held her close while they wept. He could have gone on holding her until time was shattered by eternity's hammer, but all too soon Arin released him and stepped out of his arms. Turning away, she took a few slow steps along the beach. Not knowing what else to do, he followed. Another few steps, and she bent down, and burrowing her fingers into the sand, plucked a shell from its sea-soaked grave and washed it off in the leading edge of the tide. She murmured, "This is a nice one," and held it out to him.

"It's beautiful." The shell—coiled like a snail's, but much larger—nestled in his palm, gleaming pure white in the afternoon sun, and shimmering like a pearl. The beauty of it humbled him. *It makes my beads look gaudy by comparison.* He started to give it back to her, but she shook her head and closed his fingers around it.

"Take it with you, since you no longer have the other one."

Jacob swallowed and promised, "I'll bring it back to you when I can."

"I will wait."

*   *   *   *   *

Simon arrived in Caesarea that same evening, eager to get started. When he reached his informant's house, however, he found out that trouble had preceded him. "A mob from Jerusalem attacked and robbed one of Caesar's servants," his informant told him. "Beat the fellow half to death. Cumanus was forced to retaliate. The word is that he's sent squads of soldiers to the villages nearest Jerusalem to ransack them."

"That is nothing to me," Simon answered. "I have authorization to bring ben Lathan to justice, and that is what I will do."

"You want to proceed tonight?"

"No," the steward answered. "We will wait until morning. I want a clear view of ben Lathan's face when his sentence is carried out. You do know where he's staying, don't you?"

"As of this morning, he was at the house of a man named Phillip, who is also called the Evangelist."

"Evangelist?"

"He's one of that Nazarene sect. He preaches all over the area."

Simon folded his arms, and smiling said, "There's an interesting bit of news. So ben Lathan is also in league with those trouble-makers. That will only make things easier for me."

His informant stroked his beard. "I don't know that he's one of them, sir...."

Simon waved him off. "Doesn't matter. For my purposes, he is." He thought for a minute before adding, "Go ahead and ask the leader of the synagogue for an audience tonight. I want to talk to him first. The rest will wait until morning."

* * * * *

Jacob savored every bit of the food the women had prepared. *This will be the last meal I eat with my family for a long time.* Between bites he told them all that had happened to him after he was captured. He sat where he could see Arin clearly, and when he told of how he had preached in the prison, and how men had called upon the name of the Lord because of it, her eyes glowed. "The guards also listened to the words the Spirit gave me to say," he continued. "And the commander of the prison happened to be the son of the woman who rescued me."

Phillip smiled. "'Happened to be'? There are no coincidences, Jacob. The Lord planned the whole thing."

Jacob glanced at his father, who suddenly seemed fascinated with the appearance of his food. *So he is still not part of the Way.* He said, "Then His plan was just in time. I wouldn't have survived another night in the prison, the way things were." He shook his head. "But there is still something I don't understand, and it bothers me. Why was Simon so insistent on bringing me back to Jerusalem? He had other apprentices before me, and he didn't pursue them."

Without looking up, Caleb said, "Revenge."

Jacob frowned as he tore a piece of his bread apart and dipped it in the sauce. "I don't understand, Father. Revenge for what?"

"According to what I was told, your Grandfather ruined the career of another money changer, and the man was forced out of Jerusalem. This happened many years ago, when I was still a child. Simon was that man's son." Caleb shook his head with remorse. "I imagine Simon spent all his life looking for some way to retaliate, and I fell right into it when I offered to apprentice you to him." Then he frowned, remembering. "Come to think of it, he approached me. He must have gotten wind that I was looking for a position for you." He rubbed at his forehead, as if to erase the memory. "He planned to use you to destroy me."

"But why you?" Jacob asked. "If Grandfather was the one to blame, why come after you?"

"Eye for an eye," Caleb replied. "His father was ruined, destroying Simon's chance to have his own table in the Temple. So he came after me, set out to destroy my livelihood, thereby getting back at my father, ruining us both in the process. You were just the finishing touch on his scheme. He had me financially. He wanted to break my spirit, too."

After dinner came a time of prayer. Jacob heard Gedeon's voice raised to Heaven, along with the others. *He has put his faith in the Christ. Lord, I thank You for that. You have given me many reasons to rejoice tonight.*

But what about my father?

* * * * *

It wasn't the first time Caleb had found himself in the middle of a group of Jesus' followers listening to them pray and worship. And he was certainly no stranger to worship itself, having worked in the Temple for so many years. But tonight something stirred in him. He peeked through nearly-closed eyes at the others. Jacob and Jonathan stood side by side, arms upraised. Most of the women sat, but Arin knelt with her head touching the floor. Gallus knelt across from Caleb, both arms lifted high, and he felt a shock of sympathetic pain course through him. Gedeon had told him the former soldier's story. *He had his hand cut off so he could be one of them.* Phillip knelt beside him, his hands cupped in front of him. The attitude of his body reminded him of something. *Of what?* With another jolt he remembered. *The blind beggar at Siloam.*

He and Phillip had both witnessed it, had seen Jesus of Nazareth kneel in front of the beggar and daub his sightless eyes with mud. They had followed the man to the pool of Siloam, watched him grope his way to the water and wash. And the man could see. His eyes were opened.

Just like Miriam's ears. Reuel was healed. So was my father. Jesus must have known my father hated him, but he came anyway. Why? Because Miriam asked him to? What was it he said to his followers when he healed that beggar? With stunning clarity, Jesus' words rang in his ears as if it were yesterday. *"While I am in the world, I am the light of the world."* He swallowed hard. At least the beggar had faith to follow the prophet's instructions. *I had more reason to believe than he did.* Almost without thought, Caleb lifted his own hands. "Forgive me, Lord, for I have been blind, and my darkness far exceeds that of the beggar. You are the light of the world. Open my eyes, that I may see."

Heaven heard. Light flooded Caleb's soul, sweeping away darkness and fear, sweeping away his sin. A voice whispered to his heart, sure and strong, "This day you are My son." With a shout of raw joy, he sprang to his feet and sang, "Give thanks to the Lord, for He is good. His love endures forever. Give thanks to the God of Gods. His love endures forever...." By the time he sang the second "forever", everyone else had joined him. He opened his eyes once more. Jacob and Jonathan both had tears streaming down their faces—tears that mirrored his own.

* * * * *

A little later, just when Jacob was becoming painfully aware that time was getting away from him, Phillip said, "Caleb, why don't you and your boys go outside for a while?" Caleb nodded and headed for the door, with Jonathan following. When Caleb glanced back, Jacob said, "I'll be right there."

"No goodbyes tonight," Arin warned him with a shake of her head when he took her hand. "If you can't come back here, send word to us, and we will see you off when you sail." Then she smiled. "Your prayers for your father were answered." She raised up on tiptoe and kissed his cheek. "Go talk with him, Jacob."

He let his eyes linger on hers a moment longer before turning to go outside. Caleb and Jonathan both waited just beyond the door. When he joined them, Caleb said, "Let's go up to the roof."

The evening was fine and clear, with a bright, waning moon. They sat down on the rooftop, suspended between the silver light washing the sky, and the tide pulsing below. Caleb cleared his throat and rubbed at the stubble on his jaw with one hand. "I hardly know what to say. A year ago, I would never have expected to be sitting here with my two sons." He shook his head in wonderment. "It means more to me than I can tell you. And... and the Lord has accepted me. Now I understand. I understand why your mother...how she could.... " his words faltered. ""Your mother is one of the most courageous people I've ever known. I hope you two can forgive me for what I did."

Jacob was quick to reassure him, but Jonathan hung his head. Finally he said, "At first I didn't want to forgive you, even though Mother spoke well of you. I didn't understand how you could send us away." He raised his eyes, "And to be honest, I didn't want to claim you as my father. Reuel raised me. He was with me every day."

Caleb nodded. "He did well. I will always be grateful to him."

Jonathan said, "These past few weeks have taught me much. I saw that you had a heart that longed to do good. And I saw how you were deceived." The beginnings

As I am Known

of a smile played at his mouth. "Now that you are my brother, as well as my father, I guess I have to forgive you."

Caleb chuckled. "Well said, son. I deserve that."

Jacob broke in, "Father, I'm going to have to leave soon, and I don't know if I'll be able to come back. Will you bless me before I go?"

"I don't know if there will be an inheritance...."

"That's not what I mean. Knowing that you love me—that you came looking for me—is inheritance enough. All I want is your blessing."

He waited while his father searched his face. Finally, Caleb said. "I will come to you in the morning, and give you my blessing then." When Jacob looked away in disappointment, Caleb said, "I want time to think about it and pray."

Jacob stood up. "I need to go. Perhaps they'll let me come again tomorrow."

Caleb stood with him, and caught him up in an embrace. "Whether they do or not, I will come to you in the morning, son. You have my word."

"And I'll come with him." Jonathan added.

Caleb reached out to him with one hand, and the three of them held each other until Jacob pulled away. "Until tomorrow, then," he murmured. When he reached the bottom of the stairs, he trotted off into the night, back toward Caesarea.

Caesarea Maritime was a modern, Roman-style seaport, with its streets laid out in a logical grid. Once he reached the city, it only took him a few minutes to locate the street for the inn where they were staying. There he stopped in his tracks, his breath caught in his throat. A familiar figure stood several houses away with his back turned. *Simon! Or is it?* Without thinking, Jacob retreated into the shadow of a doorway. *Is that him?* He rubbed at his eyes and peered into the night. The man he was watching wore the same kind of clothing he remembered seeing on the steward. *But it's been a year since I've seen him, and there may be many people here who dress like that.* Still, he waited.

Moments later, the man stepped into the yellow circle of light cast from a nearby house. At the same time, he turned. Lamplight, coupled with moonlight showed him the steward's face clearly, the angry set of his face, the prominent vein on the forehead. *What is he doing here? He looks like he's waiting for someone.* Whatever the steward's business, Jacob decided it couldn't be good. Just as he made up his mind to exit his doorway and go around in a different direction to the inn, another man came out and joined Simon where he waited.

Jacob was too far away to hear everything, but his heart skipped a beat when Simon said, "...ben Lathan. First thing in the morning?" The next thing he was able to make out was, "...and the son, too...."

The other man said something that sounded like, "Corruption of blood?"

Simon laughed and nodded his head. "The sins of the father...."

The two men shook hands, and Simon came down the street. Jacob shrank back into the shadow as far as he could. His palms had gone clammy, but he dared not wipe them off. He dared not move at all. In a fair fight, he thought he could probably beat Simon, but he didn't want to risk it, not in a strange city, certainly not as a slave. If he lost, or even if he got the better of him and Simon cried out for help, Jacob was as good as dead. No one would take the word of a slave against the word of the steward of the High Priest. And by the time the lady Helena found out, it might be too late. *Lord,* he prayed, *shield me from my enemy. Hide me in the shadow of your wing.*

Simon passed by him without so much as a glance in his direction. Jacob waited until he was out of sight before he abandoned his hiding place and sprinted to the inn. "Nikos," he gasped when he found the bodyguard. "Has the lady Helena gone to bed yet?"

"She has not," he answered. "What's the matter, Jacob? You look like you've seen a ghost. Did you have bad news of your family?"

"Not exactly." Jacob bent over with his hands on his knees, heaving for breath. "I saw someone on the way here. I need to talk to her, if she'll see me."

Nikos studied Jacob for a long moment, apparently trying to decide whether disturbing his mistress would be prudent. Finally he shrugged. "I'll ask her, but this had better be important."

Jacob nodded. "It's on my head. I understand."

Nikos knocked at the door and opened it. "Jacob has returned, Lady. He wants to know if you will talk to him." He glanced back toward Jacob who was still panting from his run. "It appears to be somewhat urgent." He nodded and stepped aside. "She will see you."

"Thanks, Nikos," He straightened his robes and went in, then halted in shock. The lady Helena was seated on a stool in the middle of the room. Her maid was combing out her hair, which flowed in silver ripples to her waist. Jacob had never seen a woman's hair unbound and unveiled. Even Roman and Greek women covered their heads in public, and they wore it up in braids. He felt his face go hot, and averted his eyes. "Thank you for seeing me, lady."

"What is this about, Jacob? How is your family?"

"They are well, thank you," he answered.

"And your sister? Is she all right?"

"She was injured in the riot," he answered, "but she will recover."

"You had good news then," she said. "Why did you want to talk to me?"

"I saw someone on the way here," he said, still careful to not look at her. "Simon, the steward of Caiaphas."

"The one who hired Phineas to come after you?" When Jacob nodded, she probed, "Are you sure it was him?"

"I had a good look at him. He was with another man, and I heard some of what they said." He related what he overheard, and told her what his father had said about Simon's quest for vengeance.

"This is a serious matter," she said when he finished.

Jacob's heart swelled with hope. *She understands. Surely she can help me.*

"You can look at me now." The maid had plaited her hair for the night, and covered it with a veil. Helena stood up. "Do you understand what 'corruption of blood' means?"

He nodded. "I believe so. It means that if a man breaks the law, his family is guilty by association, and they can also be punished."

"That is correct." Helena steepled her fingers and tapped them against her lips as she began to pace. "I wonder how he knows you're in Caesarea." To Jacob's questioning look, she said, "He did say, 'and the son, too.'"

Jacob chewed at his lower lip. "He did, but he may have meant my brother, Jonathan. If Simon's been watching my father, he may have seen my brother. We look a lot alike."

"And he said, 'first thing in the morning.'" She stopped her pacing and turned to him. "What did the other man look like?"

Jacob closed his eyes, trying to remember. "He was wearing a Pharisee's robes, and he was older than my father—maybe forty or forty-five. Some gray in his beard. About Simon's height."

Helena sighed. "I don't know many of the Jews here." She held up one finger. "But you said he lives on this street, or at least that he met Simon on this street." Turning to Nikos, she said, "Go talk to the innkeeper. See what you can find out."

With a nod, Nikos was gone. Jacob said, "Lady, may I please go to my family tonight and warn them?"

She shook her head. "You may not. It's far too dangerous. If I send anyone, it will be Nikos." She sat down again. "The problem is that I dare not touch Simon. Were he a lesser man, Phineas for example, I'd have him arrested—at least until your father could go away. However, he is Caiaphas' steward, so I have to assume Caiaphas sent him. If that is true, all our lives could be in danger."

"But you're a citizen of Rome," Jacob protested.

"So is Stephanus," she answered, and explained, "He's one of the emperor's trusted servants. Two days ago a mob attacked him. They robbed and beat him. The procurator is in Caesarea because of it. Citizenship has its advantages, but this far from Rome, those advantages do not always afford full protection. If I cross swords with Caiaphas, I am almost sure to lose."

Jacob's heart sank. "Then you can do nothing. I'm sorry, lady—sorry I disturbed you."

She wheeled around to face him. "I am *disturbed* that you think so little of me." He felt the burn from the fire in her amber eyes. "You told me that one of your friends is a former legionary. If he were here, he would no doubt tell you that in battle, every man is assigned a station, and that each man must hold his station until the battle is done, or until his commander issues new orders. You have your station, Jacob, and I have mine. You're not the only one who hears from his Commander." Her expression softened. "I prayed about you, about what to do with you, from the moment Tertius told me of your plight. I am following my Commander's orders. He has instructed me to keep you out of harm's way, and that is what I will do."

Shamed, Jacob hung his head. "I understand, lady. But my brother and father are in mortal danger."

She nodded. "It is likely they are. You will have to take that up with Him. Jacob, I believe there is more going on here than this matter with Simon. This isn't just about you and your family. We are in a war we cannot see." Now she approached him and laid a hand on his shoulder. "We will do whatever may be done, but we have to leave the outcome to the Lord. It's not in our hands."

Chapter 18

Jacob spent the night on his knees. Several times during the long, dark hours, he was tempted to get up and go out, to run to Phillip's house, despite Helena's forbidding, to risk whatever punishment she might see fit to inflict on him for his disobedience. But each time, a quiet inner voice urged him to be still. In the prison, he had learned to trust that voice. *You preserved my life, Lord. I belong to You, and I will obey.* Still, the battle was hard fought. He worshipped, and he interceded for his family, pleading for his father and brother, that God would keep them safe. When the rosy veil of dawn brightened the eastern sky, weariness had settled deep into his bones, but his heart was at peace. *The Lord has a plan in this,* he reassured himself. *He will work it out.*

Nikos stuck his head in the door a few minutes after Jacob murmured his final 'amen' and said, "We must go now. I'm taking you to Demos' ship."

The room did a slow spin around him. Jacob clutched at a nearby table for balance. "We sail today?"

"Demos hasn't sent for us," Nikos answered. "The lady Helena ordered me to take you to him for safekeeping. Then I will go to your family and warn them."

Things were not turning out as he thought they would, but Jacob said, "Let's go, then. We're wasting time."

The two of them hurried out of the inn, and once they were in the street, Jacob dashed off toward the wharf, with Nikos close on his heels. On the way, they passed the synagogue, where a crowd had already gathered, and was moving away to the north, Simon striding along in the middle of them, making some kind of speech, urging them on. "There he is. That's Simon." Jacob stopped short to point, causing Nikos to barrel into him. He fell to the ground, skinning both knees. "We're going to be too late," Jacob panted.

Nikos hauled him up by the arm. "Get going. Hurry!"

"You go on to my uncle's," Jacob said. "I'll go to the ship by myself."

"No good," Nikos shook his head. "I promised the lady Helena I'd personally see you there first. Now go!"

Spurred by the Greek's command, Jacob took off again, ignoring the pain it cost him to run. It seemed to take an eternity to reach the wharf, and far too long for Nikos to locate Demos and explain the situation to him. But at last, he turned to Jacob. "Now tell me where your uncle lives."

Jacob pointed north. "That way, about a mile up the beach." He described the house, and pleaded, "Hurry, Nikos. Get them away from there." He lowered himself onto a crate and bowed his head, panting from the run. *Oh, Nikos, please, please hurry!*

Moments later, Demos sat down next to him. "You all right, lad?" Jacob could only manage a nod. Demos passed him a dipper. "Here's some water. Drink it up." Jacob hadn't realized he was thirsty until the cool, sweet liquid hit his parched throat. He didn't refuse seconds.

"You want to tell me what's going on?" Demos asked. "How did you get yourself in the middle of such a mess? I can see you're not used to being a slave."

Jacob knew Demos was trying to distract him from worry, but he complied. "It's a long story, but I'll make it as short as I can." And he began to explain what had happened to him, from his escape from Jerusalem, to his kidnapping by Phineas.

When he mentioned the man-hunter's name, Demos stopped him. "Phineas, you say? Dresses in gray, walks with a limp?"

"You know him?"

"He bought passage on my ship a few months ago," the captain answered. "He was on his way to Cyprus. He wouldn't tell me what his business was there, but I learned from a friend that he was searching for a couple of preachers. My friend thought he meant them evil, and so I went ahead of Phineas when we got to the island and warned them."

Jacob's stomach turned over. "Who were the preachers?"

"A fellow from Tarsus named Saul, and a Cypriot named Jonathan—some call him Barnabas."

A sudden rash of gooseflesh prickled Jacob's arms and raised the hairs on his neck. "My best friend was with those two men." He stood up, gazing out toward the city. From the wharf, all appeared deceptively peaceful and business-as-usual. "That's how Phineas found me," he murmured. "He got to John Mark." He turned back to Demos. "Did he hurt anyone while he was there?"

"Not to my knowledge. I had him watched. He came to the island alone, and he left alone. We had no report of anyone being injured by him."

Jacob crossed his arms and sighed, then uncrossed them again and ran his fingers through his hair. Demos said, "If you want, I'll send one of my men out to see what's going on and have him report back."

Jacob dropped back down onto the crate. "I can't ask that of you. Too many people have been hurt because of me."

Demos grunted, and leaning forward with his elbows on his knees, combed his short, graying beard with his fingers. "The way I see it, lad, no one's been hurt because of you. There's something bigger going on. You're just one little piece of it."

"Lady Helena said something like that last night," he answered. "She said this was a war."

Demos nodded. "A wise woman, that one." Straightening up, he put his fingers to his lips and blew a shrill whistle. "Erastus!"

A burly seaman with arms like tree trunks waded toward them through the barrels and crates. "Sir?"

"You know the Evangelist, don't you?" When the seaman nodded, Demos said, "He lives a mile up the beach. There's some kind of a ruckus going on there. Go have a look and report back."

Erastus glowered. "Somebody bothering him?"

"Him or one of his relatives," Demos answered. "See what you can find out."

When he was gone, Jacob asked, "You know my uncle?"

Demos nodded and smiled. "He's the reason I follow the Christ."

* * * * *

Running on sand was far harder than Nikos would have guessed. It sucked and dragged at his feet, making one mile feel like four. By the time he came in sight of Phillip's house, his lungs were on fire. *And I'm too late.* The mob was already there. They had surrounded the house, and their angry shouts carried perfectly all the way to the water.

He stopped to study the situation, wiping his face on his sleeve. *Now what?* Seconds later, the door opened, and a man stepped out. Feral cries of triumph erupted from the crowd when he appeared. *That has to be Jacob's father,* Nikos told himself.

The fellow Jacob had identified as Simon seized Jacob's father by the arm and dragged him into the midst of the mob, which turned as one man and started back toward the city, carrying him along with them like an evil riptide. But Simon wasn't satisfied. "Stop!" he screamed. "We must take his son, too. They are both guilty!"

Enraged for Jacob's sake, Nikos charged up the path to the house. "You will not!" he roared, shoving Simon away from the door.

He tried to barrel his way through the throng to Jacob's father, but Caleb looked back, his eyes wild with fear, his mouth already bloodied and cried, "Save my son! Save my son!"

Nikos turned back toward the house. More than a half dozen had surrounded a man with pale yellow hair, who was fighting them off with a ferocity that Nikos recognized and admired. *That has to be Gallus.* A woman's scream sounded from inside the house. Simon had gone in with several others, and they were dragging a young man out with them. *Jacob's brother.*

Nikos waded into that bunch, wresting the boy from Simon. "Let him go!"

"No!" Simon screeched. "He is mine!"

At that moment, Gallus won free of his battle and fought his way through to Nikos. His blue eyes met Nikos' black ones for a bare instant, warrior to warrior, and he spun Simon around to face him. Simon took one look at him, and at the damage he had done to the men who thought to beat him, and screamed, "I'll see you crucified!"

"Not if you are dead," Gallus answered with a humorless smile. "Now let the boy go."

But it was Jonathan himself who punched and shoved at Simon until he was free. Simon fell to the ground, scrambled up, and ran after the mob, shouting for them to come back and take the boy. They ignored him. He had whipped them into a frenzy at dawn with his accusations of blasphemy and inciting the riot in Jerusalem. And Caiaphas had been right about one thing—the people wanted to punish someone. They had seized the culprit, and they would not be swayed from their purpose.

Jonathan started after them, shouting for his father, and it took both Nikos and Gallus to stop him. "No, Jonathan," Gallus said, holding onto him with a firm grip, "you must not."

"They'll kill him," he panted, trying to wrench himself away.

"They will kill *you*," Nikos told him. "They planned from the start to kill you both."

About halfway to the city, the mob stopped moving. Several stooped to pick up stones from the ground. "Get the boy inside," Nikos said. "He shouldn't see this." The two of them wrestled Jonathan, who was howling with rage, back into the house.

Once inside, Gallus cuffed the side of his head, "Control yourself, boy," he growled, "You're frightening the women and dishonoring your father."

With a sob Jonathan sank to his knees, put his forehead to the floor, and covered his face. Nikos looked around him. An older man sat in one corner, his arms around four young girls who clung to him, all of them weeping. Nikos nodded toward him and asked, "Is he the one they call the Evangelist?"

"No, he isn't here," Gallus answered. "Phillip and his wife, Leah, and Joel went into the city last night to visit with Leah's brother." Then he held out his right hand, "Thank you for your help. I could not have saved him without you. May I ask your name?"

Clasping his hand in his own, the Greek answered, "I am Nikos, bodyguard to the lady Helena."

"Jacob's mistress?"

"Yes. On the way back to the inn last night, Jacob overheard Simon plotting with another man against his father. I asked around and found out that the other man is the leader of the synagogue here. I set out at dawn to bring you warning, but the mob was ahead of me."

"And what of Jacob?"

"He is safe. He is aboard a ship docked at the wharf. They have orders to set sail if they run into trouble."

Gallus went back to the door and opened it. His mouth fell open. "I don't believe it."

"What? What is happening?" Nikos shouldered into the doorway to see.

"There's a woman out there. It looks like she's trying to stop them. Is that the lady Helena?"

Nikos' face went hot. "She didn't tell me she was going to do this. And who is that man with her?" He bolted out of the house.

Gallus turned to the others. "Everyone stay here," he ordered them. "Stay here and *pray*."

By the time Nikos reached the scene, the mob had ceased stoning their victim. The lady Helena moved, cool as a snowdrift, between his body and the angry crowd. "I am a Roman citizen," she announced in clear, ringing tones. "I have worshipped the Lord for many years. I helped to build the synagogue in Caesarea Philippi."

"Are you the lady Helena of Berea?" someone in the crowd shouted. "The one who's related to Caesar?"

"I am," she said. "And you are...?"

Instead of answering, that one shook his head, and dropping his stone, retreated a few steps before turning and running away. About a dozen others followed him. Several more dropped their stones, but remained where they were. Simon stepped forward. "What right do you have to stop us?" he demanded. "I come under the authority of Caiaphas."

"And I have come at the request of Cumanus, the procurator," she answered. She gestured to the man with her, who was now kneeling over Caleb's bleeding body. "This the procurator's personal physician, Titus Albans."

Titus laid an ear to Caleb's chest and gestured for quiet. He tried a second time, and a third. At last he raised his head. "We are too late, lady. He is dead."

Helena walked right up to Simon, her lovely eyes now red with suppressed tears. "You got what you wanted. Now let us bury him."

"Not quite," he smirked. "I will have his sons, too." By this time, about half of the crowd had dispersed. Nikos shouldered through those who remained and went to stand beside his mistress.

"Really?" she took another step closer, stopped and cocked her head as if listening. When she spoke again, she lowered her voice till it was little more than a whisper. "I know some things about you, Simon. Shall I tell them?" She gestured to the crowd. "Shall I tell them what you do to boys?" Simon's face went white, and he looked like he might vomit. "Shall I tell them about the idols you keep hidden in your room? How you defile yourself, and then go into the Temple?"

Helena repeated, "The man is dead. I suggest you leave it at that. If any harm comes to either of his sons, I will expose you for what you are."

With a snarl of impotent rage, he backed away from her. "You won't live forever, you know."

"Nor will you," she answered. "May the Lord judge you."

At that, he stalked away, and the rest of the crowd went with him. Nikos turned to see Gallus kneeling over Caleb's body, weeping as if for a lost brother. *Someone is going to have to tell Jacob,* he thought sadly.

*   *   *   *   *

On the *Phoenix,* Jacob occupied himself by washing his skinned knees with a clean wet cloth Demos gave him, and picking the gravel and dirt out of the wounds. He continued to pray under his breath as he did so. *Thank You for allowing me to see my mother again.* He sniffed, and daubed at his right knee, wincing at the sting. *Even if I never see her again, at least You brought us together that one time.* With a start he remembered her letter, which had gone forgotten in all the excitement. Jacob sat up and opened his purse, pulling out the scroll. *Zerah must have written this for her.* He broke the seal and unrolled the paper.

> *To my dear son, Jacob,*
>
> *Phillip has sent us word of what became of you after you were taken. I am sorry such extreme measures were necessary to save you from that evil man, but what is most important is that you are alive and well. I have prayed for you every day of your life, and will continue to do so as long as I have breath.*
>
> *Your father was here. I think by the time he left again, we were at peace with each other. He was always a good man—now he is becoming a strong one. He loves you with his whole heart, Jacob. He gave up everything to go looking for you.*
>
> *By the time you read this, I will have gone home to Antioch. My husband needs me, and I've been away from my other children for too long. Zerah gave me one of your bead necklaces, a red one on a purple cord. I hope that is all right. It is a lovely thing, and I will treasure it.*
>
> *Write to me, if you are able. Be strong in the Lord. Serve your mistress as if you were serving Him. I am so thankful I had a chance to see you again, to get a glimpse of the man I knew you would become. I love you.*
> *Your Mother.*

The last few lines were smudged where drops of water had fallen on them. *Tears.* Jacob wiped at his own eyes, then frowning, examined the letter again. *This is not Zerah's handwriting.* He read the missive once more, and rolled it back up. *I will have to write to her after today. Whatever happens here, she'll need to know.*

* * * * *

Arin stood up to get a cup of water for her sisters to share. Except for their sniffing, the house had gone unnaturally quiet. She took her father's cup from the shelf, since it was the biggest, and filled it with water from the pitcher. *It's nearly empty. We need to draw more sometime today—and soon.* Her heart quailed at the thought of walking all the way into town. Would the mob be gone? Sudden shame for her cowardice seized her, and her hands shook when she picked up the cup. *They're out there killing Jacob's father. They're stoning him, the way Papa's friend was stoned.* A single tear tracked down her face. *I'm glad Papa wasn't here to see this.*

She took a sip from the cup, refilled it, and took it to her grandfather, who nodded his thanks and passed it around among the younger girls. Arin turned away and went to the door. She put one hand on the latch, wondering if she dared open it. She glanced at Gedeon, who shook his head and said quietly, "Let me." With gentle hands, he untangled himself from the girls' clinging arms, and stood up. When Prisca whimpered, he said, "It's all right, little one. I'm going to help Arin. I'll be back in a minute."

He crossed the room with the stiff gait of a much older man. "Get behind me," he murmured as he opened the door. She peered out over his shoulder. No one was near the house. About a half mile away, atop a small rise, she could see the mob. Gedeon watched for what seemed a long time before he said, "They're just standing there. And some of them are leaving." He let out a long breath. "It must be over."

Closing the door again, he turned to her, and reached out, stroking a stray hair from her face. "My poor little girl. You've lost your betrothed and your father-in-law, all at once." Arin fell into his arms, and they held each other and cried. Gedeon alternately prayed over her and hummed an old lullaby he used to sing to her when she was little. She buried her face in his robe, taking comfort in the circle of his arms, his rumbling voice, and the familiar smell of him—a grandfather smell of outdoors, and wine, and the oil he used on his hair. Despite her sorrow, she felt the tension seep out of her.

"Open the door! Open the door!" A shout from outside separated them, and Gedeon yanked at the latch. Arin stepped back as Gallus hurried in, followed by a large man she didn't recognize. Between them they carried Caleb's battered body.

"Clear the table," Gallus ordered her, and she rushed to take away the bowls and pitcher. Another stranger followed them in, older and slimmer than the first, and finally a woman with regal bearing, dressed in fine, white linen.

"Papa!" Prisca screamed, and jumped up. The older stranger turned at the sound of her voice. He got down on one knee and intercepted her flight to her father, and while the others were laying Caleb out on the table, he said, "Prisca, look at me." When her gaze finally shifted to him, he asked, "Do you remember me?"

She nodded, her chest heaving with suppressed sobs. "You're the doctor. You bought our house."

"That's right. I took care of you when you were hurt, remember?" She nodded again. "Now your papa is hurt, and I have to take care of him."

Her eyes were deep pools of fear. "Is he going to die?"

The physician took both her hands in his. "He may, but I am going to do everything I can to stop it. Understand? And I may have to hurt him some more, in order to help him."

"Like when you put the bindings around me, and it made my ribs sore?"

"Something like that, yes." He stood up and said to Gedeon. "Is there somewhere she can go where she won't see this?"

"Come, Prisca," Gedeon took her by the hand. He turned to the other girls. "Salome, Lyssa, come with me. Let's go out into the garden."

When he had led them all outside, the doctor said to Arin. "I need you to build up the fire. Get it as hot as you can."

She nodded and fled outside to gather another armful of wood. By the time she came in again, she began to understand what he intended to do. Caleb's lower left leg was a mangled mess of blood and shattered bone. "It'll be easier on him if I do it while he's unconscious," the doctor was saying. "As for his internal injuries, either he will recover, or he won't."

Arin put the wood down, and Gallus stooped to help her, the two of them frantically blowing on the flame. Suddenly, he sat up. "Where's Jonathan?"

Arin gasped, "Jonathan! I haven't seen him since you left."

Muttering a curse under his breath, he stood, and stalking to the door, flung it open and started out. "Gallus!" The physician stopped him. "You can't leave now. You and Nikos must hold him down."

The soldier remained where he was, murmuring something under his breath in a language Arin didn't recognize. Finally the tense set of his shoulders relaxed, and with a sigh of resignation, he shook his head. "I wouldn't even know where to look for him."

"He went to find Jacob," Arin answered, her voice harsh from blowing on the flames.

He turned abruptly. "He told you this?"

"No," she answered, poking at the fire to encourage it, "but that's where I'd go if I were Jonathan."

She wiped at her damp forehead, and as she leaned over to blow on the flame again, the doctor laid the blade of a long, sturdy knife into the coals. He asked her, "Is this all the water you have in the house?"

She nodded, her face flushed with shame. "They came so early.... I wasn't able...." Fresh tears sprang to her eyes.

"It's not your fault," he reassured her. "Do you have wine?"

"Those two jars in the corner," she pointed. "I can run get more water now...."

"We can't wait," he answered. "Bring me one of the wine jars."

Arin jumped up to do his bidding, and Mina came to tend the fire in her place. The doctor took the jar she handed him, and poured wine liberally on Caleb's wounds. "This gash on his arm will have to be stitched," he murmured. Turning to Arin, he asked, "Can you give me a strand or two of your hair?"

She nodded, and without thinking, uncovered her head, and worked through her braid with frantic fingers to loosen it. She separated three hairs and pulled them out, laid them in her palm and offered them to him. Only afterward did it dawn on her that she had uncovered her head in a roomful of men. She watched, fascinated, while the physician threaded his needle and stitched the gash in Caleb's arm. "You sew very neatly," she murmured.

"Why, thank you," he answered. "I try, but I'm no expert like you ladies." He turned and looked at the knife. "Now for the difficult part." To Gallus and the stranger, he said, "You two to take hold of him while I do this, in case he thrashes." He gave Arin a pointed look. "This will be bad. You may want to go outside."

"Thank you, sir, but no. I will stay."

"As you wish. In that case, be ready with the wine when I call for it." He plucked the knife from the fire. "Here we go."

Arin turned her face away. She heard a snapping sound as the knife cut through bone, and Caleb screamed once in bitter agony. She squeezed her eyes shut. *Lord, strengthen him. Help him through this.* A hissing sound followed, and Arin's nose caught the smell of cooking flesh. She bit down on her lower lip as she felt her legs weaken and concentrated on the feel of the cool jar in her hands. *Lord, please don't let me fall!*

"Wine!" the doctor ordered, and she opened her eyes, surprised to see so little blood, and poured the remaining contents of the jar on the freshly cauterized stump. The big stranger named Nikos was just ducking out the door, carrying the mess that had been Caleb's lower leg.

"I brought bandages with me," the doctor told her. "They're in that bag over by the door."

She dug into his bag and found several rolls of white cloth strips. When she handed them over, he said, "One more thing. Get some olive oil, and I'll show you how to dress the wound." Arin took the jar of oil from the shelf. When he had taught her how to anoint and wrap the wound, he said, "You must change the bandages every day until this is healed. Every single day, understand? Use clean bandages each time. And take a good look at the wound. If it grows red and puffy, send for me. I'll be in the city for a while yet." He laid a gentle hand on her shoulder. "What's your name?"

"Arin."

"Well, Arin, it's been a pleasure having you assist me. You did a good job." At that moment, Gedeon came in again with the younger girls in tow. The physician picked up his bag and went to the door, where he stopped and said, "I understand you are a praying family. This would be a good time to get to it." With that, he was gone.

* * * * *

Jacob had just finished reading his mother's letter when Erastus appeared at the end of the wharf. He stood up to get a better look. There was someone with him, following just behind him. As they neared the *Phoenix,* Jacob shouted, "Jonathan!" and scrambled to the gangplank. Running to his brother, he gripped his arms. "What's happened? Where is Father?"

A breathless sob tore through Jonathan. "They took him, Jacob. They took him, and... and they stoned him." He sank to his knees. "I couldn't stop them." He lowered his head and cried bitterly.

Jacob groaned. *Nikos didn't get there in time. I should have gone last night. Lord, why? Why did You let them do this?* Too shocked to weep, he hauled his brother to his feet. "Tell me what happened."

"They came just after first light, came banging on the door. They demanded that we—father and I—come out to them. They said if we didn't come out, they would come in. Phillip and his wife, and Uncle Joel were gone. They had spent the night in the city. The little girls were so frightened, Jacob. They were all crying.... Father told me to stay where I was, and he opened the door... and he went out. Some man came in and dragged me out, too, but a big fellow with black hair showed up...."

"Nikos," Jacob said.

"I guess so. He and Gallus got me away from him. They shoved me back inside and ordered me to stay there. Jacob, they killed our father. No one could stop them. I couldn't stop them." With a harsh cry, he collapsed into Jacob's arms, and the two young men clung to each other and wept.

* * * * *

Soon after the doctor left, Arin remembered the woman who had come in with him. She looked up to see the lady seated across the rooms on the cushions. When their eyes met, the lady beckoned to her. "Sit here with me a little while." She patted the cushion next to hers. Arin sank down, suddenly aware of just how tired she was. "You are a strong young woman," she said, "but I would expect no less from Jacob's betrothed."

Arin stared at her. "How... how do you know about that?"

The woman nodded toward the black-haired Greek who had helped Gallus carry Caleb inside. "Nikos told me."

Then Arin understood. "You are the lady Helena."

"Yes, my dear, I am."

The two women appraised each other frankly, until Arin lowered her eyes. "I have you to thank for saving his life."

"Arin," Gallus called to her, "We're ready to move him now. Where should we put him?"

She answered, "My parents' room will be best. It's quieter in there." To Helena she said, "And you brought a physician. You've saved my father-in-law as well."

"That remains to be seen," Helena answered. "His recovery will be long and slow—if he recovers."

"But you did what you could." She bowed her head. "I'm surprised they didn't kill him."

"They intended to," Nikos said as he came back out of her parents' room. "The lady Helena stopped them before they could finish the job. It was a clever bit of acting," he added, "having Albans pronounce him dead."

"I assure you, Nikos, it was no act," Helena said. "He *was* dead. His heart had stopped. But while you were carrying him here, he started breathing again." She turned her attention back to Arin. "I wonder if you would indulge my curiosity. Are you and Jacob still betrothed?"

Arin colored to the roots of her hair. "We are. I told him I would wait for him."

Helena nodded. "There are few believers in Berea. We need someone with his gifts to come and help us." She reached out and took Arin's hand. "If you ask me to release him now, I will. I think the danger from Simon is over. But if you are willing, I want to take him with me—for a few years at least."

Arin's heart felt like it would crack under the weight of her choice. *Father, how can I refuse You anything, when You have given me all I have?* Blinking back her tears she said, "He belongs to the Lord."

With the gentlest of smiles, Helena said, "True, but you still haven't given me an answer."

"Send him back to me when it's time," she closed her eyes with a sigh, "when the Lord releases him."

Helena leaned forward and kissed her cheek. "As I said, you are a strong young woman. Thank you." She released Arin's hand and stood up. "Nikos, take me back to the inn, and go get Jacob. Let him have the rest of the day here." With a polite nod to Gedeon and Mina, she swept out the door.

* * * * *

Jacob and Jonathan started back up the beach toward Phillip's house, trailed closely by Erastus. "I can't believe Demos let you go," the seaman muttered. "The lady Helena will skin his hide, and probably yours, too."

"I don't care," Jacob answered. "I just want to see my father one last time." *But there won't be a blessing. Grandfather took it from me long ago. He set the wheel in motion when he made Father vow to send me away. I wonder if he would have done differently if he could have seen the end of it?* He kept his head down as he plodded through the sand.

"You'd better start caring now," Erastus remarked. "That looks like the lady herself coming this way."

Jacob's head snapped up. There was no mistaking the stately woman gliding toward them along the water's edge, or the muscular block of a man who followed close behind her.

"Well, Jacob," she remarked as they met, "what's this? I ordered Demos to keep you on his ship."

""It is my doing, lady," he answered. "I am going to pay my last respects to my father."

"No, I don't think you are," she replied.

Jacob's hands curled into fists at his side. "Lady Helena, forgive me, but I *will* go to him...."

"Calm down." Her quiet words cut like a steel blade. "You misunderstand. I am not happy to see you here, but I was going to send you to your uncle's house anyway. Your father is alive." Jacob's knees nearly buckled under him. Jonathan clutched his arm with shaking hands and held him up.

Helena said to Jonathan, "You are obviously his brother. Go on, then—go see your father. Jacob, I will send for you when Demos is ready to sail. Until that time, you remain with your family—and don't you dare disobey me again."

"Yes, lady," Jacob gasped. "Thank you!"

* * * * *

Caleb woke up just after sunset. One eye cracked open in his battered face. "Father?" Jacob took his hand. "Father, we're here—Jonathan, and Prisca, and I. We're all here."

Caleb moved his hand to touch Jacob's face, and opened his other eye, which was blood-red. "You're safe," he breathed. "All three of you—safe."

Prisca kissed the one spot on his forehead that wasn't bruised. "The doctor had to hurt you, Papa, but you're going to get well now."

"My brave girl," he smiled. His gaze went to Jonathan. "And you got away from them."

"I had help," he answered. "I'll tell you about it when you're better."

Caleb nodded, and the movement made him wince with pain. "I should have died," he moaned.

"No, Papa," Jonathan answered, "The enemy meant to kill you, but he was thwarted. The Lord means you to live."

"There is a purpose He intends for you," Jacob added.

Caleb swallowed. "I nearly lost each of you. But He gave you back to me." A tear rolled down his battered cheek. "He gave you back."

Phillip put his head in the door. "I thought I heard your voice." He came in and stood over the bed. "How do you feel?"

His swollen lips cracked a smile, "Worse than I look."

"That bad?" Phillip sat down at the foot of the bed. "Caleb, I'm sorry I wasn't here earlier...."

"You couldn't have stopped them," Jonathan told him. "They were too many."

Caleb said, "They might have stoned you, too. The leader of the synagogue looked... disappointed that you were gone."

Phillip got up with a sigh. "I'm just glad you're still with us. I lost one friend this way already, and that is one too many." He went to the door. "Call if you need anything."

Caleb turned his head toward Jacob. "Come closer, son." Jacob felt a thrill race though him as he understood his intent, and he leaned toward his father. Caleb laid a hand atop his head. "May the Lord bless you. May your life be long in His service, and may He fulfill all His purpose in you. May you find favor with the Lord, so that even your enemies praise you. May your marriage be a happy one. May your wife be like a well-watered vine, lovely and fruitful. May your table be crowded with strong sons and beautiful daughters. And may they bring you the riches of joy that you have brought to me."

Jacob's tears fell freely on his father's shoulder. "I love you," he whispered.

"And I love you, son."

    *   *   *   *   *

Two days later, Nikos came knocking at the door. "It's time to go, Jacob," he said. "Demos is waiting."

Jacob said hurried goodbyes to everyone. He kissed Leah and Lyssa, and—with Gallus' permission—kissed Mina, who blushed and kissed him back. He hugged Joel, and Phillip, then ducked into the bedroom, and laying his head briefly on his father's chest, told him goodbye.

"I've decided to take Gedeon up on his offer," Caleb said. "I'm going to Ephesus. After all, I have another son to look after."

Jacob nodded. "I'll write to you when I can."

Coming back out, he caught Prisca up in his arms and held her close. "Take care of Papa."

"Will you come back and see me?" she asked.

"When I can," he answered. "But while I'm gone, remember that I love you."

He embraced Gedeon. "Sir, I cannot thank you enough for all you've done. You were truly a grandfather to me."

"Thank you, son." Gedeon's hold on him, though brief, was fierce. "God bless you in all your ways."

Jacob turned to Jonathan, who shook his head. "I'm seeing you to the ship."

"So am I," Arin said. "We'd better get going."

*   *   *   *   *

On their way down the beach, Jacob said to Jonathan, "Let me ask you something." He pulled the scroll from his purse. "I got a letter from Mama, but I was wondering who wrote it."

Jonathan laughed. "Who do you think wrote it, if it's from Mama?"

"I know it's from her, but who *wrote* it? Do you recognize the handwriting?"

Jonathan unrolled it and gave it a cursory glance. "She did."

Now Arin laughed. "You should see your face, Jacob. You look like somebody slapped the back of your head!"

Jonathan grinned and did just that, then skipped away, just out of reach. "Hey!" Jacob exclaimed. "Come back here!"

Arin gave him a sidelong glance. "There's something I haven't told you. If we're going to marry, you should know."

Jacob felt his heart turn over inside him. "What is it?"

"I can read and write, too."

"Woman!" he exclaimed, raking his fingers through his hair, "Don't scare me like that!" Arin laughed and took his hand.

The mood was light all the way to the wharf, but when they got there, when

As I am Known

they came in sight of the ship that would bear him away, Jacob's steps slowed. "It's all right, Beloved," Arin reassured him. "The hand of the Lord is on you."

They stopped at the bottom of the gangplank. Nikos went ahead of them into the ship. There was the lady Helena, talking with an older man Jacob presumed to be the other passenger Demos had been waiting for. He turned to his brother. "When you go home to our mother, give her my love, and tell her I'll write to her." He and Jonathan embraced. "I will miss you, my brother."

"And I you," Jonathan replied. "Come to us in Antioch, if you can."

Then it was Arin's turn. Jacob told her with a lopsided smile, "I expect you to write to me."

"You know I will," she answered. He started to say something more, but she put her fingers to his lips. "No need," she whispered.

He nodded, then bent down and brushed her lips with his. He pulled her close. "I'll come back to you as soon as I can, Beloved."

Arin nodded against his chest, then released her hold on him and stepped back, whispering, "Go now."

He turned away, drew a deep breath, and walked up the gangplank. Apparently, they were only waiting for him. Seconds after he boarded, the ship was loosed from its moorings and heading out to sea. Jacob stood on the deck, while his brother and his betrothed shrank in the distance. He held up one hand in farewell, and Jonathan returned the gesture. Arin, however, remained still as a statue, watching. Somehow he knew she would go on watching until the tip of the tallest mast was swallowed up in the horizon.

Epilogue
Twelve years later:

Arin stood staring out to sea, her arms crossed against a nipping north wind. It was her habit now, every evening at sunset, to walk down to the shore and send her prayers flying out over the waves. *I know it doesn't matter to You where I pray, Lord, but my heart wants to be out here.*

So much had changed since Jacob sailed off to Berea. Zerah died four years later. Gallus wrote and told them that he and Mina were still living in his house with Odelia. Grandmother Eunice passed away soon after that. Arin thought, *At least Grandfather is still strong.* He continued to come every year, and sometimes Caleb and Prisca came with him. Last year, he brought Andrew, who had grown into a tall, handsome boy with a quick smile and a sprinkling of freckles across his nose.

And deep sorrow had touched them. Arin's mother died in childbirth. *It's been almost ten years now.* Leah left behind a baby daughter for the rest of the family to cuddle and spoil. They named her after her mother, for she had her hazel eyes and easy temperament. The baby was now a sturdy little girl—gifted with prophecy, just like her sisters.

But not everyone to whom they prophesied would listen. Just last month, Saul—now calling himself Paul—was at the house with his traveling companion, a physician named Luke. Other believers from the city had gathered at the house, as well as a prophet named Agabus, from Judea. Fresh tears filled Arin's eyes as she remembered that meeting. Agabus took Paul's belt, tied his own hands and feet with it, and said that the Holy Spirit was telling him the Jews in Jerusalem would in the same way bind the belt's owner. Paul, he said, would be handed over to the Gentiles.

The word rang true in Arin's spirit. She took Paul's right hand and implored him, weeping all the while, not to go. But even her love for her friend would not sway him. He kissed her forehead, his own eyes swimming with tears. "Please don't cry. You're breaking my heart." Then he declared to the rest of them that he was ready to be bound and even to die for the Lord.

"He is gone," she whispered into the wind. "We will never see him again." Days after he left, Arin received a message from Jacob. *"We won't be coming to Caesarea this year,"* it said. *"The lady Helena is not in good health and cannot travel. I am sorry, Beloved. She did tell me that she has been setting aside wages for me, as if she'd hired me, and that the money will be given to me when she's gone. I don't think it will be much longer.*

"The church here thrives, and Paul's last visit helped us greatly, though it was far too brief. I hope he will come again. Greet him for me the next time he passes your way. I will come to you as soon as I can."

Arin drew in a deep breath and murmured, "'Hope deferred makes the heart sick.' But You have seen me through it, Lord. My heart isn't sick, only waiting." She started to turn, and felt the tip of her toe hit a lump in the sand. Bending down, she dug it out. It was a shell similar to the one she gave Jacob. She had long since stopped collecting them, preferring now to simply watch the rolling sea. "I have learned, Lord. I have learned to trust You. We are in Your hands, and it is enough." With that, she cocked her arm back, hurled the shell out into the sea, and watched it disappear into the waves. Then she turned and started back to the house.

Author's Note:

The riot in Jerusalem really happened, in AD 48. It is not mentioned in scripture, but the historians, Josephus and Eusebius both wrote about it, and Josephus gives the causes for the riot and its aftermath, including the incident with Caesar's servant, Stephanus, in Caesarea. I have tried to follow his account.

At that time, Jerusalem was a city of about three hundred thousand. During Passover, the crowds of pilgrims swelled those numbers to between two and three million. Rioting during the Feast was something the Romans and Jews both feared, and for good reason. This incident may have been the worst riot in history, in terms of casualties. No fewer than twenty, and possibly as many as thirty thousand people were trampled or crushed to death in Jerusalem's narrow streets. Josephus adds that no family in Palestine was unaffected. Every household suffered loss, and what should have been a time of celebration turned to a time of mourning.

Saul and Barnabas actually left on their journey around AD 45. I have them going out two years later. My apologies to historical purists.

Phillip in this story is known as The Evangelist. This is not the Phillip who was one of the Twelve, but rather one of seven men who, along with Stephen, the church's first martyr, was appointed to oversee food distribution to the widows among Jerusalem's Christian community. (See Acts 6:5-6) Phillip preached to the Ethiopian eunuch (Acts 28:26-40), and according to Acts 21:8-9, had four virgin daughters who prophesied.

Eusebius suggests that Phillip eventually gave his daughters in marriage, leading me to wonder how old they were when they began to prophesy, since girls at that time married young. So I wrote them as children. "I will pour out my Spirit on all people. Your sons and daughters will prophesy, your young men will see visions, your old men will dream dreams. (Acts 2:17)